On THIN ICE

BETH BOLDEN

AUTHOR NOTE

On Thin Ice and the Portland Evergreens series take place in the wider Beth Bolden universe: a universe that is more inclusive and welcoming than our own.

In Beth-world, the first professional athlete to come out of the closet was Colin O'Connor (*The Rainbow Clause*), and after this happened, approximately ten years ago, there have been numerous players, coaches, and even owners who are living their best queer lives freely.

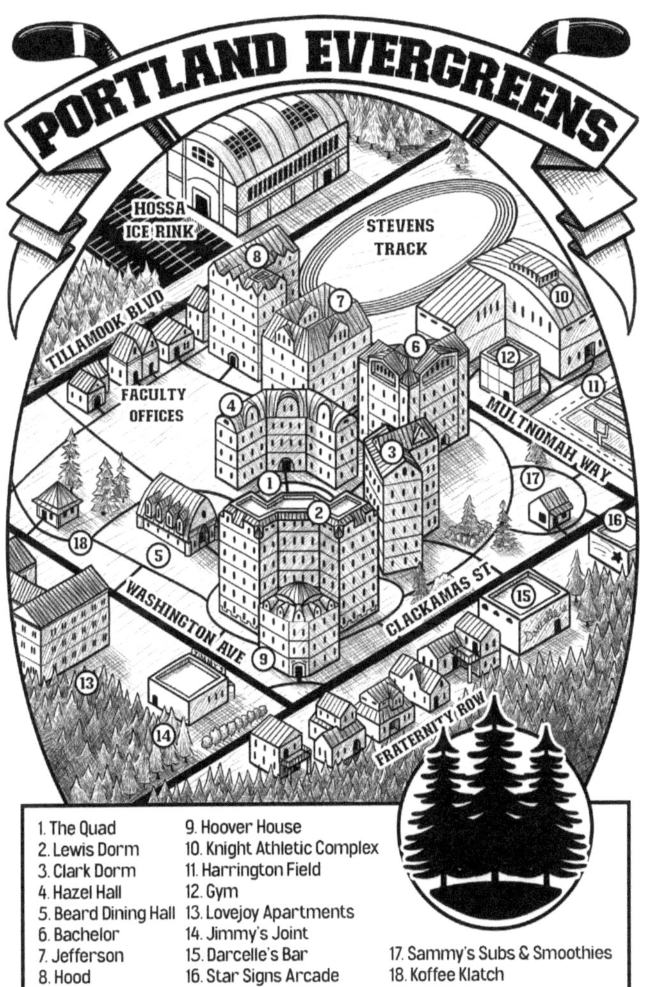

PORTLAND EVERGREENS
HOSSA ICE RINK
STEVENS TRACK
TILLAMOOK BLVD
FACULTY OFFICES
MULTNOMAH WAY
WASHINGTON AVE
CLACKAMAS ST
FRATERNITY ROW
1. The Quad
2. Lewis Dorm
3. Clark Dorm
4. Hazel Hall
5. Beard Dining Hall
6. Bachelor
7. Jefferson
8. Hood
9. Hoover House
10. Knight Athletic Complex
11. Harrington Field
12. Gym
13. Lovejoy Apartments
14. Jimmy's Joint
15. Darcelle's Bar
16. Star Signs Arcade
17. Sammy's Subs & Smoothies
18. Koffee Klatch

CHAPTER 1

"Is that who I think—"

Finn barely got half his question out before Elliott abruptly stopped, right there, in the middle of the ice, and smacked a hand right across his mouth.

It was the annual Evergreens fundraiser, when they invited the rest of the student body and Portland U's professors and staff out onto the ice. The staff had dropped half a dozen big silver reflecting disco balls all around the rink, the lights were flashing to an upbeat pop mix, and the ice was full of people barely managing to stay upright.

"Don't," Elliott warned.

Finn shook his hand off. Annoyed, despite knowing better. "I wasn't—"

But predictably Ell didn't let him get *that* out either, interrupting him first. "You don't need to start shit. Not tonight."

"It's not *me* who dislikes him," Finn reminded his friend sulkily.

He didn't give a shit about Jacob Braun, despite listening to his dad bitch about him at every possible opportunity.

"I'm just saying the last thing we need is for you to go up to him and start something." Elliott said this quite reasonably as they started to skate again, barely gliding along with the very slowly moving crowd.

Finn rolled his eyes. Out of the pair of them, it was usually Elliott pushing the buttons of everyone around him. Especially his linemate and their teammate Malcolm. Though Finn had noticed that lately their sniping at each other had taken on a whole new dimension, full of heat.

Finn knew it was only a matter of time before they fucked—if they hadn't already, and Elliott hadn't told him yet. And if he *hadn't* told Finn, then that meant it wasn't just fucking. For either of them.

As far as Finn was concerned, *that* was the real problem, not Jacob Braun skulking over by the far wall, big arms crossed over his even bigger chest, thick dark beard obscuring the expression on his face.

"I'm hardly going to go challenge him to a duel over my father's honor," Finn said dryly.

"What honor?" Elliott retorted, his tone even drier. "Morgan just didn't like that he couldn't score on Braun."

Finn knew that. It wasn't hard to figure out what had pissed off Morgan Reynolds.

"And now you know why I'm not tempted to go over there and kick his ass."

Elliott nodded, his eyes twinkling suddenly with amusement. "Or you could go over there and flirt with him. He's hot, even if he's old."

"He's not *that* old," Finn said, not sure why he was insisting on this point. "He had to retire early. A hip injury, I think? He's maybe thirty-four? Thirty-five?"

"He kind of reminds me of—" This time Elliott stopped himself abruptly.

"Don't say Mal," Finn teased. But he could see it. The height. The breadth of Braun's shoulders. The messy dark hair, the beard Mal could surely grow if he ever allowed it. That intense stare. Even if it was brown instead of blue. "Now I see why you wanted to go flirt with him."

"I didn't want to go flirt with him," Elliott claimed. "I wanted *you* to go flirt with him. Imagine how pissed off that'd make your dad."

Finn could imagine just how that'd go. The disapproval that seemed to permanently reside on his dad's face deepening even further. Even thinking of the texts he'd get made him not even want to *look* at Jacob Braun.

Because Ell was right. Jacob Braun was kind of hot, in that reclusive, brooding mountain man kind of way.

"Don't need to flirt with Jacob Braun to annoy him," Finn said as lightly as he could.

Which . . .frankly . . .was not that light, when it came down to it.

Elliott patted him on the shoulder but Finn didn't feel all that reassured. "I know," he said quietly.

For half a rotation, they didn't speak, but Finn had a feeling if he looked up, he'd see Jacob Braun's gaze on him. He could feel it, burning into him.

He knew he lived in town, in one of the gigantic houses perched in the West Hills. Once or twice, he'd seen him around the facility, but they'd never spoken.

Maybe because Jacob didn't give a shit that his issue had been with Finn's dad. Maybe Finn was included in his dislike, anyway.

Nick, the other goalie on the Evergreens, said he'd asked him for a training session, but Jacob had said he didn't do that, and that was the end of it.

Finn had half-expected Coach Blackburn to try to convince Jacob, but apparently he hadn't. Or if he had, it hadn't turned out the way Coach B had wanted, and so Finn had never heard about it.

Even his father had only mentioned Jacob's presence in Portland once.

"You know," Elliott said again, "you *could* go over there."

"Ell," Finn warned.

"Not to flirt. Or to fight."

"And here I thought those were your only two modes," Finn said.

Elliott made a disgruntled noise. "That's not true."

"When it comes to Malcolm, yeah," Finn said, turning the subject onto his friend because that was easier and way more comfortable than thinking about what he might say to Jacob Braun.

Sorry my dad's such an asshole? Don't worry, he's like that with me too?

It wasn't exactly a state secret, but Finn still couldn't imagine walking up to Braun and admitting that.

"I know what you're doing and it's not going to work," Elliott said primly.

"So you're not gonna tell me, then."

"There's nothing to tell." But Elliott was a shitty liar, and from the waver in his voice and the sudden blissful expression on his face, Finn knew there was a hell of a lot to tell.

He hoped that Mal wouldn't inadvertently break Elliott's heart—or that they wouldn't somehow break each other in this mess.

If he needed another reason to *not* go over to where Braun was leaning against the wall, that was it.

It was too complicated. Messy.

Besides, he was right here. If Jacob wanted to do more than just stare, *he* could come over and talk to Finn.

It had been a mistake to come tonight. Jacob knew that now. He pushed open the door to the outside and took a deep gulp of fresh air.

Not because of the Reynolds boy, though *that* hadn't helped, either.

Seeing Finn, looking like a young shadow of his father, had brought back a lot of memories, good *and* bad.

But the rink itself had done more than enough. Even the scent of it had brought it all back. What felt like every moment, flashing in technicolor across his memory, good and bad and fantastic and awful.

Moira had told him that it would be good for him to come tonight, but he was pretty sure that when she asked him how it had gone during their next session, he was going to tell her it had been a complete fucking disaster.

He'd dutifully paid his money—all going to support the hockey team, of course, and he'd laced his skates up. Carefully stretched his hip. Gotten on the ice.

It hadn't been his first time skating since his retirement, not by a long shot, and he'd thought maybe the rink, with its festive atmosphere, would feel different. *Better.*

It hadn't.

The moment his blades had touched it, Jacob had wanted to fall to his knees and beat his fists against the ice, in turns thankful and furious.

Relieved and regretful.

Even with six months of therapy and his admittedly great support system, Jacob couldn't say he was managing any of his feelings about hockey all that well.

He couldn't imagine what it would be like without Moira and without his brother and his family. Without his agent, Mark. Without Sophie, who handled his PR.

No wonder a lot of ex-players turned to drugs and booze to cope.

He'd made it nearly to the sidewalk when he noticed someone sitting on one of the concrete benches lining the walk up to Hossa Rink. A streetlight was partially shining on him, the caramel-colored mop of hair on the guy's head unmistakable.

That head was bent down, over a dimmed screen, and as Jacob passed, he saw an unmistakable flash of unbearable frustration cross over his face before it was wiped clean.

Shit.

He should leave it alone. He should keep walking and not invite more pain. He should pretend he hadn't seen him, and just keep going—

"Hey."

He found himself in front of Finn, opening his mouth before he could snatch the greeting back.

Finn glanced up.

In this light, he didn't look much like his father at all. Except for the hair, which he wore longer, letting it curl around his forehead, his ears. Morgan had always kept it cropped short, like the melting pot of browns and blonds and hints of red, all tangled up in swirls and loops, made him too soft.

The curls didn't make Finn look soft, they made him look—

Jacob cut that thought off hard and fast. This was *Morgan's son.*

"Decided you hadn't done enough by just staring at me, huh?" Finn asked.

Jacob couldn't help the wince. Considered denying Finn's accusation. But he didn't. "No. Sorry. I'll—"

He went to turn, but Finn caught his arm.

Jacob looked down at the hand curled around his plaid jacket. He could feel the warmth and power of it even through the fabric. Up close, Finn didn't look as young as Jacob had imagined he might. He'd grown up even in the six months or so since they'd last seen each other. He was a man now, despite the haunting insecurities hiding in the corners of his gaze.

He should *really* go.

But Finn's grayish-green eyes were clear in the streetlight, looking directly at him. "No, *I'm* sorry," he said.

Jacob wasn't sure either of them were really all that sorry, but maybe it was better to preserve the fiction.

"Well, uh, I thought—" He started and then stopped. Started again. Papered over his own awkwardness with the reminder words had never been his strong suit. "Thought I should say hi, at least."

"Hi," Finn said wryly.

"Right." He could tell Finn to tell his old man hi for him, too, but the last time they'd seen each other, Jacob had still been playing, in his last All Star Game, and Morgan had been newly retired, and the one time they'd actually come face-to-face, Morgan had told him to go fuck himself.

Jacob, blood hot, might have shoved a hard elbow into his gut and told him he wasn't taking names right now, and even if he was, he wouldn't want his balls to freeze off.

Not his best moment. Not Morgan's, either, but then Morgan had always seemed to enjoy their feud more than Jacob had.

"Uh, how's . . .uh . . ." Jacob rubbed his neck and shot Finn a sheepish look. "I guess your dad's doing just fine."

If Morgan Reynolds had struggled with retirement, it had never been public—or even private—knowledge.

He'd gone straight from success to even more success. Investing in companies, buying into an AHL team, gracing ESPN with all his very important insights.

Jacob hadn't wanted to keep resenting the asshole, but it had been hard when he'd been so tangled up and Morgan was seemingly just fucking fine.

As always.

"Of course he is." Finn sounded like he resented this fine-ness too. Something he and the boy had in common.

He's not a boy. Not from this angle.

Not from any angle.

Jacob dragged his mind—and his uncooperative dick—back from the certain insanity of thinking just how well Finn Reynolds had grown up.

"He would be," Jacob commiserated, shooting Finn a reassuring smile. "Has he ever not been just fine?"

"No." Finn chuckled. "No. I wish I knew how he does it."

"Hey, me too, kid," Jacob said, patting him awkwardly on the shoulder. And then winced, again. *God*, he'd just called him a kid. Finn was frowning now, and probably not because he'd touched him.

"I'm twenty-one," Finn said. "Not a kid."

Jacob, despite the mess he always made of shit when he said anything out loud, *at least* knew that it would be a fucking disaster to say that he'd called him a kid out of self-preservation—it was easier, simpler, and way less full of dangerous land mines than thinking of how he'd grown up. How gorgeous he was.

Because he was. Breathtaking, actually, in this light, and it was taking everything in Jacob to ignore that burn of attraction.

If things were terrible *now*, imagine how bad they could be if he said that shit *out loud*?

"No, not a kid," Jacob finally agreed, because that was the only way to give himself an easy out.

"Don't even say you remember when I was born. I know you don't. You and my dad didn't start playing against each other until I was . . .what . . .six? Seven?"

Jacob grimaced. He did not want to go down this road.

There was no way this particular path wasn't emblazoned, in flashing neon letters, *Jacob Braun is a dirty old man.*

"Something like that." Jacob shoved his hands into his pockets.

"Well, there you go." Finn flashed him a grin.

Except it did *not* make Jacob feel any better.

"I'm glad you came tonight," Finn continued, like he couldn't tell Jacob was shutting down. Or maybe he just didn't give a shit. Morgan had been like that. He was the king of pushing and pushing and pushing until he pushed someone right off the cliff of good sense.

And because Morgan was Morgan, he'd laugh at you all the way down. Like it was all some great joke.

Not for the first time, Jacob thought that if it had been hard to play against someone like that, how hard would it have been to grow up with him as your father?

"Ah, well, not much going on these days." It was the opposite of how busy Morgan seemed to be, in retirement, and Jacob wanted to snatch the words back and pretend that he too had his fingers in many important and lucrative opportunities.

But Finn didn't look judgmental, only sympathetic. "Must've sucked, when your hip gave out."

"Wasn't fun," Jacob admitted.

He'd thought he'd had a few decent years left—maybe he'd have spent some time as a backup, but it would have been time on the ice.

"My dad said you were one of the best to play the position," Finn said.

Jacob smiled, aware of what Finn was doing. "I bet he said that with a whole lot more four-letter words."

Finn laughed, the sound seemingly startled out of him. Like he hadn't expected Jacob to call him on his polite bullshit. Well, Jacob hadn't expected to do it either—hadn't expected *any* of this. Certainly not the unsettling awareness of Finn residing in his gut.

"Yep," Finn agreed. "But it's still true. The more he hated you? The better you were, in his eyes."

"Sounds about right," Jacob said. It was how he'd always managed to deal with the feud. Even when he hadn't liked it, he'd at least been able to acknowledge it was ultimately Morgan's greatest compliment.

The one time Morgan had come up with his therapist, Moira, Jacob had muttered offhandedly about if anyone needed to talk to anyone, it was probably Morgan. "Everyone needs therapy, Jacob," Moira had said gently. "Well, he needs it more than everyone else," Jacob had insisted.

And if that was true, what did that say about *Finn*?

He is not your business or your problem. He is definitely not a solution either, or a very convenient and attractive distraction from all the shit you're carrying around.

If it happened—and it wasn't going to—Morgan would take it as just another insult in a very long list. He'd fly to Portland to beat Jacob's face in and probably drag his adult son, who knew how to make his own choices, back to New York by his ear.

"You guys are . . .uh . . .good this year," Jacob said. "You're playing good."

Finn rolled his eyes. "Haven't caught you at a game, yet."

He wasn't about to tell Morgan's son that he was still struggling to return to an ice rink. Not that Finn was necessarily his father's biggest fan either, but it wouldn't be too surprising if that knowledge slipped out. Even inadvertently, Jacob didn't need Morgan to know just how much he was struggling.

"I . . .uh . . .I've been following on TV. And online." That wasn't a lie. Sometimes when the silence of his house felt like it was going to eat him alive, he switched on a game.

"Then you know I'm *not* playing good," Finn said flatly.

"That's . . .*no*," Jacob stammered, guilt washing over him. Had he paid attention to Finn's play? Well, yes, because he'd been a goalie too, and also because he was Finn. He'd been interested.

He hadn't thought Finn was really taking advantage of his good instincts, but he hadn't believed he was *bad* either.

And suddenly it occurred to Jacob why Finn might feel that way.

"Morgan's not—"

"Don't give me that *he wouldn't* bullshit. You know exactly how my father is. More than anyone else," Finn said bitterly. "All the way across the country. Going to college instead of going into juniors, like him. Different position. Doesn't matter. I can't escape him."

This is not your problem.

"I never could either," Jacob said gently.

"You didn't *try* to," Finn snapped.

But he had. He'd tried to make nice with Morgan so many times, and a few times he'd thought they'd actually gotten to a decent place, sharing late-night drinks after a game or even once having dinner a few years back. And then they'd play again, and once they were back on the ice, everything always changed.

The difference between him and Finn was that he could escape Morgan Reynolds. He never had to think about him or probably ever talk to him again, if he didn't want to.

Finn didn't have that luxury.

"Well, from one ex-goalie to another, I don't think you're playing bad," Jacob said. Maybe it wouldn't make any difference what he said. Maybe Finn wasn't his problem. But he couldn't turn away from all that obvious pain without saying a goddamn thing.

"Sure," Finn scoffed. He stood, and for a split second, Jacob was sure he was going to stalk away, and that would be the end of this weird conversation.

But then Finn turned back. "You really don't think I'm playing shitty? I know we're winning, but—"

Jacob's heart ached.

He didn't want it to, but he felt the painful echo anyway.

"You're not. But listen to your instincts more, okay?"

"What instincts?" That bitterness was back in spades.

And now *Jacob* wanted to fly to New York and beat the shit out of *Morgan* for making his son feel this way.

"You got 'em," Jacob said.

"Then help me," Finn said.

It was the last thing Jacob expected him to say.

It seemed it was also the last thing Finn had expected to say, too, because the shock on his face mirrored exactly how Jacob felt.

"What?"

"You heard me." But Finn was recovering faster from the surprise, because he seemed strangely sure now. "Help me. Make me a better goalie. You were one of the best to play the game, and I *know* I could be better, but I . . ." Finn trailed off.

He's not your problem, he's not your problem, he's definitely not your problem. You've got enough of those on your own . . .

"No," Jacob said. He'd wanted to reject the suggestion more gently, but in the end all that came out was that terrible bark.

Finn didn't look fazed though. "You could help me," he said.

He *could*. But helping Finn would mean a whole lot of other things. Like getting back on the ice, regularly. Like *seeing him* regularly. And while Jacob had no idea if this recent and very messy attraction was reciprocated *and* he'd always believed in his own ironclad self-control, he was not going to risk it.

There were so many other, *better,* people out there who could help Finn.

"I can't," Jacob said firmly.

"But—"

"No."

Jacob had wanted this awkward conversation to end but he was still disappointed—in Finn but more in himself—when Finn took in his last rejection, shot him a venomous glare, and then stalked off.

"Fuck," Jacob muttered out loud.

Now the father *and* the son hated him.

CHAPTER 2

Finn couldn't breathe.

He'd learned to live like this most of the time. The inescapable pressure digging into him, not just with its weight but with *claws*. Some days were worse than others. And today was a bad day.

His dad's words, sent innocuously over text, were a litany in his head, over and over, undeniable and unacceptable.

You're lucky you have such a great offense behind you.

You're lucky you have such a great offense behind you.

You're lucky you have such a great offense behind you.

Morgan Reynolds didn't have to say the rest. Finn could hear it, even louder and even clearer.

You're lucky they're fucking bailing you out, because you can't do it on your own.

Would it have been easier to *not* follow in his dad's footsteps?

No question.

But in a sweetly painful twist, Finn actually loved playing hockey. *Wanted* to play hockey, not just to make his dad happy or proud, neither of which he thought he'd actually done.

At first, coaches had always wanted to put him in his dad's center position, but he'd had no feel for it. Then they'd decided to try him on defense, until one day in his early teens, when he'd stayed late at the rink, helping a friend out who was perfecting a specifically angled shot.

His dad had come to pick him up—one of the few times he'd actually been *present* in Finn's life, ironically—and the next day, he'd marched right over to the coach and told him that if he didn't put Finn in the goal, he was stupider than Morgan thought he was.

Finn had become a goalie that day.

The joy he'd experienced finding his right place on the ice had been short-lived, and sometimes Finn felt like he was chasing it every single day, every single practice, every single game.

He strode back and forth in front of the bar, wishing he was anywhere else. But he'd learned well enough that there wasn't a place to run that was far enough.

He'd come all the way across the country, because just going to college hadn't been enough difference from his dad's career trajectory. He'd needed to be even farther away. Three thousand fucking miles away.

But what was three thousand miles when a text could cross that distance as easy as breathing?

Breathing, *ha*.

The expectations settled over him, inescapable and pressing into him, making even taking a deep breath impossible.

Someday, his father liked to say, karma always comes round.

He'd always worried that all this shit, the baggage he carried around because he couldn't figure out how to set it down, would make it impossible for him to keep playing as well as he *knew* he could.

That day was here.

Every game he started, Finn felt like a ticking time bomb.

One day, he'd go off.

One day soon.

"Hey, what's going on? Everything okay?"

Finn turned and was both surprised—and not surprised—to see that Elliott had followed him.

Surprised because Elliott should be inside, enjoying his new boyfriend, Mal. It had only been a few weeks since the fundraiser, but they'd seemingly settled into the honeymoon phase.

Not surprised because if anyone had an inkling of how he felt, it was probably Elliott.

Elliott would probably be drafted in the first round. He was one of the most promising talents in years. And yet he carried that pressure like he was built to do it, never letting it faze him, whereas all it did was push Finn farther and farther into the ground, bogging him down until it felt like he could barely catch his breath and barely move his feet forward.

It was unfair, but Finn loved Elliott and couldn't blame him for it.

"No," Finn said shortly. He didn't need to go into details, at least with Elliott. He'd know exactly what was wrong.

"What happened?" Elliott put a hand on his shoulder, worry creasing his handsome face.

Finn both wanted to tell him and not tell him at the same time. Ell would understand, and that would soothe some of the ache. But then Ell would also know the depth of his humiliation.

"Dad saw the score from last night and just texted."

"What did he say?" Elliott asked, frowning.

Finn *could* tell him, it turned out, but he couldn't quite look him in the eye when he did it. He stared instead at his sneakers, at a fraying shoelace. "Oh, just a comment about how lucky I am that I have such a great offense behind me, ready to bail me out every time."

"Is that really what he said?" Elliott sounded skeptical, and okay, *that* was worse. Now they thought he was all overreacting. That he was a goddamn drama queen *and* a goddamn mess.

Finn pulled his phone out of his pocket. Let Elliott see it right there, in undeniable black and white.

"Finn," Elliott said kindly, after he handed the phone back, "you gotta stop letting him matter."

Finn didn't know how to even begin to do that. Probably because to everyone else on earth, every other single person in the hockey community, Morgan Reynolds was a goddamn god.

He *mattered*.

How was Finn supposed to fight that inevitability?

Anger surged through him—at himself, and at fate, more than Elliott, but unfortunately for Elliott he was going to have to bear the brunt of it.

"Oh? That's all I should do? Just tell myself he doesn't matter? That *Morgan Reynolds* doesn't matter? And I'll be alright? God, why didn't I think of that before?"

Elliott looked appropriately guilty, at least. "I know it's not easy."

But Elliott's expression didn't assuage Finn's anger. Especially when the knowledge, lodged hard and inescapable in his breastbone, told him that Elliott *had* been there and he'd gotten everything he'd wanted, in the end.

It had never been fair, but the gulf between fair and unfair had never felt as wide as it did right now.

"Damn straight it's not easy. What if someone had told you to just leave Mal alone? Would you have? Oh wait, I know you wouldn't have, because we *all* said it. We all told you to stop harassing him, but you didn't. You kept at him. Because you wanted him and you weren't willing to settle for less."

I wish I could settle for less.

Do something else.

But Finn couldn't. Ice was in his Reynolds blood, as much as he wished it wasn't. He'd fight for every inch, even though maybe he should've given up.

"I might've settled," Elliott protested, but they both knew the truth.

He'd never have given Mal up.

Just the way Finn refused to give up on his hockey dream.

It was why he'd gone completely insane and asked Jacob Braun to coach him.

Jacob was at the top of a very, *very* short list of people who'd never let Morgan get to him. And Finn had wondered—*hoped*—that he might be willing to impart some wisdom to Finn about how to accomplish that, along with making him a better goalie.

But Jacob had turned him down flat, like it was nothing, like he didn't matter, just like his father did, sometimes.

Finn's blood boiled, just thinking of it.

"You did what it took to get his attention," Finn said. He began to pace. Thinking, maybe, of something he shouldn't be thinking of. "It was a little insane, and we all knew it. *You* even knew it, but you did it anyway. And it fucking worked."

Throwing the Hail Mary was not supposed to work.

But sometimes it did.

Which was why football teams, down at the end of a game, always tried it.

"What are you thinking of doing, Finn?" Elliott asked suspiciously.

"Nothing," Finn said. *Lied.*

Because he was thinking of pulling his own Elliott. His own Hail Mary.

"Don't do something stupid or insane because I did and it worked," Elliott warned.

"You still don't have a fucking leg to stand on here," Finn reminded him.

Nobody was going to talk him out of this.

Jacob didn't want to give him the time of day? Jacob didn't want to coach him?

He was going to make saying no *impossible.*

He was Morgan Reynolds' son; he'd cut his teeth on impossible.

"I know," Elliott said, "but there was every chance it wouldn't work. It still might not. We might end up on separate coasts, doing this whole long-distance thing."

Finn rolled his eyes. "And you'll still be in love."

"Well, yeah," Elliott said. At least he seemed to be aware of how fucking weak his argument was.

"Exactly. Are you really going to stand here and tell me not to fight like hell for what I want? What I *deserve*?"

Elliott finally nodded. "Yeah. I mean . . .*yeah*. It's true. You want something? Don't let anything stop you."

If Elliott knew what he was planning, he'd definitely stop him. But that was the beauty of Elliott *not* knowing.

"Or anybody," Finn said with satisfaction. "I'm glad for you and Mal, I am. But I gotta go, okay? Tell Ramsey I'll see him tomorrow, at practice."

"Are you sure—" Elliott made one last-ditch attempt.

It was pointless. He probably knew it. But Finn loved him for the attempt, even as he easily brushed him off.

"Seriously. I'll be fine." *I'll be fine, now.* "Go inside. Enjoy your boyfriend."

He took off down the street, pulling his phone out again. Jacob lived somewhere near here. It shouldn't be that hard to find the address or to get someone to give it to him.

Finn had a lot of connections because of his last name, but it still took hours more than he'd thought it would. The passing time didn't do anything but solidify his determination and make him intent and focused on getting exactly what he wanted.

Elliott got Malcolm into his bed, finally?

Well, Finn was going to get Jacob to teach him exactly how to pretend Morgan Reynolds didn't exist.

How to let his opinions slip right through him, like phantom smoke.

By the time he got the address, he was so keyed up his fingers were trembling and he gripped the steering wheel of his SUV hard as he drove up the private road to Jacob Braun's house.

It was big, bigger than he'd expected and set back behind a wall of trees, another forest stretching out behind it.

Isolated, that was what Finn thought when he saw it.

If Jacob could be an island, then Finn could find a way to be one too.

Finn parked and jumped out. He could hear the faint strains of music—some kind of seventies rock, he thought—echoing between the trees, so he knew someone had to be home.

Still, he was surprised when he pounded on the big wooden slab doors and nobody came to open them.

He knocked again, louder this time.

Nothing.

But Finn hadn't come all this way to strike out.

He slipped around the side of the house, laughed at the fancy wrought iron gate, and climbed it easily, falling to his feet on the other side.

There were lights down the winding path, and the roof of a gazebo just peeking out from between the trees.

Finn let his determination power him down to where he'd find Jacob—and hopefully a future where he could actually fucking *breathe*.

Nothing was going to stop him now.

Jacob hated meetings about his career—or his *non*-career, he supposed he could call it now—and so when his agent and his PR rep wanted one, he did everything to make it as palatable as he could.

Andina was one of his favorite restaurants and had a nice private room he could call up and reserve. So instead of suffering through this hell on Zoom or even in a conference room, at least Jacob was doing it over a glass of heavenly wine and the best lamb shank he'd ever put in his mouth.

"At least when you make us fly in," Sophie said wryly, "you feed us well."

"It's only because he hates these," Mark said, shooting Jacob a knowing glance.

"*He* also prefers it when you don't talk about him in third person when he's right fucking here," Jacob retorted without heat.

"I know, darling, but it's the truth," Sophie said, her smile kind.

Jacob took a long sip of wine. "Complaining about coming to Portland or complimenting me on my restaurant choice doesn't tell me where we're at with the foundation."

Early on in their therapy sessions, Moira had identified that he was specifically struggling with having too much time. Not having any purpose, now that his career had ended. They'd talked about a lot of options. Coaching—which he wasn't *against*, but didn't feel ready for. Jacob ignored the pulse of guilt fluttering through him at how he'd turned Finn down. It had been almost two weeks ago now, but instead of moving on, he was still thinking about it. Wondering how he could've done it.

Wondering if he might've been able to banish those shadows from Finn's beautiful eyes. Wondering if he could've gotten Finn to stop worrying so much and just *play*.

But that ship had sailed and wasn't coming back, if Finn's angry expression and Reynolds blood was any indication. Morgan had never let a single fucking thing go, ever. Every shot Jacob had blocked, Morgan had blamed him for, forever.

Coaching, that wasn't for him. Not now.

Maybe someday.

Of course he'd probably never get an opportunity to help Finn get his head screwed on straight, because by the time Jacob got *his* shit in order, it would be too late.

Finn would be . . .well, whatever it would be.

Coaching had been out. The next suggestion Moira had was founding or volunteering for a charity, and she'd let that thought linger, without other distractions, for a few weeks, letting Jacob really consider the possibility. And he'd decided he *liked* that idea. Of giving back. Especially giving back to kids who didn't have anyone else to believe in them.

"I'm still going through resumes for the director," Sophie said.

Jacob frowned. "I thought we'd narrowed it down to five possibilities." *He'd* sent in his top five candidates after reviewing the resumes Sophie had forwarded him.

"Yes. Sorry. I got some new advice from that non-profit course I'm taking," Sophie said, not sounding very sorry at all. "It made me want to take a different approach to the process."

Jacob told himself not to get pissed. But it was six months since he'd brought Sophie and Mark this idea, and this was as far as they'd gotten. *Looking* at resumes to hire someone to help get his foundation off the ground.

"And," Sophie added, more gently this time, reaching for his hand and patting it, "we still haven't discussed how you want to handle the inevitable questions."

"Yes, we did," Jacob said. Okay, Sophie was technically right. They hadn't discussed it. When Sophie had asked him, he'd only said, *tell them the goddamned truth and then move the fuck on.*

Frustratingly, she did not think this was a very good strategy to come out of the closet. Even worse, Jacob was beginning to wonder if she might be right.

"You told me to just drop the unvarnished truth. Say, *yes,* Jacob Braun is gay. And then leave it at that." Sophie shot him a look, the meaning of which he understood perfectly. *Maybe it's true, but it's also bullshit, and it's not going to work, and you know it, too.*

"I did." Jacob internally winced. He'd said that on a particularly bad day, a few months back, and unsurprisingly, Sophie had made sure they didn't revisit the conversation until now. Until he was a glass and a half of superb wine into dinner.

"You've said more than once retiring from hockey was a blessing and a curse. So let's focus on the blessing. You can come out, now," Mark said soothingly.

"Right." Jacob stared at his wineglass. He didn't think it was full enough to be having this conversation.

"So, *yes,* we need to talk about the process of you coming out, that's what we have to tackle before we do *anything,*" Sophie said firmly.

"Does there really have to be a process?" Jacob questioned. "Don't the kids today just live their lives?"

Sophie made a face and took a long drink of *her* wine, so he guessed not. Or that much easier version of upcoming events wasn't in the cards for him. "Yes and no," she said. "Kids, yes. Not guys who spent their whole career closeted."

"I never had a beard. I never faked it with a woman," Jacob said. He'd never been willing to go there. Even to dispel the rumors that had, *yes*, followed him. Which was why he didn't understand why they couldn't just confirm them.

"No, you didn't," Mark agreed. Though Mark had half-heartedly suggested it once or twice or ten times. Every time those rumors cropped up. Clearly his agent hadn't liked the idea any more than Jacob had, because while he *had* mentioned it, he'd never pushed Jacob to do it.

"Then why can't we just say, yep, everyone was right about me? I don't want it to be some big deal."

"Jacob, it *is* a big deal," Sophie said gently.

"Only to me," Jacob argued. "To everyone else, it shouldn't even matter. Besides, who cares if I start a LGBTQ charitable foundation? Does that *have* to mean I'm queer? Those kids need support too. More support, in fact."

"I know, but Jacob, there's going to be questions. And if you don't establish this upfront, the questions might overtake the whole point of the foundation. And I *know* you don't want that. You want the foundation and its cause front and center, not your own sexuality." Sophie's expression was empathetic. She was absolutely cutthroat and killer at her job, but with an unexpectedly soft heart she didn't show to just anyone. But she'd shown it to Jacob early on, and they'd always gotten along as a result.

"Fine, *fine*," Jacob agreed. "We'll do it your way. But only because I'm not doing this to bring even more attention to myself."

"God forbid," Sophie said, her tone dry *and* affectionate.

"Told you he'd see reason," Mark said.

"*He* is still right here," Jacob retorted. "And *he* is willing only because he wants to actually help the kids."

Sophie chuckled. "We'll make it painless."

"Relatively," Mark added.

Approval received, Sophie and Mark let Jacob sit back and drink his wine as they argued over which way they were going to turn his life upside down.

Mark was right; he'd seen this as one of the major advantages of retiring. Of course he'd also had this ridiculous dream that he could just *live* and stop hiding and that would be good enough.

He should've known better that Sophie—and Mark—would want it to be more than that.

"I don't want to give an interview. I don't want to go on TV. I definitely don't want to do a series of TikToks," Jacob interrupted after they'd gotten so far in the weeds he was actually physically uncomfortable, shifting in his seat.

"But social media—"

"Isn't for me. Which is why I hired you to begin with," Jacob finished for her.

Sophie made a face. "Okay. We'll go back to the drawing board. Figure out some new, less invasive ideas, and send them over."

He nodded. "And while you're at it, send me the new resumes. I want to pick a director while you're working on the coming out plan."

Sophie didn't look particularly pleased about this, but it was Mark who spoke up. "You sure that's the best use of your time?"

"Use of time? All I have is time. You asked me to start reaching out to old friends and teammates about support and I did that. They're ready to donate. But they can't do it if there's no actual foundation." Frustration leaked into his voice and he didn't hold back. "We *need* to get this going."

"We will, we really will. I promise you that we will," Sophie assured him, reaching out and gripping his hand.

"What about Morgan Reynolds?" Mark asked.

Jacob wasn't proud of how he froze. Hoped that both of them would incorrectly attribute his deer-in-the-headlights expression to their years-long feud, not the fact that he'd just had a run-in with Finn.

"Oh, Mark, we keep talking about this," Sophie complained, shooting the guy a long-suffering look.

"I know, but think of the publicity it'd generate—Jacob's old enemy, supporting him now that they're both retired. Plus, it'd be great PR for Morgan too, with his son being gay."

Jacob had *known* that was true. It had been right there in the back of his mind during their whole conversation, and afterwards, too. When he'd jerked off in the shower two days after their run-in, and he'd had to actively *not* think about what Finn might feel like under his hands and his tongue and wrapped around his dick.

Regardless, he'd been trying to pretend that it wasn't a factor. That it didn't matter to him one way or the other.

Liar.

What he needed to do was find a hookup, or even better, find a guy he actually *liked*, and with whatever new plan Sophie came up with, maybe now he wouldn't scare him off with how deep in the fucking closet he was.

Regular sex might cure him of this sudden Finn affliction before it could get even more out of hand.

"You're not contacting Morgan," Jacob said firmly, "and I'm *definitely* not contacting Morgan."

"Oh come on, that's water *long* passed under the bridge," Mark said.

Jacob might've agreed, but Morgan had gotten more pissed at him the longer they played against each other, not less. He supposed that when you were chasing legacy and statistics and records, anyone standing in your way was an enemy to be defeated.

But Jacob had never been willing to just go down.

Especially if his spot in the history books was at risk.

"No, it's not, at all. If you'd seen their last run-in—where was it, Jacob?"

"Last All Star game."

Sophie shot Mark a triumphant look. "Even Jacob got pissed. Jacob was playing but Morgan was there as what . . .an analyst? A special guest? Anyway, they ran into each other and . . .*well*, I'm glad I was there. That's all I'll say about that."

"Morgan got pissed first," Jacob muttered sullenly. He wasn't particularly proud of how Morgan tended to bring out the worst in him.

Kinda like his son, just in a totally different way.

"Morgan always got pissed first," Mark pointed out.

Specifically not saying how Jacob hadn't had to rise to the bait. The truth was, he usually hadn't, but he'd been in low levels of pain with his hip that night, and thinking that this might really be it, and when Morgan had started running his mouth like he liked to do . . .well, was it any surprise he'd lost his shit?

"All I'm saying is that it was a bad idea to put them in the same room back then, and nothing's changed. Doesn't matter if his son's gay."

"He didn't—he doesn't—" Jacob could barely get the question out, even as he knew it wasn't something he should be asking.

He doesn't think less of Finn because he's gay?

Despite popular opinion, he'd never been that eager to kick Morgan Reynolds' ass, but he *would*—in fact he'd barely manage to hold himself back—if Morgan was shitty to Finn about his sexuality.

"Not that I've heard," Sophie said, hearing the question he hadn't quite been able to get out. "Finn's here though, isn't he? In Portland?"

If Sophie hadn't heard anything then there was nothing to hear. Her ears picked up goddamn everything. It was a blessing and a curse.

"Sophie," Jacob warned. He wanted her on his side on this. Not deciding that Mark was right about this after all.

"Yes," Mark said, "which is why this is a golden opportunity."

"Maybe Morgan's mellowed." Sophie directed this mostly to Jacob, who just rolled his eyes.

"He's Morgan Reynolds. He doesn't know *how* to mellow," Jacob argued. "We're not calling him. End of story."

"What about the son? What's his name? Finn?" Sophie asked.

"We're not calling him either." Jacob finished his wine, hoping that he'd sounded certain enough that the next time they met, Sophie wouldn't show up with a surprise Finn Reynolds.

"Oh come on, *he* doesn't hate you," Mark complained.

No. Which is the whole fucking problem.

If Sophie or Mark decided to drag Finn into this goddamn mess, he'd probably want something in return—like private coaching—and Jacob was not only *not* doing that, he was absolutely not doing that with Finn.

"Jacob—" Sophie started to cajole, and even worse he *knew* that tone in her voice. She always deployed it when she thought she might have a chance in hell of convincing him to change his mind.

"No," Jacob interrupted before she could get going. "No. We're not doing this with either Reynolds. We *are*, however, doing this with a director that we're *at least* going to be partway to hiring by the time we meet in a few weeks."

"Fine," Sophie said, setting her napkin on the table. "If you're decided."

"I'm decided," Jacob said firmly.

Half an hour later they were going their separate ways—Sophie and Mark to the hotel they were staying in only a few blocks away from the restaurant, and Jacob in his car, heading to his home far up in the West Hills.

He'd had high hopes for this meeting. He'd thought they were getting closer, way closer than they actually were, and as he parked in the garage, lifting himself out of the low-slung Audi, he found his frustration boiling over.

Huffing under his breath, Jacob strode into the house trying to calm himself. But it didn't work. It didn't always work.

Forcing himself to take a breath, then another, he leaned across the long marble slab that was his kitchen island and mentally ran down the list he and Moira had compiled early on.

Things he enjoyed. Things that relaxed him. Things that kept him focused, but not on his frustration.

Slightly calmer, and with a plan—he was *always* better with a plan—he walked over to the enormous wine rack that spanned one side of the living room. He'd bought this house two years before retirement, already knowing he'd want some place that he could carve out for *just* him. The open floor plan had appealed to him after spending so many years on the road, crammed into tiny hotel room boxes.

But the open floor plan had had another benefit, which was he'd gotten a metal artist to design and create scaffolding across one wall that displayed a portion of his wine collection.

Pulling out a bottle here or there, he finally found what he was looking for and grabbed a corkscrew, opening the wine in a few easy, experienced twists. Bypassing his normal glasses, he picked a cheaper stemless option from the cabinet and headed out the back door.

Another benefit of this house had been the extensive property behind it, leading up to an enforced forest preserve, which meant he would never lose the privacy buffer—or the peace and quiet—of the woods.

He'd built the meandering path down to the clearing himself, but he'd had the hot tub brought in and the gazebo put up by others. The sound system had been wired last year, when he'd discovered that sometimes he liked the quiet, but other times, music was a nice change of a pace. A reminder that he wasn't alone in the world, the way it felt sometimes.

Today he wanted the music, to tune out the noise in his own fucking head. He picked a station he liked on his phone and Stevie Nicks' soothing voice echoed through the otherwise silent woods.

He deposited the bottle and the glass down on the railing and pulled the lid off the hot tub, checking the settings to make sure they were exactly as he liked them.

The first few times he'd felt too vulnerable getting in naked, but the whole point of the setup was to be alone, and now he felt comfortable in the bubble of privacy he'd created. So he shed his clothes right there. Shoes and socks, then his pants, buttons coming apart and his shirt opening as he let every item of clothing fall to the wood deck.

He poured himself a glass of wine and, setting it on the side of the tub, slipped in. Tilted his head back and let contentment finally take him over.

Fucking bliss.

CHAPTER 3

Finn had spent the last few hours contemplating how to convince Jacob's *no* to become a *yes*.

He had envisioned meeting Jacob a lot of ways. Jacob opening his door, a flat stare, probably not very happy at Finn just showing up, unannounced.

He had not expected a naked Jacob Braun, eyes closed, steam curling around his bare chest, in a hot tub in the middle of the fucking forest.

Finn stopped abruptly, wincing at the sound of a twig breaking under his foot.

He was still going to do this. The hot tub and the surge of heat at the sight of the man weren't going to change anything. But he'd still wanted a moment to . . .well, to collect himself. To re-tailor his approach to this new situation.

But then Jacob's eyes opened and his gaze pinned Finn in place.

Shit.

He wasn't going to get a moment.

He wasn't even going to get a second, because Jacob was rising from the tub and *holy fuck*, as droplets streamed down his body, Finn was pretty sure he was naked. *All the way down . . .*

The water was lapping at his lower abs when he stopped abruptly, like he'd just realized he was about to give Finn a free show.

A show you'd like very much to see.

He'd always thought Jacob Braun was attractive; he'd need to be blind to not see that even though Jacob was retired now, he was *still* crazy fucking hot.

Finn's pulse accelerated as Jacob's dark brows slammed together. He didn't look happy Finn was here, in his backyard. Of course, he hadn't said that he wasn't happy, but did he have to?

He hadn't said anything at all. *But then, neither have you.*

"I . . . uh . . ."

Jacob's frown deepened.

Not a great first attempt.

Finn tried again. "I'm sorry—I should've—"

"Should've?"

Finn grimaced. "Shouldn't have come here like this. I should've—"

"Shouldn't have come at all? Yeah, how about we try that one?" Jacob said dryly. He settled back into the hot tub, and Finn knew he was being dismissed.

He didn't want to be dismissed. Before he'd realized the precarious position Jacob was in, he'd been beyond determined to convince Jacob to change his mind.

Was that possibly harder now? Yes, it was.

But that didn't change any of the fundamentals.

Finn still wanted Jacob to coach him.

Finn still *needed* Jacob to coach him.

So instead of leaving, he pushed forward, heading towards the small open gazebo over the hot tub.

Jacob watched him as he walked closer, not saying a word, but his eyes following him with intent.

When Finn got to the edge of the deck, he stopped. Cleared his throat.

"What happened to *shouldn't have come at all?*" Jacob asked calmly.

"I came here to ask you a question and I knew I couldn't just not ask, even if I . . .uh . . .interrupted your . . .um . . .your private time."

Jacob's eyebrow lifted. "A guy can't get naked in his own hot tub on his own goddamn property?"

"*Obviously,* yes." Finn didn't retreat, but he did reposition. "I *am* sorry I interrupted uh, your private time. That wasn't my intention."

Jacob's arms spread out onto either side of the edge of the tub, skin damp and rippling with muscle.

Finn swallowed hard. This would be a hell of a lot easier if Jacob wasn't hot—if Finn wasn't attracted—if Jacob wasn't *naked.*

But Jacob was hot, Finn was attracted, and Jacob was *definitely* naked.

Jacob didn't seem all that angry anymore. More amused. "You walked into my backyard, which *does* have a fence, by the way, so I'm unsure what your intention was."

"I needed to talk to you. And when I knocked nobody answered, but I did hear the music and I thought—"

"You thought you'd just wander down and see what I was up to?"

"Uh, well, sure? And if you really want to be sure that fence is enough, maybe build it a bit higher next time."

Jacob picked up his wineglass and sipped the dark red liquid. "So what was important enough for you to jump my fence?"

"Coach me."

Jacob didn't look surprised. "I told you no already. Meant it too."

"You *have* to," Finn said. Begged, more accurately.

For the first time since he'd shown up unceremoniously in Jacob's backyard, he actually looked annoyed. "Oh, I do?"

Okay, he probably shouldn't have phrased it that way.

"You're the only one I've ever met who was largely unimpressed by my father. I need—I *want*—to know how you do it. I want to know how you never seemed to falter. How you were always able to shake off someone scoring on you and re-focus."

"There's lots of mindset coaches out there," Jacob reminded him. "That's not me."

"I know, I've been to them. I changed coasts. I changed colleges. I even fucking changed positions—"

"You're a natural goalie. Morgan wasn't wrong about that," Jacob said.

And maybe that should've made him feel better, but it didn't. Not really.

"It's not enough," Finn said. His throat felt tight but he managed to get the words out anyway. That was it, laid bare.

It wasn't enough. Maybe it wouldn't ever be enough.

"I wish I could help you, but I can't." Jacob's face closed over, but that wasn't enough either. Not enough to make Finn stop.

He wanted this too badly—not just for his father, anymore, but for *him*—and over the last few weeks, ever since he'd surprised himself by asking Jacob to coach him, he'd become convinced that the only way to accomplish every goal he'd set for himself was to get Jacob on board.

"You can, you're just saying no because . . ."

"Because?" Jacob asked, darkly amused. "Oh, please, enlighten me, kid."

"I'm not a kid. I'm twenty-one. And I want a career like you."

"Even if my career got cut short?"

"When you were on the ice, nobody could touch you, *ever*. Not even my dad. He hated you because you were better than he was."

"That's not necessarily true," Jacob said wryly.

"Yes—"

"No," Jacob interrupted, his voice firming. "No. He wasn't better or worse than me, but you're right, his bullshit mostly didn't bother me. *Mostly*. Because there were definitely a few times he got to me."

"That time you almost punched him in the face?"

Jacob chuckled. "Yeah. That's one of them. I'm just saying, *kid*, don't be like me. I'm not . . ."

Finn wasn't going to accept it. Either Jacob's no, or the disparaging tone he talked about his career with.

"Tell me why you won't, and we'll deal with it. It's not money—"

"No."

"It's not because you got other things going on."

"Ouch," Jacob said.

"Is it my dad? Because I'm his son?"

"No, I never cared about what Morgan thinks," Jacob said.

That was kind of what Finn had always figured anyway. That was how Jacob stayed unbothered by Morgan's antics. He truly didn't give a shit.

"But," Jacob continued, "I don't want to invite Morgan's bullshit either."

It wasn't like Finn hadn't tried not giving a shit. He had.

He'd just never evolved to that higher plane of being, despite all his efforts.

"Then what the fuck is it?" Finn wanted to know. If Jacob would tell him why then he could deal with it. He could get around it and convince Jacob to change his mind.

Jacob hesitated. He took another long drink of his wine. He looked everywhere but at Finn.

"I just think it's a bad idea. I'm not a coach. And you're—"

"I'm what?"

Jacob straight up looked away.

"Not 'cause I'm hopeless, right?" Finn pushed. He didn't think he was hopeless. He'd worked too hard. And as insane as it made him, Morgan had been right about goalie being the right position for him.

He just needed Jacob to help him get out of his own god-damn way *and* to help him elevate his skills.

"Hardly," Jacob said.

"Then what is it?"

"I'm not a coach. I can't be. And I definitely can't be *your* coach," Jacob said. Then looked like he immediately regretted it.

"Why not?"

But Jacob didn't answer, and Finn had a feeling this was the reason.

Whatever lay behind that last issue.

"If it's not because I'm a Reynolds, and not because I'm hopeless, it's not because . . ." Finn paused. Disbelieving it could *really* be about his sexuality. His dad had offhandedly mentioned Jacob being gay half a dozen times, even to the point of saying, when he'd retired early, that maybe he could come out now.

Of course he'd said it in that typical Morgan way, but Finn had gotten fairly good at reading between his dad's words.

It *couldn't* be because he was gay, too, unless . . .

Well.

Finn had a feeling that Jacob's reticence meant he wouldn't easily admit his attraction, but he had options.

Including the most obvious one.

It wasn't exactly warm—being early December in Portland—but Finn slipped his jacket off and let it fall to the deck.

"What are you doing?" Jacob didn't just sound annoyed now. Or wry. Or over this whole conversation. He seemed . . . tense.

Funny, because Finn hadn't been sure the heat spiking inside him every time their eyes met might not be just in his head. But based on what he'd said *and* the tremor of Jacob's hand as he grabbed the bottle of wine and refilled his glass, Finn was beginning to wonder if he'd read this situation all wrong.

Finn stripped his T-shirt off. "I'm getting into your hot tub." No, he wasn't. He only wanted to call Jacob's bluff.

But Jacob didn't know that.

"No, you're sure as hell not." He was totally panicking now.

He wasn't even trying to hide it anymore as Finn toed his shoes off.

"You don't want me to get in there, do you?"

"Of course not! It's my fucking hot tub and I'm—"

"You're naked. And you don't like it, but you'd like me to be naked too." Finn's hands strayed down to the button of his jeans. He didn't flick the button open, but he knew he wouldn't have to.

"No." Jacob hesitated. "I don't want you to be naked, at all. I swear . . ." He muttered something under his breath that might've been *dirty old man.*

"You're not old, and I certainly hope you're dirty," Finn teased. "Even if it's not for me."

"It's just been . . ." Jacob swallowed hard. "Awhile for me, okay? And you're making it hard—"

"I hope that's true, too."

"Ugh," Jacob complained. "I'd ask why you're doing this, but I already know."

"Yep," Finn said cheerfully.

"If I coach you, nothing else is happening."

Finn lifted his hands over his head. "I didn't say it was." Though he was a little disappointed. Who *wouldn't* want Jacob Braun in their bed?

But if the coaching was all that was on offer, he'd take that, no questions asked.

Jacob flushed. Or maybe it was the hot water he was currently hiding in. "Right, no. Of course not. I just—"

"We can keep it professional. Don't worry, I'll keep my hands to myself," Finn promised.

"That . . .I didn't say yes," Jacob argued.

"Surely I can do something for you, too. We'll make it an exchange. You coach me to be a great goalie and to pretend like Morgan Reynolds doesn't exist, and I'll—"

"Don't you dare say you'll hop in my bed," Jacob said between clenched teeth.

He hadn't been about to, but *that* was an idea. For a split second, Finn let himself contemplate that *very* enjoyable exchange.

But he shook his head. "I wasn't going to," Finn said. "What *do* you need help with?"

"If only you had this confidence when you're between the pipes," Jacob groused.

"I know. It's a character flaw." Finn paused. "One we're going to correct."

"Oh, we are, are we?" Jacob rolled his eyes. Sipped his wine. "What if there *was* something you could help me with?"

"That's what I keep saying," Finn said.

Jacob tapped his fingers on the edge of the tub. "You came out."

"Was I ever *in*?" Finn wondered. He'd never made some big announcement or anything. He'd just lived his life. Never worried about what people would say about *that*. He hadn't any extra bandwidth, not when he'd spent so many hours and brain cells focused on being Morgan Reynolds' son.

Being gay had felt easier, weirdly enough.

"I'm trying to get there." Jacob sounded strangely apologetic, like it was *his* character flaw that he'd been stuck in the closet—even though it was more a symptom of the times and the career he'd chosen than him being a good, or a bad, person.

"Okay," Finn said.

"I think I could use some advice and guidance that's not coming from my agent or my PR. They're overly focused on making a big deal out of it—"

"It's not a big deal?" Finn wondered. Not judging, but genuinely curious.

"I just want to fucking live. I couldn't for so long and . . .and I'm ready now."

Finn nodded. He didn't know what that felt like—but then maybe he did, after all. He just wanted to be able to pull his skates on, pick up his stick and take his place on the ice without that litany of questions. Questions he asked. Questions everyone else asked.

And maybe he couldn't silence those. But he could silence his own fucking brain.

"Here I thought you were going to ask me to do something *hard*," Finn said.

"Finn—" Jacob warned.

Finn laughed. "Not *that*, God, not what I meant. You really need to stop worrying I'm going to seduce you." *Though that would be fun.*

"I'm not," Jacob said flatly.

"Okay, worrying that you're going to lose all your self-control and seduce *me*." *And that would be even* more *fun.*

Jacob choked on his wine. "That wasn't; *I wasn't.*"

"Well, then stop acting like it. I'm hot. You're hot. Maybe we're both attracted but that doesn't mean we have to act on it. We're going to keep it professional. I get it. It's disappointing, but I get it."

Jacob stared at him.

"Too much honesty?" Finn was aware he was babbling now, but it was hard to stop himself. "Trust me, I'm not *that* irresistible. And neither are you."

Maybe that was even more disappointing. But when Finn thought about trading the chance to play hockey free and clear, no pressure, no frustration, no self-recrimination, for the possibility of a few nights in Jacob's bed, it was no contest.

Finn didn't say it though, because every guy had an ego and maybe Jacob Braun was chill, but he was still a man, wasn't he?

Oh, he sure fucking is.

"No?" Jacob asked dryly.

"No." Finn picked up his T-shirt, pulling it back on, and then shrugged his jacket on. Leaned over and shoved his feet back into his sneakers.

"Alright. But the moment it doesn't work out—"

"It's going to work out," Finn said confidently.

"Again, we've gotta find that confidence on the ice," Jacob said.

"That's *your* job," Finn retorted. And now his own ego was smarting, because Jacob was right. He was confident everywhere else, but once the horn sounded, it evaporated. Finn told himself it was a good thing—not humiliating at all—that Jacob had identified this so easily, so quickly.

"Nope, it's yours still, kid."

"Don't call me that."

Jacob's smile was amused. "Fine. No *kid*. Probably better that way."

"Better if you don't want to think of yourself as a dirty old man, anyway."

Jacob sighed. "Can you forget you heard that?"

"No way."

"You'll pay for it," Jacob warned.

Finn had kind of assumed he would. "But if it makes me better, am I really paying for it?"

Jacob didn't say anything, just stared at him flatly. Like he already wanted to throttle him. Finn told himself that was a much better alternative than wanting to do anything else, but it wasn't quite convincing enough.

It'll need to be.

"This your phone?" Finn asked, gesturing towards the one sitting next to the bottle. If he pushed Jacob any harder, he might tell him to get the fuck off his property without agreeing to anything—coaching *or* sex—and that would be a real problem.

"Yes, but don't," Jacob said. Sighed as Finn's hand closed around it. But he handed it to the guy instead.

"Just wanted to give you my phone number, old man," Finn said. "No need to overreact."

"I wasn't," Jacob insisted. But he unlocked it and handed it to Finn anyway. "Just put your number in, and don't do anything crazy like send me gay porn."

"But gay porn is so fun," Finn said. It was also so fun to work Jacob up. To make that flush climb up his chest to his cheeks.

But that way, probably—okay, almost certainly—lay disaster.

He'd need to remember that.

"This isn't about fun," Jacob said, and Finn decided that was just the reminder he needed.

It wasn't about fun. It was about their futures.

And if Jacob wanted his even half as much as Finn wanted his own, then he'd want it an awful lot.

He typed in his number to a text and pressed send.

"There," Finn said, handing the phone back. "Now we're all set. When do we start?"

Jacob groaned.

"Tomorrow? Is that too soon?"

"Yes. No." Jacob groaned again. "I gotta think about this."

"Not if you're going to do it," Finn clarified.

"No. *How* I'm going to do it," Jacob said.

Finn breathed out a sigh of relief. "Okay. Yeah. How. Well, let me know, okay?"

"Okay," Jacob said. Paused. "Now get out and let me enjoy this wine."

Finn wasn't stupid. Having gotten exactly what he'd come for, he got out.

CHAPTER 4

"You're looking a little pale this morning," Bryan observed wryly as they rounded a turn in Forest Park.

His brother would know, because nobody else knew him as well as Bryan and Bryan was also a doctor. Admittedly, he specialized in pediatrics and children didn't tend to get hangovers from a bottle and a half of red wine, but still. He'd know.

Since Jacob had retired, Monday mornings were their running time. Usually they tried to make it twice more during the week, though that day changed depending on Bryan's schedule. Not just with his work, but his family.

Jacob had two small, very adorable nieces, Jacqueline and Krista, who had yet to get the memo that their uncle was not very cool.

"I got a little carried away with this cab sauv. A really delicious smoky fruit. You'd have liked it, but unfortunately I drank the whole goddamn bottle," Jacob admitted.

"That's not like you."

Jacob had debated whether he'd tell his brother about the late-night visitor who had systematically demolished a few of his walls—and seemed hell-bent on destroying some more in the weeks and months to come.

You really need to stop worrying I'm going to seduce you.

If Finn had any inkling how laughably easy it might've been, maybe he would've proposed that exchange.

Sex for coaching.

But Jacob knew he'd never have taken the offer, even if he wanted to.

Things were complicated enough between him and anyone with Reynolds as a last name without adding fucking to the equation.

"I had someone show up last night. At the house."

Bryan glanced over at him. "A hookup? Good. You need—"

Jacob interrupted him because that was the last thing he wanted to hear. Especially not right now when he was trying to focus on *not* saying fuck it and just taking it. "No. Not a hookup. Uh . . .Finn Reynolds. That's who showed up."

Bryan did a double take. "Not . . .well, *that's* awkward."

"Yep. Morgan's son. He's a goalie for the local college's hockey team. Really pretty decent goalie, I think."

"You think?" Bryan's question seemed innocent enough, but Jacob knew better.

"I might've watched him a bit," Jacob conceded, breath coming out in faster pants. "Mostly out of curiosity. And then we ran into each other when I went to their fundraiser a few weeks back."

"Mostly?"

It was annoying how Bryan always knew what he wasn't saying.

"He's not a child, you know. I'm not—I wouldn't—I *don't*."

"Hey, I didn't say *anything*." Bryan threw his arms up in mock innocence as they took another turn, moving deeper into the forest.

Jacob had set a bit of a punishing pace—the reason he wasn't going to touch with a ten-foot pole—but Bryan seemed to be keeping up just fine. He might've not had a career as a professional athlete, but he'd kept himself fit.

"He's twenty-one, and besides, it's not like that."

"Yeah, 'cause Morgan would murder you. Might murder you, anyway, frankly, but this would only add more fuel to the fire."

"I can't imagine Finn telling him," Jacob said. "Even about the coaching."

"So that's what he wanted, huh? Not to get into your pants, but to get into your mind?" Bryan snorted.

"Something like that."

"And you're going to do it." It was a statement, not a question.

"Well . . ." He'd said he would. Even though he'd said no initially, he *did* want to help Finn with all the demons plaguing him, despite all the very good reasons not to. And then there was the fact that Finn could also help *him*.

A fact he might not have even considered except that he'd only been in his hot tub, drinking wine because the meeting with Sophie and Mark had frustrated him so much. Maybe Finn wasn't an expert on image, but he could give Jacob a different perspective.

"You're going to do it," Bryan repeated, this time with a smile tilting the side of his mouth.

"Yeah."

"Well, God help you," Bryan teased.

"I know," Jacob grumbled. He pushed his sweaty hair back from his forehead. "Except I don't know how to be a fucking coach. I don't know how to teach him how to not give a shit about his dad."

"Let me guess—he came to you because his impression of the situation is that Morgan was always bothered by you, but you didn't give a crap about Morgan."

Jacob nodded.

"Well, that'll be an interesting conversation."

"It's not that I was *bothered* by Morgan."

"No, but we both know it was more complicated than that. Maybe the world didn't know about it because you didn't spout off about the dickhead every chance you got, but he bothered you."

And there it was, in a nutshell.

"I *can* teach him to block out noise, though. I can teach him to be a good—a *great*—goalie."

"That you can, little brother." Bryan patted him on the shoulder. "But I bet I can still take you down today." He gestured to the top of the hill they were heading towards and then took the fuck off, finding a new gear.

Jacob made an outraged noise and pushed his legs harder, faster, lungs bellowing.

They raced up the side of the gently rolling hill, and by the time they got to the top, he was breathing hard and his legs were burning, but he felt better, too, like he'd sweated out the last vestiges of the wine.

"I hate it when you're right," Jacob told his brother when he'd finally caught his breath.

"Hey, it was to your benefit, too," Bryan teased. "So you're really going to do this and not tell Morgan."

"If he'd even take my call—"

Bryan interrupted him. "He's going to find out. And then he's going to be really, *really* pissed."

"Why?" Jacob asked even though he knew exactly why Morgan might be pissed. "It's not like *he* can teach Finn how to be a better goalie. And he's Morgan so he'll want his son to be the best. Even if that means I'm involved."

"So you *do* want to tell him."

"No." Jacob let out a hard breath. "Because he'll assume . . .because we all know what he'll assume, and it won't be *that* far from the truth, probably."

"That far, huh?" Bryan teased.

"It's not going to happen. There's a line I won't be crossing. A line I won't let *him* cross."

"You told him that?"

"Yes," Jacob said. Sighed. "I'm gonna have to find a better coping mechanism than a bottle of wine, though."

"Hard running, that'll do it," Bryan suggested, a light in his eyes. "Trust me, I know."

He and his ex-wife Marlena had gotten divorced five years ago, when she'd taken a once-in-a-lifetime job working at a brain injury study clinic in Switzerland. Their marriage had been over before that, but when Marlena had decided to move, taking the job, they'd agreed to co-parent, only.

And Bryan, with the primary custody of Jacqueline and Krista, found himself a single parent with not much time or energy to devote to dating. It didn't matter that he was bi and would've been happy with either sex. Even though the reasons for his dry spell were different than Jacob's, they'd both found themselves in the same position. Single. Alone. Sexless.

"I keep thinking, I come out, and maybe I'll finally find a guy who's willing to put up with me for more than just a night," Jacob said.

"But you're not really making much progress on that," Bryan guessed.

"Nope. I get Sophie and Mark's hesitancy, I do, but it's driving me crazy now. I've . . .I'm ready. And I feel like now that I'm finally there, they keep throwing up roadblocks."

"They trying to keep you in the closet?"

"The opposite." Jacob hesitated. Wiped his face down. Pulled a water bottle out of the light pack he wore. "They keep putting together crazier and crazier coming out plans. And I wondered, is that why all their suggestions suck? *Are* they trying to hold me back?"

"Holding you back is still holding you back."

"Well, I'm going to be getting a different perspective on the whole thing," Jacob said wryly.

"Let me guess—that's what Finn's going to be giving you. Not his dick."

"Not his dick," Jacob agreed. He ignored the pulse of disappointment and instead said, "Race you to the bottom?"

Bryan groaned, but the moment Jacob took off, he was hot on his heels.

"Where you off to in such a hurry?"

Finn had hoped he'd be able to slip off unnoticed at the end of the team's weight room session.

Jacob had texted him around noon and said to come to his place again at seven-thirty.

Their weight room session was supposed to last until then, but Finn figured if he took it a bit easy and ducked out five or so minutes early nobody would notice.

But of course Ramsey noticed.

There wasn't anything Ramsey wasn't aware of.

Including him sneaking out, apparently.

At least Finn believed that Ramsey cornered him in the hall-way outside the weight room, duffel bag on his arm, sweatshirt hood pulled up over his head.

"Uh . . .just have something I gotta handle," Finn said. Not meeting Ramsey's eyes, because that piercing light blue saw and cataloged everything.

Some of their teammates—even teammates who'd played with the guy for years—still stupidly thought he was just some pretty boy player, out for a good time. But Finn had long since suspected that was just a front Ramsey put on so nobody would see what he was really doing.

What was he really doing? Well, Finn wasn't *sure*, but he was fairly convinced Ramsey just liked organizing everything and everyone around him. Making sure it worked the "right" way. AKA the way Ramsey wanted it to. And since Ramsey also seemed to understand what people fundamentally needed—not even necessarily what they wanted—those scenarios were ones everyone usually ended up happy with.

Ramsey had set up Brody and Dean, Brody's football-playing boyfriend, as roommates, thinking, Finn was fairly certain, that they'd find their way into the same bed.

He'd gently pushed and prodded Elliott to see past the frozen, unyielding walls Malcom had put up, until they too had ended up happy together.

"What do you need to handle?" Ramsey asked casually.

But nothing with Ramsey was casual. Finn had figured that out. If Ramsey didn't think he saw through his little stunts with foosball and all the other things he did to try to put Finn's mind at ease, well . . .

Finn would've called him out on it ages ago, but the problem was that they *worked*. Even when Finn knew exactly what Ramsey was up to, they worked. Not always, and not as a long-term solution, but well enough that he'd manage not to implode this season. *Yet*.

"Just a thing," Finn said evasively.

"A hockey thing?"

Finn made a face. "Not everything is your business, Ramsey."

But Ramsey just shrugged, like they both weren't *very* aware of the fact he thought differently.

"Just curious. You seem like you're heading somewhere in a hurry. Kind of like a few days ago, when you raced off from drag brunch at Darcelle's."

Fucking Elliott and his huge ass mouth.

"I didn't—"

"You sure did." Ramsey's tone firmed. He was always so relaxed and easygoing until he revealed that he was all steel underneath. It was easy to forget he'd been a foster kid, who'd been forced to make his own way in the world.

But Finn, who'd been forged in a different kind of fire, but still a fire, always remembered.

"You gonna tell me what's going on with you?" Ramsey asked.

So I can fix it, was the unspoken end of Ramsey's question.

But Finn didn't need Ramsey's fixes. He needed to figure it out on his own, and he'd taken steps to do that.

"No," Finn said bluntly.

Ramsey made a face. "Are you really gonna be like that?"

"Are you really gonna be this fucking pushy?" Finn wanted to know.

"Hey, we're on the same side here. I just . . .I'm worried about you." Ramsey reached out and gripped his arm reassuringly. He meant it. That was Ramsey's magic; he wanted better for you than sometimes you even wanted for yourself. Reached higher than you'd ever dream to climb.

But not Finn. Not this time.

"You don't need to be, not anymore." Finn remembered what Jacob had said about him just last night.

We gotta find that confidence on the ice.

They would. Together. Finn felt sure of it. He could already see the end of this agony, and he'd never been as ready as he was right now to put it all behind him.

No matter the cost. Whatever it ended up being, he'd pay it, willingly.

"What are you doing?" Ramsey asked again. Like phrasing it differently would give him an answer this time.

"What I have to do," Finn said and turned and walked off.

Finn wasn't stupid enough to think the conversation was permanently over, but at least Ramsey didn't follow him.

It was about a fifteen-minute drive over the winding West Hills to get to Jacob's house.

He hadn't known what to expect last night when he'd come here, but this remote home, set way back from the road, its jagged but graceful peaks looking like it belonged in the forest where it sat, was not what he'd imagined.

It had been a good reminder then—and was still a good reminder now—that he didn't know Jacob Braun all that well.

Most of what he'd learned about the man was reading between the lines of what his dad said about him, not from the half a dozen times he'd met the man in person over the years.

Finn parked his SUV, grabbed his bag, and made his way to the house.

This time when he knocked on the front door, it opened immediately, like Jacob had been waiting for him.

Something fizzed inside him at that thought, but Finn shoved the thought away.

He wasn't here to seduce or be seduced.

He was here to become the best version of himself.

CHAPTER 5

"Hey," Jacob said, opening the door and gesturing him inside. He was wearing a plain navy blue T-shirt and a pair of loose gray sweatpants. His hair was lighter, less black than chestnut brown, the ambient light in the house picking up little hints of red in it. But his beard was dark as ever, even though it looked to Finn like he'd trimmed it.

"Hey," Finn said, suddenly nervous.

He wasn't sure if that was due to him realizing just how little he didn't know about Jacob Braun—or whether Jacob's appearance, clothed or naked, apparently had the same effect on his cock.

Unfortunately.

Jacob was eyeing him up and down. They were dressed similarly. He'd just thrown on the sweatshirt because of the early December chill, but otherwise, he was dressed to work out.

But would they be working out? It was a big house, but surely not big enough to hold any ice. They'd need to figure out a solution for on-ice practice. Maybe Jacob had some connections they could use, or Finn could ask Coach B how they could use Hossa Rink during off hours.

These were all things, Finn realized belatedly, they should've discussed last night. Not how badly they wanted to hop on each other's dicks.

"What are we up to tonight?" Finn asked, shifting from one foot to the other, because Jacob's silence was freaking him out a little.

"You still want to do this?"

"Are you serious?"

"It's a serious question." Jacob hesitated. "Maybe why I said no at first bothered you. Maybe you don't want to be alone with me."

Finn rolled his eyes. "I'm not worried about you at all. I'm only worried that . . ." Suddenly the emotion of it felt too close to the surface. What *if* he had to keep going this way? What if there was never an end to this relentless pressure? What if he never felt comfortable on the ice again? What if all this bullshit ended up chasing him away from hockey? What if, even worse, it meant that he never succeeded?

He'd been drafted in the third round by the Tampa Sentinels. Everyone had said, at a volume impossible to tune out, that he'd only been taken that high because of his last name. And even if they hadn't said it, Finn would've believed it.

When he'd changed colleges last year, moving from the east to the west coast, they'd barely seemed to care. He'd been worried they'd insist he move to the AHL or another one of the development leagues, thinking that would be a better use of his time than a new college. But they hadn't said a word, and that had ended up feeling even worse.

Morgan had pointed out, bluntly, that to get them to give a shit, he needed to have a killer season.

"I'm so close. I'm so fucking close." *To making it. To falling right off that edge. I need a hand, to pull me up, and it's sure not gonna be my dad's.*

Jacob stared at him, like he *knew* how close to falling apart Finn was.

Like he not only understood it, but that he'd experienced it, too.

"Okay."

It was all Jacob said, and he turned abruptly and started walking farther into the house. Finn followed, eyes barely taking in the floor-to-ceiling windows that framed the picture-perfect woods, barely visible in the darkness.

Jacob took him to a door and then a staircase, narrow and winding, that led down.

Maybe he should've hesitated. Maybe he *was* about to be murdered, in Jacob's serial killer basement.

But to Finn's surprise the narrowness ended abruptly, in a large gym that might've taken up the whole downstairs level of the house.

One side of the room was lined with shelves, full of memorabilia and awards from when Jacob had played. Framed jerseys lined another wall. Jacob's, and several other famous players, including some who'd been teammates and some who hadn't.

Finn was not surprised that a Morgan Reynolds' jersey was not included in the display. His dad had played for a division rival and even more than that, there'd been so much venom exchanged between the two of them over the years.

Half the gym was devoted to equipment. Finn took in the treadmill, the rower, and an elliptical. A huge cushy looking mat, with stacks of weights.

But the other side was entirely different. There were only two pieces of equipment. A full-sized goal and a machine that Finn recognized could randomly shoot pucks.

The concrete floor was smooth, and might not be exactly like ice, but it would be close enough, on skates. *Roller*, not ice.

"Here," Jacob said, speaking up from behind Finn. He pointed to a bench pushed all the way to one side of the room. There was one set of in-line roller skates underneath that looked well-used. Jacob's, then.

And another pair, still nestled in a box.

"How'd you know my shoe size?" Finn asked, walking over to the bench. He'd practiced like this before. Not everyone had access to ice year-round. His dad had a setup like this in their Italian villa.

"Not that hard to find out," Jacob said. "Your equipment manager was all too happy to tell me when I texted him this morning."

Marcus could be a bit of a chatterbox.

"Did you tell him why?"

"I agreed to send over a signed puck, and *why* never even crossed his lips," Jacob said.

Finn didn't need to hear more. He understood, had watched it with his dad too many times to count. Most regular people froze and then became completely pliant when faced with a famous person. They couldn't even help it.

"You ever get tired of it?" Finn wondered as he sat on the bench, toeing off his sneakers and pulling over the skates.

"All the fucking time?" Jacob sighed. "Of course when it's convenient, no. And that's worse. Makes me a hypocrite."

"But a cute one?" Finn teased.

Jacob made a face. Like he was trying to be anything *but* cute. "I thought we said—"

"Listen, you have to stop worrying about this. I . . ." Finn hesitated. "I make jokes, 'cause it's easier than feeling all the bullshit I feel. So get used to it."

"Alright," Jacob said stiffly. He looked like he wanted to ask what the bullshit was but he didn't. Maybe he already knew—or could guess.

Finn laced up the skates. "Any particular drill you want to run after I get stretched out?"

"Nope—I wanna see what you've got."

"But you've seen me . . ." Finn trailed off as he got his first skate laced up. Suddenly, he was nervous. What if he *was* crap? What if that was what Jacob said, when he finally saw him in action?

What if he said forget it, that he couldn't help Finn after all?

"Hey, cut that shit out." In a second, before Finn could even react, Jacob was across the room, right in front of him, hand smacking him on the shoulder.

"I—"

"No. You wanna be confident, *be* confident. Don't think, I'm gonna play in front of Jacob and he's gonna think I'm shitty. Instead, I'm gonna play in front of Jacob and he's going to see that I'm better than he thought I was. *I'm* gonna see I'm better than I thought I was." Jacob hesitated. "I can't be the first person to tell you that. Not if you've seen any mindset coaches."

"No," Finn admitted.

"But you're still doing it."

"I got . . ." It was hard to admit, but maybe necessary. "I got sloppy. Complacent. Easier to let myself flail around than fight this all the time. I'm . . .I'm *tired* of fighting it."

Jacob's gaze—that hard flinty darkness—softened a bit. "Doesn't help to hear that you're gonna be fighting that insecurity forever, does it?"

"No." That had been his breaking point. That it would never change. Never go away. That he'd be pushing against it for as long as he played. And once he'd realized that, it had been easy to let it creep back in.

Easy to let it take back ahold of him, like it had never left.

"But we're gonna find a way that it's not so loud. That it's not so tough to fight against," Jacob said, and he *did* sound confident that was true. "'Cause I'm gonna tell you, it's not that I let things slide off easy. It never came easy. You give a shit about being good? It's *never* gonna be easy."

Finn wanted to be angry at Jacob's bluntness, but it was hard when he was right.

He nodded, and Jacob raised up. "Stretch out and get yourself ready." And to Finn's surprise, he joined him on the bench, pulling on the worn pair of skates.

Finn glanced at him.

"How am I gonna show you if I don't do it myself?" Jacob asked wryly.

"Lots of coaches don't."

"Well, I'm no coach," Jacob said with finality.

Finn didn't know if that pronouncement was meant for him or for Jacob himself, but he decided there was no point in arguing. He was only here by Jacob's good graces, and if those evaporated . . .

He finished lacing up his skates and began his regular stretching routine.

Trying to ignore Jacob as he did the same.

Even as he tried to focus, it was almost impossible *not* to look at the muscular curve of Jacob's ass in those gray sweatpants as it slowly rose and fell.

Finn tore his gaze away, digging his fingers into his palms. He wasn't here for sex, even though it felt like it had crawled, uninvited, into every moment of silence that fell between them.

"You ready?" Jacob asked, interrupting his litany of *don't think about it, don't think about it, don't think about it . . .*

"Uh, yeah. Yeah, I think so."

Jacob shot him a look.

"I'm ready," Finn revised.

Maybe he didn't feel supremely confident, but he could fake it at least well enough that Jacob might believe it. And if he was very, very good, maybe even *he'd* believe it.

Jacob had a variety of sticks on a rack on the wall, behind the goal. Finn skated over, testing out the new skates, and after a minute perusing the selection, picked one.

"No pads?"

Jacob tossed him a pair of form-fitting ones, one after the other. Finn caught them easily out of the air, raising a questioning eyebrow.

He knew perfectly well this wasn't the normal setup he wore. Jacob knew it too.

But Jacob's eyes gleamed knowingly. "Wanna see what we're dealing with. But put the helmet on."

Finn made a face. "But—"

"Let's see how you do without your gear," Jacob said. "But I'm not about to let you take a puck to the head."

"But—"

"I'm interested in how you move without it." He moved over to the machine and checked its feeder.

"Those aren't cheap," Finn said, picking up one of the helmets on the shelf. Slipping it on. "And they're hard to find."

"Good thing I'm rich then," Jacob said dryly.

"You need to find someone to spend all that money on," Finn teased.

Jacob grimaced.

"Or not?"

"No . . .no, I want to." This was not what they were supposed to be discussing, Finn knew it. Jacob knew it too, from the deepening crease between his brows.

But that didn't stop Finn from saying. "What's stopping you?"

He really didn't want to know. But he asked anyway as he strapped on the kneepads and maneuvered into the goal. Getting a feel for the space as Jacob repositioned the machine another foot back.

"The closet?" Jacob asked, the edge of his voice hard.

"That shouldn't stop you," Finn said. "Not if there was someone you really liked."

It wouldn't stop me. Even for a second.

Jacob rolled his eyes. "Stop digging, Reynolds."

Finn had told himself he wasn't, but maybe he was, a little. A guy like Jacob—rich and famous and hot, would have guys pounding at his door at a chance to pound—

He cut that thought off hard and fast.

Ignored how his fingers were shaking a little as he curled them around the stick.

"Ready," Finn said, nodding at Jacob.

Hoping he was. Ignoring the insidious voice deep inside that said he wasn't.

"It's set at three-quarter speed. For now," Jacob said, and Finn raised his chin.

Even at partial speed, the pucks came in hard and fast.

He wasn't as used to the in-line skates or the concrete beneath him as he was the ice. And playing without the pads he usually relied on meant he had to react quicker, more instinctually, not letting them take the easy shots.

Three shots in, his forehead was already damp as his focus narrowed to three things.

The stick he gripped in his hand, the next puck coming at him, and Jacob standing there, expression opaque.

Finn had been doing drills like this since he'd started playing goalie, but it had been a long time since he was pushed this hard or for this long.

His last coach and also Coach B both knew he had the basics down and both believed in quality of practice, not necessarily quantity.

But Jacob clearly believed differently. Because he left Finn in there longer than he'd ever dreamed, until sweat was running down his face, down his back, until he felt broken down, until all that was left was the puck and the goal.

Not even Jacob.

He didn't even register anymore.

It became a test, one Finn was determined, with every aching muscle in his body, to pass.

Finally, the machine clicked on an empty chamber, and Jacob reached over, turning it off.

"Hundred pucks," Jacob said casually. "Not easy, is it?" He wandered over to a mini fridge set against the wall and grabbed a bottle of water, tossing it over in Finn's direction. He caught it with his free hand, because his other hand seemed permanently clamped around his stick. He tried to loosen it, but his fingers cramped, rejecting the idea it was over.

"No," Finn said with a short, humorless laugh. He finally got his hand to loosen, letting the stick clatter to the floor. Pushed the helmet off and chugged half the water, set it down, and yanked his T-shirt up and off, wiping off his face.

When Jacob's gaze traced over his abs, his chest, at least the pulse of attraction was easier to ignore since he was fucking exhausted.

They'd have a chance in hell of not acting on the heat between them if Jacob kept working him this hard.

"You weren't terrible," Jacob said matter-of-factly. "By the time we're done, I want you to be able to make it through that whole stretch without a single goal."

"Seriously?" Finn spluttered. He'd let in maybe a dozen or so shots. But considering the difficulties—the sheer number of pucks shot at him and the lack of pads he usually relied on—he'd been pretty proud of how low that number actually was.

"I do it a couple times a week, still," Jacob said. Like that wasn't completely fucking certifiable.

"You do realize you're retired, right?" Finn said, annoyance coupled with frustration making him crueler than he'd ever wanted to be.

"Oh, I realize it," Jacob said, not insulted, even though maybe he should've been. "But it keeps the mind sharp and the body primed and ready to go. It reminds me to lead with my instincts. You got there, towards the end. You let all that shit and your baggage drop and you just *played*. You gotta get into that headspace every single damn time you take the ice."

"I—"

"I know," Jacob said as he started gathering the pucks up into the machine's hopper. "It's gonna take time."

"I was gonna say I can't do that. It's fucking impossible."

Jacob shot him a look that spoke volumes. Like, *you can't say that word here.* Like, *you're never allowed to give up that easily.* Like, *I'm not fucking giving up on you that easy.*

"Yeah? Okay." Jacob didn't argue though. Not with words.

He skated over, and his big body moved with a state of grace that Finn could barely believe. Before Finn could react, he plucked the helmet right off Finn's head, apparently not caring about Finn's sweat slicked inside. He picked up the stick Finn had dropped and tested the weight.

"Not my favorite, but it'll be fine. A challenge," Jacob said, his eyes suddenly not flinty but *hot*. He hip-checked Finn out of the way and gestured towards the machine. "Turn it on, okay? And turn the speed up to full."

Exhaustion was making him slow—not just mentally but physically. "Are you joking?"

Jacob made an exasperated noise. "Do I look like I'm joking?"

"Listen, I know you're good, you don't have to prove any-thing—"

"You think that's what this is about?" Jacob laughed. "Oh baby, I'm not proving anything to you. Or to anyone else. I'm proving it to *me*."

It occurred to Finn, as he found the speed switch, chang-ing the setting, and then re-loaded the pucks, watching Jacob prepare himself out of the corner of his eye, that he couldn't actually remember the last time he'd set out to prove something to himself. To *just* himself.

His team, his coach, the hockey community, his *dad*, they were always there, in his head, cluttering up his motivation until it was all twisted up.

That, Finn knew as he finished loading the pucks, was the biggest problem. And Jacob hadn't even had to fucking tell him. He'd just *showed* him.

"You ready?" Finn asked. Jacob nodded and he pressed the start button.

And then Jacob proceeded to keep *showing* him.

He moved so naturally, so easily Finn thought he could skate right onto the ice today and give a performance that wouldn't only be sufficient, it would be extraordinary.

It wasn't until the nineteenth puck, Jacob having easily swatted away the first eighteen, that the only crack in Jacob's armor appeared.

It was a corner shot, when Jacob had just been on the opposite side. Finn knew exactly how he'd have relied on his hips to push him over, quick enough that he could easily deflect the puck.

But Jacob clearly knew he couldn't. He didn't move that way at all. Instead his stick shot out, and even though he was moving slower and more carefully than Finn ever would've, he still managed to catch the puck on the far edge of the blade, barely flicking it away.

Finn had been sure that shot was going to get by him, and each subsequent puck that forced Jacob into that position, he held his breath, waiting for him to move just a fraction too slow this time around.

But he didn't.

Jacob knew exactly what his capabilities were. Had practiced with them enough that he knew exactly what he could and could not do.

It was an impressive display, and Finn shouldn't have been turned on—this was *hockey*, not sex, after all—but the incredible control he showed over his body made him inevitably wonder what else Jacob was capable of.

He'd be great in bed. Focused and intent, with the kind of control Finn would long to break down, to *own*.

When Jacob finally finished, accomplishing what Finn hadn't, Finn couldn't even be mad.

Okay, he was a *little* mad because he wouldn't ever be getting an invitation to Jacob's bed.

"Shit, man, that was crazy good," Finn said as Jacob lifted his helmet, wiped his own face with his T-shirt.

Finn didn't ignore the ripples of his abs or the trail of dark hair that led down to his sweatpants. He was long past not looking.

"Good, but you saw, I'm sure," Jacob said, barely out of breath.

It was annoying, because Finn was in good shape—in *great* shape—but it was also aspirational. If Jacob could do this at thirty-five, with a bum hip, then Finn could do it too. He could be *this* good.

It felt like the first positive thought he'd had to hold on to in so fucking long.

The first bit of light in a long darkness.

"Yeah," Finn said. But he didn't want to focus on that. He wanted to focus on what was *possible*.

Because suddenly, the whole universe felt possible.

"And now you know why I retired."

Ironically, Jacob appeared to have lost his own confidence after that. Which was fucking baffling.

"Yeah, you don't have the range you used to, but you *still* did it. You worked around it, and you were amazing. Absolutely fucking amazing—"

"Let's not get carried away," Jacob said dryly. He went for his own water and guzzled it down.

"I don't see why I shouldn't," Finn argued. *Let me have this.* "Why'd you retire?"

"You saw it," Jacob said simply.

"But you compensated for it."

"Yeah. But it takes attention and focus to do that. Takes attention and focus away from what matters. I wasn't the same goalie I was before."

"Still damn good," Finn muttered.

"And really good players would learn how to take advantage." Jacob hesitated. "If your dad had still been playing, you don't think he wouldn't have shot towards that opposite corner every single damn time?"

He would've. It would've been the only smart thing to do, against a partially hampered goalie, even a goalie who'd figured out how to *mostly* get around it. And Morgan wouldn't have even been wrong to do it.

"See, you get it," Jacob said, and Finn really hated the heavy resignation in his tone.

"I do," Finn said, and something in his voice must've finally caught Jacob's attention, because he lifted his head, their eyes meeting.

"Yeah?"

"Watching you do that, like you just did, it . . ." Finn took a deep breath. "I feel different. Not a *lot* different, but different."

"A good start then." Jacob motioned to the goal. "Come on, let's try it again."

Finn didn't argue. Just took the helmet and the stick.

It was easier to sink into that headspace this time around, now that he understood it a little better.

And he was deep into the hundred shots before he mistimed slightly, and one slipped by him.

Finn growled deep in his throat, annoyed with himself, but Jacob called out, his presence registering for the first time in what felt like dozens of shots, "It's all good. Re-focus. Finish strong."

And he did, not letting in a single other puck for the rest of the series.

"Better," Jacob said, when it was finally over, giving Finn a single nod of approval that he'd probably see when he closed his eyes tonight, exhausted and wrung out but still caught on the man in front of him.

"Thanks," Finn said. Suddenly realizing just *how* tired he was.

He skated over to the bench and hunched over, untying his skates. Jacob followed him, gingerly setting himself down.

"You alright?" Finn asked, glancing over as Jacob winced, shifting around on the hard bench like he was trying to find a more comfortable position.

"Oh yeah. Just . . . just a little stiff. Should've stretched while you were doing your second round, but I got caught up . . ."

Finn wondered if Jacob had gotten caught up the same way he had, when he'd watched Jacob.

But before he could open his mouth and ask this potentially very stupid question, real pain crossed over Jacob's face.

"What is it? You okay?" Worry spiked inside Finn. Did Jacob *not* normally do this and he'd only done it today in order to coach Finn? Had he been doing it to show off and now he'd fucked up his hip even more?

If that was true, then Finn shouldn't feel guilty—that was all on Jacob. But guilt swamped him anyway.

"I . . .*ugh* . . .just normally use the sauna right after, to prevent it from—" Jacob exhaled sharply. "To prevent it from locking up."

"Like it's doing right now?" Finn didn't tell him that he shouldn't have waited through his second round. He didn't have to; Jacob already knew.

"Yeah," Jacob ground out. He glanced over at a small door, set into the other side of the gym that Finn assumed led to his sauna.

He bent down, like he was going to unlace his skates, but his wince was obvious.

Finn didn't think; he just acted.

Slid down to the floor at Jacob's feet, fingers picking at the knots he'd tied into the laces. Reached up and put a hand on Jacob's knee, for leverage. Froze when *he* froze.

"This okay?" Finn asked, worried that somehow he'd hurt him more.

"I . . ." Jacob trailed off, his dark eyes intent on Finn's. "You don't have to do this."

"Yeah, I know. But I want to." The lace finally came untied, and Finn braced Jacob's foot against his thigh, pulling sharply.

When he glanced back up, Jacob's cheeks were flushed. And Finn didn't think it was from the exercise.

"Don't get used to it, though, me on my knees for you," Finn teased.

The flush deepened, going dark red. "I wouldn't. I *won't*."

If Finn was Elliott or Ramsey he'd probably keep pushing. Say something about how he probably looked good like this, but even though he hoped it was true, he didn't say it out loud.

The solid warmth of Jacob's knee under his palm and the way Jacob gazed down at him—like he was afraid to look and also afraid to look away—was enough of a tease.

Finn's fingers were shaking slightly as he reached for the lace of Jacob's other skate.

He knew he should let go of Jacob's knee, but he didn't want to. Liked how solid and warm it felt under his touch. Wished he could slide his fingers up farther, and then farther still, wondering what he might find hiding under Jacob's sweatpants.

You're here for hockey—not for sex.

The reminder was a bucketful of ice-cold water dumped on his head. But more importantly, on his crotch.

He picked at the knot, loosening it and then finally untangling it completely.

Finn got the skate off a minute later, and there was no reason to stay here, bent down at Jacob's feet, so he lifted himself. Considered offering a hand to Jacob, to help him up, but Jacob shot him a look full of wry embarrassment when he considered it. Like he knew what Finn was thinking and it was the last thing he wanted.

But the shaky way he lifted himself to his feet changed Finn's mind.

"Hey," he said, reaching out and wrapping an arm around Jacob's waist. It was narrow, unlike his much broader shoulders, and a knowing heat streaked through him.

"I'm good," Jacob said, making a half-hearted attempt to shake him off, but Finn was determined and wouldn't be dissuaded.

"No," Finn said firmly. "Let me help you."

"God, I'm not—" Jacob muttered a whole string of four-letter words under his breath. "I'm not a fucking invalid."

"Not at all," Finn said. "You headed to the sauna?"

Jacob shot him a look that might've been hotter than the steam inside. "Yeah. But—"

"No buts," Finn said. "I could use it too."

Jacob's gaze drifted down to Finn's sweatpants. "You gonna wear those in?"

"No," Finn said. Trying—and failing—not to be excited about the prospect of a naked Jacob again. "And neither are you."

"You seem very sure about this," Jacob said bluntly.

"It's just a little skin." *Gorgeous skin, but you'll live.*

"It'll be fine," Finn said.

"Not playing with fire?"

Finn let Jacob shake him off this time, only because Jacob had the wall to lean on as he hit the instrument panel for the sauna, turning it on.

Finn had already shed his T-shirt, and he wasted no time pushing down his sweatpants, fingers tucking into the elastic waistband of his boxer briefs.

Jacob was looking everywhere but at him. "We're doing pretty fucking great," he muttered. "First coaching session and we're already getting naked, together."

"Think of it as necessary medical treatment," Finn teased, letting his briefs fall. Jacob was studiously staring at the door, even as he pulled it open and walked in.

He'd sat down on the wooden bench, arranging himself in what he hoped was both a flattering yet not flirtatious pose, by the time the door opened again.

Finn knew he should avert his eyes. It was only polite. And he did, technically, but not before being graced by the glory of *shoulders—chest—abs—dick—thighs—calves.*

It wasn't a sight he'd forget anytime soon. In fact, Finn already knew that much later tonight, in the shower, what he'd be thinking about when he touched himself.

Maybe Jacob had been right and this was playing with fire.

Jacob settled down on the bench next to him, with at least two feet as a buffer between his naked thigh and Finn's. Finn supposed he should be relieved and not disappointed that he hadn't taken the bench opposite him.

At least he wouldn't be missing anything when he closed his eyes and let the crown of his head hit the back wall.

"That better?" Finn asked.

"Yeah," Jacob said, and Finn could hear the receding tension in his voice. The alleviation of the pain.

"Good," Finn said.

Jacob didn't say anything else for a long moment, and Finn decided that sitting in silence, just soaking in the heat, was okay, too. That was the purpose of this, anyway.

He'd just remind himself of how it had felt the second time around. How his confidence had grown. How he'd been able to shake off the one puck he'd let score. That was way better to dwell on than the fact that only a few feet away, Jacob was naked.

And so are you.

But Jacob had other ideas than letting him visualize. "I didn't want you to see that," Jacob said.

"It's fine," Finn said. "Not like I've never been around an injury before."

"I know, but . . ." Jacob trailed off, but Finn had a pretty damn good idea of what he'd been about to say.

I know, but those guys weren't attracted to you.

Finn was no longer quite as certain that them being bluntly honest about their mutual attraction had been the right move.

How long would it take before one—or both—of them decided the pleasure would be worth the risk and the mess?

"You didn't embarrass yourself," Finn reassured him.

He wanted to reach out and touch him, but that would be even worse now that he was naked than it had been before, through the thick fabric of his sweatpants. Instead, Finn tucked his hand under his own thigh and reminded himself again that he'd be keeping his touch to himself.

"Sure," Jacob said sarcastically.

Finn considered and then discarded half a dozen ways of convincing him that was true.

Or you could be very stupid and be blunt again.

"Trust me, I'm still gonna be thinking about you, later tonight. Bum hip and all."

Jacob seemingly choked on air. "I don't need to know about that."

Finn took a risk and glanced over at him. *His* eyes were still closed, but his hands were clenched fists resting on the top of his bare thighs.

"Just making sure you know it wasn't actually a turn-off," Finn said, forcing his voice to remain light.

"Good to know." Jacob's voice was cold. Flat. But Finn couldn't take it personally, not when he knew exactly why.

"Next time—tell me, okay?"

Jacob grunted, but Finn had a feeling that it wouldn't be a problem again.

Finn decided if they were being blunt about sex, they could be blunt about hockey, too. "You good getting back on the ice with me? Giving me some pointers?"

"Would Gavin—Coach Blackburn—be okay with that?" Finn heard the waver in Jacob's voice.

"Didn't Coach B *offer to* bring you on as a coach at the beginning of the year?"

Jacob was quiet for so long that Finn almost wondered if he'd fallen asleep. Some people could do that in a sauna. Not Finn, but maybe Jacob was built that way.

"Yeah. I said no. For good reasons, but . . ."

"But?"

Jacob sighed. "Finn, I know we agreed I'd do this, and I do think I can help but . . ."

"You can't keep starting to give me a goddamn reason and then saying *but* without finishing," Finn objected.

"I know. I'm sorry." Jacob took a deep breath. "I don't talk about this—well, except with Moira and my brother, I guess. But, I don't know if I can go back on the ice."

"Not medically," Finn clarified.

"Not medically," Jacob agreed.

Finn looked over at him, right in the eyes. He wasn't surprised to see Jacob looking back at him. "I'm sorry. I had no idea. I wouldn't have—"

"No, that's not why I told you," Jacob said. "I told you because . . .well, because I think this might be good for me, but it's not gonna be easy and you might have to be patient. I guess if you can tolerate my hip and the way it locks up, you can deal with this bullshit too."

"I can," Finn reassured him.

"I'd *like* to come to practice. And to games. But . . .but it's hard. I'll get there, but it sucks in the meantime."

"That why you stayed on the wall during the fundraiser? Staring at me?"

Jacob chuckled. "Uh, yeah. Number one for sure, number two . . .you'd grown up."

"Oh, that's what you decided, huh? That I was all grown-up and fair game?"

"Uh. No. Yes." Jacob went bright red, and Finn knew it wasn't entirely due to the steam.

Finn decided to let him off the hook. "I can be patient. At least if we're working together here, like this."

"You need more though," Jacob objected.

Finn tamped down his outraged ego, as Jacob made a face and kept going. "Not like that. Not like it sounded. I mean to really help you, I *should* be at practices. At games. It's what you meant. It's what you wanted."

It was, but how selfish and demanding would Finn be if he told Jacob to just get over it? People liked to say that to him, sometimes. That he should be *grateful* that his dad was Morgan

Reynolds and surely it was easy to just change his perspective. Like Finn hadn't tried to do that a hundred times already. A *thousand*.

"Yeah, but I can work at your speed," Finn said. "It's way better than nothing. Way better than the way I've been playing."

Jacob nodded. He didn't look one-hundred-percent convinced and unfortunately it wasn't as easy to persuade him as it was about Finn's attraction. All that would've taken was a few blunt words and maybe a picture, post-jerkoff session.

But this was trickier.

"Trust me," Finn said, and Jacob nodded again.

"What if you just came to practice? Didn't come out on the ice?" The moment the question was out of his mouth Finn wanted to take it back—it made him sound so freaking desperate for even the barest scrap of Jacob's attention. But he didn't. Because he *needed* every single goddam scrap.

Jacob frowned but didn't immediately dismiss the idea, not like Finn had imagined he might. "You think your coach would be okay with that?"

"I can ask, but I can't imagine Coach B would be mad about it."

"Alright. No promises. But I'll try to do it this week. And let me be the one to ask, okay?"

"You sure?" Finn did regret it now, because he'd pushed him into this.

But Jacob just nodded. "Yeah, I'll see what I can do," Jacob said. Finn reminded himself that if Jacob didn't want to do this, he didn't have to. If he didn't want Finn around, he'd just tell him to fuck off—or not bother texting him in the first place.

Finn didn't think Jacob would do that, though. Not now. But still, that didn't mean he was ready to go back to the ice. Maybe he would be someday.

But he wasn't today, and Finn needed to make his peace with it.

CHAPTER 6

Jacob had told Finn he'd think about practice, and he'd meant it, but to his surprise, the thought lingered.

Through him seeing Finn off. Through his shower.

All evening, through the TV he watched, forcibly trying to turn his goddamn mind off.

He was lying in bed, staring at the dark ceiling, when he suddenly wondered if the reason the thought kept hanging around was because he *wanted* to do it.

Maybe not go one-on-one with Finn. Maybe not go to every practice. But to strap his skates back on and see what he could do to help? Yes.

The last thought he had before falling asleep was that he'd call Coach Blackburn—*Gavin*, the man had insisted Jacob call him, when they'd met up earlier this fall—first thing in the morning.

It didn't happen, though.

Instead, he cycled through everything he could find, giving himself anything and everything to do but make the phone call. He wanted it, yes, but it also terrified the shit out of him.

"Stop this," he told himself as he finished wiping out his nearly bare refrigerator. "You're braver than this."

Was he though?

Moira would've told him there was nothing to be gained by being hard on himself, but it was hard when Jacob could look back over the morning and see every fucking thing he'd done to avoid making the phone call.

Wallowing in bed, which he'd excused because he'd had restless sleep—thanks to the dream of a naked, sweaty Finn dancing in his head.

Extra-long workout, even though his hip had been screaming from the night before.

Followed by an equally lengthy shower and breakfast.

Then scouring the kitchen and the fridge, even though his cleaning service was supposed to be stopping by tomorrow.

Jacob collapsed onto the couch and pulled his phone out. Stared at the screen for a long moment.

Then finally dialed.

He really hoped that he'd just have to leave a voicemail but a kind, gruff voice answered on the second ring.

Jacob made a face, glad he wasn't on FaceTime.

"Jacob, I'm glad you called," Gavin said, sounding pleased and surprised.

Jacob made another face. "Yeah," he said. "I . . .uh . . ." *Stop this fucking waffling. Either you wanna help Finn or you don't.* "I was wondering if that offer from earlier in the year was still open. Helping out with some coaching."

"Sure is," Gavin said. He didn't ask specifically, but Jacob knew he had to be wondering. "The offer's always open, if you want to stop by practice. I can send you a schedule, so you can just drop by whenever, or if you have a more specific timeframe in mind . . ."

Jacob wasn't stupid; he knew Gavin was digging to know exactly what had motivated this change of attitude.

He shouldn't tell him about him and Finn—not that there was anything specific to tell. But anytime he paired up with a Reynolds it would undoubtedly be big news in the hockey community.

Still, Gavin was Finn's coach. He should know the truth. Maybe if he even knew some of what Jacob was trying with him, he could reinforce the ideas.

"I'm hoping to come to at least one practice a week." He could manage that, right? He could. He *would*. "Specifically to work with Finn. And uh . . .the other goalie."

There was a long pause. Jacob told himself he was imagining things—it was *just* silence. But it felt loaded, like there was a whole list of admonitions Gavin was thinking and then discarding.

"Finn and Nick?"

"Yes, Nick." He hadn't even known the other guy's name, even though he'd technically asked for one-on-one coaching before Finn ever had. But sure, he could help him, too.

Gavin chuckled wryly. "So Finn got to you, huh?"

"You could say that. You know—"

"Oh, I know," Gavin said. Of course he'd know about him and Morgan. *Everyone* knew.

"I don't suppose we could keep this sort of under wraps?"

"Like give you a heads-up when I know Morgan's coming into town?"

"He does that?" Finn hadn't mentioned it, but that might explain why Finn felt like he was slowly being crushed to death under the pressure.

Unsurprisingly, Morgan never took his foot off the gas.

"Oh yeah, he swings by at least every few weeks." Gavin paused. "I've told him it doesn't help. He laughed that right off."

"He would," Jacob muttered.

"You'd know."

Jacob sighed. "Yeah, I would. So he swings by, and what? Makes his son feel like shit and then fucks off, leaving you to pick up the pieces?"

"To be clear, I don't think he *realizes* that's what happens after he takes off, but yeah."

"How can he not know?" Jacob was reconsidering not flying to New York to beat Morgan's ass. He'd deserved it for years, for all the shit he'd pulled with Jacob, and now there was Finn—and that *really* pissed Jacob off.

"Probably because he thinks he's helping."

"He's not," Jacob said flatly.

"I know that. Finn knows that. Now you know that. *He* doesn't know that."

"Ugh. And you've talked to him?" Jacob considered that maybe the next one to tell Morgan to leave Finn alone might have to be him, but what good was that going to do? Morgan had never listened to him, and he couldn't imagine that changing now.

"Mentioned it a couple of times."

"Okay. Well, if you know he's coming, yeah, give me a heads-up. I don't want to make things harder on Finn."

"No, you're trying to do the opposite," Gavin guessed.

"Yeah." He didn't know if he could, but damnit he was going to try.

Hadn't even realized just how determined he was to try until this phone call today. Last night he'd felt it too, but hadn't wanted to look too closely at it. Probably because he'd been afraid. Worried that his desire to help was caught up in an entirely different kind of desire.

You need to get laid. By someone not named Finn Reynolds.

"I'm glad," Gavin said. "He's got good instincts, when he listens to them."

"That's what I'm telling him."

"Good. I'll send the schedule, but you're welcome anytime."

"What about non-practice ice time?" Jacob couldn't believe he'd asked the question. Before this conversation, he hadn't even been sure he could go to a practice. But now, here he was asking about *more* ice time.

Moira would be proud. Confused, probably, but proud.

"I can arrange that, too." Gavin paused. "You're not gonna wear the kid out, are you?"

Jacob choked on air. Because of the *wear him out* or the *kid*—he wasn't entirely sure. Both, maybe.

"No. *No*," he repeated with as much certainty as he could.

"Okay, good. You know the line. And he's young. Hungry."

"He sure is." Jacob wished Finn was a little less hungry. A little less honest, too, because the more they talked about what they *weren't* doing, the more obvious it became that if Jacob crossed that line, Finn wouldn't turn him away.

"I'm sure glad you're doing this," Gavin said, "and if you need anything else, you just let me know, right?"

"Right. Will do," Jacob said.

A different brain maybe. A new hip. And don't get me started on my libido.

After he hung up with Gavin, Jacob pulled up his email and shot Moira a quick message.

Helping out a local guy who's trying to improve his skills. Gonna get back on the ice. Why am I not more freaked out about this?

He should've known that tossing something like that Moira's direction would get him a phone call.

She called five minutes later, just as he was heading into his office to deal with some other business.

"Who's this local guy?" she asked.

Ugh, of course, she was going to start with that.

"Funny story," Jacob said. "It's . . .uh . . .Finn Reynolds. He plays for a local college and asked for help and I figured why not?"

A vast oversimplification, but even though Moira was his therapist and he trusted her because she'd seen him through some tough times, he didn't want to confess everything. Like how Finn had called his bluff by nearly getting naked. Like how Jacob was attracted to him even though he didn't want to be. Nevermind that hearing about Morgan's treatment, inadvertent or not, and how it tore Finn down made Jacob want to kick his ass harder than he'd ever been tempted when Morgan's insults had been flung in *his* direction.

"Finn Reynolds. You mean *Morgan's* son? That Finn Reynolds?" It took Moira a second, but she got there.

She'd have gotten there faster, but he knew she normally saw football players, not hockey players. Jacob was her first.

"Yep."

"Well, this is a development," Moira said. "Do you want to talk about it?" He'd been working with her long enough that he knew what she actually meant was, *do you need to talk about it?*

"No, not necessarily." He was hoping they didn't have to go there, though that was probably a pipe dream.

"Jacob, this Morgan Reynolds has come up more than once."

"I thought it was just the once—"

"No," Moira corrected gently. "More than once. And one session, you spent quite a bit of time telling me about how you wanted to be his friend—how you *tried* to be his friend—but he insisted on continuing your feud. On and off the ice."

"Well, that's not really why I messaged you. I really just wanted to know why I could barely get on the ice at the fundraiser and now? I'm asking Finn's coach if I can come to practice. About additional ice time," Jacob said, awkwardly changing the subject.

"And you don't think those two things are related? Finn's last name and your sudden desire to get back on the ice?"

"It's not a *desire*. I do want to help him, and the ice part is kind of non-negotiable."

"Ah," Moira said. One of those noises she made that said about a hundred things, just not out loud.

"It's just . . .I was curious." Jacob knew how stupid it sounded.

"My guess is, you found something that was more important, more compelling, than your fear or your regret. Your desire to help this boy."

"He's not a boy." The words escaped out of Jacob before he could snatch them back. He wasn't used to being so circumspect with Moira. That was what he told himself anyway, why he'd said anything at all when he'd been determined that he wouldn't touch on Finn as a person.

"Is there something you're not telling me?" she asked archly. She could always sense it. He should've known better than to try to hide anything.

You did. That's why you emailed instead of asking her to call you.

"No. Nothing's happened. Nothing's *happening*."

Moira clucked, and then a second later said. "Oh, Jacob, he's cute, isn't he? I just googled him. Really cute. And you've been single a long time now."

"Moira," Jacob said weakly. They hadn't *not* discussed his sex life, but he'd tried to only allude to his interminable dry spell.

"And he's twenty-one. As well as being the child of a very famous hockey player. He's not a kid. You're right about that."

Jacob made a face, hoping it wouldn't get worse, but of course, she kept going.

"If you want to talk about it—"

"No," Jacob said. "No. It's not . . . no. I'm just helping him with hockey, that's all."

"You're not the kind of man who'd be attracted to some-one *because* they're young," Moira reminded him. "If you like him, it's because you like him."

"I don't," Jacob said, pretty sure that was a lie. How could he not, when Finn had seen him at his worst and he'd reacted with grace and compassion and even some gentle teasing? It had all done what almost nothing else could: forced him out of his own head.

"Right, of course not. But if you *did* . . ."

Jacob didn't want to pick up her bait. He did not. But he did anyway. "And if I did?"

"If you did, *one*, I'd tell you to tread lightly, because it could get messy with the father, and *two*, to trust yourself. Your own instincts."

Ironically, what he kept telling Finn to do.

"Well, I don't, and I won't. It's not happening."

"Alright, Jacob," Moira agreed quietly.

"But you think that's it, then? I want to help him more than I'm afraid?"

"It's likely. And that's a good thing. A very good thing."

"It feels good." It did, after so long spinning his wheels.

"And I'm sure there's some part of you that wants to make it right, with Morgan, and you can't, so Finn is a good substitute."

"Finn's not a substitute for *anyone*," Jacob growled.

Moira just laughed, though. "There you go," she said lightly, "already proving me right."

He didn't ask what she believed, but he was afraid he'd already guessed.

⇝⇝⇁ ⇜⇜⇜

Finn hadn't heard from Jacob in a few days, but from the way they'd left things, he hadn't really been sure he *would* see Jacob at practice.

Or maybe ever again. Had he pushed too hard?

Finn had worried that he'd done exactly what he'd told himself *not* to do.

So he was unbelievably surprised when he skated onto the ice to finish his warmups before practice started, and there Jacob was, in a lightweight gray zip-up and black track pants, skating around the ice like it was nothing.

Like his voice had never wavered, the other night, just talking about coming back.

That he hadn't said he couldn't, because now he was.

"Hey," Finn said, skating over. "I didn't think you'd be here."

Jacob looked up at him. Shrugged. "Wasn't sure I would be either. Wasn't sure so I didn't mention it."

"Coach's okay with it?"

"Yep. Even sent me the schedule. And he got me in touch with the facilities manager here. We'll have some non-practice ice time, too."

"Really?" Finn could barely believe it. "Are you sure? I don't want to push you. Not if it's something you're not comfortable with."

"I know my limits," Jacob said firmly.

"Alright." Finn smiled then extended his arms. "You gonna kick my ass again?"

Jacob chuckled. "You need your ass kicked?"

"Actually . . ." He'd wanted to text Jacob this more than once but then he'd worried it would be too pushy—or would make Jacob think he was trying to make this thing between them about more than just hockey. "It's going good. Better."

"Yeah? When's the next game?"

Finn smiled even wider. Enjoying that he was totally going to catch Jacob pretending ignorance—but he knew better. They *both* knew better.

"Oh so you were just telling *someone else* Coach sent you the schedule," Finn teased, nudging him.

There were so many layers of fabric and cushion between them, but he felt it like they were still naked in the sauna.

It would be so much easier if this electric chemistry faded but Finn was beginning to think that no matter how many times he reminded himself to focus on hockey, it would always be there, lurking in the background.

"I . . .well, yeah," Jacob said, sounding flustered. "He did send it. But Gavin could be starting the other goalie."

"Nick? He's a freshman. He'll get a start every so often, to give me a breather, but mostly . . .it's on me."

"How'd you feel about that?"

For a second, Finn considered lying. If Jacob was his dad or Coach or one of the other players, he'd have put on a confident front, talking some bullshit about what a great opportunity it was to get more work.

But Jacob knew. He'd been there. Surely there'd been some time in his career when a team had leaned on him maybe a little too hard.

"Not great," he admitted. "You know how it is."

"I do. If you ever need to take a break in practice, you tell me." Finn was sure he saw approval in his eyes. For Finn's honesty?

"I'm good," Finn said and meant it. If Jacob was actually *here*, and willing to help—he was going to give him every minute he could.

"You warmed up?"

"Give me ten," Finn said, and Jacob nodded.

He went through his final stretches, making an effort to shift his focus from excitement—he'd *come*, he was *here*—to the headspace he sank into every time he took the ice.

By that point, Coach had taken the ice, Zach skating closely behind him, and out of the corner of his eye, Finn watched as they greeted Jacob. When they'd finished with him, moving over to where the lines had started to arrive on the ice, Mal and Elliott snarking at each other and Ivan rolling his eyes, Finn headed over in Jacob's direction.

He'd set up next to the goal. Had a stick in his hands now and was moving a few pucks kitty-corner to it.

"You ready?" Jacob asked, and Finn nodded.

"Okay, some footwork first," Jacob said. "Your speed, but we'll get faster. That's the idea. Compress your reaction time, your physical response, and then we'll work on stringing some movements together."

He was a Reynolds, so he had good technique. His father would have never stood for anything else and had always hired the best coaches to come in and make sure that Finn not only had a grasp on the basics, but that he excelled at them.

They drilled footwork until Finn's thighs were aching and his calves were burning. Jacob had the same intensity and single-minded focus of the other night, and it helped Finn too. Physical effort leading to mental focus.

"Good." Jacob tapped his stick on the ice. "Now faster."

He did it again and again.

When Jacob finally let him stop for a quick break, Finn pushed his helmet and his sweaty hair back, squirting Gatorade into his mouth.

"You good?" Jacob asked, and Finn nodded.

"You know, it doesn't take a single day of practice to go from good to great. It's a hundred times repeating the same time drills. A thousand. Until it's second nature."

Finn nodded.

"Let's work on your transitions."

Finn hated transitions, even though he knew how they could change an entire defensive stand. They were a bitch to drill, but apparently Jacob had decided to throw him in the deep end.

Hoping to make him a better goalie, for sure, but maybe also hoping to exhaust them both enough they couldn't even think about sex.

But even as tired as Finn was—and he knew he'd be more worn-out after this—the awareness of Jacob as a man, not just a coach, sizzled under his skin.

"You've got better movement, your positioning is better, and what does that mean?" Jacob asked.

"First save's better," Finn said, finishing his Gatorade and slipping his mask back on.

"If you've got better control on your first save, then your rebound is better. More deliberate, less instinctual."

"Right," Finn said.

"Position," Jacob barked.

Finn got ready, and what followed was much like what they'd done at Jacob's house, but more intense somehow.

Maybe because Jacob wasn't behind the machine, removed from the action. He *was* the action, peppering him with pucks, sometimes one right after another, over and over again, getting right up into his face, until it felt like there was nothing but Jacob's dark brown gaze challenging his.

"Good. Good." Finally Jacob stopped. He'd run out of pucks, for the third time, and Finn let out a hard breath. "You've got great technique, but you've been relying on your instincts."

"I thought I didn't listen to them enough," Finn complained.

Jacob grinned. "Different kind of instincts. There's a feel for the puck, for the players. How they're going to approach, the way they might take the shot, etcetera. But when you block, when you commit physically to a save? That's preparation. Execution. Recovery." He paused. "But you've got the ability and the foundation. I can see why the Sentinels took you in the third."

Finn's jaw dropped. "What?"

Jacob's smile morphed into a smirk. "Don't tell me you thought it was because your last name was Reynolds."

"Well, yeah, I did. So did everyone else."

"You gotta stop giving a shit what other people say. Listen to me. Listen to your coach over there. Listen to your teammates. But most of all, listen to yourself. Block the rest out. Let their words just bounce off you."

"You do that?"

Jacob shrugged. "Mostly, yeah. Can't say I never let anyone rile me up."

"My dad. More than once." Finn knew he shouldn't have brought it up, but it was true, wasn't it? And that was exactly what Finn was looking for—some magic bullet of advice that would mean he no longer gave a shit that his dad was Morgan Reynolds.

"Your dad is a special case," Jacob said with a reluctant sigh. "He's . . .he tries to get around that wall you build. Dig under your skin. You know that."

"Yeah." He knew. Probably better than anyone else. Eventually it had pushed his mom away, and she'd left.

It was what had given Finn the idea to move across country.

But distance to Morgan was nothing.

"But I also know this," Jacob said, and he reached out, gripping Finn's arm through its heavy pad. "Your dad is fucking proud of you. Does a shit job of showing it, but he is."

Finn rolled his eyes. It was easier than arguing. Than saying the blunt words, *No, he isn't.*

"Don't do that. He *is*. I know. He told me. More than once."

"You? He *hates* you," Finn said, and wished, the moment the words were out of his mouth, that he hadn't said them. Jacob knew it was true, of course, but he didn't need to say them.

Didn't need to lash out, when all Jacob was doing was trying to help.

"I know." Jacob said it matter-of-factly. "But that doesn't mean he didn't say it. Told me that someday, you'd be me, holding some hockey god back from breaking his own records."

"He did not," Finn said.

"He did," Jacob argued. "How did Morgan become the best?"

"I don't know," Finn retorted. He'd wanted Jacob to help him, but it turned out, he didn't actually *want* to talk about this.

"Yeah, you do. You just don't want to talk about it or think about it—but that's not doing you any fucking favors. You can't ignore him and hope that it'll mean you'll stop giving a shit."

"Yeah?" Finn felt temper spiking in him. Dredged up from that place inside him, the one Jacob was right, the place he tried to pretend didn't exist.

The one that Jacob was forcing him to look at.

Jacob shot him a look, skated around the goal. Like he needed an extra minute. But that was Finn, who felt dangerously close to the edge of losing it. He was tired, but not tired enough.

"Has it helped so far?" Jacob wondered. But then he pushed more, because he knew, of course, that it hadn't. "Come on, Finn. You know this. How did your dad become the best?"

"He had talent. Skill. But he worked his ass off, too."

"Exactly. He drilled constantly. He never took a day off. He pushed himself every single moment. He never accepted less."

Which is why he's never accepted you.

That yawning chasm of hurt threatened to reach up and devour him whole.

Finn swallowed hard, pushing it back down, but he didn't know how long he'd be able to hold it at bay.

But like Jacob knew, he drew close again, and this time it was his hands that pushed up Finn's helmet. He turned his head, but Jacob reached out. Forced his gaze back. "I'm telling you this, I'm *reminding* you of this, because this is what he's like. To himself. To others. To every other person. You're not special, Finn."

The pain screamed.

"Don't you think I know that?" His voice felt raw. Exposed.

"Not the way you think I mean. I mean, your dad's hard on everyone. But he's the hardest on himself. Once you accept that, once you accept that his approval isn't ever coming, because he doesn't even fucking accept *himself*, it's easier to brush him off."

Finn knew that, of course. Nobody was as good as Morgan if they didn't have a force inside, pushing them as hard as possible. But it had never occurred to him that as unrelenting as Morgan was towards Finn, the spotlight he shone inside himself was even brighter. Not ever letting a single thing go.

"That's . . ." Finn trailed off.

"Sounds really fucking miserable? Yeah." Jacob let go of his chin, but Finn could feel the ghost of his touch, even after it was gone. "Just remember that, okay?"

"That's what you did?"

"I wanna say, yeah, but I didn't even realize that until the very end. Until it felt like he got angrier and angrier and it bothered me that I couldn't figure out why. Most guys I played with and against, they mellowed as they got older. But not Morgan. Never Morgan."

"No," Finn agreed.

"That's when I realized that he couldn't accept less. He couldn't figure out how to do it. And that changed things."

"Didn't change the way you never let him score on you," Finn said, swallowing the lump in his throat. It was easier to tease than to talk about it.

It hurt to even consider the possibility that his dad would *never* accept he'd done his best, no question about that, but if he could stop worrying about it, and start worrying about living up to his *own* expectations, instead?

Well.

"Fuck no," Jacob said, chuckling. "Let him win by getting to me? Never."

Finn realized that was what he'd been doing.

Unlike Jacob, he'd been letting Morgan win. In every way. He'd won by dictating their relationship. By dictating Finn's own feelings about it. By controlling the way Finn felt about himself. About his capabilities. Even about his own goddamn future.

Finn nodded. Realizing what Jacob was saying without really saying it.

"Got it," Finn said quietly.

"Think you do. Now let's go again. I want you to think about your angles. Shifting your hips, angling into the movement, before you move, that gives you the kind of control I want to see."

Finn nodded, but to Finn's surprise Jacob reached out, and his hand was warm, firm, even through all the layers he wore. "God, it fucking sucks, okay? I get it. I get it more than anyone. But you're so much more than a Reynolds."

Jacob was so fucking earnest, his brown eyes so warm on Finn's face. But Finn wanted him to say it again. Again and again and again.

"I am?"

"Anyone else would've let this beat them down. Let it beat them. But you never did. You fought, every inch of the way."

"And now you're telling me not to fight."

"Don't fight *him*. Fight for you? Yeah. I wanna see you do it."

Finn flashed him a smile. He'd never imagined it, but by shining a light on that spot, by not pretending it didn't exist, by acknowledging it, and starting the process of coming to grips with it, he did feel better. Less out of control.

More hopeful.

"I wanna do it, too," Finn said.

"You've got this," Jacob agreed.

"So that was the surprise you were sneaking off for," Ramsey said.

Finn looked up. He'd showered and changed after practice, moving slowly, in deference to the ache in his muscles.

"You convinced Jacob Braun to coach you," Ramsey continued, settling down on the bench next to Finn. "What did you promise him?"

Practically nothing.

Jacob had said something about getting his temperature on the coming out process, but so far there'd been nothing about that. He hadn't even brought it up again, but he *had* been completely committed to helping Finn.

"I just asked and he said yes," Finn said.

Ramsey shot him a look. "I don't believe you," he said. "Are you fucking him?"

"Ramsey," Finn warned.

"I mean it, are you fucking him? 'Cause you probably could. He thinks he's sly about it, probably, but the way he looks at you a little too long? And all those years of painful repression? He's ripe for the picking, Reynolds."

Don't remind me.

"We're not fucking," was all Finn actually said.

"But you could be."

"Ramsey," Finn repeated. "Don't."

"I'm just saying, he's hot. Don't tell me you didn't notice."

"I noticed," Finn said dryly. "But this is about way more than getting off. He's *helping* me, and I fucking need it, okay? Way more than a few orgasms."

Ramsey grinned. "Would it be just a few though?"

Finn punched him in the arm. "You're actually the worst."

"So I hear. But seriously, why can't you do both?"

"I don't know, because some of us aren't controlled by our dicks?" But even though Ramsey absolutely gave that impression, loud and clear and front and center, Finn had realized long ago how hard he worked to keep the playboy front up. It was more misdirection from the king of it.

"I'm hurt. Really hurt," Ramsey teased.

"Truly suffering. I can tell." Finn reached out to grab his bag. Winced a little as a muscle he hadn't even known he had pulled. Jacob had worked him over good.

And he'd work you over some more, if you asked real nice.

Great. Now his subconscious sounded exactly like Ramsey.

"Maybe I am."

The seriousness in Ramsey's voice caught Finn's attention. He turned back to the other guy. "You are not." But suddenly Finn wasn't sure.

"I just can't believe you figured out the solution to your problems before I did. I knew Braun lived here, but I never considered it." Ramsey looked earnest and also impressed, which was kind of terrifying. "Maybe because it was so fucking messy, I didn't think it would be a good idea."

"I'm definitely not telling my dad. Which means *you're* not telling my dad."

Not that he'd actually thought Ramsey would. In fact, whenever Morgan came into town, Finn could always count on Ramsey playing interference. He'd been hurt by it and more than a little embarrassed, the first time he'd realized what Ramsey was doing, but those feelings had long since faded into gratitude.

But then, by relying on Ramsey to keep Morgan out of his hair, all Finn had really been doing was avoiding the problem.

Not embracing it. Not like Jacob wanted him to do.

"I wouldn't dream of it," Ramsey said. "And next time he shows up—"

"I'll handle him," Finn said resolutely. Would it suck? Without a doubt. But if he didn't grasp the problem and learn to live with the sting, learn to *accept* the sting, he'd never be able to move past it.

Jacob was right about that.

"What? Why?" Ramsey looked annoyed, probably because he'd surprised him twice now.

And nobody ever surprised Ramsey.

"It's time I man up, deal with him on my own."

"But—"

"No." Finn patted Ramsey on the arm. "Thanks for what you've done. But I gotta . . .I gotta deal with this in my own way. On my own terms."

Ramsey looked floored. "Who are you? Did Jacob perform brain-swapping surgery with someone else? Is his dick *that* good?"

"His dick's not anything." In fact, he was very much trying to *not* think about Jacob's dick, thank you very much.

"God, you really mean that." Ramsey made a face. "I'm almost disappointed."

"You want it, you go get it." Finn regretted the words as soon as they were out of his mouth. He didn't want Ramsey propositioning Jacob. He didn't want Ramsey anywhere near Jacob.

First, Ramsey would chew Jacob up and then, because he was Ramsey, casually but kindly discard him after. And Jacob deserved better than that, deserved better than a few orgasms.

Second, because Finn *really* didn't want to share.

It was unfair, but there it was.

"You don't mean that." Ramsey called him on his bluff, grinning.

Finn made a face. "I don't mean that."

"See? I told you that you wanted him." Ramsey slung an arm around Finn's shoulders. "It's so much better when we're honest about these things."

It sounded painfully like what Finn had told Jacob the night they'd agreed to this exchange. But it hadn't really *felt* better. Instead, it felt like really fucking unfair, because if they wanted each other, couldn't they just take each other?

No. Absolutely not.

"Or not," Finn said wryly.

"Aw."

"It's not happening. No matter how you push and prod and attempt to maneuver us into it."

Ramsey made a transparently sad face. "I'm offended."

"Oh come on, you *know* you're the master at moving us around like fucking chess pieces." Finn picked up his bag and headed towards the door to the locker room.

"Well, *yeah*. I'm offended that you'd call it an *attempt*," Ramsey teased.

Finn wanted to tell him he was wrong, that sometimes it *was* just an attempt, that he didn't get to dictate to everyone, but then, where *had* he gone wrong recently?

Behind him, he knew he'd see Mal and Elliott's heads close together, miraculously on the same page after over a year of intense bickering. And later that night, if he popped into Sammy's or the library, he'd probably see Brody studying with his boyfriend, Dean, the way they looked at each other making their mutual affection blatantly obvious.

"I'm not a project for you to fix," Finn said. "Or even worse, to pair up."

He gestured behind him at where Mal and Elliott probably were.

"But that worked out, didn't it?" Ramsey nudged him. "See? Better to just bow to the inevitable."

CHAPTER 7

"I can't believe I got a babysitter for this," Bryan said, the teasing glint in his eyes making it clear that he was totally giving Jacob shit.

"It's good for you to have a night off." From the start, Jacob had pretended that this was for *Bryan*—a fun evening out, he'd referred to it when texting his brother earlier in the day. But the truth was, they were here for *Jacob* and they both knew it.

"But at a hockey game? A *college* hockey game? In Salem?"

"The Evergreens are good this year," Jacob said.

"Yeah, that's why we're here. Because the Evergreens are good this year," Bryan deadpanned. He glanced over at Finn, standing in the goal. "So, how's he doing?"

Finn already had his helmet on, his literal game face on, and Jacob couldn't see his face, his eyes. Root out how he was feeling. He'd texted him earlier today, and Finn had just sent a thumbs-up.

"We've been working on fundamentals, which he's pretty good at already," Jacob said. "Honestly, his only really bad habit is doubting himself."

"Ah," Bryan said knowingly.

Jacob had attended the one practice this week, and all things considered, it *had* gone well. Afterwards, he'd considered offering for Finn to come back to the house later in the week, but he'd chickened out at the last moment, deleting the text invite letter by letter, like it had never existed at all. Next week he'd already booked ice for the two of them, mid-morning, when Finn wasn't in class.

That felt reasonably safer than his own basement gym, where nobody might ever see what happened there but the two of them.

Still he'd spent days pretending like he wasn't watching his phone, gazing at the empty screen like a lovesick teenager with his first fucking crush. He'd told himself the whole time he had this handled, but considering he'd driven an hour south to see Finn play in an away game *and* dragged his brother along, Jacob was beginning to think he was full of shit.

This morning, Bryan had seemed like a good safety net. Surely his older brother would call him out, delivering a much-needed lecture about why this whole thing was a terrible fucking idea.

But with every knowing look Bryan shot in his direction, it seemed more likely that Bryan would invoke some medical professional bullshit and tell him he needed to get laid.

"Does he know you showed up tonight?" Bryan asked after the puck dropped.

Jacob tore his gaze away from the action on the ice as the line changed.

"No, I didn't tell him." He wasn't going to tell Bryan how long he stared at his phone this afternoon, thinking about how he'd phrase it, and what Finn might say back. *I want to see you, even if it's only on the ice* had seemed like a monumentally bad choice, but he'd been tempted to send it anyway.

He'd punished himself for it by blocking two hundred shots and then sweating out all his bad impulses in the sauna after.

Bryan raised an eyebrow. "You didn't tell him."

"I didn't want to . . .it was easier . . ." Jacob cleared his throat. "Better this way."

"Easier, huh? So you didn't chicken out?"

"No. *No.*" Jacob's attention snapped back to the ice as the Phantoms charged towards the goal Finn guarded.

He could read Finn's mind in every twitch of his body. Every blink Jacob couldn't see but could only sense.

Jacob tensed as Finn blocked one shot, then another, then finally smothered the puck by falling on it.

"That was good, yeah?" Bryan asked, patting Jacob's arm.

"You know shit about hockey, but yeah. Pretty good. He controlled the execution and then the recovery, so he could block the rebound shots."

"And here I was thinking it was just about you throwing your big hulking body around," Bryan teased, even though thanks to Jacob, he'd been around hockey for twenty-plus years now.

Jacob rolled his eyes. "You know that's not true."

"Well, yeah, but it's fun to get a rise out of you. About hockey or about . . ." Bryan trailed off, gaze skimming across the ice and resting on Finn.

"Don't start."

"I've never seen you like this, all tense and shaky over a hockey game. Which means it's not just a hockey game—"

"Maybe I just want him to play well so I don't have to keep coaching him," Jacob snapped.

He took a breath and opened his mouth to apologize, but before he could, he realized Bryan was actually laughing.

"You don't actually believe that," Bryan said between chuckles. "No—you don't. Which is why you brought me. As what?"

"Sanity. Logic. A voice of reason." Jacob didn't want to admit it, but maybe if Bryan knew, he *might* err on the side of those things, instead of telling him he needed to get laid.

"Ah."

On the ice, one of Finn's teammates—Jacob was pretty sure it was one of the first line forwards, the smaller, quicker one; sue him, he may have studied the lineup on the Portland U website—darted in and drilled an absolute beaut of a shot right past the opposing goalie's skate.

Jacob shot to his feet, yelling his approval at the gorgeous fucking goal the Evergreens had just scored.

Finn added his own approval, tapping his stick on the ice.

"You were right, they *are* good," Bryan said, when the crowd calmed down. Even though they were at Salem University's rink, the Evergreens clearly traveled well, because it felt like half the fans were wearing their signature forest green.

"Told you the babysitter would be worth it," Jacob said smugly.

But the Phantoms' winger won the face-off and immediately made a hard push into the Evergreens' defensive zone, swarming across the ice.

Jacob froze, watching intently as Finn moved, shifting into his stance just a second too late. Ramsey surged over, flicking a shot away, but the Phantoms' center grabbed the puck.

Finn barely pushed it away, Brody catching it and passing it back over to one of their forwards.

"Shit," Jacob muttered under his breath, hoping that Finn might have at least a moment of reprieve to reset, physically and emotionally, before he had to defend the goal again.

He leaned forward, fingers digging into his knee, breath in his throat as Finn popped up and Jacob thought, *he's not going to make it, he can't make it* . . .but before he could think the rest, the horn sounded. The period was over.

"He's good, right?" Bryan asked, then glanced over. "Better question: are *you* okay?"

Jacob didn't know. He'd been worrying about going to the game because of his *own* shit, but just sitting here, only waiting and watching, was the most excruciating experience he could imagine.

Bryan reached over and put a hand on his. Which was still shaking. "Come on. Go talk to him. You can do that right?"

Jacob didn't know that either. He wanted to, he knew that much.

Would Gavin turn him away if he went down to the tunnel, asked to be let into the locker room? He could probably make it that far, on his face alone, though he hated to trade on it like that.

But would he do it to talk to Finn, to reassure him? To reassure *himself*?

Jacob shot to his feet.

"Good," Bryan said, nodding with approval.

"And here I brought you to talk me out of stupid ideas," Jacob muttered under his breath as he got to the aisle and headed down the stairs, dodging people as he jogged, trying to meet Finn at the barrier before he went into the tunnel and the locker room for the intermission.

He reached the wall just as Finn trudged by.

"Hey," he said, and Finn glanced up. He'd pushed his helmet back, curls slicked with sweat, eyes wide and surprised as he realized who was standing in front of him.

"You're here." Finn stopped.

"Yeah," Jacob said.

You fucking came all the way down here to talk to him. So talk to him.

"Uh," he continued, forcing the words out. Far too aware of the people around them, listening in.

Finn's lips quirked up. He motioned to the security by the door. "Come on," he said to Jacob.

The security guard looked dubious.

"Don't you know who this is?" Finn asked, conversationally. "This is Jacob Braun. He won the Cup *and* the Vezina twice."

The guy gave a nod and opened the door.

Jacob slipped through the door, carefully walking across the ice to the tunnel where Finn was waiting for him, and to his surprise, the assistant coach was, too. He wasn't one-hundred-percent sure, but Jacob thought his name was Zach.

"You should've told Coach you'd be here," Zach offered.

"You should've told *me* you'd be here," Finn said, lifting his chin and meeting Jacob's gaze straight on, heat meeting heat.

Jacob flushed. Felt caught out, like a guy with a crush who'd just been discovered.

You're allowed to be here.

Well. Sort of.

"It was a last-minute thing," Jacob said.

Finn didn't look convinced.

Zach gave him a look. "I'll let Coach know you'll be a minute." Then he walked on, leaving the two of them alone in the tunnel.

"That last bit was rough," Jacob said.

"Yeah."

He hadn't meant to lead with a criticism. Or for that to *sound* like a criticism. *Get your fucking shit together, Braun.*

"But you got through it," Jacob said, awkwardly patting him on the shoulder. Touching anyone else didn't feel like navigating a minefield, but it did when he touched Finn.

Like he might want to keep touching. Might want to strip off all these stupid pads, the jersey, and all those layers beneath.

Until he could feel the skin underneath.

"Thanks," Finn said. "Any more backhanded compliments in your arsenal?"

Jacob let out an unsteady breath. "I told you, I'm *not* good at this. I want to be good at it, though, for you, to help you, to make this easier. Better. Less . . ."

Finn turned to him, his hazel eyes glowing green against his flushed cheeks. "Then just fucking do it, man."

It was the same kind of blunt advice Jacob might've given Finn, but instead he'd turned the tables on him.

Resolve solidified deep down.

Bryan's voice echoed inside him, reminding him why he'd gone to all this trouble to come down here. Not to criticize. Not to give Finn an awkward pat on the back and some meaningless *rah-rah* speech.

He'd come here for a purpose—and it wasn't any of that shit.

"Hey," Jacob said and gently pushed him back against the wall of the tunnel, gear and all, "*hey*, look at me."

Finn did, the heat in his eyes still searing Jacob raw.

"I came down here to ask if you're okay."

Finn opened his mouth and Jacob was ninety-nine point-nine-percent sure that he was about to give him a flippant, non-serious answer. But then Finn paused. Hesitated. Considered it. "Yeah," he said quietly.

"And I came down here to tell you that, no matter what you think, that *yes*, you're okay," Jacob said. "You're okay. You handled that. Not everything has to be perfect to be handled. You don't have to be perfect to be okay."

Finn moistened his lips, and Jacob's eyes were drawn to them, helplessly.

Not here, not now.

Jacob mentally rephrased: *Actually, not at all.*

"I don't," he said, and it was half a question, half a statement.

"You don't. You got this," Jacob said and patted him on the shoulder pad, his touch lingering this time.

"And here I thought you weren't going to bother with meaningless platitudes," Finn said.

Jacob laughed. Tightened his grip on Finn's shoulder. "Who says it's meaningless?"

"I—"

"No," Jacob said earnestly. "I *mean* it. You got this. You can handle these guys. But more importantly, I know you can handle yourself."

"You believe that." Finn had the nerve to sound surprised.

"I sure fucking do. That's what I really came down here to say."

Finn's chin lifted and his eyes flashed with something else now. Not the heat of a challenge, but a warm affection, and an understanding.

And that scared the shit out of Jacob, even more than the desire to touch and to feel Finn's bare skin against his.

"Thanks," Finn said.

"Good luck out there." Jacob patted him one last time.

"You're not coming into the locker room?"

Jacob shook his head. "Not today. But maybe someday."

"Alright," Finn said, and there was that understanding in his eyes again.

Like he understood that Jacob wasn't ready for that, yet.

He wasn't wrong.

There was still a part of Jacob that longed to be the one on the bench, sweat slicking his skin, checking every piece of his gear and getting mentally ready for another period.

He didn't need that desire to grow claws and rake at him, relentlessly, even more than it already was.

Though funny enough, as Jacob retraced his steps, coming down here *had* helped. He felt more settled already, like a piece of him that he'd been missing forever had finally locked into place again.

Happy, he realized as he headed back towards where Bryan was sitting, he was *happy* again. He hadn't thought he'd like coaching. But maybe it wasn't off the menu, forever.

"So, how was it?" Bryan asked him when he got back to their seats.

Bryan had taken the opportunity to go grab drinks and a pretzel nearly the size of his head.

"I thought doctors were against salt," Jacob said, because it was so much easier to talk about Bryan's eating habits than to tell him the truth about how that had just gone.

Pretty good. And a total fucking disaster.

Bryan smacked him on the back of his head. "Don't change the subject. Besides, this is my night out, and if I can't get laid, and they don't even have beer here, I'm going to eat this fucking pretzel."

"Fair," Jacob said. "Don't—"

"You mean, don't mention that *you* could get laid, because you could, you absolutely could."

"You didn't even see us together," Jacob protested.

"Yeah, didn't need to. You wouldn't be so torn up about this if it was just you. You'd slink off and lick your wounds. You wouldn't be sitting here, looking torn, like you're only five seconds away from listening to the devil on your shoulder."

"I am not," Jacob said. But for someone who'd always had ironclad self-control, he wasn't doing a very good job of exercising it right now.

"What does Moira think?"

"Ugh," Jacob said, really not wanting to tell him.

Bryan took a big bite of pretzel. Offered it up to Jacob. He tore off a piece, but didn't pop it in his mouth, instead rolling it between his fingers, like it might solve all the mysteries of the universe.

Or maybe just *this* mystery.

"You do realize, Morgan *hates* me. He thinks I'm personally responsible for denying him the record he really wanted. If he caught me—caught *us*—" Jacob hesitated. "He'd flip his shit. Not just on me, but on Finn, and he doesn't need more of that crap from his dad."

"Well, that's stupid," Bryan said.

"I know, it's none of his business—"

"No," Bryan interrupted. "Why he hates you. You were just *one goalie* he played against. How is it your fault he didn't get the record he wanted?"

"We were in the same division, so we did play pretty often against each other," Jacob offered.

Bryan smacked him again. "You're smarter than to parrot his stupid ass reasons back at me."

"Thanks," Jacob said dryly.

"I mean, it's not your fault. He *knows* it's not your fault. You're just a convenient external excuse. If he blames you, he can't blame himself."

That truth settled hard and inescapable inside Jacob's gut.

Morgan *would* blame himself, if given half a moment. Jacob had told Finn the truth: Morgan might be hard on everyone around him, but he'd always been twice as hard on himself.

"Maybe," Bryan added, "it was even self-preservation to hate you."

"Let's not go that far," Jacob muttered.

"I'm just saying, you two should clear the air."

"And then, what, he's going to be perfectly alright with me fucking his son? I don't think so."

Bryan laughed. "There's a *lot* of room between hating you and applauding whatever you and Finn get up to together."

Jacob shoved the mashed-up pretzel into his mouth, chewed and swallowed. "You're incredibly annoying."

"And incredibly right," Bryan said smugly. "Just think about it."

Like Jacob was going to be doing anything else.

Every time Finn took the ice, he was focused.

It was too much of a habit to *not* be focused. An instinct by now to pull his mind in, to set it at its primary task for the next twenty minutes of play.

But now felt slightly different. *Better.*

Just like Jacob had said. *I want to help you. Make it better. Easier.*

And he'd done it.

There *was* a voice in Finn's head that always wanted him to be perfect, that had trouble sloughing off less-than-perfect defense. But now he reminded himself, *it doesn't have to be perfect to be okay* and that was more freeing than he'd imagined it might be.

Malcolm won the puck in the starting face-off, and it was clear, from what he'd heard in the locker room and now by Mal and Elliott and Ivan's behavior, they felt like they'd been sitting back too much.

They were pushing now, aggressively, and that was Elliott's favorite way to play, so he was flying across the ice, pestering the Phantom's defenders, skating circles around them, Mal swarming with him, the three of them working in tandem to keep the puck on that side of the ice.

But Finn didn't relax. He couldn't. He *wouldn't*.

His eyes followed the puck, watching it across the ice as he kept his body both relaxed and primed, ready to make his first move if that was required.

But it wasn't. Not now.

Especially not when Mal slipped between two defenders, and lightning quick got a shot off just above the goalie's right shoulder.

Elliott's scream of victory was louder than if he'd scored himself, and he jumped into Mal's arms as he pumped his fist in the air.

But even though the Evergreens' second goal gave him a little extra breathing room, Finn stayed ready.

As expected, the puck eventually came back over the line, their second defensive line trying to steal it away, trying to interfere with the play setup.

Finn tracked the puck with his eyes, breath quickening. Trying to predict when and how it would be shot so he could get half a second of extra jump on his reaction.

Luckily for him, their left winger hadn't learned yet just how much he was telegraphing his actions, and Finn shot to the side of the goal, controlled and *in* control, and shot a leg out, stopping the first shot, then was able to recover without a single millisecond hesitation to take on the rebound.

The puck drifted into the paint, and Finn reached out, smothering it with his glove.

Coach B took advantage of the momentum and swapped lines, and Finn held on to the puck a second longer, before using his stick to bat it towards Ramsey, who passed it onto their third line center.

With their offense's intent to be aggressive, Finn knew sometimes the puck could get away, but not this time. This time, the Evergreens ended the period with twice as many shots on goal as the Phantoms.

And this time, Finn told himself he wasn't disappointed when Jacob didn't jog down the stairs to the ice, to meet him in the tunnel—even as he reminded himself that he'd gotten what he'd needed out of him, anyway.

Even though he didn't *need* him, he found he wanted him anyway. Still, he settled for Zach kneeling in front of him in the locker room, parsing out the defensive scheme and making sure that Finn hadn't noticed any holes.

It shouldn't have felt like settling for Zach to pat him on the knee, telling him that he was killing it tonight, that he'd never looked so dominant in the net, but it did, anyway.

But a surprisingly loud part of him wanted to know not what Zach or even Coach B thought of his performance, but what *Jacob* thought.

It was annoying and a little frustrating, but Finn was able to bat it away, and re-focus on what mattered now: getting through the last period of the game.

CHAPTER 8

"Killer performance tonight by Finn—who proved to us that he's only getting better in the net," Coach said, giving him a solid nod of approval, as they sat in the locker room after the final buzzer, Finn having delivered his third shutout of the season.

Finn lifted a hand, acknowledging the compliment and the resulting cheer.

"Frankly, we're all coming together, getting better and better," Coach continued when the noise finally died down. "Also want to call out our offense, for really getting going in the second period. Ell, you had that sweet goal in the first, but you followed it up and didn't lose the momentum. In fact—you built on it, and that's what I want to see. What the scouts want to see."

Elliott looked over at Malcolm, who looked like he was trying not to grin proudly at his boyfriend. "I had the perfect person pushing me," he said.

Ivan made a vomiting noise. "You guys are disgusting. Save the lovey-dovey shit for the bedroom."

"I couldn't agree more," Coach said. "But yes, you're better when you push each other. When you *all* push each other."

"We're gonna keep doing it, Coach," Brody said in that quiet, determined way of his.

"Yep," Ramsey agreed.

"Good, 'cause the tough part of the season is coming up. We're second in the conference, but I really want that first seed with its bye week in the playoffs. And I want *you* to have it, too, to rest and recover and to prepare for what's to come. Let's agree that we're attacking each and every game like it matters, because it does."

The resulting cheer was even louder and Finn nodded, because he too felt like they were playing their best hockey—but they could be even better. *He* could be even better. Sure, he'd recorded the shutout tonight, but there was always another level he could push himself to.

And he wasn't even doing it *just* for this team, but to prove to the Sentinels that he deserved their time and attention and resources. He was ready to move on from Portland, but they held all the cards.

Morgan had been telling him for months to push them.

But it was more than that, Finn realized.

He needed not to push, but to *prove*.

"Really," Coach B said as he meandered over to where Finn was stripping his equipment off, one piece at a time, "it was a great game, Reynolds."

Coach patted him on the shoulder, all warm reassurance, but Finn was stuck on how different it had felt when Jacob had touched him. It hadn't been warm; it had been *hot*.

That was going to become a problem. He could see it coming, and honestly, part of him didn't even care anymore that it would be messy. That it would make everything infinitely more difficult, because it wasn't like resisting was all that easy, either.

"Thanks, Coach," Finn said, grateful at the acknowledgment of a job well done.

"You seemed . . .calmer out there. Different, in some way." Coach paused. "Zach mentioned you saw Jacob between the first and second period. Is he . . .that's working?"

Finn wanted to know what he'd held himself back from saying but knowing Coach he wouldn't divulge it. But Finn could guess.

"It's going pretty good," Finn said. *I hope it'll be going even better soon.* But just like how Coach didn't want Mal and Elliott's relationship invading the locker room, he wasn't going to want to hear about how Finn had a major hard-on for the ex-NHL star giving him private coaching. In fact, he'd probably warn Finn off, then overload him with good-intentioned and likely logically sound advice that he'd have to blow off, and that would add an extra layer of guilt that Finn didn't need.

So he didn't say anything.

"Good, good. I'm glad. I wasn't sure . . .you didn't need more pressure, but a pressure *valve* and I hoped he might be the right tool."

He's got the right tool alright.

Finn snapped his mind back from the danger zone. "So far it's working out."

"If he wanted to be on the bench, in the locker room, how would you feel about that?" Coach's question was casual, like it didn't mean anything, but Finn caught the sharpness in his gaze. It was a big deal to invite a new entity permanently into these sacred spaces. Could change the chemistry for the better—or for the worse.

Coach would be cautious.

"What he said was helpful, between the periods," Finn answered honestly. "I wouldn't be against it but . . ." He hesitated, because Jacob hadn't really talked a lot about his feelings surrounding retirement, but he'd said enough that Finn knew a part of him was struggling with it. And part of *him* didn't want to be the one to divulge Jacob's secrets to Coach. "But I don't know how he'd feel about that."

"Right." Comprehension dawned across Coach's face. "Understood. I'll talk to him."

Finn nodded.

"Alright, get dressed," Coach said, patting him again.

Coach B had turned to walk away before Finn found himself saying, "Would it be okay if I didn't take the bus back?"

Coach looked back, over his shoulder, his gaze narrowing. "You want to drive back with Jacob? Go over the game?"

"Something like that."

Finn could feel the heat building between him and Jacob, as surely as the pressure inside him had built. Maybe they could be each other's release valves.

God knew Jacob probably needed it, and *Finn* could even use it at this point, though he could probably find a lot of guys casually willing to do it. But he didn't want that. Not now. Not anymore.

"Alright," Coach said. "If Jacob's fine with it."

Jacob probably wouldn't be. He'd probably freak out and panic a little and claim it was a bad idea. But Finn already knew he had the power to convince him to change his mind. He couldn't—*wouldn't*—abuse it, but it was there, all the same, just waiting to be used.

And Finn intended to use it tonight.

He showered and changed, sure that when he exited the visiting rink, Jacob would be waiting outside.

Sure enough, there he was, lounging against one of the decorative trees lining the walkway to the front door. There was another guy with him, and for a second, Finn internally panicked. Had Jacob brought a *date* to his game tonight?

But after the sudden, painful wave of jealousy ebbed, Finn looked closer and realized they were both a similar height and had that same familiar dark brown hair on their heads. The other guy's was neater, and had a few speckles of gray on the temples, but it was still the same. And then the other guy swung his head around, probably reacting to Jacob seeing him approach, and their faces were so alike Finn knew this had to be a brother.

Jacob had brought his brother to his game. To meet him? To see him?

This did add a wrinkle to the request Jacob drive him home, but Finn decided this was even better.

Jacob would probably insist it didn't mean anything, but Finn knew better, and exhilaration swamped him, eating every bit of jealousy away.

"Hey," Jacob said as he walked up to the pair of them. "Great game."

"Thanks." Finn turned to the other guy, who was definitely smirking now, and held out his hand. "I'm Finn Reynolds."

"Bryan Braun, and I know exactly who you are," he said, shaking Finn's hand and still grinning.

"I just bet you do." Finn chuckled, especially delighted at how uncomfortable Jacob looked by this whole exchange.

"None of that," Jacob said firmly, shoving his hands into his pockets.

"Aw, we're just getting to know each other," Finn teased. "And we're going to keep doing it too, 'cause I need a ride home."

"A ride home? What about the team bus you took here? The bus you're *supposed* to be taking home?"

Yep, Finn had been dead-on right about the panic. Though that seemed like quite a bit of an overreaction now, because what was he going to do to seduce Jacob with his *brother* in the car with them?

He shrugged. "Coach said I could drive home with you." Grinning, he nudged Jacob with his shoulder. "You know, break down the game together."

"Sounds like a pretty boring time," Bryan inserted. "Glad I drove myself."

Oh shit. No wonder Jacob was panicking.

Jacob frowned. Finn knew he'd probably not wiped his relief off his face quickly enough and he'd probably seen it. Known exactly why he'd been happy about this turn of events.

"You should take the bus back," Jacob said.

"Nope," Finn said. "I really don't think I should."

Bryan laughed. "Brother," he said, patting Jacob on the shoulder, "you just remember what I told you. I'll check in tomorrow. It was great to finally meet you, Finn."

Then he was walking away, and Finn resisted the urge to do a fist pump. *Finally meet you.* Which meant Jacob *had* been talking about him.

"Don't freak out about that," Jacob muttered. "It doesn't mean anything."

"No?" Finn grinned.

"No. Means nothing."

"Somehow, I don't believe you." Finn nudged him again. "Come on, drive me home. Would it kill you?"

"It might. He *might*," Jacob said darkly, and Finn knew he was thinking about his dad.

"Come on, don't be overdramatic. Imagine how happy Morgan's going to be that I'm a great goalie. Uplifting the Reynolds name and all that utter bullshit."

"You were *already* a great goalie," Jacob said. "You cleared this with Gavin?"

"Gavin? Oh, you mean Coach B?"

Jacob nodded, compressing his lips together. Like he didn't need a reminder that Finn's *coach* was his contemporary and he was not only allowed to call him by his first name, but he was welcome to do it.

"Yep. He's good with it." They started walking towards the parking lot. "He asked me if I wanted you to come into the locker room during games."

"Oh . . . I . . . uh . . ."

"Don't worry, I didn't tell him," Finn said wryly.

Jacob didn't say anything, just nodded as he unlocked the door of a dark blue Mercedes SUV.

They got in, and Jacob started the car.

"I think it would be really hard to retire before you were ready. Even when it would've been so much easier for me to *not* play hockey—to do just about anything else, honestly—I still wanted to do it, and I still thought it was worth it."

"Yeah."

Finn made a face. "Clearly you don't want to talk about it. Guess I can't blame you for that." It was going to be a long hour, though, if Jacob didn't want to talk to him. If he really believed that staying silent would somehow keep Finn at arm's length.

As Jacob pulled onto the highway heading north towards Portland, he stayed silent.

Finn opened his mouth—maybe Jacob didn't want to talk about his retirement but the game had to be allowed territory, right?—but before he could bring up anything, Jacob actually spoke.

"It *was* hard to retire before I wanted to. But it's been weird since. Because on one hand, I'm *happy*. Really happy. The possibility of coming out, of living honestly?"

"You could've done it before now," Finn said, making sure his tone was free of judgment.

"And let that be all anyone ever wanted to say about me? No. I didn't want that. For others, that's fine, but I'm too private." Jacob drummed fingers against the steering wheel. Still looking like he didn't want to discuss this.

Finn nodded. "Makes sense."

"So I *am* happy. Relieved almost. No more worrying about getting outed. If the one or two guys I hook up with every year will blab, despite the NDA they sign."

Finn froze. "Wait," he said. "*One* or *two* hookups *a year*?"

"You *would* focus on that," Jacob said dryly.

"No wonder you're happy. I'd be fucking thrilled."

"Sex isn't everything." Jacob cleared his throat, and Finn watched as his fingers tightened on the wheel, his knuckles going white.

"That's what people say when they haven't had a lot of really, really good sex," Finn teased, because he couldn't help himself.

Maybe it wasn't fair—but he'd been right, hadn't he? *God*, if anyone needed a pressure valve release, it was Jacob Braun.

"You're twenty-one years old. Don't tell me *you've* had a lot of really, really good sex," Jacob said and then looked like he immediately regretted saying anything at all. "Nevermind. Don't answer that. *Please* don't answer that."

"Oh, but I *want* to," Finn said, just to see Jacob's reaction. He was rewarded by a tightening of that glorious jaw.

His profile was black and white in the dim light of the car, illuminated briefly every once in awhile as a car passed them on the freeway. His dark beard was thick and looked soft, but Finn's fingers itched to feel his face. To trace its shape. He'd be handsome, maybe even beautiful, without it.

And with it? He was still so fucking hot.

"The answer is that I guess I don't know," Finn continued. "I've had what I *thought* was really good sex, but when you're eighteen and anyone but you touches your dick, it feels great."

"Or when you're twenty-one and anyone but you touches your dick," Jacob deadpanned.

Finn had to give him that. "True," he said.

Speaking of his dick, it was undeniably interested in this conversation, thickening in his slacks. He resisted the urge to shift in the seat and give away that all it took to give him a hard-on was listening to Jacob Braun say the word *dick*.

He'd finagled his way into this car with the idea of seducing Jacob. That it would be easy-ish. Now Finn knew just how easy it would be. Jacob was probably panting for it. But now he also knew just how complicated it was too, because it wouldn't just be a hookup to Jacob. It would be the start of the rest of his life. A life lived openly and freely.

Finn wanted to be ready for that, but he didn't know if he was. He was still so fucking tangled up with all Morgan's crap. Was he ready to take more baggage on? Ready to take *Jacob's* baggage on?

He changed the subject, telling himself that it was the only sane thing to do in this situation.

Besides, his balls would thank him later.

"So you're happy because you can finally live the way you've wanted to, but you know it came at a steep price."

Jacob glanced over at him, and Finn caught the surprise on his face. Had he really expected Finn to push? To keep talking about sex until there was nothing to do but pull over and go at each other on the side of I-5?

Frankly, it had been tempting, so Finn understood the assumption a little too well.

"Basically yeah," Jacob admitted. "Every moment I think how happy I am, how happy I *could* be, in that hazy future I want, the guilt at what I paid for it kills me. It's . . .it's complicated."

Finn told himself that was why it had been smart to change the subject. This thing was messy enough, with even the thought of Morgan lingering between them like a bad smell.

"But you still want to come out," Finn said.

Jacob nodded. "I'm working on it, anyway. Mostly because my PR rep, Sophie, tells me if I want to publicize this foundation I'm starting, I have to do that first."

"What kind of foundation?"

"Support for LGBT kids who want to participate in athletics," Jacob said.

It was exactly the kind of thing that he'd imagined Jacob might do, but he was still surprised at how touched he was. "That's awesome," Finn said. "We need more of that."

"We do," Jacob said. Finn had changed the subject once himself, so he could hardly be annoyed when Jacob did it, now. "You want to talk about that last bit before the end of the first period?"

He didn't. Especially because it had worked out, in the end. But ostensibly this was why he'd hitched a ride with Jacob. Ignoring the voice inside him that argued, claiming that he'd just wanted *more* time with the guy, no matter *what* they talked about, Finn nodded.

For the next forty-five minutes, he and Jacob broke down the game, going over a number of plays. If Finn had worried that Jacob would be overly critical, he wasn't. He didn't hesitate to call him out if he deserved it but he never rubbed the mistakes in, and he didn't hold back on compliments, of which there were a surprising number.

When Finn commented on that, when they were only maybe five minutes away from campus, Jacob shot him a surprised look. "You didn't think there'd be a lot to compliment in your game?" he said.

"Well, no, not exactly," Finn hedged.

"Don't tell me you thought I'd be like your dad, because if you'd thought that, you'd never have come to me in the first place," Jacob muttered.

"Maybe I came to you because you're hot, and I was craving some of your 'special' one-on-one tutoring," Finn teased.

Jacob rolled his eyes. "Don't change the subject."

"Yeah, I got a shutout, but—"

"No buts," Jacob said insistently. "You got the shutout, you got the win, so you take it. Accept it. Celebrate it. Then we move on."

"Okay."

"Remember what I told you between the first and second period?"

"Not everything has to be perfect to be handled."

"Exactly." Jacob's chin rose. "You handled your shit today. Was it all perfect? It never is. There's always room for improvement, for growth. That's what keeps us moving forward. But there's also room to acknowledge everything you did right."

"Thanks," Finn said quietly.

Jacob pulled over in front of the quad. "This okay?" he asked. "I realized, I wasn't sure where you lived . . ."

"You asking to be invited up?" Finn teased.

"Don't do that," Jacob said and he reached over, cupping his chin with a big warm hand. Calloused in all the right places. Finn felt the thrill of it all the way down. "Don't deflect with a joke."

His hand dropped.

"I . . ." But he had been. It was easier to change the subject, to tease Jacob with something sexual, than it was to accept that he was good.

That he deserved the shutout tonight.

That he was, in fact, *good enough*.

"Sit here, for a minute, and just accept it, okay? I want you to actually say it. Out loud. Finn Reynolds is a good goalie. Finn Reynolds is a *great* goalie."

Finn nearly made a joke, again, about how Jacob was going to swell more than just his ego, but he bit his tongue at the last moment. Because Jacob was right. He didn't want to just sit here and accept it. To say it.

He wouldn't say he was more comfortable with the status quo of believing the bullshit his dad didn't say, but lingered between the lines of his texts anyway, because none of that had ever been *comfortable*. But it was easier, maybe. Something he'd accepted.

"Finn Reynolds is a good goalie." He said it slowly, cautiously. Not quite believing it.

But Jacob nodded. "Again."

"Finn Reynolds is a good goalie." It came easier the second time. "Finn Reynolds is a great goalie."

"There you go," Jacob said softly, approval and an undeniable affection glowing in his dark eyes. "I knew you could do it. You're tough, you're strong, you're determined, and you're willing to put the work in. With all that, plus your natural skill, there's nothing you can't do, Finn."

But there was *one thing* Finn couldn't do. Shouldn't do.

He leaned over the console, closer to Jacob. Close enough he could nearly smell the scent of the trees on his plaid shirt. The fabric would be warm from his body. He could lean in even closer, flick open a button or two, find the skin underneath.

It would be glorious skin. Finn had already seen it once, when they'd been in the sauna, even as he'd tried not to look.

But this time maybe he could touch.

Jacob didn't move away. His Adam's apple bobbed as he swallowed hard.

The air thickened between them. It felt inevitable that Finn would cross the final distance separating them, and Jacob, too long without any of the release he must need, would let him.

It would be so good. Maybe even the really, really good sex Finn had been teasing him about earlier.

Finn tried to remember his earlier hesitation, when he'd acknowledged to himself that Jacob deserved someone who could be free and easy with him, the way he wanted to be, now. With Morgan, that wouldn't be possible. Maybe his dad might accept Jacob making him a better goalie.

Morgan would never accept this.

Their relationship, already strained, would implode.

You'll never get that approval you've always craved. He'll be silently disapproving, forever.

But even that didn't stop Finn. He leaned in another inch, and Jacob's eyelashes fluttered. They were thick and dark, curling on the ends. His chest was rising and falling rapidly with his breath, and Finn knew if he pressed a hand to his heart, he'd feel it racing.

So easy to curl his fingertips in the fabric. Undo those buttons.

Jacob would let him.

Would even welcome it.

The fate of our self-control shouldn't be in my hands, Finn thought. Not when this charged moment, in the dark, with Jacob's woodsy scent all around them, felt like the hottest sex he'd ever had, and they hadn't even touched each other.

How was he supposed to resist when everything about this was electrifying? When it was the most exciting thing that had ever happened to him?

"Finn," Jacob murmured, his voice rough around the edges.

"Yeah?"

Finn's fingers drifted down to his arm, circled it, the hard firmness and its inherent warmth soaking into his palm.

But Jacob didn't say anything else. Finn leaned in, and even before their lips brushed, he was already drowning in the taste of him.

But before he could actually experience it, a buzzing shook the car.

Shook them apart.

Jacob sprang back, horror written across his face.

He doesn't want you.

Correction: *he doesn't want to want you.*

Finn knew it, but the truth still hit him like a bucketful of ice-cold water.

Jacob scrambled back, pulling his phone out of his pocket. That was what had buzzed, then.

He answered it, and Finn tried to ignore the way Jacob's fingers were trembling around it. He dug his own fisted hands into his thighs, also pretending they weren't shaking the exact same goddamn way.

"Hey," Jacob said. "Oh. *Oh*. Well that's…unexpected. Good, but unexpected." He paused. "Sure. I can do that. I…I'll make the reservation. Yeah. Same place. Same time. Alright. See you then."

He clicked the phone off and set it on the console. He looked over in Finn's direction, but Finn realized he was staring over his shoulder. That he wasn't even *looking* at him. "That was Sophie."

"Who's Sophie?"

"My PR rep." He paused. "She and Mark, my agent, are coming into town this week and we're going to have one of our dinner meetings on Tuesday night. I…I want you to be there, Finn."

Finn wasn't stupid enough to believe it was because Jacob had acknowledged this was inevitable, and he wanted to introduce two of the most important people in his life to Finn.

No, it was time for Finn to earn *his* part of the bargain they'd struck.

Finn moistened his lips. Pretended that if they hadn't just gotten interrupted, he might've been able to taste Jacob on them, now. "Okay," he said.

"I'll text you the address of the restaurant. We'll meet at seven. I know you have school and homework. Maybe even practice?"

Finn wanted to laugh wretchedly. What a time to be reminded that he was still in *college*. Maybe Jacob wanted it, but he sure fucking didn't.

"It's fine. I'm free. We have Tuesday off. No practice."

"Okay. Okay. Good."

Jacob had still not looked him in the eye.

It was impossible to believe it was better this way, not when it felt so shitty.

"Finn . . ."

"Don't," Finn said sharply. If Jacob apologized . . .if he let him down easily, *kindly*, Finn was going to scream. "Just don't, okay?"

"Okay," Jacob said.

For a long moment, neither of them said anything. But Finn, who knew he should get out of this goddamn car and away from temptation, didn't move.

"I just . . .I want you to speak up in the meeting, okay? If you don't like what they say. You know me—"

"And they don't?" Finn interrupted.

"No, they do, but they have a lot of factors to consider that aren't *just* me, and how I am, how I feel, but you . . ." Jacob cleared his throat. "That's what you're there for. To have my back." *The way I have yours*, was the unspoken end of that sentence. Finn heard it, even if Jacob didn't say it.

"Yes," Finn said. He wanted to tell Jacob to fuck off, that this all had been a massive mistake, a painful tempting of fate, but it *was* working, wasn't it? He'd had a shutout tonight. He felt better about his play than he had in a long time. And Jacob would have someone at this meeting to stand up for him, to think about *him*.

Like Finn could fucking think about anyone else.

"Okay. Good. I thought . . .I thought we could at least have this." Jacob laughed, not sounding particularly amused by it.

"Right." *Get out of the car now, before you say anything else. Before you goddamn* do *anything else.* Finn put his hand on the door handle, but he didn't open it.

Then of course, Jacob chose that moment to actually *look* at him, right in the eye. "No matter what happens," Jacob said slowly, like he was carefully picking each and every word, "I'm not going to regret this."

Finn jerked and opened the door.

Melted into the night and refused to look back.

Understood a little too well how Jacob felt about retiring from hockey. That he was happy and *guilty* about being happy.

Because Finn fucking loved that he held their fate in his hands and resented the hell out of it, at the exact goddamn time.

CHAPTER 9

"You look tense," Brody said casually as he skated around the back of the net, getting his legs warmed up for practice.

Finn made a face. "I'm not tense," he argued. But he was. He definitely was.

Knew he was, even as he tried to limber himself up. He grunted at Brody, who rolled his eyes and skated off, to finish his own warmup.

He'd spent all day yesterday doing homework and getting ready for the week, but even though he'd been going through the motions, nothing had felt as real or as pressing as the thirty seconds where he and Jacob had nearly kissed.

It was a mistake. If they'd actually kissed, it would have been an enormous mistake.

Finn kept telling himself that, reminding himself—and his dick—that they'd dodged a bullet. Keeping Jacob in the coach box was better than any of the alternatives. Now he wouldn't ever have to disappoint his dad with his shit choices in men. Now he wouldn't be distracted from hockey. According to Zach, the Sentinels' scouts had been in the audience at the game. They'd even sent him an email, congratulating him on the shutout and telling him how good he looked.

"In control" was the phrase they'd used, and Finn could see how they might think that was true.

But it wasn't true.

When Jacob had sent a text yesterday evening about grabbing some ice time for just the two of them Thursday morning, he'd been so tempted to reply with some version of the same text he kept typing out in his mind: **what the fuck was that and why did we stop?**

But he knew why they'd stopped.

He didn't need Jacob to answer the question. He *knew*.

"And here I thought you getting some on the regular might loosen you up some."

Brody was back, now, and he had a look in his eye that promised he wasn't going to let this go.

"Getting some according to who?" Finn asked, but he already knew. Ramsey had decided that not only was Jacob coaching him, he was fucking him. It was not very surprising that he'd tell Brody, his best friend on the team.

What *was* surprising was that Brody—who before his football player boyfriend had practically been a virgin—was giving him shit about this.

"You're not?" Brody questioned.

"I'm not." Finn took a deep breath, wishing for patience. For sanity. "We're not. He's just coaching me."

"Well, the point remains. You're playing better than I've ever seen you. You were in the zone Saturday night," Brody said.

"Thanks."

"So why *are* you tense?" Brody paused, clearly hesitating because he wasn't sure he wanted to bring up the *D* word. "Is your dad in town?"

Finn shook his head. He didn't want to talk about it.

"Then what the fuck?" Brody asked, voice kind.

"It doesn't matter," Finn muttered.

"Do you—" Brody cut off his question. "Oh. I get it. You *wish* it was like that, and it's not."

"You are disgustingly smart," Finn muttered. "It's better if it's *not* like that."

"Maybe," Brody agreed.

"Are you kidding—my dad would lose his fucking mind if he knew Jacob was just coaching me, nevermind anything else."

"I thought Jacob was supposed to be making you care less what your dad thinks," Brody remarked mildly. "It's not his business who coaches you, or who you spend your time with."

Finn frowned. "Well, *I* know that, but I don't think anybody's ever given him that memo."

Brody shot him a knowing look. "I'd imagine that there's someone out there who could." And he skated away, like a total asshole.

Not leaving Finn in any better of a mood than he'd been before.

He didn't know if Brody meant him or Jacob—but both of those options frustrated him. He didn't want Jacob sticking up for him, like he couldn't stick up for himself. And if he *did* stick up for himself . . .well, it wasn't like Finn hadn't ever done it before.

But it never got easier.

His frustration didn't end, though.

He went through his own drills. Incorporating some of the new moves Jacob had taught him, but that only reminded him, unbearably, of how Jacob looked when he'd shown him. How strong and broad and totally fucking capable—of recording a shutout, and of decimating the last of Finn's precarious self-control.

Then Zach skated over and told Finn they were going to run a shootout drill.

Not Finn's favorite thing in the world.

But the last thing he wanted was for Zach—or anyone else—to know how much this drill pissed him off. Made him doubt himself.

He'd been doing this for years and years, and he'd hated it from the beginning, and he'd probably always hate it.

It was one thing to be scored on during a game—when that was the opposing team's entire purpose for being on the fucking ice. It was another entirely when it was guys he respected and trusted, exposing him in front of everyone. Every crack and seam that he hoped they might miss. Broken open for everyone to see.

"Alright," Finn said, because what else was he supposed to do? Beg Zach to leave it alone, when he was already in a shit mood?

He wasn't going to do that.

He was a hockey player, a *goalie*, and this was his only purpose.

If he couldn't do this, he couldn't do anything.

Finn tightened the grip on his stick and centered himself, watching the group on the other side of the ice.

"Mal," Zach called out, and Mal separated from the group, heading towards Finn's side of the ice with long, lazy swoops, skating deceptively easy.

But Mal was anything but easy. It wasn't hard to be fooled by his approach, and Finn had seen so many goalies get sucked into the matter-of-fact way he skated.

Then suddenly, he hit an edge, changing direction and taking off with a speed that nobody ever expected a guy of Mal's size to possess.

But Finn knew he had it and had been waiting for it.

He watched his eyes, as they slid up to his shoulder and then back down like he was trying to decide where he was going to go. But he knew, already, and Finn knew he knew.

It was only a matter of guessing which angle he'd already chosen.

"Come on, Mal," Elliott shouted from the other side of the ice. "Stop fucking around!"

Mal's grin turned shades of evil, and impossibly, he found a new closing speed and shot the puck, a dart off his stick.

Finn hit the ice, half a second too late to deflect it off his leg pad.

"Fuck," Finn muttered as it hit the net.

Elliott yelled at the other end in excitement and joy.

Zach must have called his name next—Finn couldn't hear anything but the roaring in his ears—because Ell took off, then, his celebration not slowing him down even a fraction.

He was crazy fast and never bothered to try to hide it, not like Malcolm.

No, he was out for blood immediately.

No matter how Finn told himself it wasn't personal and this was *Elliott* and he loved him, the brother he'd never had, it was almost impossible to remember that by the time Elliott took his shot, the puck's speed tucking it just between his legs as he collapsed down in an attempt to deflect.

"That's it," Zach called out, clapping. He glanced over at Finn. "You good?" he asked.

Like Finn was going to say he wasn't good.

"Fine," he said between clenched teeth.

"Alright," Zach said with a nod.

Ivan went next. And he actually did manage to deflect *his* shot, making Ivan mutter in Russian under his breath.

The rest of the team went, Ramsey flicking a sick shot above his shoulder, proving why he was so difficult to defend against. Because he was *that* good of a defenseman, and since he knew all the tricks, he knew just how to get around all of them.

By the time it was over, Finn felt raw and exposed, one big nerve.

Like he was a parody of a goalie, a pretender in pads.

Grinding his teeth together, he didn't hang around on the ice, heading to the locker room the moment the drill was over.

"Hey, Finn," Elliott called out but Finn ignored him.

"Just let him go," he heard Zach say behind him, and that stung, even more, pinpricks of pain digging into the wall of numbness he'd attempted to erect.

Everyone let him go.

He shucked off his equipment, resisting every urge he felt to just throw it.

To take his stick and to destroy something.

Maybe even himself.

He was supposed to be above this, *over* this. But he wasn't. It hurt more, now, when he'd believed he might finally be past it, than it had before.

The only fucking blessing was that his dad hadn't had to see that—or any of the hockey media who always liked to say that he was only a shadow of a Reynolds, the "lite" version of Morgan.

Didn't matter that they played different positions. The media liked to chip away at him, anyway, like he was indestructible, but he'd never been.

No matter how much he wished otherwise.

He took a shower, standing in the stall forever, letting the hot water wash down his body, hoping for a benediction or a blessing. Hoping to be washed clean of all his sins.

But it didn't work.

Especially when he walked back into the locker room and Ramsey was sitting on the bench like he'd been waiting for him.

"Hey," Ramsey said.

"Hey," Finn said shortly.

"You know we don't think any less of you, right? We know how solid you are." Ramsey's voice was so gentle and careful, and Finn hadn't thought it was possible, but now he felt even worse.

Overreacting and overemotional.

"Right," Finn said, swallowing the lump in his throat.

"It's taken us almost a whole fucking season to be able to do that to you." Ramsey kept going because he didn't know when to stop. That was Ramsey for you. "You realize that, right?"

He realized it, sure, but it wasn't like that really helped.

"Yeah," Finn said.

Ramsey shrugged, like he'd done what he could and he didn't know what else to do.

Finn burned under his skin. Anger and frustration and all that fucking lust that he hadn't been able to scorch off.

He wanted to call Jacob and say, *fuck doing the right thing. Just do me. Make me forget. Make me not think for a whole evening.*

But he couldn't. And not just because Jacob would chuckle in that uncomfortably tight way he did whenever Finn pushed and then say, even more gently than Ramsey, "You know we can't."

Yeah, he fucking knew it.

He was walking to his dorm room in only a T-shirt, hoping the heat of his anger would dissipate with the freezing air of an unexpectedly rain-less December night in Portland when his phone rang.

For a second, Finn froze. What if it was Morgan?

You'll just ignore the call, he reminded himself. *Like you've done a dozen times before.*

But it wasn't Morgan. It was Jacob.

Finn didn't know if that was better or worse, but he was in no mood to be a fucking saint, so he picked up.

"Hey," he said shortly. "What did I tell you about actual phone calls?"

"They make me look really old." Jacob chuckled—but self-consciously, not uncomfortably, not like Finn had pushed him into a place he didn't want to live in. That was something, at least. "I know. I thought I'd risk it. You didn't answer my text and I wanted to make sure we were still on for dinner tomorrow night."

"Yeah, I'll be there," Finn said shortly.

The dinner where Jacob would plan his coming out. The coming out that he'd share with his eventual, yet-to-be-named boyfriend.

Everything burned.

Finn didn't want to be that boyfriend; he *didn't*. It would be a mess, a true fucking disaster. But he already knew it would hurt if he ever saw Jacob and the phantom boyfriend out to-gether.

He'd wish it was his hand Jacob was holding; his ear Jacob was murmuring into. His body that Jacob took apart when they returned to Jacob's house, to Jacob's bed.

"You okay?"

Ramsey had essentially asked the same question, and he'd ig-nored him. He should ignore Jacob too, but the pull, inevitable and nearly irresistible, to confess how terrible practice had been, was hard to ignore.

Jacob would understand. It felt like Jacob was the *only* one who could understand.

"No. No. Not really." Finn choked back a sob. Leaned against a tree, halfway to his dorm. "Had an absolute shit practice."

There was a long silence on the other end.

"You want to talk about it?" Jacob asked.

Did he want to talk about it? No, he wanted to do anything *but* talk about it.

"No," Finn said. "No, no, I can't, I don't . . ."

"I got you," Jacob said. "You still on campus?"

"Yeah," Finn said.

"Don't go anywhere. I'm coming to get you."

Finn almost asked if Jacob was going to take him to his house and finally fuck him, but he was afraid to ask.

Afraid Jacob would say no. Even more afraid Jacob would say yes.

"Alright," Finn said. But whatever they did, he could admit he was breathing a little easier. Feeling less like the only way to deal with the burning rage lodged under his breastbone was to turn to this tree and decimate it with his fists.

"Just wait right there. Where I dropped you off Saturday night, okay?" Jacob said.

"Okay."

"Give me fifteen." Then Jacob was gone.

Finn leaned against the tree and tried to steady his breathing.

⋙⋙⇉ ⇇⋘⋘

"I can't believe you're gonna bail out on me after I fed you," Bryan said, teasing good-naturedly as he soaped up the pan he'd used to cook the pasta in.

"Sorry," Jacob said. "I just . . ."

"Need to go play knight in shining armor?" Bryan said, raising an eyebrow.

"Something like that," Jacob muttered.

"Well, go say goodbye to the girls, and tell them your booty call's more important than beating them on Mario Kart," Bryan said.

"Bry," Jacob said, frustrated.

Bryan looked at him. "I just don't like to see you lie to yourself like this. You're obsessed with this kid."

"God, please don't call him that."

"Okay, you're obsessed with this *guy*. Pretending you're not, that you can keep things . . .what, on just a coaching level . . .is just lying to yourself."

"Maybe I like lying to myself," Jacob said.

Bryan shot him a look that said he'd never believe it. Not in a million fucking years.

"Okay, I hate lying to myself, but what else is there to do? I can't . . .I *can't*."

"Why not?"

Oh God, for so many reasons. "I don't even have time to go into all the reasons it's a bad idea. Obviously Morgan."

"Obviously," Bryan said dryly.

"He's younger than me. A lot younger. He's got this whole life ahead of him, a whole NHL career, which I think is gonna be pretty damn spectacular, if he can stop worrying about how it stacks up against Morgan's."

"Maybe he's not looking for a white knight *or* a happily ever after," Bryan pointed out, setting the pan on the drying rack on the counter. "You ever think about that? You're actually the worst at taking good things and just *enjoying* them."

"I know," Jacob said.

"Just . . . if he wants you and you want him, why can't you just enjoy it?"

Why couldn't he? Well, of all the reasons he was planning to come out, that was one of the most important. He'd said for nearly as long as he'd been retired that one of the few advantages of retiring early was coming out and finding a boyfriend and enjoying a real relationship for the first time in his life.

That wasn't going to be in the cards with Finn.

Even if, deep down, he wanted Finn to be that guy, so much it hurt.

Finn didn't fit into the mold. He was too young, too eager for the rest of his life to begin. And named Reynolds to boot.

"You know what I want," Jacob said. "We've talked about it."

"You *thought* you wanted that. And there's no reason you can't have it, eventually. But I'm telling you, as the older, wiser one in this scenario—"

"You're barely eighteen months older," Jacob interrupted.

Bryan shot him a grin. "Still older. I'm telling you—enjoy him. It doesn't come around very often, like this, and you should get that chance, just the same as everyone else."

"I'll think about it," Jacob said and pulled his brother into a quick half-hug. "I'll go say goodbye to the girls."

Jackie and Krista were already deep in their Mario Kart battle, and he dropped kisses on their heads and a minute later was out the door, wrapping himself up in his coat as he headed towards his car.

Luckily, the school was only a few blocks away from Bryan's house, and only a few minutes later he was pulling up to the curb where he'd dropped Finn off just two days ago.

Finn was waiting, too, hands shoved in his jeans pockets, duffel over one shoulder.

He slid in, putting the bag in the backseat before he settled into the passenger seat.

"Where's your coat? You're gonna get fucking pneumonia on a clear night like this," Jacob complained.

Someone had to worry about Finn, if he wasn't going to worry about himself.

"I was hot," Finn said.

Jacob made a disgruntled noise and cranked the heater up.

"Where are we going?" Finn asked when they were halfway to their destination.

He'd probably guessed they weren't going to Jacob's house since he'd deliberately turned the opposite direction. Jacob had wanted to ask him what had been so bad about the practice, but he knew how those could feel. It was always better to wait until someone was ready to talk.

"What I always did after a really bad practice or a shitty game," Jacob said. He pulled into the parking lot.

"Dairy Queen?"

"It's impossible to be sad when you're eating ice cream," Jacob said. "Come on."

Finn grumbled under his breath, but when he emerged from the car, he'd grabbed a sweatshirt from his bag and was shrugging it on. "Is that like scientifically proven?" he wondered as they walked into the store.

"We're getting milkshakes 'cause we're not staying," Jacob said, refusing to answer Finn's teasing question.

Teasing was better than the look of concentrated doom he'd worn when he'd gotten in the car.

"You gonna at least ask me what flavor I want?" Finn asked, nudging him with a shoulder.

"Well, obviously," Jacob said.

"Marshmallow." Finn said it so fast Jacob did a double take.

"Is that even a flavor they *have* here?"

"Obviously," Finn said and marched right up to the register like this wasn't the first time he'd done this.

Well, maybe it wasn't only Jacob who got milkshakes when he was having a bad day.

He walked up to the register and then turned to Jacob. "Let me guess," he said, green eyes glittering, "you want chocolate."

"Why do I feel like that's a bad choice all of a sudden?"

"It's basic, is what it is," Finn said. But he ordered the chocolate milkshake along with his marshmallow abomination, and before Jacob could grab his wallet or protest, he'd paid for both of them.

"Call it a thank you for dropping whatever you were doing," Finn murmured as they waited for their shakes to be made.

"I wasn't . . .well, truthfully, you saved me from Jackie and Krista kicking my ass at Mario Kart," Jacob said.

Finn raised an eyebrow. "Jackie and Krista?"

"My nieces. Seven and ten. They're much, much better than I am," Jacob admitted.

"At everything or just Mario Kart?"

Jacob wasn't particularly surprised that Finn had asked about them. Curiosity was partially responsible of course, but Jacob understood too how much easier it was for Finn to talk about something else than what was really bothering him.

"Pretty much everything," Jacob said sheepishly. "They're amazing and brilliant and beautiful, and just . . ." He trailed off when he realized just how doting he sounded.

Finn smiled. "That's why you moved here, after you retired."

"Yeah," Jacob said. "Bryan's a single dad, and I want to support him, right, but also . . .you have a chance to be with those little girls, you're not gonna miss it."

After they picked up their shakes they walked outside, Finn sucking noisily on his straw. "So what's the next step in the 'Jacob Braun feel-better plan'?"

"How do you know there's a plan?" Jacob unlocked the door and they both slipped inside.

Finn rolled his eyes as he started the car. "There's *clearly* a plan."

"Fine, fine, there's a plan, okay?" Jacob started the car.

It was only a five-minute drive to the overlook, but he drove it in silence, only listening as Finn gnawed at his straw.

If he looked over, he'd see it in Finn's mouth and he really, *really* didn't need to see anything in Finn's mouth. It would feed the worst of his fantasies and they already felt out of control.

Jacob parked at the overlook, ignoring the sign that claimed it closed at dusk. Led Finn towards the low chain-link barrier and over it.

"Look at you, Braun," Finn teased. "Such a lawbreaker."

He *did* sound lighter, but Jacob also knew whatever had made him sound so much worse less than an hour earlier didn't just evaporate.

You had to suck out the poison, first.

Metaphorically, he reminded himself. *There will be no* actual *sucking.*

"Hey, we're not doing anything *really* bad," Jacob said as they walked out towards the overlook.

"No? Disappointing."

Jacob took a drink of his milkshake so he wouldn't have to answer that—or defend himself.

The chocolate was rich on his tongue, stirring up all the memories of when he'd needed one of these.

It was a good reminder of why they were here.

"I did this after every bad practice. Every wretched game." Jacob stopped at the edge of the cliff. Portland in all her shimmering golden glory was laid out beneath them, and because for once it wasn't raining, the stars created a sparkling canopy overhead.

"You never played here," Finn said matter-of-factly.

Changing the subject again. On Saturday night, Jacob had called him out for deflecting, but he wasn't going to do it tonight.

"I didn't," Jacob said. "But they had overlooks in Pittsburgh. Milkshakes, too."

"Funny how that works." Finn took a deep breath. Let it out again.

Jacob heard it and hoped that it was helping. Decided that he'd be safe offering a little more.

"And," he said, "after I retired and moved here, I did this enough times. Plenty of bad days, even though I wasn't playing anymore."

"Because you weren't playing anymore," Finn guessed.

Jacob nodded. Finn still hadn't looked over at him. He was still gazing out at the lights below, and he told himself that was better.

Easier, anyway.

This was supposed to be for Finn's peace of mind, and if he could find it that was the most important thing.

"It's ironic, isn't it," Finn said, "I needed it because I *am* playing, and you needed it because you're not anymore."

"Hockey's a blessing and a curse," Jacob said pragmatically.

Finn sighed.

"You wanna talk about it?" Jacob said after a long moment. He was nearly done with his milkshake, and he had a feeling Finn was nearly done with his, too, since the cup was dangling at the end of his fingers, at his side.

"Not really." Finn finally looked over and made a face. "Tell me more about Jackie and . . .Trista?"

"Krista. Ugh, they're just . . .so smart. More than book smart. They always seem to know when I'm in a bad mood, and they just . . .miraculously drag me out of it, I don't even know how. Every time, I would've sworn to you nobody on earth could, but they just push and tease and cuddle up to me, and the next thing I know, I'm smiling and even laughing. Wrestling with them on the ground. Letting them doodle all over my face. Losing spectacularly to them at Mario Kart."

"I think I could probably give them a run for their money."

"You'd think so, but you'd lose, anyway," Jacob said.

Finn flashed him a smile, and it reminded him of how Jackie and Krista always managed it with him, and now he'd done it too.

Maybe not as effortlessly as them, but things with his nieces were so much simpler. The situation with Finn was layered. Messy.

"Sounds like it. Maybe I could . . ." Finn trailed off, and Jacob had a feeling he was thinking of saying, *Maybe I could meet them someday.*

But why would he have a reason to? He wouldn't.

Jacob was just his coach.

"Maybe you could meet them someday," Jacob said, because he was an idiot and a total sucker for attempting to eradicate that melancholy tone out of Finn's voice.

"I'd like that a lot," Finn said, shooting him a small smile.

"You've met Bryan already, after all." Jacob knew he was trying to justify it, even though there was no real reason.

"Yeah," Finn agreed. He let out another unsteady breath. "Zach had us run a shootout drill today."

"Ah." Jacob reached over and took Finn's empty cup and tossed both of them into a nearby trash can.

"Did you always hate those too?"

"I didn't *like* them," Jacob said. "But I understood why they were necessary. They make you better. They make your offense better."

"Ugh, not you too," Finn complained.

"Okay, why do you hate them?"

Finn shot him a look. "You know why."

"Yeah, maybe. But I want you to say it." *Out loud,* Jacob didn't add, *so you can hear how ridiculous it sounds.*

"I hate them because it makes me look bad. Foolish. Outmatched. Over and over again. And it means that not only will *I* know that, the whole team's gonna know that, too."

Finn got to the end of this and then winced. He shot Jacob a rueful look. "It's really stupid, isn't it?"

"Not stupid. Do you really believe you're bad? Foolish? Outmatched?"

Finn shook his head.

"And does the team believe that?"

"No," Finn said quietly.

"There you go. It does suck. You want to do well. You want to show them you've earned their respect and their belief in what you can do. But one drill isn't enough to change any of that, not even close. You know that, Finn."

"I also . . . just . . ." Finn stopped. Looked over at Jacob. "Why does this have to suck so much?"

"Playing hockey?"

"No, no, no." Finn hesitated. "You know what."

"Ah. Well." Jacob shoved his hands into his pockets. They'd managed to *not* get deep into the weeds tonight, unlike Saturday. He'd been doing his best to steer them clear, but maybe there was no real steering them clear. Not when he felt the way he did. Not when the attraction flared between them, every time Jacob looked over at Finn. Not when he knew how much Finn felt it, too.

"I shouldn't have pushed Saturday." Finn sounded morose again.

And Jacob hated that, even more.

"None of that," Jacob said and grabbed the metaphorical red-hot potato in his hands, tugging Finn into a tight hard hug. He'd hugged teammates like this a thousand times over the years, and it should've felt the same. It didn't. But he was going to at least pretend—one day at a time—that it did.

Finn let him go. "You came even though you were worried," he said.

"Worried about you? Yeah, I was." He had been. He'd heard the sound of Finn's voice and he'd been there, too, more times than he wanted to remember.

He'd wanted to take the pain away. Bear it for Finn, even if it was only for a little while.

"Worried about this," Finn said, gesturing between them.

"*This* isn't going to stop me," Jacob said firmly.

Finn stared at him for a long moment. "You're a good guy. A . . .a good coach."

Jacob thought maybe he'd wanted to say something else, but he'd settled for the simple, easy, non-problematic answer instead.

He should be happy that Finn had.

But he found himself wondering what Finn had wanted to say instead, long after he dropped him off.

CHAPTER 10

FINN HAD HIS CLOSET open, staring at the contents within, temptation warring inside him as he tried to decide what to wear to this dinner tonight, when his phone rang.

Before, when he'd glanced at the screen, he might've let it go to voicemail.

Then might've eventually replied to his dad when he sent a follow-up text, and then another.

Avoidance had not been a particularly good strategy, though. It had pissed Morgan off, and in some ways, Finn wondered if it made him push him harder. Plus, it wasn't like it made Finn feel any better either. He'd still been drowning under all that pressure.

"Hey, Dad," he said, tucking his phone between his ear and his shoulder, flicking through the clothes hanging in his closet.

The restaurant Jacob had texted him the address of was dressier, not that much in Portland required more than jeans.

He *could* wear jeans and a nice sweater.

Or he could make Jacob swallow his tongue.

He'd intended the former, until last night, when Jacob had taken him out for milkshakes and it felt like things had shifted between them.

Now he was conflicted.

If they crossed the line, it would be so messy. That hadn't changed. But that wasn't all Finn saw anymore. The tantalizing possibilities of what it could *also* be danced just out of reach.

"Great game Saturday," Morgan said.

"Yeah," Finn said.

There was a weird pause on the other end of the phone. Like his dad hadn't expected him to agree.

Or maybe he just hadn't expected him to answer the goddamn phone.

"Didn't expect to get you," Morgan said, and hesitation had crept into his dad's normally purely confident tone.

"Yeah," Finn said.

"Finn," his dad said sternly. "This is serious."

Finn was five seconds away from pretending ignorance and saying, *oh yeah, really? I had no fucking idea.* But he remembered what Jacob had said Saturday. Not just the pressure of Jacob's fingers on his chin, but how Jacob had told him he liked to deflect.

That would be all that comment would do. Deflect, with the added benefit of pissing his father off.

"No shit, Dad," Finn said.

There was another long pause.

"Are you okay? What are you doing?"

"I'm fine. Trying to decide what to wear to this dinner," Finn said. He didn't say who it was with, because his dad would totally lose his shit.

"A date?"

Finn laughed. "No. Not exactly. But . . .I wouldn't mind it if it *was*."

And he wouldn't. He realized that now. Maybe Jacob *was* serious. Finn wasn't sure he *wasn't* serious, anymore.

"I didn't realize you dated during the season."

"I said it wasn't a date," Finn reminded him firmly. "Only that I'd *like* it to be. And let me remind you that you *married* Mom during the season."

Obviously Finn had not been present then, but even now, he thought that might be one of the more uncharacteristic things Morgan Reynolds had ever done.

Of course, uncharacteristic didn't mean successful and they'd gotten divorced when Finn was five.

He and his mom talked much less than he and his dad, for a few reasons. *One*, Morgan seemed virtually incapable of leaving him the fuck alone, and *two*, his mom had remarried a studio exec in Hollywood and had two young sons. He knew his mom loved him, but she was so busy.

Finn didn't resent that exactly, but he couldn't say he *liked* it either.

Morgan cleared his throat. "I like to think you've learned from my mistakes."

"Mistakes? You?"

Normally that kind of comment might piss his dad off. But then that was usually when he *finally* got ahold of Finn, and also after Finn had probably made half a dozen other flippant remarks all designed to rile him up.

But this time, he only chuckled under his breath. "You know I make them, every once in awhile."

"Every once in awhile," Finn retorted mildly.

"I didn't call you to talk about me," Morgan reminded him.

No, of course he hadn't.

"Right," Finn said. Pulled out a suit, fingers sliding along the fabric. Would he dare? He *wanted* to dare.

If he dared, he had a feeling that tonight would end very differently than Saturday. Than last night. If he wanted it.

And he *wanted* it. Wanted Jacob.

"It really was a great game," Morgan said. "Other than that little bit right before the end of the first period. But you recovered well."

"I know," Finn said matter-of-factly. Suddenly wondered if his dad had seen Jacob on the camera as he'd come down to the ice from the stands. Or if the broadcast had already panned away, going to commercial break. But if he had, that's what Morgan would've led with, first thing.

"Do you want to talk about it?"

"Not particularly. I learned what I needed to from it."

His dad was silent again, and Finn knew he'd surprised him again.

Considering how Morgan could be, Finn decided that was a positive.

"You hear from the Sentinels?"

Finn ground his teeth together. Of course, he wouldn't just give up; he'd keep pushing.

"They emailed me. They're happy with how I'm progressing," Finn said. Trying to stay calm and only mostly succeeding.

"Nothing about camp next year?"

"No," Finn said, through clenched teeth.

"I'm heading to Tampa next week, actually, I could talk to them an—"

"No," Finn said.

"But—"

"Don't say you only want to help. Don't say you're only doing it for me," Finn said. And he was annoyed now. Annoyed because it always started this way, reasonable and conversational, and it *always* devolved into this pseudo-pressure bullshit.

Morgan said nothing.

"I'm handling this," Finn said firmly. "They drafted *me*, not you, though I'm sure they fucking wish I was more of a chip off the old block than I actually am."

"Finn," Morgan said and he sounded so reasonable and so *not* annoyed it only made Finn's temper flare hotter.

"I have this," Finn repeated. "I *have* this."

Maybe for the very first fucking time he wasn't just saying the words, hoping that his dad would accept them long enough to get off his back, but he might actually believe them.

He *did* have this. He was growing. He was learning. He was changing. Jacob was giving him a much-needed new perspective on how to handle this work, this job.

This career.

He didn't have to be Morgan. He could be Finn and that was absolutely fucking *okay*.

"You do," Morgan said. For once it actually sounded like he agreed. Grudgingly, maybe, but that belief was all he'd ever wanted. "I told you, you played great last night. Honestly, great the last few weeks. What's different? You've changed—"

"No," Finn said. "We're not doing this."

Morgan actually had the nerve to sound hurt. "I'm not asking because of *me*. I'm asking because of you. Because I give a shit about you. You're my son."

"You're fucking asking because you're worried I'm going to make you look bad. Don't worry; I'm not gonna embarrass the Reynolds name."

"That's not—I'm not—" Morgan broke off with a muttered *fuck*. "Don't do that, Finn."

"Then don't be an overbearing ass."

Morgan took a short huffing breath, like he was desperately trying to rein in his temper, and a voice inside Finn, a voice that sounded suspiciously just like Jacob's, told him that maybe he should do the same.

For a long moment, there was nothing, only silence. Finn half-expected his dad to just tell him he had to go and hang up, but he didn't. He changed the subject instead.

"Tell me about this dinner," Morgan said. "This guy you're going to dinner with. The dinner that's not the date that you'd like to be."

"Yes, I know what you're asking about." Finn rolled his eyes and stared at the suit he'd pulled out. The options of what he could wear with it.

Was he trying to give Jacob a heart attack? Melt his defenses one breath at a time?

Ramsey would tell him to just fucking go for it.

He wanted to be brave like Ramsey. Fearless.

"What's he like? How'd you meet him?"

Finn could hear the effort in his dad's voice and told himself that if Morgan was trying this hard, he should at least reciprocate.

"He's a bit older. Nice. I'm giving him some advice now, but I'm . . .yeah, I'm hoping for more."

"Not a hockey player, then," Morgan stated, rather than asked.

But as angry as his dad could make him, Finn didn't want to lie. Outright or otherwise. "He runs this foundation. Or he's starting this foundation, I guess. Wants some advice from a queer perspective."

There, that was about as factually accurate as Finn could get without telling Morgan the whole truth.

"A do-gooder, then. He *must* be nice."

"He is," Finn said.

He wanted to tell his father that Jacob was nice, but firm. That he wanted better for Finn than sometimes Finn wanted for himself. That he pushed him, but in all the right ways. Ways that made him feel brilliant and capable and strong, not weak or hopeless or forever lagging behind.

"So what's the problem, then?"

"Who says there's a problem?" Finn asked.

"You said *you'd* like it to be a date, but it's not. Why isn't it?"

"Dad, not everything's a problem that you can fix."

"Maybe not, but tell me anyway."

Finn sighed. "He thinks he's too old for me."

There was a long drawn-out silence. Then, "How old is too old?"

"He's uh . . .mid-thirties?"

"Well, I like him already," Morgan said, and Finn had to bite his lip so he didn't laugh. So that Morgan wouldn't interrogate him about why that was so fucking hilarious.

"Why?"

"Because he's not *that* old, but he's conscious of it. Doesn't want to take advantage of you. Thoughtful. Makes me like him. If he's putting you above getting off."

"*Dad.*"

"Just saying." Morgan didn't sound regretful at all. "Sounds like a great guy, honestly. You should tell him how you feel."

"I . . ." Well. He hadn't because he'd been sure it was a bad idea. But now that he was no longer so convinced. . .now that he was thinking of what he really wanted, of just giving up the fight and going for it . . .

"With your *words*, Finn," his dad said dryly.

"I'm pretty sure he's aware."

"Well, he cares about you, doesn't he?"

Finn let out a huff of annoyance. "I don't know why you're asking *me* that."

"I think it'd take a strong man to know how you feel and care about you, in return, and do nothing."

"Yeah, he's a fucking boy scout," Finn muttered.

"You know how to drive just about anyone 'round the bend, Finn."

"That your way of saying wear the suit?"

Morgan's attention sharpened. "Which suit?"

"The one I had made in London last year." The one that fit him like a fucking glove, that made his shoulders broad and his hips narrow and hugged his thighs and ass like it had been made for them—which it had.

"You woke up today and chose murder, huh?" Morgan sounded delighted by this. "You *are* a Reynolds."

"That's what my passport says, anyway," Finn said. Normally a comment like that would fill him with bitterness, but not today.

Today, he was shockingly, ridiculously pleased that his father approved of his methods. Even if they were underhand. Frankly, *more* probably because they *were* underhand.

"You got this," Morgan said encouragingly. "You want him? Don't let him get away."

Someday, if this actually all worked out . . .

If by some fucking miracle, he and Jacob figured their shit out, *and* if they got in deep enough that there was no way around finally telling Morgan, and if he didn't immediately commit murder . . .

Well, that was a lot of *ifs*, but if they ever got to that place, Finn was going to remind Morgan of this conversation.

Of how he'd once said, *You want him? Don't let him get away.*

"Noted," Finn said, amused by even the possibility of throwing that comment back into his dad's face.

"And don't tell me how it goes, after," Morgan said.

"Don't worry, I wasn't planning on it."

"Good." Morgan paused. "And I meant it. You're playing great, Finn. Keep it up."

After Finn hung up, he told himself firmly and at length that the *keep it up* was not a threat and not a reminder, but instead, it was Morgan attempting to be supportive.

Jacob would probably tell him to stop wondering which it was and just decide what *Finn* wanted it to mean and then move on.

He wanted to take the advice. More than anything. *Then do it*, that Jacob voice in his head murmured. *And while you're at it, come over tonight looking so good I forget my own name.*

Finn grinned at the mirror.

"Sure thing," he said.

Finn was late. Less than five minutes, yes, but it felt like a fucking eternity.

You should have picked him up. You should have driven to the college and picked him up.

Jacob paced in front of the restaurant, knowing he should go inside—Mark and Sophie were already at the table, waiting—but he didn't want to. Not until Finn got here.

But after he'd texted the address, Finn had sent him a thumbs-up.

Why *hadn't* he insisted?

The truth, despite insidiously worming its way through his consciousness, was still hard to acknowledge: *if you picked him up, this would feel more like a date than it already does.*

It wasn't like last night hadn't felt like a date. An impromptu date, maybe. He'd picked Finn up and driven them somewhere and then driven them back. Finn had even managed to make it out of the car with only a friendly smile and an agreement to see him for dinner, tomorrow night.

Finally giving up on the last bit of his self-control, Jacob pulled his phone out of his pocket. Apparently it wasn't cool to actually *call* anyone these days, but he could text. Make sure that Finn was on his way. *Make sure he's okay.*

But before he could do anything other than pull their text convo up, a car pulled up to the curb and the back door opened.

Jacob's grip on his phone tightened as the figure emerged from the car.

Finn was undeniably attractive, every single day, no matter what he was wearing.

He looked gorgeous in sweats, a hood pulled over his wind-blown curls. Sweaty. Exhausted.

But this . . .

Jacob's breath came in unsteady pants.

What is he trying to do to me?

He was terrified of the answer.

"Hey," Finn said, tilting his chin up and meeting Jacob's eyes straight on.

Jacob wasn't proud but he fucking stared.

The gray suit with its faint hint of check fit Finn like a glove. It framed him, flawlessly tailored to his shoulders, to his arms. Jacob's gaze skittered lower, his sharp intake of breath loud between them. The pants were slim, tracing the curves of his thighs, his legs, his calves. If he turned around, Jacob had no doubt the fabric would cup his ass like it had been painted on.

And underneath, the moss green knit polo was thin and clingy, drawing attention to his pecs, his chest, his abs. The color made his eyes glow, brought out the slight reddish-gold tinge of his curls.

Jacob knew he could clean up fairly well; he'd even tried tonight to take more care than he normally did.

But *Finn*.

Jacob didn't know whether to curse or fall to his knees in abject praise.

"You alright there?" There was the slightest hint of a dimple in Finn's cheek as he grinned at him, like he knew just how delicious he looked. And since he no doubt owned a mirror, *he knew*.

Which meant he'd done this—done this to Jacob—entirely on purpose.

"Do you know what you're doing?" The words came out rougher and harsher than he'd intended.

But Finn's smile didn't waver. "Not really, no, but it seemed like a good idea, anyway."

"To drive me *insane?*" Jacob questioned and took his arm, sparks racing along his fingertips as they dug into the fabric.

"Is that what I'm doing?" That dimple deepened.

"You know exactly what you're doing," Jacob ground out.

But Finn only continued to look absolutely fucking delighted. "Are we going in to dinner?"

"I'm tempted to dump you back in a car and send you home. Insist you take that suit off."

"Oh, I bet you'd like taking it off a whole lot," Finn purred under his breath.

That was the whole fucking problem, wasn't it? As mouthwatering as Finn looked in the suit, he'd look even better out of it. Lying in Jacob's bed without a single fucking stitch on, as Jacob looked his fill.

"You're playing with fire," Jacob told him.

And we're gonna get burned.

"And you're not?" Finn reached up and cupped his *bare* cheek. And okay, yes, he'd shaved his beard off. It had begun to look a little straggly plus it made him look even older, and as he'd stared in his mirror tonight, he'd thought, *it can always grow back.*

And maybe he'd been thinking, in the back of his mind, of the way Finn touched him sometimes, the way he was doing now, fingers curled around his jawline.

He'd wondered how it would feel, skin to skin, with nothing in the way.

He knew now.

"I . . .it was time," Jacob stuttered. Didn't want Finn to know that it had anything to do with him, even though Finn had just made it plenty clear that every mouthwatering inch of his look tonight was entirely for Jacob.

"I like it," Finn said and patted his cheek. "Like the beard, too, but this is nice."

"I . . ." *Tell him it wasn't for him.* But Jacob couldn't get the words out.

Instead he changed the subject to something that felt reasonably safer.

Dinner.

"Come on," Jacob said, "Sophie and Mark are waiting for us inside."

Finn nodded and followed him inside, weaving through the restaurant until they reached the private dining room he'd reserved.

Sophie pinned him with a look the moment he entered. "What's going on, Jacob? Who are we waiting for?"

Finn stepped out from behind Jacob and Sophie looked more than a little surprised.

Mark said, "Well, you certainly had us convinced last time that you weren't going this route."

Finn glanced over at him. "You talked about me?"

"Uh, only the Reynolds as an abstract concept," Jacob said, suddenly uncomfortable. This had seemed like such a good idea last night—better, anyway, than the really catastrophically bad idea of finally letting himself kiss Finn—but maybe it wasn't.

Maybe it had just seemed less bad in comparison.

"I'm Finn," Finn said, extending a hand. "Nice to meet both of you."

"Sophie," she said, shooting him a pleased smile.

"Mark," his agent said, shaking Finn's hand next. "So when you categorically refused to work with either the father or the son, did you already know Finn here?"

Jacob winced as Finn shot him a pleased look as he took his seat.

"No. Not really," Jacob admitted. "But . . .circumstances changed."

"Clearly," Sophie murmured.

"Can I get the matching set?" Mark wondered.

"Finn's only here as a sounding board," Jacob said firmly. "Finn and Finn *only*. You can't breathe a word to anyone he was here. Especially anyone who might get back to Morgan."

"Ooooh," Sophie teased, "a *secret rendezvous*. Sexy. I like it."

"Not sexy . . .not . . ." Jacob trailed off.

But Sophie and Mark weren't stupid and they knew him well. Surely they could see how he could barely tear his eyes away from Finn in that delectable suit.

"Alright," Sophie said kindly, clearly taking pity on him and patting his hand supportively. He knew later, probably tomorrow, she'd call and pin him down. He'd probably tell her how he felt about Finn long before he ever confessed it to Finn himself.

Of course, if he kept his head about him, he'd *never* confess to Finn how he felt.

Someday, he'd end up with that boyfriend who he'd be out for, and this whole thing with Finn would fade like a fever dream.

But Jacob already knew, a solid deep down certainty, that no matter how great or hot or kind the boyfriend was, Finn would linger forever in the back of his mind. The one that got away.

"Jacob?"

Jacob's attention returned to the table, feeling short of breath and acutely aware of how shitty that would be. "What?"

Mark shot him an impatient look. "Did you bring wine or should we order something from the wine list?" He waved the folio in front of him.

"I . . .uh . . .I'll pick something out," Jacob said, plucking it from Mark's fingers. Focusing on a purpose might keep his brain from short-circuiting over the realization he hadn't wanted to have.

He glanced over at Finn from under the cover of the wine list. He was laughing at something Sophie said, and Jacob's dick twitching was not new. But his heart was clenching too, and that *was*.

Morgan would absolutely kill him. But when had he ever given a shit about what Morgan did and didn't like?

"So you're some kind of wine expert, huh?" Finn asked, leaning over, making Jacob light-headed with how good he smelled.

Like candy-coated sin.

"Don't let him tell you any differently," Mark said.

"It's a hobby," Jacob said modestly.

"Surprised he hasn't told you about his collection yet," Sophie said.

"I did see some wine when I was at your house, on that big wall in your living room?" Finn questioned.

Jacob internally winced as Sophie pounced. "You were at Jacob's house?"

Finn grinned, clearly aware of why she wanted to know. "Oh, yeah. Jacob's working with me, one-on-one." He winked, and Jacob nearly groaned.

He would ask Finn what he was trying to do, but it was obvious. He was trying to wear Jacob down. He was trying to *seduce* him.

The only question was if Jacob was going to let himself be seduced.

The waiter approached, and Jacob blindly picked a merlot that sounded good—not even bothering to consult the flavor profile in his wine app, even though he rarely didn't. But if he took his attention away from Finn for even a second, what was he going to say? *Do?*

"Now, what's the news?" Jacob asked after the waiter promised to bring out the sommelier with their wine.

"I think we might have a solution for you," Sophie said excitedly.

"You do?"

"You know Neal Fisher?" she asked.

"Wasn't he a football player? Kicker, yeah?" Jacob wondered. Not sure if he was remembering the right guy.

"Yeah, he missed that field goal at the end of the Super Bowl a few years ago. Riptide released him after that, even though he'd been a great player for them," Mark said.

"I remember. And then he ended up on some football show on ESPN." Jacob also remembered that he was gay and gorgeous, though not really Jacob's type.

Who was he fucking kidding? If he'd had a type before now, his type was currently sitting next to him.

"He's doing a podcast now," Sophie said.

"Good for him?" Jacob didn't want to go on a podcast, even if Neal Fisher was the one doing the podcasting.

Finn nudged his foot under the table.

"It's a great podcast. All about the intersection of queerness and athletics, and he touches a lot on other topics related to professional sports, like how tough retirement can be."

"I'm glad he's talking about it," Jacob said grudgingly.

Sophie skewered him with a single look. "He wants to have you on, Jacob. And the conversation would *mostly* talk about your emotional health post-retirement, but I thought this would be a great, really a *wonderful*, opportunity to come out in a very understated, easy way. The conversation wouldn't focus on that, but it would be easy enough to slide in."

"It'd still make a lot of fucking headlines," Jacob said. Wishing the wine would get here. He needed a fucking drink.

"Jacob," Mark said bluntly, "there's going to be a lot of fucking headlines no matter what you do. You tell the truth, any part of it, no matter how you downplay it, and it's going to be news. Everyone's going to be talking about it."

"Don't promise me a good time or anything," Jacob muttered. It made his skin crawl, the thought of everyone gossiping about it, tearing his private life apart one soundbite, one headline, at a time. Especially when he'd spent so long, so fucking long, trying to stay out of the spotlight so nobody would put two and two together and get four.

He turned to Finn, but already knew he wasn't going to like what he said, based on the wry smile he was wearing.

"Mark isn't wrong," Finn said. "Everyone's going to talk about it. But it'll be one time, and then it won't be news anymore. And frankly, it's *less* news than it used to be. Maybe if you'd come out ages ago, when you were playing . . ." Finn must have figured out that going down *that* road was going to do him no favors, so he stopped. "I'm just saying, this sounds like a good possibility. Maybe you shouldn't dismiss it outright."

"It'll be an easy, comfortable, sympathetic environment," Sophie chimed in, clearly sensing that this was the time to strike. To close the deal.

"And you can talk about the foundation while you're on. Neal does a lot of work with kids and athletics. He's got this huge field complex down in LA, hosts all these kids' teams, a lot of them queer," Mark said.

"I'll think about it," Jacob said and realized that he *might* mean it.

"Not for too long," Sophie said. "Promise me you won't just put me off forever. You know you can't get the ball rolling on the foundation until we take this step. You *know* that."

Jacob turned to Finn. "Is that true?"

Finn shrugged. "I'm not an expert, but yeah, I'd assume there would be a *lot* of questions if you suddenly rolled out a foundation designed to support queer athletes and you hadn't said a word about your own sexuality." His gaze softened. "There'd be a lot of talk. Mark's right; there's going to be talk no matter what. But if there's no story . . .nothing to question, to wonder about, that's better."

Imagine if the world figured out that I was falling head over heels for Morgan Reynolds' son? What kind of chaos would that cause?

Jacob could only fucking imagine how invasive everything would get then. Every frame of every fight between Jacob and Morgan would get dredged up. Every set of ugly words they'd exchanged. The last time they'd met publicly, at his last All Star Game, when he'd had to be held back from punching Morgan in the face.

Then because Morgan was Morgan, he wouldn't be able to keep his trap shut, and he'd say something designed to piss Jacob off. Maybe even designed to piss Finn off, too. That wouldn't surprise Jacob, particularly.

It would get so ugly, their private business played out for a salivating public.

"Alright," Jacob said, clearing his throat. Hating how tight it had suddenly gotten. Why did it only feel like there were two choices: *the one that got away* and *becoming the hottest gossip in the NHL?*

It wasn't fair at all, but then Jacob knew life wasn't particularly fair.

The wine arrived then, and Jacob, aware of Sophie's knowing gaze falling on him, tried to pretend like everything was normal.

But nothing was normal.

Finn was next to him, looking and smelling so good Jacob wanted to cry with it.

"Why do I feel like there's something you're not telling me?" Sophie wondered when Finn excused himself halfway through dinner to use the restroom.

"There's nothing," Jacob said.

"You *like* him. A lot. And I guarantee he isn't going to wear that suit for just anyone, Jacob," she said.

"It's just a suit."

A suit designed to bring me to my knees.

"No offense, but that's not *just* a suit," Mark said. "I asked him where he got it. That's a custom Burberry suit. Do you have any idea what that costs? How hard it is to get them to make you one? And he wore it to dinner *with you.*"

Jacob's throat felt dry and tight. "Maybe he likes it."

"Maybe he wanted *you* to like it," Sophie said, not surprisingly hitting the nail right on the head. "Do you have any idea what you're playing with here?"

Fire. Red-hot fire.

"Morgan is going to lose his mind," Mark said.

"It's not his business. Finn is a grown man." *Not a kid.* "An adult." He'd laughingly produced his driver's license to prove he was of drinking age when the waiter had asked.

"It's cute that you think the age has anything to do with how pissed off Morgan's going to be," Sophie said. "You didn't want us to *mention* anything about the foundation to his people. You forbade us to even bring it up. And then the next time we meet, you show up with *his son*, and it's clear something's going on between you. Jacob, you need to—"

But she never got to say what it was he needed to do, because Finn arrived back at the table again, and she covered up her concern with another throwaway comment in his direction.

Finn shot him a questioning look, but didn't say anything.

Not until they'd wrapped up the meal and Sophie and Mark had gone their separate ways—after Sophie trading numbers with Finn, under the pretext she'd take a look over his social media—Finn turned to him, his curls gilded by the golden light hanging above the table.

"What was that Sophie was saying before I walked back in?" Finn asked as he stood, reaching for his suit jacket.

Jacob didn't know if it was better or worse when he gracefully slid it on. The jacket covered up the *pecs-chest-abs* that clingy polo revealed, but then once it was on, it accentuated the gorgeous slope of his shoulders.

"Not sure what you're talking about." He grabbed his own jacket.

Jacob looked away. It had been easier when Sophie and Mark were here—as a buffer or maybe a distraction? Now that they were gone and it was just him and Finn, the air had thickened and he was reminded, painfully, of every time that had come before. Of how close they'd been to kissing on Saturday.

Last night had been easier, or had that just been a comfortable lie he'd told himself? Jacob didn't know.

But he did know that once it happened, there was going to be no way to pretend it hadn't.

"Oh come on," Finn objected teasingly. He nudged Jacob's side as they walked out the front door. "You know what I'm talking about. I came back from the bathroom and Sophie handled it well, like a pro, but she totally clammed up. She was warning you off, wasn't she?"

Jacob shot him a look as they approached the valet stand.

He knew he should give Finn a ride home, but if he'd been afraid picking him up would feel date-like, taking him home while he was wearing that suit was even worse.

"Oh, Mr. Braun," the young valet said with a worshipful look on his face as soon as he spotted him. "I'll go grab your car right now."

"Thanks," Jacob said dryly.

"She was warning you off, wasn't she?" Finn persisted.

"She was speaking plain common sense," Jacob practically growled. Why couldn't Finn just let this go?

Probably for the exact same goddamn reason you can't either.

"Do you always do that?" Finn asked.

"What?"

"Listen to common sense."

Jacob nearly laughed. "The exact fucking opposite, at least when it comes to you. I sat here three weeks ago and told both of them under no circumstances would either you *or* Morgan be part of the foundation rollout, and then that exact same goddamn night, what do I do? Agree to coach you. Agree to do just about anything you goddamn want."

Finn smiled, the corner of his mouth tilting into an impossibly charming smirk. "That was the same night?"

There was no point in pretending. "Yes," Jacob ground out.

The valet arrived then with Jacob's car, pulling up to the curb, his face melting into a smile when he saw Jacob.

"Someone's got a crush," Finn murmured under his breath. That was all the warning Jacob got before Finn slid right up next to him and put a hand around his waist, fingers curling into the leather of his belt. Finn gazed up at him, and Jacob froze, very aware of how this looked.

"Hey baby, you gonna finally take me home?" Finn cooed.

Jacob opened his mouth and then snapped it shut again.

He wanted to throttle Finn and also pull him in even closer, the warmth of his body unbearably enticing.

And maybe it was time to finally choose. Finn had pushed him, yes, but he'd *wanted* to be pushed.

"Yes," Jacob said. He handed the admittedly disappointed-looking valet a folded bill and deposited Finn into the passenger seat before walking around towards the driver's door.

After the door shut behind him, he pinned Finn with a look. "What are you doing?" he asked.

"Two birds, one stone," Finn said. "First, I wanted to temper that poor guy's expectations of you, and second, I wanted you to take me home."

"I'd have done that anyway," Jacob grumbled, starting the car.

"No, I mean, I want you to take me back to *your* house."

"Not happening." Not that Jacob couldn't be unbearably tempted if he was only dropping Finn off at the college. Saturday night had happened, hadn't it?

"I mean, it seems only right and fair," Finn said. "I never got my hot tub moment."

"For good reason." Jacob's hands tightened on the wheel. But he didn't pull out yet. He should. He should just put the car into drive and head in the direction of the college.

But he didn't.

Kind of like he hadn't pulled away Saturday, when Finn's intent became clear.

"I'm just saying, the night shouldn't end any other way but you and me in the hot tub."

"Stop asking," Jacob grumbled, but he heard how tempted he sounded.

"What if I promise to stay on my side?" Finn offered. His grin turned wicked. "I won't touch you, unless you want me to."

Finn seemed to be laboring under the mistaken impression that Jacob wasn't burning for him—touching or no touching.

"You have a lot of faith in my self-control," Jacob pointed out.

"Not really," Finn said cheerfully.

So that was the game then. Push Jacob until he gave in, *gratefully*, and Finn got what he wanted.

But it wouldn't just be Finn, would it? Because Jacob wanted this too. So badly, it was practically a miracle he hadn't pulled Finn up a dozen times during dinner—every time he was funny or charming or kind or heart-stoppingly gorgeous—and dragged him to the bathroom.

Self-control, my ass.

Jacob let out a breath. Then another. There was every indication that this would be a massive disaster, a garbage fire in the making. But before it blew up, it promised to be very, *very* good.

And, a voice inside him that sounded remarkably like his brother's said, *you haven't had enough of those very bad, very good things in your life. You've been so fucking careful. Enjoy this while it lasts. Whatever it is.*

He put the car into drive and pulled out, heading not towards the college but his house.

CHAPTER 11

FINN WAS PRETTY SURE he meant it.

I won't touch you, unless you want me to.

All the way up until they arrived at the gazebo-topped hot tub and Jacob shed his jacket, then leaned over and began to fold the cover back.

The drive here had been conducted in almost total silence. Finn had stopped pushing, because he had a feeling he'd pushed Jacob just about as far as he could.

Maybe tonight they would just really climb into the hot tub and keep to their respective sides, and that would be the beginning and the end of it.

He'd be disappointed, sure, but Finn was starting to understand that the *goal* wasn't even the enjoyable part of this. Just spending time with Jacob was amazing, in a way that he'd never experienced before.

The man had a dry sense of humor that Finn loved, and his kind smile lit Finn up from the inside out. That wasn't even going into how much Jacob had supported him and was just plain *there* for him. Believed in him, in a way Finn didn't think anyone else ever had.

If this had been just about sex, Finn was fairly sure he could've convinced Jacob to go for it pretty early on. But now, they were wading, metaphorically and soon to be literally, into waters that Finn wasn't familiar with.

He *liked* Jacob. And he was pretty sure that his dad was right, and the reason Jacob kept insisting that they couldn't hook up was because he liked him too. More than he should.

That realization added both clarity and complexity.

"And here I thought I was the king of overthinking everything."

Jacob's words interrupted Finn's thoughts.

He'd toed his shoes off now, not just removed his jacket, and he was leaning down, pulling his socks off too.

"No," Finn said, swallowing hard. When he'd conceived of this plan, it had seemed more arousing and less terrifying.

Well, truthfully when he'd conceived of it, he hadn't been entirely sure he could convince Jacob to take him back to his house, nevermind to get naked together in his hot tub.

But Jacob's fingers were currently unbuttoning his shirt, and Finn could see his bare feet peeping out from under his slacks. It felt painfully intimate.

"Don't tell me you've gotten cold feet," Jacob said casually. "You can't be worried about what you look like. You wore that suit, didn't you?"

"Did you like it?"

But Finn knew he had. Had watched as Jacob had taken him in, eyes dilating, chest rising and falling sharply as he'd stared. He'd caught him staring all night, and Jacob's gaze had been more intoxicating than any of the wine he'd drunk.

"You know I did. Kind of hated it, too," Jacob said. He grinned fiercely, and something deep inside Finn throbbed. "You should take it off."

"I . . . I can do that." Finn swallowed hard. Shrugged out of his jacket, hanging it carefully on the back of a chair. Then followed suit, by discarding his shoes and socks.

They matched now, at least until Jacob finished unbuttoning his dark gray shirt, muscles rippling as he took it off, revealing the strength of his upper body.

"Come on, now," Jacob teased. He didn't linger at his belt but unbuckled it with sure fingers that weren't shaking. Not like Finn's.

Jacob's belt hit the deck. Then his pants pooled around his ankles.

Ironically, just a few days ago Finn had tried to claim that Jacob had no experience with good sex, but he was beginning to think that was him, now. Because none of his hookups had ever felt like this.

Finn had a feeling that if he confessed the truth, Jacob would tell him that he'd been toying with boys, not fucking with men—and he probably wouldn't be wrong, but it was more than that, too.

Everything about this felt different.

He'd never been this hot for anyone before—*God*, those powerful thighs and chest and shoulders and all his olive-toned skin smooth, only a trail of dark hair leading to his black boxer briefs which . . . Finn swallowed hard, again. They clung to him in the best kind of way, making it very obvious that this striptease was affecting him as strongly as it was affecting Finn.

But Jacob still tucked his fingers into the waistband and, without a single hesitation, tugged his underwear down.

Finn jerked, like he'd just been shocked.

He'd been so sure that he'd be the one daring Jacob to cross the line, and here he was, without a stitch on, climbing into the hot tub without an ounce of visible shame.

He's got nothing to be ashamed of. Not a goddamn thing.

Jacob settled down into the hot water with a happy sigh. He shot Finn a blunt look. "You coming?" he asked.

He didn't have to point out that this had been all Finn's idea—three weeks ago, when he'd first tried to call Jacob's bluff, and now tonight. And he was the one who was still mostly clothed. The one still waffling.

Finn gathered his dignity—and his courage. "Yeah."

If his dad could see him about to do this, he'd lose his shit. But he'd also tell him that a Reynolds didn't back down from a challenge, *ever.*

He tugged his shirt off, laying it next to his jacket. Trying to emulate Jacob, he didn't hesitate. Just unbuttoned and un-zipped his pants, letting them fall to the wooden deck.

The sharp intake of breath from the vicinity of the hot tub told him that even his matter-of-fact stripping act was having its desired effect.

He didn't let himself think. Just stripped his briefs off, any shame he felt at being so completely fucking hard doused by the sharp heat spiking through him at how Jacob was looking at him now.

Finn climbed in, and like he'd promised, he kept to the op-posite side.

"That wasn't so hard, was it?" Jacob asked, tilting his head back, his newly shorn face swathed with steam.

He'd looked great with the beard. He looked even better without it. Younger, Finn realized, and had to wonder if that was why Jacob had shaved.

"I don't know," Finn said, "it's pretty hard."

Jacob's face settled into a satisfied, smug smile. "There he is. Welcome back."

Finn glared, but the only heat in it was the heat pooling in his belly. At how much he wanted to glide over to Jacob's side of the hot tub and break his promise.

"I'm sure," Jacob said, unexpectedly chatty tonight, "you thought all you had to do was wear that suit and I would just fall to my knees, eternally fucking grateful."

Finn told himself he shouldn't be embarrassed at how transparent he'd been. He wanted this, he could own up to it.

"Something like that." Finn drummed his fingers against the edge of the hot tub. Morgan's words from earlier echoed in his head. *You should tell him how you feel. With your words, Finn.*

Point taken, Dad, now get out of my head. At least for this next part.

"I wasn't very subtle, was I?" Finn continued, gathering the rest of his courage.

"No." Jacob chuckled.

"I didn't want to be," Finn said. "I wanted you to know. I wanted you Saturday. I wanted you last night. I wanted you three weeks ago. I want you *now*."

Jacob froze. "That wasn't subtle either," he said, finally. Which wasn't really a *no*, but it wasn't a *yes*, either. Or a *hell yes, get your hot ass over here so I can finally touch you.*

"No, but it was time I was honest." Finn hesitated. *Be honest with me, too.* "Don't you think?"

There was always a moment between Jacob resisting and Jacob melting where he appeared to visibly fight the urge.

He was doing it now, practically squirming on the bench, underneath the water.

Finn slid closer.

Jacob's dark eyes pinned him in place. Or would've, if he wasn't as determined as he was. He kept sliding, anyway.

"What happened to *I won't touch you?*" Jacob asked.

They weren't touching. Not yet.

"It was *I won't touch you, unless you ask me to,*" Finn corrected gently. He slid his arm behind Jacob's shoulders. His skin almost brushing Jacob's. *Almost.*

Jacob didn't say anything. Just stared at Finn. Well, at Finn's shoulder, more like. Like he was afraid to look right at him, of what might happen if he did.

Finn knew it would only take a little push to topple over the last of Jacob's self-control. It was evident, right there in the heavy rise and fall of his chest, the dilation of his pupils, the heat of his gaze as it skimmed over what he could see of Finn's naked body.

"I think you want it just as bad as I do . . ." Finn murmured, leaning in, willing Jacob to ask. Willing him to admit it.

But that was all Finn got out before Jacob was suddenly gone, leaving him hanging there, all alone.

One moment Jacob was there, right there with him, begging him with his eyes, and then he was gone, sliding away in the water, leaving Finn stunned and disappointed.

"You don't get to do this," Jacob said sternly, staring at him from across the hot tub. It wasn't very big, but it felt like a million fucking miles.

"What? Seduce you?" Subtlety, truly, had gone right out the window.

Probably the moment Finn had decided to wear *that* suit tonight.

"Yes," Jacob said, nodding, his expression grave. "Do you even know what you're doing?"

"I'm not a virgin." Finn could barely say it without pouting.

"What I mean is . . .do you have any idea the can of worms you're opening up? Do you *know* how messy this could get?"

Finn licked his lips. "I've thought about it," he admitted.

"Your dad will hate this. He will literally hate it. And he won't just punish me, but you too."

"I really—"

"I don't want to talk about him right now, either," Jacob said wryly. "I've got a hard-on the size of fucking Canada, and the last person I want to be talking about right now is your dad but we have to. Before we do this, we *have* to."

Finn gave up on not sulking. "Yeah, so?" he said, crossing his arms over his chest.

"Obviously we don't have to tell him right away, but I'm telling you, right now, Finn, I want . . ." Jacob's voice cracked. "I *want* you. And not just for the night, or in bed, or to have that really, really good sex you aren't sure you've ever had. I can't stop thinking about you. How we fit together. Despite every reason that says we shouldn't."

"I know what I'm giving up," Finn could admit it, barely. "What . . .what he'd say, if he found out."

And funny enough, it was the advice Jacob had given him about acknowledging that his dad might *never* really approve that helped make this more palatable.

He was going to wish Finn was different either way, so why *shouldn't* Finn have this?

"If this is what I think it could be, he's going to find out. We'll have to tell him, eventually." Jacob paused. "I didn't spend all these years in the closet just to come out and then hide my boyfriend. I don't think it needs to be now, that kind of commitment, but I want that . . .someday. With you."

Finn's mouth was dry, now. Bone dry. He should be less turned on right now, not more, but he was. Incredibly.

Just from Jacob saying the word *boyfriend*. Finn had never particularly wanted one before, but now that he'd seen what it could be like with Jacob, it was shockingly appealing.

"You look surprised," Jacob said, making a face. "Did I freak you out—I didn't mean to freak you—"

Finn flung himself forward with such force he nearly stumbled. But Jacob didn't nearly catch him, he caught him. Physically. Metaphorically. His mind, his body, and his heart.

After he did, Jacob's arms closed around him firm and tight, like he wasn't going to let him go, not anytime soon, and to Finn, nothing had ever made as much sense as tilting his head up and kissing him.

For a moment, Jacob froze, his fingertips digging into Finn's damp skin, lips not moving.

But then his touch shifted, sliding up Finn's bare back, and he was kissing him back, the gentle, fierce possessiveness of his lips telling Finn everything he needed to know.

Finn sank into him, into the water and into Jacob's embrace. His tongue slipped into Jacob's mouth, and they both groaned as the kiss went from tentative to gentle to intense to wild.

Finn slid fully into Jacob's lap, his lips still moving against Jacob's, not willing even for a single second, to stop. His blood was hot and getting hotter, his cock brushing against Jacob's taut, muscular stomach, and he thought, for a split second, *it's too good, I can't take anymore, it's already so damn good.*

But the thought had just crossed his mind when Jacob had the nerve to pull back.

"Wait, wait," Jacob said breathlessly, his dark eyes huge.

"What, *why?*" Finn said, his own breathing not exactly steady. He curled his hand around Jacob's shoulder, glorying in how large and firm it felt.

He only wanted to get closer, to feel every inch of Jacob's skin pressed against his. In fact, he wasn't even sure he *could* get as close as he wanted.

From the way Jacob kept stroking his back—from the sensitive skin on his spine right under his hairline, all the way down to the top of his bare ass—Finn wondered if he felt the exact same goddamn way. But he'd stopped them, hadn't he?

"I just . . ." Jacob kissed him again, all too briefly. "I just want to make sure you're—"

"I wouldn't have kissed you otherwise."

Jacob chuckled and his fingertips skated lower, barely brushing down the curve of his ass. Finn's cock got impossibly harder, his stomach clenching with arousal. "I really want you. So much, it's made me sure I can handle this. But I want you to be sure, too."

Finn considered just kissing Jacob again. Making it clear, without words, that he'd never been surer of anything in his whole goddamn life. That he knew, without a doubt, if he gave Jacob his heart, he'd treat it carefully.

But the words were clearly important to Jacob. So Finn said them. "I'm sure," he said. "Of you. And me. Of us together."

The only warning Finn got was how Jacob straight-up trembled at the way Finn said *us together*, and then Jacob was kissing him. Fiercely. Passionately.

❧ ❧

If Jacob worried Finn wouldn't be as into this as he was, the way he kissed him answered every single question and incinerated every single doubt.

"You feel so good," Finn murmured into his mouth as they kissed.

Finn thought *he* felt good? Finn felt like goddamn heaven in his arms, like everything he'd ever wanted and told himself he couldn't have.

He'd expected that maybe if he fell off the wagon of self-denial, he might get this *once*. Maybe twice.

Mostly he hadn't expected that it would happen at all.

He'd been worried Finn would decide the pleasure wasn't worth the pain. That *he* wasn't worth it.

But Finn was *here*, right now, kissing him back like he never wanted to stop, tongue sliding against his, body pressing into Jacob's, making these addictive little noises in the back of his throat.

Jacob slid his mouth along Finn's neck, trying not to leave a mark, even though he *very* much wanted to leave all the marks.

"I thought about this, after you left the first time," Jacob admitted, panting into his skin. It was damp and hot and tasted so goddamn sweet under his tongue. And then there was the curve of his ass, impossibly sweeter as his palm cupped it, stroked it.

Finn squirmed in his lap. "Yeah?"

"Wished you'd called me on my bluff, taken all of your clothes off, and gotten in with me," Jacob said roughly.

"I should've," Finn said, and his lips, red and wet from Jacob's mouth, quirked into a grin. "Should've done this, too."

Suddenly his hand was sliding down, finding Jacob's cock, hard and aching, under the water.

Jacob swore as pleasure spiked.

"We—I—*but*," Jacob protested as Finn stroked him.

"No wonder you only had one or two hookups a year. If you were this difficult for them, I'm not surprised," Finn teased. "Come on, I know you want this. I can *feel* it."

"But—"

"Don't worry about the hot tub. Or cleaning it. Or anything else. Just let me," Finn murmured and leaned in closer.

Jacob groaned and kissed him. He didn't want to be difficult; he wanted to be *easy*. To just lie back and enjoy Finn all around him, his mouth lush and real and his hand stroking his cock like he'd been born to do it. Teasing touches, like he wanted to do this for as long as he could, not just spinning the pleasure out for Jacob but for *himself.*

"Wait," Finn said, pulling back, and Jacob nearly chased his mouth with his own. "I've got a better idea."

"Does it involve getting out of this hot tub, because I can't promise—" It was cold outside, and while he was harder than he could remember being in forever, he couldn't *guarantee* that the situation wouldn't change on the walk back to the house.

"No," Finn said and glanced up at the ledge. "Just scoot up there a bit."

Jacob had a feeling he knew what Finn wanted, and his whole body shook with anticipation as he lifted himself out of the tub, settling on the edge.

It *was* cold on his upper body, but then Finn drifted between his legs and licked a stripe up his dick with his tongue, and Jacob forgot everything that wasn't Finn and his mouth and how absolutely, insanely perfect it felt around him.

Hotter than the hot tub, surrounding him, drawing out his pleasure in long leisurely sucks, like he didn't want to go anywhere.

Jacob sure didn't.

He thought he could sit here like this forever, floating in pure fucking bliss. He risked looking down and felt everything inside him pulse at the sight of Finn with his mouth full of his cock.

But Finn's mouth tilted up in that smirk—the one that promised he was up to no good, and that Jacob would probably like it, probably *love* it, honestly—and then his mouth was sink-ing deeper, the tips of his fingers brushing Jacob's balls, and the easy, lazy pleasure he'd been enjoying morphed into white-hot electricity, racing up his spine.

Finn sucked harder, and Jacob trembled. Knew he was teetering right on the edge, even as he wanted to make it last. Part of him wanted to wring every bit out of it, because there'd never be a first time ever again. But then the other part of him screamed even louder, *there's gonna be a lot more times, you stupid blockhead.*

Jacob's hands drifted down to Finn's curls and slid into the damp strands, digging into his scalp as Finn tried to wring his orgasm out of him.

"Should've known you'd be good at this. If I'd known, I'd have never been able to keep my hands off," Jacob ground out.

Finn's gaze flicked up and their eyes held together as Jacob tipped over the edge, coming in long, endless pulses down Finn's throat.

"Never say I don't have great ideas," Finn said as he stood on slightly wobbly legs and leaned in, kissing Jacob.

Jacob groaned in the back of his throat. It shouldn't have been so hot to taste his own come on Finn's tongue, but he loved it.

Finn's hard cock pressed into his thigh, and Jacob, still on the high of his own orgasm, reached for it with sluggish fingers.

"God, yes," Finn said, moaning. "I'm so fucking close."

For a split second, Jacob nearly suggested they switch places, because he'd love nothing more than to return the favor, but then he decided he could do one better.

"Come on. Let's go in the house," Jacob said and lifted himself out of the tub, gasping as his body adjusted to the cold air outside.

He kept towels in a little cupboard on the deck and he pulled one out and wrapped it around himself, then grabbed another as Finn muttered under his breath.

"Don't tell me we're doing this because you've got some misplaced romantic notion that you need to make love to me on a bed," Finn complained. "Believe me, I would be *very* happy with some down and dirty hot tub fucking right now."

"Just trust me," Jacob said, pulse beginning to race at Finn's words.

The truth was, he wanted it all. The slow romantic fucking, rose petals crushed beneath their bodies, and the hot, dirty fucking—barely able to shed their clothes before they were on each other, horny and starving. He wanted *every-thing.*

And you're gonna get it, if you're really fucking lucky.

The stone path was cold underneath his bare wet feet as he led Finn up towards the house. He let himself in the back door using the code and wasted zero time pushing Finn onto the living room sofa. Wet towel and all.

"See?" Jacob teased as he leaned in, pressing his body against his. Trying to warm them both up. "You're just fine. Bless being twenty-one."

"I don't think I could get soft even at the North fucking Pole," Finn retorted, but he was smiling.

Then his smile morphed into something else as Jacob sank to his knees and got his first taste of Finn's cock.

It twitched against his tongue, and Jacob groaned at the taste of his precome. Wanting more. Needing more.

"So good at this," Finn murmured, fingers carding through Jacob's hair. "Why do you think I was so fucking desperate? God, yeah, baby, just like that."

Jacob took him deeper, washing away the chemical taste of the hot tub, until all his senses were full of Finn and only Finn.

His fingers slipped lower, caressing his balls, and to his surprise, Finn scooted down, widening his stance. Opening himself up for whatever Jacob wanted to do to him.

When Jacob glanced up, there was only heat and approval and trust in his eyes.

It was a gift, the most incredible gift Jacob could remember being given, and he wasn't going to take it for granted and he sure fucking wasn't going to waste it.

Raising his hand to Finn's lips, he felt a pulse of remembered pleasure as he slipped his fingers into that hot, perfect mouth.

"Fuck, that's so hot," Finn groaned as Jacob finally pulled them out and tucked them right under his balls, pressing his saliva-wet thumb against his hole. Not pushing in, just rotating it around. Giving Finn the sensation of penetration without actually doing it.

Finn's cock twitched against his tongue, giving its own approval, as Jacob finally pushed his thumb in. He wanted to push more than his thumb in. He wanted to bend Finn over this couch and slide his cock right in, into the hot clasp of this gorgeous ass.

Fuck him until he couldn't even remember his own goddamn name.

But they had no lube and they hadn't discussed testing or results or anything else.

Jacob had to remind himself of those very important facts—and the additional fact that they had all the goddamn time in the world to fuck—as Finn's ass pulled him in closer, clenching around him.

Finn cried out, and that was all the warning he got before the cock in his mouth jerked and then Finn was coming.

"Oh my God," Finn murmured with a sharp exhale as he came back down, Jacob licking him clean. "I need you in me like *yesterday.*"

Jacob's fingers trembled at his admission. "Can't arrange for yesterday, but I *can* promise that if you give me another few minutes, I can make you forget your own name."

Finn's smile was slow, lazy and very, very satisfied. Not only, Jacob realized, with the pleasure he'd just experienced, but the promise he'd just been given. "Yeah?"

"Yeah," Jacob said and pulled himself up from the floor, collapsing next to Finn on the couch.

Finn glanced down at his half-hard cock. And yeah, maybe a few minutes was not as optimistic as he'd imagined it was.

"Don't tell me I make you feel young again," Finn teased, running his fingertips down his chest, tracing the ridges of abs, humming in approval as they tensed under his touch.

"Is that a cliche?" Jacob wondered. Not really caring if it was, because it was also true.

"If it is, it's one I'm personally going to enjoy very much." Finn grinned. "That was . . .well, you were there, I don't need to tell you."

Jacob pressed a kiss to the side of Finn's head, lips lingering there. "Doesn't mean I don't like hearing it."

"Maybe we're making some progress on that concept of very, *very* good sex," Finn said.

Jacob certainly thought so.

But it wasn't just the sex, though that was definitely going to become addicting.

"I meant it, you know?" Jacob said softly.

Finn turned to him, looking surprised, but at least he didn't look disappointed. "I didn't think you *didn't*."

"Why does it feel like there's a *but* there."

"Oh, there's a but there," Finn teased again. "Do I need to give you a personal introduction, because I thought you were already intimately familiar . . ."

"Finn," Jacob said, faux-sternly.

Deflecting again. Jacob could hear it in his voice and there was part of him, already aroused enough, that he wasn't sure he even cared.

If you lead him into your bedroom right now and lay him out on your bed, sink your fingers and then your cock into him, nobody will care. Neither of you will give a shit about him brushing you off.

It was so tempting. Jacob nearly did it.

But he didn't. Because he hadn't just wanted even the really, *really* good sex. He wanted more. He had for a while now. And it turned out he wanted it with the last person on earth he could have it with but there was no changing his mind—or his heart—now.

"I know you want it," Finn said. Nearly whined. And Jacob knew if he glanced down, he'd probably see that Finn's cock was hardening again. Already.

Just like his own.

"I want *you*," Jacob said.

Finn's gaze softened. "You really mean that."

"When have I ever meant otherwise?"

Finn was quiet for a long moment. "It would be easier if you found what you're looking for someplace else."

"Easier, maybe, but not better," Jacob said.

"Might mean you have to wait longer to trumpet him to the skies."

"I knew that, when I kissed you." He had. Knew exactly the kind of messy waters they were both wading into. But he'd chosen Finn anyway, and he wanted to believe Finn had chosen him too.

That this wasn't just about getting off.

Though that had been spectacular. Off-the-fucking-charts. Re-aligning his whole universe, frankly.

"I said I was sure," Finn said, "and I'm still sure. Never done more than hook up, and I didn't even think I wanted more, but then we met. And weirdly, it changed."

Finn's gaze was honest, uncompromising. Those clear eyes hid nothing. No deflections this time. And no goddamn walls.

"Weirdly, huh?"

Finn smacked him in the bicep, which strangely didn't affect his arousal, slowly ratcheting up, even a little. "Commitment's never been a turn-on for me before."

"Can't say it has for me either but now . . ."

"Now . . ." Finn trailed off, the corner of his mouth tilting up. "Now, all I have to say is, Jacob Braun, take me to bed."

Like there was a chance in hell of Jacob not doing it then.

He rose to his feet and tugged Finn after him, leading them up the stairs and into his bedroom.

Finn didn't waste a moment. He climbed right on the bed, then pushed himself up on all fours, making Jacob groan low in his throat at the sight of that back and that perfectly curved ass, right there, for the taking.

"I've been tested and I'm on PrEP," Finn said as Jacob went with shaking hands to rummage in a drawer by the bed. "If you want to forget the condom."

"You're sure?" Jacob asked, glancing over at him.

"I thought earlier that I couldn't get you close enough. I still can't. I *need* you, Jacob," Finn said, his voice edging into pleading territory.

"Okay. I'm the same—it's been . . .a while . . .since I did this," Jacob said.

But he knew what he was doing. And he knew how to make Finn scream. He'd already begun learning his body—what it wanted, but even more, what it needed.

He slicked up his fingers and notched himself behind Finn on the bed, clean hand trailing down the spine of his back. "You're beautiful," he murmured into his skin, pressing a kiss on every freckle he could find.

"Here I was kidding about the rose petals—" Finn gasped, losing his words and probably his whole train of thought when Jacob circled his hole and slid in his thumb. Deeper this time, wiggling it around in a tight circular motion as he opened him up.

"Yes, *yes*, the dirty fucking, *please*," Finn begged.

Jacob had just finished telling himself—and telling Finn, not in those exact words but hopefully his meaning had been clear enough—that they could have both.

And he intended to have both.

He kept his gentle kisses up as his fingers pressed into Finn's hole, spearing him deep, feeling him shake and tremble against his bigger body.

Jacob knew he'd hit the right spot when he froze and then cried out.

"Oh fuck me," Finn begged. "Oh, *God*."

"I'm gonna give you exactly what you need," Jacob promised. He could hear the waver in his own voice, a corresponding, echoing need rising in him. He'd never been harder in his whole life, and he needed to be in there, right now, giving Finn everything he was pleading for.

"Then give it to me," Finn cried.

Jacob gave one last firm thrust and then pulled his fingers out, scissoring Finn's tight, hot hole as he went. He slicked up his cock, told himself he'd go slow, and then as he began to slide inside, promptly lost his whole goddamn mind.

Sex was good. Sex was fine.

Then there was this, which came so far past the realm of *good* or *fine* that they had transported to a whole other universe.

By the time he thrust all the way into Finn, they were both shaking.

"So fucking amazing," Jacob choked out as he tried to gently stroke Finn's hip. Make sure he was okay. Make sure he was ready for more.

Finn glanced back, the heat in his eyes burning Jacob alive. "If you don't fuck me into this mattress *right now* . . ."

Jacob didn't need a single additional word of encouragement. He knew what Finn needed, and his body, even if it was a little bit broken, could still give it to him.

He dug his fingertips into Finn's hips and thrust. Finn wailed, and it was the best sound Jacob had ever heard.

It didn't take him long to find that spot again. The one that made Finn shake all over. Once he did, Jacob dedicated himself to hitting it every single goddamn time until Finn was gasping, the only other sound in the room besides Jacob's breathing and the sound of flesh hitting flesh as he drove into him with every single bit of strength and finesse he possessed.

"Harder," Finn cried, and Jacob realized, almost belatedly, that Finn was close. Finn was balanced right on the edge, and all he needed was a little more to fall.

"I got you," Jacob said, voice rough. "And do one thing for me, beautiful?"

He thrust harder, longer, lengthening his strokes and making Finn wail.

"What?" Finn gasped.

"Touch yourself. Make yourself come on my cock."

Finn tensed, and that was all the warning Jacob got before Finn was crying out, slumping to the bed, Jacob following him. The intoxicating pull of Finn's ass, clenching around him, pulled him in and then detonating the last of his self-control. He thrust once, then twice, and then it was over.

His orgasm shuddered through him, and he collapsed onto Finn, who made only a half-hearted groan of protest.

"You're not light, you know," he said, voice muffled.

"Just give me a minute," Jacob said, chest heaving. "That was—"

"I know," Finn said, and he sounded even happier than he had before. "You're okay right? That didn't . . ."

"I'm fine. My hip is fine," Jacob said dryly and finally pulled out, rolling over, deciding that Finn's attitude about mess was preferable to his own worries.

"Okay good." Finn slung an arm across his chest and slumped down, half on top of him. "Because we're going to do that *all* the time and I don't want you to hurt yourself."

"I'm thirty-five, not a hundred and five," Jacob said. "I think I can continue fucking you well enough."

"Not well enough. *Spectacularly,*" Finn said, still sounding dazed and wondrous.

"It was pretty spectacular for me, too," Jacob admitted.

"Good." Finn paused and Jacob pried his eyes open to look at him. Finn was gazing back up at him, a mischievous look on his face. "'Cause I can't leave you unsatisfied."

And God, yes, they had agreed to that, hadn't they?

Jacob felt a thrill—both intoxicating and terrifying—spill through him.

They were going to do this. They were *already* doing this.

"Trust me, I'm not. I'm . . .honored and a little baffled and thrilled and scared," Jacob admitted.

"Baffled?"

"Why you'd want me . . .why you'd pick *me*," Jacob said.

Finn's eyes glowed. "How about this? I wouldn't want to pick anybody else."

CHAPTER 12

"You look like . . ." Ramsey trailed off, shooting Finn a sideways glance as they walked across the quad towards the library.

Finn told himself not to blush.

"Like what?" Finn asked, but he was afraid he knew. Ramsey had a sixth sense about these kinds of things, and he'd probably already guessed what he'd been up to the night before—even though he'd taken a shower at Jacob's house and borrowed a pair of sweatpants and a T-shirt from his closet before he'd dropped him at the college.

When he'd looked in the mirror this morning, he'd told himself that he didn't look any different.

But maybe he'd just been lying to himself.

"Like you had a really, *really* good night," Ramsey teased.

Finn made a face. "How can you even tell that?"

"It's a special gift."

"Special gift my ass," Finn retorted.

"Oh, so you *do* want to talk about your ass?" Ramsey raised an eyebrow. "Did it get a lot of action last night? Who am I kidding, though? *Some* action would be a *lot* for you, at least recently. I haven't seen you at a Gamma Sigma party in ages."

"This is why people get annoyed at you," Finn grumbled as he pulled the library door open.

"Because I know everything?"

"Because you *think* you know everything." Finn lowered his voice as they walked through the stacks, towards their favorite table they liked to study at.

Well, that *Finn* liked to study at. Ramsey usually just sat there, doom scrolling through Instagram and attempting to show him every progressively more stupid video he could find on TikTok.

Whenever Finn tried to remind him that he should at least pretend to study, Ramsey always said that *was* him studying.

Finn didn't really think that the Communications department only cared about social media these days, but arguing with Ramsey was usually pointless, because he never lost.

"It's true, I do think I know everything," Ramsey said, settling down in his usual spot, pulling out his phone. "For example, I *know* you spent last night with Jacob. What I *don't* know is why you're trying to pretend it didn't happen."

"I—"

Ramsey shook his head decisively. "Don't even try to lie to me."

"I wasn't," Finn said, annoyed now. He'd been in such a good mood all morning—how could he not be? Last night had been freaking incredible, everything he'd hoped it might be and so much more. And then this morning, Jacob had brought him coffee in bed, and then in the shower . . .well, for the first time in weeks, he hadn't had to just *think* about Jacob as he got himself off. He'd gotten an in-person assist.

But now, with Ramsey pushing him to confess everything, the realities of the situation were beginning to intrude.

"Sure," Ramsey said knowingly.

First, he was going to have to tell Ramsey—clearly, that was a non-negotiable—and then it would be the other guys. They'd be supportive. Surprised, probably, but supportive.

Eventually, they'd have to tell the one person that Finn really didn't want to tell. Jacob was right: they had no choice if they wanted to actually commit to this relationship.

Jacob was right about something else too. It was going to really fucking suck to do it. Finn could already imagine Morgan's betrayed expression.

Especially when Finn confessed that it wasn't just a passing thing, or a sex thing, it was a *feelings* thing. That Jacob wasn't going anywhere anytime soon.

That thought filled Finn with happiness. Okay—it filled him with 95% happiness and 5% terror.

"You're staring at that screen like it holds the mysteries of the universe. Or maybe just the mysteries of Jacob Braun's dick."

Finn shot his friend a look. "Who says there's any mysteries in Jacob Braun's dick?"

"You'd know," Ramsey said.

And goddamn it, he'd walked right into that one.

Finn set his elbows on the table and whisper-yelled, "How did you even know?"

"It's not that complicated, actually," Ramsey said smugly.

"Well, tell the rest of us so we're in on the joke," Finn muttered.

"First off, you totally have a hickey under your hairline, right by your ear." Finn's fingers flew up to it, where Jacob had lazily kissed him in the shower this morning. Maybe it had been too soon for the mark to develop before he'd left Jacob's house, but now everyone could see it, like a big scarlet J. Ramsey shot him another one of those infuriatingly smug looks. "And since you've brushed off even a suggestion of a hookup lately, I guessed it would have to be Jacob, because clearly, he's the only one you're interested in kissing. Next up, your shoulders are relaxed."

"I was relaxed before."

"No, you were tense as hell. A good night of sex and your shoulders smooth out just there . . ." Ramsey reached over and ran his fingers up his shoulders. "See? Relaxed."

"Fine. Okay." Finn gave his friend a sharp nod.

"But mostly, more than anything else, I was walking out of Hood this morning and saw Jacob drop you off. And when he did, you leaned in and kissed him. Wasn't a quick kiss either. Seemed serious."

It seems serious, Finn wanted to tell him, *and it seemed like the best idea in the world last night but now I'm . . .panicking. Just a little. And mostly, almost entirely, because of this whole interrogation.*

"That explains it, then," Finn said, then logged into his laptop and started on his assigned reading, enjoying as Ramsey squirmed, for the first time today.

He let him go for five minutes and then ten, pretending to ignore as Ramsey shot him look after look, eyes flicking up from his phone every so often.

Finally, Ramsey gave in and tossed the phone onto the desk. "Are you really not going to tell me about it?"

"I don't know what you mean," Finn said, barely able to keep the grin off his face.

"You know what I mean," Ramsey hissed. "You're not going to tell me how you finally got him—*Jacob freaking Braun*—into bed and you're not going to tell me if it's actually serious? Was last night not the first time, because it sure seemed like the first time, but maybe I'm wrong, that *does* happen sometimes—"

Finn took pity on his friend, for whom rambling *definitely* did not come naturally. "You were right. It was the first time."

"I knew it," Ramsey announced triumphantly only to be shushed by two adjoining tables.

"You're going to get us kicked out," Finn said.

"Wouldn't be the first time. Did I ever tell you about the *last* time I got kicked out of the library—"

It wasn't even a contest; it would be way worse to hear all the details of Ramsey's last conquest—in the library no less—than to confess the truth of last night.

"I thought you wanted to hear about me and Jacob," Finn interrupted.

Ramsey's eyes gleamed as he leaned across the table. "Well, tell me then."

"We went to dinner."

"Like a date?" Ramsey looked horrified, then remembered, probably just in time, that Finn *wasn't* him, and wasn't allergic to commitment. *Oh you've got no idea*, Finn thought.

"No, not a date. A dinner meeting, with his agent and his PR rep. He's . . .uh . . .starting a foundation."

"And he has to come out first," Ramsey finished before Finn could decide just how much he should say about Jacob's future plans. "Because it's a LGBT-leaning organization, and he doesn't want more people speculating on his sexuality than talking about the charity work he's trying to do."

"How do you know that?" Finn asked, mystified. "Were you masquerading as one of the waiters last night or something?"

"My major is Communications," Ramsey said pointedly, like he actually did fuck all with his major.

"Anyway, yes, good guess. I was there because Jacob wanted my take on their plans."

Ramsey nodded in approval. "Damn. I would've thought he wasn't that good. But he pulled it off."

"That *is* why he invited me."

"Sure," Ramsey said easily. "Not just because he's crazy about you."

"*Anyway*, yes, he invited me. I wore the Burberry suit—"

"Wait, you pulled out the *Burberry* for Jacob? You must've been pretty fucking desperate to go for the big guns. Was he really putting up that much of a fight?"

"Yes and no," Finn said, attempting to find his dignity. It shouldn't be humiliating to admit to Ramsey he'd gone to dinner intending to seduce Jacob, especially when it had worked. After all, he'd done it, he should *own* it.

"Oh, he was," Ramsey said annoyingly. "But you got him in the end, didn't you? God bless that suit. I wish *my* dad would buy me a custom Burberry suit that makes men forget their own names."

To hear Ramsey talk, he *did* have a dad who might behave just like Morgan Reynolds did, but Finn knew not only did he *not* have a dad like Morgan, Ramsey didn't have any dad at all.

But Ramsey was always casual and easy about it, like it was no big deal.

More than once, Finn had wondered what was *really* going on in Ramsey's head, behind all those walls and all the interference he was constantly running.

"You do pretty okay on your own, without a Burberry suit," Finn reminded him.

"True." Ramsey grinned. "So it worked."

"It worked. But it wasn't *just* the suit."

"Of course not," Ramsey said, but it was clear he didn't believe that for a second.

Finn was going to have to tell him all of it.

"So you *were* right about the coming out thing. It's not just for the foundation he's starting, but also because he just wants to, and because he wants to not worry about being public with his relationships. With . . .*any* relationship."

"He was coming out so he could get a boyfriend. Good for him." Ramsey paused. "Wait. *Wait.* He wanted—*wants*—you didn't tell him you'd *date* him, did you? Because your dad is going to lose his fucking mind."

"Probably," Finn said, which sounded more optimistic than he felt.

There was no *probably* about it. Morgan would absolutely, no questions asked, lose his shit when Finn—and Jacob, because there was no way he'd let Finn do it alone—told him the truth.

"You didn't tell him you'd be with him just to get him into bed, did you?" Ramsey actually looked concerned now.

"No. *No.*" Finn squirmed in his seat, suddenly uncomfortable. Before Jacob, he and Ramsey had shared details and notes about their hookups fairly frequently. Well, he'd shared and Ramsey had *over*shared, but the point remained. And no, he'd never really been particularly interested in more, before, but that was *before.*

With Jacob, everything was different.

"So you what . . .you *like* him?" Ramsey looked shocked for the first time, like this was the one development he hadn't been able to guess or predict.

"I do. I do like him. A lot, actually," Finn admitted, and the moment it was out of his mouth, that part of him currently panicking settled.

He *did* like Jacob. So much. Was the sex fantastic? It definitely was. But it was about more than that, for Jacob, and for Finn, too.

"Huh."

"Don't look so confused, you know what that is."

"Not what it feels like, though," Ramsey admitted.

"You will, someday," Finn promised.

Ramsey shrugged. "Maybe. Maybe not. So you're like . . .that into him, then?"

"Yeah."

"And it's mutual?"

"Seems to be. That was what was holding him back, actually. Because he's had hookups while he was in the closet, playing hockey, and he was done with that. And I wonder if . . ." Finn hesitated. "I wonder if it was more than that."

Ramsey shared a conspiratorial smile. "I bet it was. God, you wore your *Burberry* for him. The moment you told me that, I should've known it was serious."

"I thought it looked serious this morning, when we were kissing goodbye."

"Well, there's that too. Then there was the way he watched you walk away."

"What are you talking about? What way did he look at me?" Finn was suddenly painfully, horribly curious.

"I'm not telling you," Ramsey said primly. "That's for him to tell you. But yeah, he's serious."

"Then why did you ask me?" Finn asked, a little outraged.

"I wanted to know what *you* thought of how he felt," Ramsey said.

Because of course he did. Finn rolled his eyes. "You feel properly informed now?"

"Well, *partially*. You still didn't tell me about the sex. Or is that off-limits now that you're all about the feelings?"

"I . . ." Finn told himself not to turn bright red. He didn't normally. But every time he even thought about how good last night had been . . .he got hot all over. "It was really good."

"That's all I'm gonna get? You blushing like a virgin and being annoyingly vague?"

"I'm not going to ask what you want because I already know you'd be into every dirty detail," Finn retorted.

"At least I'm gonna get that there *are* dirty details. He looks like he'd be good in bed. Hard, but soft, you know?" Ramsey grinned.

Finn didn't know how Ramsey always guessed. It was some kind of superpower.

"Don't tell me I'm exactly right because you look like you're thinking about it again. So I must've been. Hard but soft, huh? Did he make you scream? Fuck you into the mattress so good you cried or did you take it into your own hands—"

"Enough," Finn said, laughing. "More the former than the latter, but I don't have any doubt that if I *wanted* to take control, he'd have given it up, gladly. He's . . .well, he's really generous. And gorgeous."

"Could've told you that," Ramsey said.

"Yes, thank you. There's a reason I had a massive boner for the guy," Finn said.

"Should've known that you'd go for the most impossible guy you could find," Ramsey said, shaking his head. "You figured out how you're gonna tell Morgan yet?"

"God, Ramsey, it just happened. We're still working things out."

"He's going to find out," Ramsey warned. "And if he finds out before you decide to tell him . . ."

Ramsey didn't need to elaborate how that would go. Finn already had a damn good idea.

"I don't know why he'd find out. We're definitely not going to tell him until we're ready. And I know *you're* not going to tell him."

"Of course not," Ramsey said.

"There you go. We have some time . . .to . . .uh . . .figure out how this works."

Ramsey raised a blond eyebrow. "What's there to figure out?"

"I know you're new to this relationship thing, but it's not perfect from the beginning. It takes work. Adjustment. And if we're going to invite my dad's wrath, we'd want to be . . ."

"Sure," Ramsey finished for him. "You'd want to be sure that you're completely, madly in love."

"Uh, yes, that," Finn said, feeling a bit of that earlier panic return again.

"See? I'm not that fucking clueless," Ramsey said cheerfully. "When you think you're at that point, give me a heads-up, because it's probably going to take both of us to figure out if you actually are."

Finn wanted to tell him he was wrong and also full of shit, but Finn *didn't* know what that felt like. Not that Ramsey did either, but *maybe* if they did put their heads together, they could come up with an answer.

"Or," Ramsey continued, tilting his head, "you could ask Jacob."

"That's not happening," Finn said.

His phone dinged, and he pulled it out of his pocket.

"Ooooh, *is* that Jacob?" Ramsey said, craning his neck so he could read the screen. Finn tilted it towards himself so Ramsey couldn't.

"Yeah," Finn said.

You wanna come over tonight? We could work.

Finn grinned.

On what? How good you fuck me into the mattress?

He could practically see the flush rising up Jacob's newly bare cheeks and also the incredulous look he shot the phone. **No,** Jacob sent back. **Hockey. You know that game you play that you'd like to get better at.**

Thought I already was, Finn texted back.

You're fucking amazing, but there's no reason you can't be even better, Jacob replied.

"See," Ramsey inserted. "I actually don't think we *do* need to consult, 'cause the way you're gazing at that phone—like maybe Jacob's dick *does* hold all the mysteries of the universe . . ."

"Don't," Finn warned, but he was smiling, still.

Couldn't stop, in fact.

And maybe that answered everything for him, already.

"Good" Jacob said as Finn batted the last puck away from the net. He'd not let a single shot through, and his curls were damp with sweat. "Now, again."

Finn laughed breathlessly as he leaned down and grabbed his water bottle. "You're kind of an asshole, you know?"

"You thought I was gonna take it easy on you now?" Jacob asked the question even though he knew Finn wouldn't have ever believed that. In fact, he probably knew the truth: Jacob was more motivated than ever to give Finn the best chance at success.

"No," Finn said, still laughing as he straightened and skated over to where Jacob was gathering the pucks back into the machine for his second attempt. He put a hand on Jacob's shoulder and leaned in.

"There you go," Jacob said, leaning back. It was just a simple touch, but it felt like everything.

Other than their brief kiss hello—which Jacob had lectured himself ahead of time *would* be brief no matter how much he wanted to kiss Finn and *keep* kissing him—they'd mostly kept things professional.

Mostly.

If his hand had slipped down to Finn's lower back and then even lower still as he'd been guiding him through a particular stretch, he was only human. Finn's ass in those thin gray sweatpants was a work of fucking art. And it wasn't like Finn had exactly been disappointed. He'd shot him a knowing look that promised that he'd be happy to return the favor later.

"I think I deserve a rest—"

"Do you?" Jacob questioned innocently.

"And," Finn continued, batting his eyes at Jacob, "I think that you should show me how it's done."

"You think so, huh?"

"If your hip can handle it anyway." Finn's voice went serious and Jacob knew that he hadn't brought up his bum hip as a way to prod him into doing it.

"My hip's fine." It was. He'd made sure to stretch it out this morning. Carefully. Deliberately. It hadn't hurt at all the night before even though he had been using it *very* enthusiastically, but it never hurt to be careful.

"Well, if it isn't bothering you then, yes, you *should* show me exactly how it's done."

Jacob finished loading the pucks back in. "Alright," he said. "If you think it'll help your motivation." He walked over to the bench and toed his sneakers off, leaning over to lace up his in-line skates.

"Not really my motivation," Finn said, then hesitated.

"No?"

"It actually helps me to see how you move. How you prepare for each shot," Finn said. "Might've watched about a thousand hours of YouTube footage. You, and a bunch of other goalies. But you were always my favorite."

"Can't imagine why," Jacob said dryly. He straightened and pulled off his sweatshirt and then his T-shirt.

Finn grinned. "Yeah, can't imagine why. Though I might've had a little—or a big—crush on Thatcher Demko, too."

"Guess I should be relieved he's married." Jacob was not jealous; he was *not* jealous. So what if Thatcher Demko was six years younger than him? He was still not jealous.

At the height of his NHL career, he could've held his own against Demko or Fleury or *anyone*.

After all, there was a reason Morgan had been so pissed off at him. Because he was *good*.

"You don't have anything to worry about." Finn put a hand on his chest, curling his fingertips into his skin, and gazed up at Jacob's face with the kind of worshipful affection that before last night had thrilled and worried him.

Now, after last night, he could tell himself: *there could be worse people for Finn to admire.*

"I wasn't *worried*." But he'd been something. He knew it. It seemed almost too good to be true that this young, hot guy with an incredible future laid out in front of him was interested in Jacob.

Moira would tell him that this worry stemmed directly from the false assumption that retirement meant your life was over, not that it was just beginning.

He knew, because she'd literally just said those exact same goddamn words this afternoon, during their Zoom session.

"Sure," Finn teased. "Kinda sounded like you were. Doing this for less than twenty-four hours and you're already convinced I'm gonna go running after Thatcher Demko."

"I think I'm safe, at least for now." Jacob shook off the worry and shot Finn a look full of the confidence that still existed inside him. It might be diminished, but it still existed. "Time for me to show you how it's done."

Finn grinned with delight. "You know watching you do this last time was the best jerkoff material I'd had for months. Maybe even *years*."

Jacob, more at home on skates than on his feet, nearly tripped. "Are you serious?"

Finn shot him a look full of heat. "Are you kidding? You're so hot and so good and so . . .*ugh*."

"What you're really saying is hockey porn is a thing," Jacob said, recovering and picking up his stick. Testing it in his grip.

"Uh, *yeah*."

"So really, this is doing it for you in all kinds of ways." Jacob discovered he liked that. He really fucking liked that.

"Yep," Finn said with a nod. He positioned himself behind the puck machine as Jacob took his own position in the net.

He did one last stretch and then nodded at Finn.

This exercise wasn't ever *easy*—Jacob did it because it was hard, because it pushed him, mentally and physically, to the edges of his limits. But somehow, knowing how Finn felt about it, how much he enjoyed watching and how much he got out of watching, it felt a little easier than normal.

Easy enough that he was actually able to point out some of his thought processes to Finn, who nodded at each comment with a serious expression and eyes full of heat.

It shouldn't have been both.

But it was, and Jacob fucking ate it up, moving better now than he felt like he'd moved in ages.

"Damn," Finn said when he deflected the last shot. "That was . . .just *damn*. The hottest thing I've ever seen."

Jacob had worried when the last puck was gone, he'd feel it. And he did, the burn in his muscles, the way he'd pushed them pushing back, but it wasn't as bad as he'd expected.

His doctor *had* said that with time he'd recover some maneuverability in the joint. That he might be able to stave off a hip replacement for another few years if he continued to keep himself active and in shape.

Probably Dr. Chandler hadn't meant this kind of activity *or* the other kind of activity he'd very enthusiastically participated in last night, but in the end it didn't matter if it was jogging or weight lifting or fucking.

"Yeah," Jacob agreed. He caught the water bottle Finn tossed him. Downed half of it.

"You sure you're retired?" Finn's gaze glowed with truth. He wasn't just sucking up, trying to get Jacob into bed—after all,

Jacob had already established he was a sure thing—he *meant* it. Every single damn word.

"Could go out there tomorrow," Finn continued, gazing up at Jacob. "You know that right?"

"Yes and no," Jacob admitted.

Finn frowned.

"Today's a good day. They wouldn't all be good days, and I never wanted . . .I wanted, I *needed* to go out on top. That mattered to me."

Finn's frown morphed into understanding. "I get it," he said. "Still, *damn*. You move so good I wanna . . ."

Jacob picked up his T-shirt and wiped the sweat off his face. "You wanna go again?"

"Do this instead," Finn said and one second he was by the puck machine and the next he was pushing Jacob into the bench, his cock burning a hard, hot line into the crease of Jacob's thigh.

He kissed him then, lush and sweet, tongue sweeping into Jacob's mouth.

Jacob dug a hand into Finn's damp curls and held on as Finn tried to wash them both away with the intensity of his passion.

"God," Finn murmured as he finally drew back, "I want you. I wanted you before—I'd probably have to be dead not to want you—but that was . . .that was the damn sexiest thing I've ever witnessed."

"Sexier than Thatcher Demko's YouTube highlights?" Jacob shouldn't have asked it, but Finn's eyes lit up.

"You're perfect," Finn said, "but even better than that, you're *mine*."

Jacob groaned as Finn's mouth found his neck and then coasted lower, skating over his collarbone, leaving a mark there.

Finn probably had no idea how utterly and completely Jacob *was* his, and that was okay. There was no rush. They had plenty of time to explore this thing between them. Well, probably not *plenty* of time, but *some* time, anyway.

Enough time.

Moira had also said that he needed to find things that he enjoyed and actually *enjoy* them, and he couldn't believe that she'd meant sex with Finn, but as he reached over, palming Finn's cock through his loose shorts, he decided following the spirit of the advice counted.

Finn lifted his head, taking Jacob's mouth again, and groaned as Jacob pushed down his shorts and then his underwear, closing his fist around Finn's length. He was damp with sweat and wet with precome at the tip, and Jacob's hand slid along the length of his cock, stroking him.

"Guaranteeing this moment is gonna be in the spank bank forever?" Finn wondered breathlessly.

"I don't know. You tell me," Jacob said. Couldn't help his own moan as Finn tucked his hand underneath the waistband of his shorts.

"Yeah," Finn said and kissed him harder.

It was not going to take very long. Jacob hadn't even realized how aroused he was until Finn had looked at him like *that* and then said, *damn that was the hottest thing I've ever seen.*

But he was, blood racing and the smell and the taste of Finn all around him, the feel of him in his hand, twitching with his own arousal. Everything was a feedback loop that pressed him closer and closer to the edge until Finn trembled and tipped over, taking Jacob with him.

Jacob cleaned up as best he could with his T-shirt, passing it to Finn when he was done, who'd slid, bonelessly, to the floor at his feet.

"Well, I'm glad about one thing," Jacob said.

"Just one thing?" Finn leaned back, resting his head against his knee.

"Okay, *many* things, but right now, one thing, really. That I already did my round, and you still have one left."

"Ugh, really?" Finn complained. "I'm all relaxed and shit now."

"It's good to work hard in all your moods. Learn how to push yourself back into that mindset," Jacob said mildly.

"I was right," Finn grumbled. "You *are* an asshole."

"An asshole who just gave you a really good orgasm though?" Jacob chuckled.

"Is that a question or a statement?" With a grunt, Finn lifted himself to his feet. Rolled his shoulders.

Was it a question or a statement?

One of his first coaches, way back when he'd been a pre-teen, had told him that if he was going to do something, he might as well do it with confidence.

Like Moira's advice earlier, Jacob was one-hundred-percent sure that Coach Nicholas had not meant sex, but if the advice fit, he couldn't see why it didn't apply just as well.

"A statement. But regardless, I can definitely do better than a sweaty handjob," Jacob said.

Finn glanced back, interest lighting up his gaze. "Is that a promise?"

"It's a reward," Jacob said, gesturing towards the machine. "Get the pucks back in and let's give it another go."

"Asshole," Finn shot back, but his voice was full of affection and something else that Jacob was pretty sure he recognized, echoing in himself. But he wasn't going to name it, because it was way too soon and it was crazy *and* it was entirely possible that he wouldn't survive telling Morgan the truth.

CHAPTER 13

"I've been thinking," Finn said, his tone a little cautious, making worry spike inside Jacob, "that you should tell Sophie you'll do Neal Fisher's podcast."

Jacob looked up at him from his spot against the boards. Finn was warming up and stretching, getting ready for their first solo practice session on ice.

This Friday was the last game before the winter break, and even after working together for three weeks, Jacob could already see the changes in Finn.

The way he held himself was different. The confidence in his eyes was different.

Over the break they'd have even more time to work together.

And even more time together for uh . . .everything else.

"Oh, you have, have you?" Jacob told himself to laugh, and it actually came out, lighter and more authentic than he'd expected. He'd only been over-obsessing about the podcast and if he should do it.

"It's a good idea and you know it," Finn said.

"Maybe." Sophie had sent him two texts about it, and he'd ignored her call on the way here, to the rink.

He knew she needed an answer, and maybe Finn wasn't wrong, it *could* be a good idea, but it was also a fucking terrifying idea, and Jacob wasn't sure he was ready to give an answer either way.

"It *is* a good idea," Finn insisted.

"Maybe you should be worrying more about this upcoming game than my PR strategy," Jacob suggested.

Finn made a face and Jacob suddenly had a very bad thought.

"Sophie got your phone number at dinner the other night, didn't she? She hasn't been prodding you to ask me about this, has she?"

Finn didn't even bother trying to lie. "She told me that you kept changing the subject whenever she'd ask about it, and if she tried to pin you down, you'd just ignore her." He shot Jacob a reproachful look.

Jacob put his gloved hands onto his hips. He wasn't proud, but it *was* a big deal, wasn't it? He should consider it like the big deal it was.

Who are you fucking kidding? Kissing Finn was probably a bigger deal, and you did that with way less introspection.

"I don't know," Jacob said, knowing he needed to meet Finn's honesty with honesty of his own.

"You don't know if it's a good idea to go on Neal Fisher's podcast to come out or you don't know if it's a good idea to come out at all?" Finn asked. There was a complete lack of judgment in his tone, and *bless him*, but Jacob was fucking crazy about this guy.

When Jacob didn't say anything—he knew he should, he knew the right answer, the *true* answer, but somehow it stuck in his throat—Finn skated over. Put his hands on Jacob's shoulders.

"I'm sure you know this," he said conversationally, "but being ready doesn't mean being without fear."

It was the most they'd touched since entering the rink.

Jacob hadn't had to tell Finn that touching or kissing or even more would be a terrible idea here. Finn understood when it was time to focus, when hockey superseded their relationship.

But that hadn't stopped Finn from kissing him in the car, before they'd walked in, his lips hot and lush against Jacob's.

"I do," Jacob said, nodding. Or at least he always had, when it had come to hockey. There'd been plenty of times he'd been so nervous he'd thought he might end up puking on the ice.

But fear had never gotten in his way of performing.

He'd never let it. Until now.

Finn knew it and he'd pointed it out as gently as possible. That feeling that Jacob tried to pretend he wasn't feeling swelled inside his heart.

"Then you know you're ready. You *want* to do this. And once it's done, it's done."

"You ever listened to the podcast?" It was easier to ask this question than to contemplate any of Finn's comments. Or to listen to the heartfelt support and loyalty in his voice.

"To Neal Fisher's podcast? Yeah. A handful of times." Finn shot him a grin. "You know when I did."

"After you heard about it at the dinner."

Finn nodded and Jacob swatted him on the chest. "Go finish warming up," he said. "We've got work to do that isn't hand-holding me through the closet door."

"But I'm happy to, you know?" Finn said, shooting Jacob one last look full of tenderness and affection as he skated back over to the net.

Jacob knew he would, freely and without judgment.

"I know," Jacob said. "And I'll think about it. I've *been* thinking about it."

But Finn was right; he'd been letting fear make him believe he wasn't ready.

He pulled his phone out of his pocket and sent a text to Moira. **I know we talked today, but can you fit me in tomorrow? I only need ten minutes.**

Yes, she texted right back. **Everything okay?**

It will be, Jacob told her.

A minute later, he got an appointment notification and was just adding it to his calendar when a noise behind him caught his attention. Zach had mentioned possibly dropping by, and he expected that was him.

"Just a second," he said, and then looked over.

But it wasn't Zach standing there.

It was Morgan.

Jacob froze as Morgan looked between him and Finn, finishing his stretches in the goal.

He knew the moment Finn saw his dad, because he froze, too.

All of them frozen, staring at each other.

Morgan unfroze first, of course. Pulled his hands out of the pockets of his leather jacket and waved at Finn like he was an assistant on one of his ESPN sets. "Get over here," he called out.

It shouldn't have pissed Jacob off.

Okay, no, that wasn't true. It *should* piss Jacob off. The resentment crawling up his throat, along with anger and bitterness, was entirely justified. He just shouldn't *say* any of it out loud because none of it was going to help the situation.

It would only piss Morgan off and make everything worse.

But it had been difficult swallowing down Morgan's bullshit before, and now it was impossible.

"Don't treat your son like that," Jacob said, turning to his old rival.

Morgan looked . . .well, *shocked*, really. That Jacob was here? That Jacob was questioning him? *How* Jacob was questioning him?

At least Morgan probably assumed that this was only about hockey.

Imagine if he knew the whole story.

"He's my fucking son, not yours," Morgan snapped, temper heating his gaze.

Finn came to an abrupt stop, ice shavings curling under his skates as he stopped right in front of the boards. He gave Jacob an apprehensive glance before he said, "Hey, Dad."

"You don't answer your fucking phone, and turns out it's because you're with him," Morgan said, shoving a thumb in Jacob's direction. "*Him.*"

Jacob gave himself a very firm lecture on how this wasn't between him and Morgan, but Morgan and Finn, and then ignored it entirely. "*He* is standing right here, and *he* has a name."

"Dad," Finn said, only a single word but Jacob could hear the warning in it. He hoped Morgan heard it too. Then he turned to Jacob. "Don't start, okay?"

"I wasn't starting anything," Jacob said. But he kinda had been. Every single fucking time when they'd been playing—even at the All Star Game after Morgan was *retired*—he'd always tried to de-escalate while Morgan didn't even know the meaning of that word. But now, he wanted to do the opposite. He wanted to finally land that punch, right into Morgan's smug, annoying face.

But he didn't, because Finn was asking him not to. With his words, yes, but with his eyes, pleading at him, too.

"Finn, what the hell is going on?" Morgan asked. "Why are you here with him? What could *he* have to teach you?"

Finn glared at him. "What could he have to teach me? Are you serious? After all the times I had to hear how fucking good he was? How he'd held you back? Kept you from breaking Gretzky's record? And now suddenly he's a piece of shit who doesn't have anything to teach me?"

Morgan ground his teeth together, gaze sliding over towards Jacob. He wouldn't look at him directly but Jacob knew what he wasn't saying. "Do you think you could forget you just heard that?"

"Nope," Jacob said. "Besides, I always knew why you hated me."

"So what, you're going to help my son now?"

"Finn," Jacob said, keeping his voice light and easy, "I want you to go over and practice your angles, please."

The look Finn shot him made it clear Jacob must think he was crazy if he was leaving them alone together. "What—"

"No," Jacob said firmly. "Let me deal with this."

"*This* has a name, asshole," Morgan said, and *now* he was looking at him. Of course. It was fine when Morgan did it, but not when Jacob copied him. "And I don't want to talk to you—though don't think you're getting off that easily here—I want to talk to Finn."

Finn looked from Jacob to his dad and then back again and nodded. "There's not much to say, Dad. I asked him to coach me. He's coaching me." Then he actually fucking skated away, tossing off one last comment over his shoulder. "Just try not to kill each other, okay?"

Morgan's expression was dubious. "He actually came to you and asked you and you said *yes*?"

"Your son's a very talented goalie. I'm just helping him out with his focus. A few of his more advanced skills. But Finn's got what it takes. With or without me." It didn't really feel good to lie about this. How it had started out exactly that way, but had turned into so much more. But Morgan already looked pissed as hell already.

Imagine how he'd feel if he knew the truth.

Morgan crossed his arms over his chest. "Without you, that's my fucking vote."

"That's the whole problem, you egotistical shit. You don't *get* a vote."

Morgan's jaw dropped. "How *dare* you, I'm gonna—"

"No blood," Finn yelled across the ice.

"I would have your ass on the ground right now, but Finn doesn't want me to do it, so I'm not," Jacob said conversationally.

"Oh, like you *almost* punched me at the last All Star Game?" No question about it, it was a taunt. Jacob knew Morgan's words were a taunt, but they still riled him up anyway.

But they could rile him up all he wanted; he didn't have to act on them.

"Never had to punch you to kick your ass," Jacob said.

Morgan went pale as a ghost.

Shit. Finn had said no blood, but even though there wasn't any visible red gushing out of Morgan right now, Jacob could still see it dripping down onto the floor. And he'd done that.

You dumbass, you're supposed to be making him hate you less, *not more.*

"Listen," Jacob said and reached out for Morgan, not to punch him, but to put a reassuring hand on his arm. But he'd barely done anything before Morgan was shucking him off, a hard look on his face.

"No," Morgan said. "We don't have to do this."

He looked tired. Jacob didn't want to sympathize with him, to wonder what *his* life had really been like after retirement. If it had been anything like Jacob's—a constant struggle to feel relevant, even to himself. If all his accomplishments, going from success to success, had only been a smoke screen. Jacob didn't want to know, and he definitely wasn't going to fucking ask, either.

But now Jacob wondered, and that was almost worse.

"We've been doing this for years," Jacob said.

"And I thought you were tired of it," Morgan said. But he was the one who looked exhausted. Worn-out and worn down in a way that he'd never looked when he was playing. Back then, he'd been full of fire; always pushing, never giving an inch, lit from within by that drive that never seemed to slow down.

But time slowed everyone down. Brought everyone down to the same fucking level. Even Morgan Reynolds.

"I've always been tired of it," Jacob admitted. It was too late for them to mend fences in more than the most superficial way. Especially when it was all going to blow up anyway, once Morgan discovered that he wasn't just coaching Finn.

That he was in love with Finn.

Jacob's knees wobbled, and they nearly gave out.

He had a feeling he must've gone just about as white as Morgan, because Morgan looked suddenly alarmed and it was him reaching out for Jacob now, steadying him.

"You alright?" he asked roughly.

"I'm fine," Jacob said. *Just freaking out because I love your son. No big deal.*

Morgan looked at him more carefully. "You don't look fine. You look like you're freaking out." He pursed his lips. Jacob knew what he was thinking. *You're freaking out because of me, and I can't figure out why.*

That was technically true, Jacob supposed. He *was* freaking out, in a very tangential way because of Morgan. But it was so much more than that. He *loved* Finn. He never wanted to leave him, and he never wanted Finn to leave him. And how were they *ever* going to get that happily ever after? It felt distant and frankly, just plain fucking impossible.

"Really, it's . . .I'm fine."

"You're a shit liar." The corner of Morgan's mouth tilted up, so much like his son's and yet so much like his own. "Always have been."

"Yeah, well you'd know," Jacob muttered.

"Come on," Morgan said and actually fucking sat down in the first row of seats and gestured next to him. "If you're gonna coach Finn, we should be able to sit next each other without wanting to commit murder."

On still wobbly legs, Jacob boosted himself over the boards. Took the seat Morgan had indicated.

"Despite what you've always believed, I never felt a single murderous inclination towards you. Wasn't ever worth it," Jacob said.

Morgan laughed. "Wish I could say the same."

"I get it, you know?" Jacob steeled himself. Morgan was going to hate this, maybe even more than anything else, even the fact that Finn had spent the last two nights in his bed, not really sleeping.

"Get what?"

"I get why you hated me. Easier to blame me than to blame yourself."

Morgan said nothing for a very long time, just stared out at the ice, towards Finn, but Jacob didn't think he was really seeing his son, because Jacob knew that look. Understood it intimately. It was a man unwillingly seeing the past play out in front of his eyes and yet unable to look away.

"Should really punch you for that one," Morgan finally said, quietly. "But I won't, because Finn said no blood, and despite what you think of me, what you think of me as a player and a father, I do love him. I want what's best for him. And if you're it, you fucking asshole, then that galls me but I'll get over it."

"I know."

"Don't fuck this up," Morgan warned.

Oh, don't worry, I'm already doing that. Regularly. With relish.

"I'll try not to," Jacob said.

Morgan's gaze didn't move, but Jacob thought he might actually be seeing Finn now. Finn as he was now, not Finn as a kid, and not as he imagined Finn might be. But Finn as he really was.

"You think he's really good?" Morgan said quietly. So quietly Jacob barely caught the words.

"Of course I fucking do," Jacob said, annoyed now. Because of course Morgan was questioning that. Why else would Finn have all these complexes? His father was the fucking origin of all of them. They'd probably blossomed from his *own* and of course, Morgan had never thought, not once, that he should protect Finn from them.

And he *should* have. He should have been a father first and a hockey player second.

"Good, it's not just me, then," Morgan said.

"What?" Jacob glanced over at him now, shocked. "You—"

"He's going to be so great, and I'm so terrified of it. Of what it'll do to him. Over time. If he'll end up like me, like . . ."

"Like?" Jacob prompted, because he was too stunned to say anything else.

"If he'll end up thinking that the best thing he ever did was on that ice and that nothing else matters," Morgan said flatly.

Well, that answered *that* question.

Jacob supposed that he shouldn't be surprised that Morgan had put up a smoke screen of happy success post-retirement. Or that it was all complete fucking bullshit.

"Well, that's stupid," Jacob pointed out.

Morgan glared.

"I mean it," Jacob continued. "'Cause from where I'm sitting, the best thing you ever did is out there right now, thinking that you don't believe he's good enough. That he'll *ever* be good enough."

Morgan swore under his breath.

"Yeah," Jacob agreed. "It *is* fucking bullshit."

Morgan was quiet again. And maybe Jacob should let him sit here in that terrible, awful silence, contemplating just how he'd fucked his son up, but Jacob had to go work, to do the work to build Finn back up again. They didn't have unlimited time, and he wasn't going to give a minute more of it to Morgan.

"Listen," Jacob said, "I know you don't like this, but make your peace with it, because it's helping him, and you *know* that. You were too good of a player to not see it now, even if it's Finn that you're looking at."

"I see it," Morgan said flatly.

"Good." He rose, but a hand on his arm stopped him, the grip firm.

"Wait," Morgan said. "You really aren't doing this to fuck with me?"

"Morgan, I promise, not everything is about you. In fact, almost *nothing* is about you."

Morgan opened his mouth and then snapped it shut again. Gave Jacob a sharp nod. "Understood," he said. He looked pissed, but also resigned.

Jacob lifted himself over the wall and skated over to where Finn was working.

"Hey," he said.

Finn paused, pushed his helmet up and gave Jacob a long leisurely glance from the top of the beanie he'd pulled on to the blades of his skates. "No blood," he said.

Jacob winced. "Might be some metaphorical blood back there." He hadn't held back from speaking a few painful truths.

"Can't say he doesn't deserve it."

"No," Jacob agreed. Of course that didn't make it easier. Finn didn't entirely understand, because he was still young and hungry and eager, his whole career spread out in front of him, a blank page he could write on at will.

But Jacob found he understood Morgan a little too well, these days.

"Is he just going to sit there?" Finn wondered.

"Maybe he wants to watch you," Jacob said and noticed as Finn's whole body tensed. "Hey, hey," he said, reaching out and giving Finn what he hoped looked like a friendly, encouraging pat to the arm. "It doesn't matter that he's here, or that he's watching. You've got this, remember?"

Finn stared at him. "You believe that?"

Jacob was annoyed at Reynolds in general, for not believing in what they should be believing in—namely, Finn's ability and his undeniable skill.

"Yes," Jacob said.

Finn didn't say anything.

"It doesn't matter if he's here or he's not here. If he's in New York or he's here, in this fucking rink. You are *still* Finn Reynolds, one of the best up-and-coming goalies. You just had a shutout and you're going to get a lot more. You had whole sequences in that game that were fucking poetic."

"Good enough I should probably believe that on my own and not need the guy I'm fucking to pump up my ego?" Finn smirked.

Jacob didn't need to tell him not to say it too loudly. Finn knew exactly what he was risking.

"Yes," Jacob agreed.

"I'll get there," Finn said. He seemed annoyed at himself, that he'd needed the reminder.

But everyone needed a reminder. Hadn't Jacob needed one, less than half an hour ago?

"Hey," he said, catching Finn's arm again, after he'd pulled down his mask. "Remember earlier when you said you'd hand-hold me out the closet door, no questions asked and no judgment?"

Finn nodded.

"Well, same goes here. If you need it, you've got it. No questions. No judgment." Jacob paused. "Now, let's see what you can do."

His dad was still sitting in the same spot when they were finished.

Jacob shot Finn a look that said, *you'd better go talk to him.*

Finn returned with, *I'd really rather not.*

But Jacob just shrugged, which Finn was almost certain meant: *I've already done my part.*

He had, and in a completely exemplary way, too. Neither he nor Morgan had been bleeding at the end of it. Sure, Jacob had claimed it was more of an imaginary bloodletting, but Finn didn't even know if his father's skin was thin enough to be pricked by Jacob's words.

"Fine," Finn grumbled.

"He's not going to go away," Jacob said under his breath.

"Yeah, which is a whole other problem."

"He's got a lot on his plate, so it's not like you'll have to deal with him constantly," Jacob said, probably optimistically.

But Finn didn't feel nearly so optimistic. He knew his dad well enough to know he lived to shove sticks into wheels.

He downed the rest of his Gatorade and skated over to where Morgan sat. He rose and came over to the boards.

"Hey," Finn said.

"Looking good," Morgan said.

"Thanks," Finn said. "If I say it's because of Jacob . . ."

"I'd believe it, but I'd also believe it's because you're good, Finn."

Finn rolled his eyes. "Did he tell you to say that?"

"Would I *ever* say something just because Braun told me to?"

"Good point. What are you doing here? You didn't tell me you were coming into town."

The hesitation before his dad answered should have been enough of a warning. But Finn had had a hard practice—if anything, since orgasms had been introduced into the equation, Jacob had been even harder on him—and he couldn't say he'd slept as much the last two nights as he should have, so he missed its importance.

"No, but I'm going to be here for a bit. Probably most of December. Some of January, too," Morgan said.

Finn froze.

"It's the holidays and I don't have a lot of commitments at the network so I figured I could stay here, in Portland." *With you,* was the unspoken end to that sentence. Finn heard it clear as day.

Finn didn't know how to react. Or what to say. He definitely couldn't say, *but I thought Jacob and I would have lots and lots of time to practice hockey and also to practice being boyfriends.*

"I've got that condo in downtown. I can stay there," his dad continued like he wasn't shocked into silence.

"Right," Finn said, finally.

"So I won't be in your hair, too much," Morgan said.

Who's he kidding? He's totally going to cramp your style.

"The uh . . .last game before my break is Friday," Finn said.

"I know," Morgan said and sent him a chiding look that reminded Finn that he probably knew his game schedule better than Finn himself.

And that was true. *God,* that was true.

He didn't want to lie to his dad, but what else was he going to do to get *any* time with Jacob?

"So you're not going to lecture me? Or are you still working your way up to that?" Finn asked. Before, when he'd let himself be controlled by the fear of disappointing Morgan, he'd have waited, agonizing at everything his dad wasn't saying. But he wasn't going to live like that, not anymore.

"About Jacob? Well . . ." Morgan made a self-deprecating shrug. "I'm not *happy* about it. I get why you didn't tell me. But then I sat here, watching you two, and I get it, now. You want to be the best. So you went to the best. It's a very Reynolds thing to do."

It was. And it wasn't, all the same.

"Right," Finn said.

Morgan shot him a look. "I thought you'd be happier that I'm not mad."

"I'm thrilled. This is my thrilled face."

"Finn," Morgan chided.

"You just . . .you have your life in New York, and I have mine here."

Finn told himself to ignore the disappointment that flashed across Morgan's face, but he wasn't expecting the hurt.

"You're telling me you don't want me here?"

"No," Finn said, hating himself. Hating that he felt this way. Why couldn't they just figure out a way to co-exist happily, peacefully? Without pain? Without all this fucking baggage?

Morgan's face cleared. "I just . . .I missed you."

"You missed me."

"Finn," Morgan repeated.

"I'm sorry, I'm just trying to work my way around to this new style of parenting."

There was that hurt again. And it suddenly, painfully, occurred to Finn that all of this was his father's way of apologizing, without actually ever saying the words.

"I'm not that shitty of a father," Morgan insisted brusquely. "No matter what you're gonna claim—or what Braun's gonna say."

"What *did* Jacob say?" Finn knew he shouldn't ask, but he couldn't swallow the question down.

"Do you really believe that I don't think you're any good?" *Goddamn it, Jacob.*

"I . . .I don't know," Finn said carefully. Told himself that he didn't, in fact, *know*, so it wasn't a lie.

His father had the nerve to look fucking shocked, like he'd just been electrocuted. "Finn, I think you're *amazing*."

"That's not the way it comes across," Finn said sullenly.

"I want . . .I want you to be the best. I want you to know what that feels like. It's . . ." His father huffed out a hard breath. "It's all I have to give you."

Finn was unpleasantly reminded of what Jacob had said to him that first night. *If he's this hard on you, how hard do you think he's on himself?*

He hadn't been able to forget that, even though he'd wanted to, more than once. And now he wouldn't be able to forget this either.

"If you really think that, you're full of more shit than I thought," Finn said angrily.

He skated off, fast, going towards the locker room, hoping that *one*, his father wouldn't be stupid enough to follow him in, and *two*, that if he was that stupid, that his famous face wouldn't be enough to grant him access.

But as he was stripping his gear off, tossing it into the laundry bin, the person who approached wasn't Morgan.

It was Jacob.

"What did he say?" Jacob asked, frustration edging his voice.

"Nothing," Finn muttered. "Nothing more than usual."

"He's trying," Jacob said.

Finn glanced up, in shock. Not expecting, after *everything*, for Jacob to ever take his dad's side.

"I mean it," Jacob said. "I don't want to, but I do."

"Well, that's helpful," Finn bit off sarcastically. He sat down on the bench.

Jacob huffed in frustration. "You know what I mean. I don't blame you for being pissed. But I think it's hard to hear what he's actually saying versus what you're expecting to hear."

"Is that what you really think?" Finn couldn't believe it. Jacob was taking his fucking *dad's* side, not his. Even after everything.

"I think sometimes you can get stuck in a shitty situation and a shitty attitude, and not know the way out," Jacob said. He hesitated, and Finn wanted to tell him to shut up, that he didn't want to hear how suddenly sympathetic he felt towards Morgan. Not when he didn't deserve it. But then Jacob kept talking. "It's not the same, I know it's not the same, but when I first retired I felt the same way. Stuck. Every day felt like an end, like the best parts of my life were already gone, and there wasn't a way to get them back. I was done, *finished*."

"You weren't, though," Finn argued. He didn't want to defend the crappy way Jacob had thought of himself—he wanted to be angry at him, for taking Morgan's side—but it was hard when he could hear the pain in Jacob's voice.

"I know, but I couldn't convince myself of that. I was stuck in that belief, and until I found Moira, who helped me see I was wrong, who gave me other things to focus on, I wasn't going to get unstuck."

"So what," Finn said, annoyed but trying not to sound annoyed, because it wasn't Jacob's fault that he was making so much fucking sense, "you want me to go to therapy, too?"

Jacob shook his head. Sat down next to him and wrapped an arm around his shoulders. It was platonic, but *just*. "I'm not saying therapy wouldn't work for you, but maybe first, just try listening to what he's saying. Interpreting it differently."

"Okay." Finn hated the idea, but maybe that was more that he could see what Jacob was saying than because he was wrong.

"What did he say to you that pissed you off?"

"He said he wanted me to be the best, because that was all he had to give me," Finn muttered. Maybe it wouldn't have hurt, wouldn't have stung nearly as badly, if Morgan hadn't just said that he *was* good. Finn had been thrilling with the validation of that, then he'd unloaded the rest and it had almost felt worse as a result.

He'd . . .expected better?

Different, definitely.

Jacob muttered something under his breath that sounded suspiciously like, *what a fucking idiot* and then said, louder, "You ever think that maybe Morgan saying that isn't about you, but is actually about him?"

"No," Finn admitted.

"I told you, as hard as he is on you, he's always been harder on himself. He doesn't know how to be any other way, which honestly, that sucks for him, you know?"

"I don't know, does it?" Finn asked.

Jacob shoved a gentle elbow into his side. "You *know* it does."

Finn sighed. "Yeah. I guess so. So you think him saying that was about him more than me."

"I'm not sure he knows how to be a good dad to you, Finn, but as much as Morgan has pissed me off throughout the years, the one thing I can't doubt is that he wants to do right by you."

Finn supposed that was true. He could acknowledge it, at least to himself, if not to Jacob. Definitely not to his dad.

"I guess . . .I guess so," Finn acknowledged. "I can see it, if I squint."

"As soon as he figured out that me working with you was to make you better, to *help* you, he didn't give a shit that it was me. And I don't have to tell you how he feels about me."

"I know," Finn said dryly.

"So when he says shit like, that's all he has to give you, it means he doesn't see his worth outside that rink. And . . .well, it's not that I'm siding with him, Finn. But I know how that feels, and it sucks."

Finn sighed. "I don't want to feel sorry for him, damnit."

"You don't have to. You can and *should* demand better from him. But you should also give him the benefit of the doubt."

"Ugh," Finn said and risked tilting his head down, resting it on Jacob's big broad shoulder. "I want to tell you that you're wrong but . . .I don't know if you are."

"Yeah," Jacob said. "He can be a real ass."

"I'm going to have to talk to him, aren't I?" Finn wasn't happy about it, but what Jacob said made sense. He *was* stuck in this horrible status quo. More of his conversations with his dad—in person, over the phone and in text—ended in frustration and anger than didn't.

It didn't feel great, though it had always been easier to place the blame on Morgan.

"Probably, yeah," Jacob said.

"You think he's still out there?"

Jacob nodded.

"Well, I'm gonna take a shower and then maybe I'll try to catch him after," Finn said, lifting himself up.

"Alright," Jacob said.

Finn turned and grasped Jacob's arm. "I . . .thank you," he murmured. He wanted, *so badly,* to lean down and kiss Jacob. To tell him, with his lips, just how much he appreciated him. Coaching him and talking to him and *believing* in him. Even when he was wrong. Especially when he was wrong.

But they'd already risked touching enough—not just in this building, but with Morgan just outside.

Still, it would've been easier to say it with a physical gesture than with his words. Words didn't feel like enough.

"You know I'm here for you," Jacob said. "For *you*, to be one-hundred-percent clear."

"I know." And Finn did. He took one last risk, reaching out and squeezing Jacob's knee.

"I'll call you later tonight?" Jacob asked hopefully.

"Call? *Call?* How old *are* you?" Finn teased.

Jacob grinned. "Old enough."

"Yeah. Call me." Finn leaned in. "Maybe we'll even go wild and FaceTime."

The heat in Jacob's eyes stayed with him all through his shower and through getting dressed.

It kept him company as he walked out towards the front—and sure enough, there was his dad, leaning against the wall, gazing at a display case full of memorabilia of past Portland Evergreens' teams.

"Hey," he said.

Morgan turned, shoving his hands into the pockets of his leather jacket.

"I—" Morgan started to say but Finn held up his hand.

"You're full of shit, you know that?" Finn interrupted him.

Morgan rolled his eyes. "Am I?"

Finn smacked him. "You sure fucking are. You're more than just hockey, you know that, right?"

"Jacob talked to you, didn't he? God, I hate that guy."

"No, you don't," Finn said, wishing it was true more than believing it. Maybe his dad really did hate Jacob. But he hoped not, because it was going to make everything going forward so much harder.

"Ugh, and then there's *that*," Morgan grumbled under his breath.

"Stop being an asshole for ten seconds, okay? Listen to me. I . . .I appreciate you're making an effort here."

"Do you, really?" Morgan questioned.

And okay, that was fair.

"Yes," Finn said firmly.

Did he love that Morgan had apparently moved to Portland because that was going to cramp the hell out of his relationship with Jacob? No, he did not. But he *could* appreciate that Morgan was trying.

How long had he wanted Morgan to be there for him, and it had never felt like he was? Or that his support had strings and requirements, benchmarks he'd always felt obligated to meet—or even worse, to exceed?

And yet here he was, giving his time and his attention and his support to Finn, without him even asking for it.

"Well, I am making an effort," Morgan said testily. And maybe that was the problem, Finn realized. They were the same, in so many ways. That Reynolds blood holding true, from father to son.

"You can just be my dad, you know," Finn reminded him as they walked out the front door together.

"I want to be," Morgan admitted, and glanced over at him, worry creasing his expression, "but I don't know how to do that."

"You must hate that," Finn joked, because it was easier to make light of it than it was to really think about what his dad was saying. *I'm trying, but I don't know how so I'm gonna fuck it up. A lot.*

Not that he hadn't already. A lot.

"It's the fucking worst," Morgan agreed. He glanced over at Finn. "I'm sorry if I do fuck it up. That I *have* fucked it up. Especially because I don't think I even knew I was doing it."

"Jacob must've *really* talked to you," Finn said.

The apology felt good. He'd needed it and hadn't even realized it, but there was more, too. More he needed. The action of continuing to show up, to be the father he'd never really been, before.

"And your mom," Morgan said hesitantly.

"Oh. I didn't know you still talked to her," Finn said.

"Sometimes, yeah." Morgan cracked a smile. "She's good at setting me straight when nobody else can."

"I'd imagine so," Finn said.

"And so are you. And . . .as much as it pains me to admit it . . .apparently Braun is too."

"How hard was that?" Finn questioned innocently.

Morgan made a face and elbowed him back. "Hard, okay? I'm never going to *like* him, but . . .I'm glad you have someone coaching you, who's helping you. You look great out there. I mean that. As a dad. And a hockey player."

"Don't worry, I don't think you'd ever be able to *not* be a hockey player."

"Probably not. But I'm trying."

"Good," Finn said, nodding.

"Come on," Morgan said, "let's grab some lunch."

CHAPTER 14

"This fucking sucks," Finn hissed under his breath as he and Jacob grabbed a booth in Sammy's.

It was after practice, three days after Morgan had shown up in Portland, apparently intending to stay for the next two months.

Finn never would've guessed that his father would be such an extraordinary cockblocker, but he was.

Every time Finn carved out time—between hockey practices and classes and homework—to spend with Jacob, his dad would text, wanting to grab coffee or have dinner or he "just happened to be driving by campus," and he'd show up at Finn's door ten minutes later.

"It's not ideal," Jacob agreed with a grimace. He looked around, taking in the students milling around the popular sub and smoothie shop, like he was making sure that Morgan wouldn't just pop up here, too.

Finn wouldn't put it past him. That was the worst part.

They were going to have to tell him, and probably sooner than they wanted—if only to get some decent alone time. And considering all of Morgan's unintentional interference, it wasn't like they'd had any time to become more comfortable in their new relationship.

"It's ridiculous," Finn said, leaning forward. He wanted to kiss Jacob so badly he was practically dying for it, and yet they couldn't.

He needed to eat something, and then he had a big study session in an hour.

"It'll be easier during the break," Jacob said optimistically. "You'll have classes and homework, sure, but we'll have plenty of time for 'coaching.'"

Finn shot him a smirk. "Jacob Braun, are you suggesting I tell my father we're working on hockey when we're actually doing something else?"

"Yes," Jacob said so emphatically that it made Finn's heart beat a little faster. It felt so good to know that he wasn't the only one suffering here.

"I miss you too," Finn said under his breath, reaching out with a foot to tap Jacob's underneath the table. Before today, he'd have claimed playing footsie was totally beneath him, but if it meant he could touch Jacob and in plain sight? He was here for it.

Jacob shot him a hot look. "I keep wanting to take you out, that's all. Treat you right."

"No, you want to drag me home to your house, to your *bed* and—"

"Finn," Jacob interrupted. "Are you *trying* to kill me? Give me the blue balls of a century?"

Finn grinned. "Guess you should've given in sooner to my seductive efforts. Then at least we've could've had a few weeks of sex before the greatest cockblocker of the century arrived in town."

"It's good that he's here and he wants to be present in your life," Jacob said.

"I know you mean that . . ." Finn leaned in even closer, watching as Jacob's eyes dilated even darker. His chest was rising and falling under his flannel and Finn wanted to strip him naked more than he wanted to take his next breath. "But I think you want more, too."

"I do," Jacob muttered. "I sure fucking do. Don't get me wrong. I'm getting the hang of FaceTime sex, but it's not the same."

"Nope," Finn agreed.

Last night, with Jacob telling him exactly how to touch himself—where and how firm and how long—and dragging out his orgasm until Finn had been begging for it, with not an ounce of shame, had been really fucking good. But it hadn't been the same as *Jacob* touching him.

He'd wanted it, and he couldn't have it, because Morgan had shown up at his dorm room, wanting to go grab dinner, and Finn had been forced to text Jacob surreptitiously and tell him their dinner date was off.

"I should've told him I had a date," Finn continued.

Jacob made a face. "And he's just going to let you leave it at that? He's not gonna want to meet the guy?"

"Oh, no, he would. And then . . ." Finn paused for dramatic effect. "Surprise!"

Jacob frowned. "We're trying *not* to get murdered here."

"No, *you're* trying not to get murdered."

"I'd think you'd have a vested interest in that too," Jacob said dryly.

"I do. I *do*. You can't fuck me breathless if you're dead."

Jacob raised an eyebrow.

"Or uh, be there to be sweet and gentlemanly and treat me right," Finn revised with a smirk.

"Better," Jacob said, nodding. "Now, before you drive me absolutely insane, let me tell you how my talk with Sophie went."

"You're going to do the podcast!" Finn was so excited, even though it hadn't been his decision. Still, he'd hoped that Jacob would agree to go on it, because after listening to it, Finn couldn't help but agree with Sophie. Neal would be the perfect, sympathetic, easy person for Jacob to come out to.

"Yes," Jacob said, nodding. "I talked to my therapist, and she agrees—I'm ready, even if I'm afraid, and we worked through some of those fears together, and after really considering it . . .I see what Sophie's saying about it being a good fit."

"You mean, what *I* said," Finn teased.

"Yes, you too," Jacob said with a smile.

"You listened to it, didn't you?"

"Might've, though it was about what I expected based on what Sophie *and* you told me. But I wasn't surprised. I've caught Neal Fisher talking before on Sunday Morning Football, and he's got a good perspective on lots of things."

"I'm proud of you," Finn said.

Jacob made a disgruntled noise. "Should you be, though?"

Jacob's name echoed as the employee called it and Finn shot him a hard look, sliding out of the booth before Jacob could.

"I'm getting the food—and then when I get back we're going to talk about that."

"Fine," Jacob huffed.

Finn picked up their sandwiches and smoothies, sliding the blackberry pomegranate acai on the table towards Jacob and keeping his own strawberry pineapple.

"So why shouldn't I be proud?" Finn questioned. Though he had a good idea of why Jacob said it. Not why he *thought* it in the first place, but at least why he'd brought it up.

"I mean, shouldn't I be doing more? Living more proudly, more freely, more . . .I don't know . . .*fuck you* to the establishment?" Jacob wondered.

Finn rolled his eyes. "Do you even *want* to say fuck you to the establishment?"

Jacob was opening his sandwich, the paper crinkling almost obscuring his words, but Finn could still hear his mumbled, "No." Then he cleared his throat and added, "I don't give a shit about the establishment."

"There you go," Finn said. "This is your fucking life. There's plenty of people out there who actually want to burn down the establishment, whatever the hell that means. There's no reason you have to do a goddamn thing. It actually annoys me that you think the only way I would be proud is if you scream to the world you're gay. I don't give a shit what anyone else thinks of you."

"But you want me to come out," Jacob countered.

Finn leaned forward, not sure if what he felt was annoyance or empathy. Maybe his issues didn't revolve around his sexuality, but how different were they, really? "I thought *you* wanted to come out. For the foundation."

"I do. I *do*. Fuck," Jacob muttered. "Why am I so screwed up about this? It's what I wanted. What I *want*."

"Doesn't mean it's not hard or scary. I want to play hockey, more than anything else, and how much does that suck for me a lot of the time?"

Jacob nodded.

"You're going to do this, and it's gonna be just fine. Honestly, you should be way more afraid of telling my dad than telling the world."

Jacob's expression turned rueful. "Honestly? I am. Doesn't mean I won't do it."

Finn nudged him again under the table, this time unable to keep his smile to himself. "See? There you go."

Jacob sighed. "Why are you so great? I thought I was totally at peace with this. I talked to my therapist. I talked to Sophie. I talked to my brother. I even talked to Mark."

"It's 'cause I'm brilliant," Finn said.

Jacob smiled. "Yeah, you kinda are. Eat your dinner. I get precisely . . ." He glanced down and checked his watch. "Twenty-six minutes before you have to be at study group."

"I told you, I could skip the study group—"

"No way. Not on my watch. I didn't go to college and I think it's big that you're doing it, Finn."

"Ugh," Finn complained after taking a huge bite of his sandwich. "This whole responsibility schtick of yours should feel less hot, but . . ."

Jacob leaned forward. "Kind of like how every single time you give me a big pep talk, I want to drag you into the nearest dark corner or utility closet with a locking door and make you come so hard you cry?"

Finn nearly choked on his smoothie. His dick was hard now, in Sammy's. That shouldn't be happening, but it was, and he had a feeling if he ran his foot up Jacob's calf and then his thigh, he'd discover he wasn't the only one. "Uh, yeah. Something like that."

"Good."

"And for the record," Finn said, "it's more like . . .thirty-six minutes?"

"Where'd you get the extra ten minutes from?"

"Everyone's always late. If I roll in on time, everyone will wonder what happened."

Jacob looked understandably confused.

"Which means," Finn continued, "that it's your absolute duty to detain me for an extra ten minutes in your car."

"Detain?

"Kiss?"

Jacob smirked. "Why didn't you just say so? It's easy. You just say, *Jacob, I'd really like to make out in the car for ten minutes.*"

"Jacob, I'd really like to make out in the car for ten minutes," Finn repeated back, making sure to keep his tone as innocent as possible. Not as dirty as he was thinking, anyway.

He was thinking about it, already, as he scarfed his sandwich down.

Jacob's hot breath against his, the windows fogging over as Finn's tongue slipped into his mouth. The way Jacob's hands would feel everywhere as they dipped under hems and peeled fabric back, desperate for a taste of bare skin.

"You look a little glazed over there," Jacob teased as he finished his smoothie.

He *was* a little glazed, his brain already in Jacob's pants, stroking the cock that he was sure was already hard and leaking for him.

Because if they ended up kissing in Jacob's car for even a few minutes, Finn knew they weren't going to be able to keep it at just that. He was too keyed up; they were *both* too keyed up.

He had to know it too. Finn could see the dark heat in his eyes as Jacob gazed at him.

"And you aren't?" Finn retorted fondly. He finished his sandwich and took a long drink of smoothie.

Jacob looked down at his watch. "We have approximately—or specifically—twenty-eight minutes."

Finn leaned over the table, his forehead only inches away from Jacob's. "Is that *your* estimate or *mine?*"

"Yours. If you want to be ten minutes late to study group, that's on you." When Jacob was being the prim, responsible one, it was hot. When he was deliberately flouting the rules, that was even hotter.

"Come on," Finn said, gathering his trash as he slid out of the booth. "I can work with twenty-eight minutes."

"What if you couldn't?" Jacob wondered as he followed him.

"I'd—*we'd*—figure something out," Finn said with determination.

Jacob's hand landed on his shoulder and then slid down, resting on the small of his back. It wasn't a kiss, but it felt good-as, at least in this moment. Finn glanced back at him and thought maybe he might understand better what Ramsey had said about the way Jacob looked at him as he'd walked away.

Because he could see it now.

Which was probably why he ended up nearly running into Mal and Elliott.

They weren't holding hands, either, but Mal's hand was occupying a very similar position on Elliott's back and the way Elliott gazed up at his boyfriend made it *very* clear they were together.

Did *he* look like that, too? When he looked up at Jacob, did he have that same lovestruck, cock-drunk expression? Like there was nobody better on earth, nobody else he wanted to talk to, nobody else he'd ever wanted to just *be* with as much as Jacob?

Maybe.

"Oh shit," Elliott said as they nearly collided, Finn barely managing to avoid it only by swerving to the side. "Sorry about that."

"Yeah," Malcolm added. He steadied Elliott first, touching him like he was precious. Then he reached out a hand towards Jacob. "You must be Jacob Braun. I've seen you around practices, during the last few weeks. Malcolm McCoy." He glanced down at Elliott. "And believe it or not, this guy is Elliott Jones, who can skate like a demon on the ice, but on land . . ."

"You love it. You love *me*," Elliott said with a grin.

There was something about the undeniable pride in his voice and his eyes as Jacob shook Malcolm's hand that pinged Finn. Reminded him completely, utterly, of how he'd just been talking to Jacob.

"Jacob Braun," Jacob said and, after a weighty pause, added, "Finn's boyfriend." He slid an arm around Finn's waist and tugged him in closer. Elliott's eyes nearly bugged out of his head. In fact, even Mal looked shocked.

He hadn't needed to say it, but when Finn glanced back at him, giving him a happy, reassuring smile, he only looked proud. Not worried or upset or conflicted, in the least.

"Feels like big news," Mal said, his matter-of-fact tone the opposite of how monumental it really was.

Elliott elbowed his boyfriend. "No shit," he hissed under his breath.

"But we're happy for you," Mal added, a ghost of a smile emerging on his face.

"Yeah, seriously happy," Elliott agreed.

It was weird to Finn that what had only been a few months back these two had been on such different wavelengths they could barely say a single civil word to each other, and now it felt like they'd completely, utterly aligned.

"Thanks," Finn said, "we're pretty happy about it." He shot another smile at Jacob so he never doubted that he *wasn't* happy that he'd told their friends the truth. "But," he added, "we're still . . .uh . . .working on some of the details, so don't go around telling everyone."

"Yeah, Elliott, don't go around telling everyone," Mal teased, nudging him.

"Hey, I wouldn't," Elliott claimed, but he was smiling, still, which meant that *yes*, he probably would. "How did your dad react?"

"Uh," Finn said.

"He doesn't know yet," Jacob admitted. "That's the details."

"Well, you've got both of our support," Mal said briskly. He shook Jacob's hand again, because of course he did.

God bless Malcolm.

"Thanks," Jacob said.

"You have a good practice, Finn?" Ell asked.

"Yeah, actually."

"Tomorrow Coach said he's going to let us at you again." Elliott rubbed his hands together in anticipation and for the first time in a long time, Finn realized he was looking forward to it, too. To a chance to show the rest of his team—and himself—that he could hold his own. That he was a damn good goalie.

"Can't wait," Finn said.

Elliott's smile softened. "Yeah? I'm happy to hear that."

"Me too," Jacob said. He paused. "Finn has a study session so we'd better run."

When they were out of Sammy's and out of earshot of Elliott and Malcolm, Finn stopped and turned to Jacob.

"You did that," Finn said and decided that if his father was lurking in the shadows he could get what he deserved and leaned in, pressing a quick kiss to Jacob's mouth.

Before he could pull away, Jacob had wrapped an arm around his waist and tugged him in closer, and Finn groaned, his mouth opening against Jacob's.

For a single glorious second, Jacob kissed him hard, his lips and his tongue and his hands making it clear to Finn—and to anyone else watching them—that they belonged together.

That Finn belonged to Jacob, and Jacob most definitely, Finn realized, belonged to *him*.

"Yeah, I did, didn't I?" Jacob said breathlessly, when he finally lifted his mouth from Finn's.

"You sure fucking did. Coming out like an ace," Finn said.

"It . . it wasn't so hard. I liked it actually."

Finn squeezed Jacob's shoulder. "Not every time is going to be as good as bragging that you're my boyfriend. And uh . . ." He paused. Smiling even harder. "That's new. That word. That's new."

Jacob flushed. "Yeah."

Finn couldn't say they hadn't both been thinking it. But it was the first time either of them had said.

"I liked it. *Like it*," Finn teased.

Jacob went even redder. "Good."

Finn leaned in, pressing his lips to Jacob's neck. "It was good *and* sexy."

Ever since Jacob had shaved off his beard, it had been so much easier to see how red he could get when he was embarrassed or turned on or when Finn deliberately went out of his way to tease him.

"Behave," Jacob said with faux-sternness, nudging him.

"You don't want me too," Finn said. He glanced down at his watch. "How much time do we have left?"

"Enough," Jacob said with absolute certainty and he reached down and took Finn's hand, leading them to his car.

Finn was half-expecting Jacob to try to preserve the ruse that he was just driving Finn across campus to his study group, but instead of going around to the driver's side, he opened the passenger door and with the tiniest, hottest smirk, gestured Finn in.

Finn slid in, moving over, and the moment the door shut behind Jacob, he was leaning over, kissing him hard.

"God," Finn murmured into Jacob's mouth, "I'm so fucking proud of you. I didn't know what you were going to say—"

"Really, I didn't know I was going to say that, until I said it." Jacob chuckled under his breath, fingers caressing Finn's cheek. "It was okay, right? That I said it to Malcolm and Elliott?"

"*More* than okay." Finn took Jacob's mouth again, groaning as his hand slid from his face down lower, tracing the sensitive tendon in his neck.

"Too many clothes," Jacob muttered, and suddenly those hands weren't gently cradling or tracing him but delving right under his sweatshirt then under his T-shirt, tracing cold patterns on his overheated skin.

Finn swung a leg over Jacob's body and wasted no time grinding down on his lap and the hard cock there.

Jacob's kiss went from hot to downright filthy, his tongue curling around Finn's.

Being spread out on Jacob's bed, naked, without a stitch of clothing between them had felt incredible. But this felt shockingly good, too. Dirty and intense, both of them driven by desperation as they moved together. Finn ground down on Jacob's cock and Jacob dug his fingers into Finn's hips, grinding up at the same time in a rhythm that he knew would eventually pull him over the edge.

"You're gonna make me come in my pants," Finn gasped.

Jacob smirked. "Am I?"

Finn tilted his head back as Jacob gripped his hips hard. He'd have bruises there tomorrow, and he wouldn't even give a fuck.

"You know you will," Finn said. "And I have to go to a *study session* after this."

"Oh, do you?"

"God, you're hot when you're evil," Finn said.

"Maybe if you ask very, very nicely, I'll switch us and get down on my knees for you—"

"In this backseat?" Finn glanced behind him dubiously. Was there even room for Jacob down there?

"Hush," Jacob said, "I'm trying to be selfless here. I'll get down on my knees for you and you can come down my throat instead."

"I wouldn't . . ." Finn gasped as Jacob's hands traveled under the waistband of his sweatpants and stroked him. "I wouldn't complain."

"Didn't think so," Jacob said smugly, and it shouldn't have so insanely arousing for him to easily maneuver Finn off his lap and to sink down in front of him.

"If you tell me you bought this car because of its roomy backseat, I'm going to come right now before you ever get your mouth on me," Finn warned. He felt breathless, totally out of control. And it wasn't only how goddamn turned on he was, either. It was everything—the pride in his voice as Jacob had said *Finn's boyfriend,* the heady emotions swirling through him, *and* the intense spike of need as Jacob pulled his sweatpants and briefs down to his knees.

"Don't tease me with a good time," Jacob said wryly, and then his mouth was on him, hot and wet and perfect.

Finn groaned and tried to stave off his inevitable orgasm, but Jacob was pushing him, coaxing him almost, giving him more pleasure than he knew what to do with. Matching the emotions he'd never experienced before.

Arousal and affection mixed inside him an intoxicating swirl, and he barely had any time to warn Jacob before he was coming in his mouth.

Jacob swallowed around him, dragging his orgasm out as long as he could, until Finn was panting and nearly crying with it.

"So fucking good," Finn muttered as Jacob unfolded himself and leaned hard against Finn's relaxed body. Jacob's mouth found his and Finn's trembling fingers undid the button and zipper of his jeans, finding his cock.

He got barely half a dozen strokes in before Jacob was shuddering, too.

"Yeah, *yeah*," Jacob agreed after he'd lifted his mouth.

His smile as he gazed down at Finn was happier and *lighter* than he'd ever seen before. *You did that.*

He was pretty sure he had and pretty sure he wanted to keep doing it, forever.

That should scare you. That should terrify the fuck out of you. But it didn't.

It only made Finn feel strong and confident. Invincible, in fact.

Jacob found some fast-food napkins and helped Finn clean up before shooting another lopsided grin. "Well, I think we made it with a few minutes to spare."

"I might actually be on time," Finn said.

"If I let you go early," Jacob pointed out, settling down next to him. He reached for Finn's now-clean hand and tangled their fingers together, squeezing them. "I know we didn't talk about telling people, at least specifically . . ."

"Elliott and Mal aren't really people. They're teammates. Friends. And Elliott will keep his trap shut, so you don't have to worry about that."

"I wasn't worried about it, though if your dad finds out from anybody but you, I can't imagine it'll help," Jacob said dryly.

"No," Finn agreed. Even though Morgan had taken the news of Jacob's coaching decently enough, he couldn't imagine the same result when Finn confessed this particular nugget of truth.

Jacob sighed. "I keep thinking we must be stupid, but then I see you, then you smile at me, then we *touch* each other, and I realize I'd do a whole lot worse to keep doing it." His voice went quiet and hushed. "I'd do a lot more to keep *you*, Finn."

Finn understood. "It would've been easier if it had been just sex."

"I really . . . really care about you," Jacob said. And he sounded so careful, but so hesitant, Finn thought he understood what he wasn't saying. Not yet, anyway.

What he felt too, lodged hard and tight and inescapable, behind his breastbone. The thing he wouldn't want to get rid of, even if he could.

"Now you're never going to get that easy boyfriend," Finn said.

"No," Jacob agreed and Finn's heart clenched, again.

CHAPTER 15

JACOB SHOULDN'T HAVE BEEN surprised to see Morgan in the hallway outside the locker room before the Evergreens' last game pre-holiday break.

But before he could ask why he was here—before he could demand that Morgan *not* go into the locker room and derail Finn's last-minute mental preparations—Morgan turned to him and said, "I see you're officially on the team, now."

Jacob was surprised for a second and then remembered the dark green jacket Finn had given him that he'd swapped for his own black puffer without a second thought. If Finn wanted his logo plastered all over him, *owning* him, then Jacob wasn't going to argue about it.

"Yeah," Jacob said. "It's . . .uh . . .easier."

Nothing was actually all that easy about this, though the easiest part seemed to be the one part they hadn't confessed to Morgan yet.

Morgan didn't look convinced. "I could still kick your ass."

"Yeah, but you won't," Jacob said with an eye roll. "You don't even *sound* like you mean it, anymore."

Morgan frowned.

"Though maybe you never really did."

That frown deepened, and Morgan opened his mouth, no doubt to dare Jacob to meet him after the game outside the rink and they'd settle this like men, not like ex-hockey players, but Jacob interrupted him before he could. "Come on," he said. "Let's go find our seats."

"You're not sitting on the bench?"

"What am I gonna do for Finn on the bench?" Jacob questioned. "Besides, he's got this. He doesn't need me—and he definitely doesn't need you."

Morgan looked like he really fucking hated that, but it was just the God's honest truth, and maybe he knew it too, because instead of arguing, Morgan actually followed him.

Now that Finn—and Gavin—knew he was coming to games, they'd gotten him special access tickets, right down by the ice, within easy reach if Finn *did* need to talk to him, during a timeout or at either intermission.

There'd been a pair waiting at the box office for Jacob, but Bryan had the kids tonight and couldn't get away, so he'd intended to sit alone.

But Morgan was right there, following him like an unexpectedly lost duckling.

Jacob sighed and turned to him. "You wanna sit with me?"

Morgan bristled.

"It sucks to watch, to *just* watch, I know. Might be better if we've got—"

"Don't you dare fucking say it won't be so bad if we've got each other," Morgan interrupted.

"Or you could go sit wherever the fuck you want, instead," Jacob said.

For a second, Jacob thought Morgan *might* do that, probably using his very famous face to get whatever the fuck he wanted, but to Jacob's surprise, he made a painful, aggrieved sigh and actually followed Jacob to their seats.

Jacob decided he wasn't going to press his luck and didn't say anything as they sat down. They could sit here in silence, and at least that would mean they wouldn't get kicked out for fighting.

Theoretically.

But to his surprise, again, Morgan turned to him as the anthem finished and said, "It's so fucking annoying how right you are. It's absolute shit to just sit here and watch."

Jacob knew he should be trying to get on his boyfriend's father's good side, even if it was basically totally fucking impossible, but despite that reminder, he couldn't keep his mouth shut.

"Funny how that's not how it seems whenever I turn on ESPN and you're right there, offering all these fucking opinions."

Morgan ground his teeth together. "At least I'm doing something with my life."

"Yeah, I guess anyone can *talk* about hockey." *What are you doing?* the voice inside Jacob screamed.

He could feel Morgan's anger taking form and shape next to him. If he chanced a glance over at him, he'd probably get punched. And this time, he might actually deserve it.

"Funny how this whole time, everyone insisted you were innocent and the nicest fucking guy and our rivalry was *my fault*, like you weren't always right there, baiting me. Just like that." But Morgan didn't sound all that pissed. More amused anything else.

Like he was more than ready to have been proven right.

Jacob winced. "I didn't mean to. Then, anyway."

"And now?"

"Uh . . .well, that was more of accidental word vomit than anything else. And, the truth, actually."

"That's just fucking great," Morgan grumbled.

"And maybe I'm pissed as hell at you for making that transition look so fucking easy when I . . .when I could barely manage it." He shouldn't have admitted it—Morgan certainly hadn't, not in as many words—but if he was going to be fully honest, someday, he needed to start somewhere.

Morgan looked at him. Even though Jacob wasn't looking back, he could feel the weight of his gaze.

"You think it's been *easy* for me?" Morgan said, the edges of his voice so brittle Jacob wondered how—and when—they might break.

"You made it *look* easy," Jacob countered.

Morgan shot him a glare. "And when did you ever buy into my bullshit, Braun?"

Jacob froze. When *had* he? He never had. He'd always seen through it. Morgan had never ruffled him, because he'd always seen his grandstanding, his temper, his one-sided feud between them for what it was: Morgan's ego fighting his own fucking insecurity.

"There you go," Morgan said wryly and then stood as the announcer began to call out the lineup.

There were Elliott and Malcom—who Jacob had met officially just yesterday—skating onto the ice, accompanied by a tall, stocky guy with a nice, easy smile.

Then Brody and Ramsey, the two starting defensemen. Ramsey was showboating, playing to the crowd as he skated onto the ice, not ignoring them like everyone else was.

Finn skated out, not even glancing up, even when the crowd roared its approval.

"That kid," Morgan muttered under his breath.

"Ramsey?" Jacob was pretty sure that Morgan wasn't talking about his own son.

Morgan nodded. "I've done some work with him. I swear to God, he deliberately distracts me every time I'm in town, insisting on these endless fucking practices. Always hitting on me, trying to hook up."

Jacob jolted. Morgan's voice was so matter-of-fact. Had Morgan slept with Ramsey? Surely Finn would know if that had happened, and if he didn't, and it *had* happened, then Jacob did not want to be who finally told him. "He does?"

"He's never hit on you?" Morgan looked surprised.

Ramsey had not, and Jacob was pretty sure that was because he'd known about Finn. From what Finn said about Ramsey, it was possible he'd known about Finn and Jacob before Finn and Jacob had.

"No," Jacob said. "I'm really impressed, Morgan. You not kicking some poor lovestruck kid to the curb when he tries to cross the line."

"I'm not . . ." Morgan huffed. "I'm not a fucking villain. For all his posturing, Ramsey's a *kid*. He's twenty-plus years younger than me. I'm not gonna . . .anyway." Suddenly Morgan looked uncomfortable like he'd confessed too many of his own truths to someone he wasn't sure would treat them with the respect they deserved.

Jacob hadn't ever heard—not even *once*—that Morgan swung his way. Had never suspected it, but found himself, jaw dropped, staring at Reynolds because his *only* issue with Ramsey hitting on him was his age. Not his sex.

Not the fact that he was a man.

"Jesus fucking Christ," Jacob said, scrubbing a hand over his face.

"Oh, stop being such a fucking prude," Morgan said, chuckling. "I can practically hear the wheels turning over there."

"Does Finn know you're into guys?" *Finn had to know,* Jacob told himself firmly.

But Morgan shook his head again. "It's not . . .it's not anything. Just happened once. Never wanted to do it with anyone else. So, no point in trying to tell Finn that we're the same, that we're both queer, because we're not."

Jacob wanted to tell him that this was fucking bullshit—if Morgan wanted to have sex with even *one* man, that meant he was queer, which meant that *yes*, he and Finn and Morgan were all very much the same—but Morgan looked so suddenly uncomfortable that Jacob decided it wasn't worth making the argument.

Clearly, he hadn't meant to bring it up, and now that he had, he regretted it.

Well, Jacob fucking regretted knowing about it, because now he was going to have to keep this secret from Finn.

"Alright," Jacob said.

"You're not gonna . . .I don't know . . .lecture me on queer-ness?"

Jacob laughed. "I have no interest in lecturing you on any-thing, Reynolds."

"Alright," Morgan said and gestured towards the ice. "Puck drop."

After that, they watched the game in silence.

The Evergreens' offense was potent, anchored by Elliott and Malcolm on the wings, and they spent much of the first period harassing the Bandits' goalie, scoring twice.

It was only at the end of the period when Ramsey got caught for a hooking penalty—Morgan swearing under his breath—that Finn got any work at all.

"They've got a good penalty kill," Jacob said to Morgan, breaking the silence, before it became too brittle with all the pressure they both felt.

"'Course they do," Morgan retorted.

They watched as the Bandits swarmed their offensive zone, despite Ramsey and Brody and the rest of the power play kill team's best efforts.

Finn stopped one shot, then another, then effortlessly slid into a third position to stop the rebound.

Morgan made a noise under his breath. Jacob looked at him, quickly, not wanting to miss a moment of the game action, and as tense as *he* felt, Morgan looked like he was about to puke.

"Do you always—" Jacob stopped abruptly as Finn dove for the puck again, smothering it with his glove. "No, don't answer that. I don't want to know."

Morgan didn't say anything, not until the horn sounded, ending the period.

The Evergreens would be on the power play for approximately thirty seconds when the second period began, but with how Finn had handled his business for the majority of it, Jacob believed he'd be okay.

"You know it's hard," Morgan said. "I'm gonna get a fucking ulcer, watching him on TV. Nevermind coming here to watch." He shook his head. "I know you don't get it, but I want it so fucking bad for him. I think all the time he shouldn't be doing this, he should do something easier, something else he's good at—and he's good at lots of things. But to tackle this . . ." Morgan sighed. "I never wanted him to be a hockey player. I knew what he'd face if he was."

"He can bear more than you think," Jacob said softly. *More than either of us think.*

Morgan made a face. "I know." He didn't need to add again that he'd know better than Jacob.

"You ever tell him any of that?"

"Of course I fucking have," Morgan said.

"No, I mean, *exactly* like that. Not so he could interpret it to mean you're ashamed of him and don't want him to play because of that."

"If you're trying to tell me I'm a shit father—"

"I'm trying to tell you," Jacob interrupted, losing his patience, "that one of the things Finn's best at, besides hockey, is believing the worst version of what people tell him. Specifically *you*. And let me tell you, you haven't done yourself any favors."

"I know," Morgan muttered.

"Some friendly advice? Tell him that. *All* of that. Just like that."

"I'm trying to be better. I know you don't believe that."

"Doesn't matter what I believe." Though that wasn't necessarily true. If Morgan continued to be a shithead, Jacob would be the first in line to suggest to Finn he put some space between himself and his dad.

"Yeah it does." Morgan sounded disgusted by this. "He trusts you. Maybe he went to you first because I didn't like you, and that sounded like a fun way to piss me off."

"And now?"

"He's playing fucking great."

"That's not me," Jacob said. Though he'd given Finn some pointers and he could see echoes of them, ghosts of his own movements, filtering into Finn's blocks. Maybe he shouldn't like seeing the undeniable imprint of him on Finn, but he did. "That's him. All I did was give him the confidence he needed to be what he was always capable of."

Morgan sighed. "I want to punch you in the face for that."

"No, you don't," Jacob said, chuckling. "You're fucking grateful, that's what you are."

Please continue to be grateful when you find out what else Finn trusts me with.

"Fine, fine," Morgan grumbled. "I'm a *little* grateful. But anyone could have done this."

"Right, of course," Jacob said. But he knew the truth.

Nobody else was going to be as good for Finn as him. He knew it was true, because nobody else was ever going to love Finn like he did.

"Thirty-six seconds left," Zach reminded the team in the locker room, right before they took the ice for the second period.

Like Finn was going to forget about the power play.

He'd been thinking about it during the whole intermission, turning over and over in his mind the way the Bandits had approached the first minute and a half and what else he knew about them as an offensive team.

What new wrinkle they might attempt with only thirty-six seconds left and twenty minutes to plan.

It was better thinking about that than thinking about how his father was sitting out in the crowd, watching him. No doubt judging him.

"You good?" Brody asked, stopping by where Finn was sitting on the bench.

"Yeah," Finn said. "Barely any action in the first."

He couldn't say he'd been *bored*, exactly, but he hadn't been disappointed to watch as Elliott and Mal and the rest of the Evergreens' offense harassed the Bandits' goalie.

"Ell and Mal have really found a new gear," Brody agreed. "I'm just trying to keep the Bandits from kicking Elliott's ass."

"Mal's not helping you with that?"

Brody grinned. "He's the first line of defense, frankly."

"I'd imagine so."

It was usually the same story. The opposing team would hit the ice determined to stop Elliott, who was the fastest, slyest scorer in their conference. There were rumblings how he'd be taken in the first round of the draft. *Early* in the first round. But what opposing teams had yet to pick up was that now Elliott had a protector, who was bigger and stronger and would absolutely lay them out if they crossed the line.

"Well, we've got you," Brody said, patting Finn on the shoulder pad. "Got your back."

Finn knew it.

Felt the whole weight of the team—but not the same kind of pressure he might have experienced before—as he entered the rink, lights flashing and the crowd applauding.

He'd always felt the team's expectations as a weight, pushing him down, making it hard sometimes to even hold his head up high, but now he was seeing it differently, and it helped.

They had his back, and he had theirs.

The puck dropped, and Finn braced, stick in front, gaze glued on Brody, who'd managed to divert it behind the goal.

He sped around the corner, battling against two of the Bandits' linemen, sticks clanging against the ice as they tried to steal the puck. Ivan joined in, shoving another player out, and Finn tensed.

They were almost around the goal now, parallel to the crease, and he was going to make a stop, because if they stole the puck they *would* take a shot.

He just had to time it perfectly.

They stole the puck from Ramsey and passed it then passed it again, and Finn knew he was going to have to make a calculated guess. It was fifty-fifty and if he guessed wrong . . .

No, he told himself, *don't go there.*

He'd seen the center shoot in the first period, and he knew they were trying to center it for him—which made sense, because Finn was pretty sure he was the best player on the team.

The right wing hesitated, twisted around, and instead of passing—instead of waiting—shot the puck.

Finn hit the ice a half-second too late, not able to deflect the puck, and it hit the back of the net.

"Hey, tough break," Ramsey said, skating over as Finn lifted himself up. "You still got this."

Finn knew his father was watching. His father *and* Jacob. But anyone could've made that decision wrong. It had been smart to wait. His instincts couldn't pay off every time—even when he wanted them to.

Did it suck that they hadn't paid off *now* with his dad watching?

Yeah, it did, but before, Finn knew it would've seriously thrown him. Instead of recovering—instead of resetting emotionally and physically—he'd already be dreading what Morgan would say to him.

But even though he knew he probably wouldn't *like* it, he could push the thought away.

It wasn't perfect, but what did Jacob always like to say?

Doesn't have to be perfect to be okay.

Finn repeated those words over and over as the game unfolded. Ivan scored, and then their third line did, too, making it four to one, but he didn't let himself relax.

He didn't get seriously challenged though. The Bandits took a few shots, but they were fairly straightforward blocks, and with Brody and Ramsey and the rest of the defense swarming around them, they hadn't been able to rebound or take multiple shots.

The game ended four to one—but it was nearly five to one, as Mal nearly bagged an empty net goal at the end, to seal it off.

He showered and changed, appreciating the way Coach and Zach and a lot of the guys patted him, respecting the effort he'd put in even though for this game, at least, he hadn't felt like everything was resting entirely on his shoulders.

He halfway expected Morgan to make another comment about that, how he was lucky it *wasn't* entirely on his shoulders, but as he finished dressing, he told himself firmly that he wasn't going to think the worst of his dad before he even *was* the worst.

"Hey, great game," Morgan said as he approached where, to his surprise, his dad was standing with Jacob.

"Thanks," Finn said, letting his dad fold him into his embrace. It was a quick, reassuring hug, but it was more than he'd expected. He met Jacob's eyes over his dad's shoulder, and the warmth in his stomach grew.

Because as good as it felt to hear his dad say it, it felt even better to have Jacob look at him like that.

Like he'd done everything Jacob could've expected—and more. And even if he hadn't, Jacob would still be here and would still be looking at him exactly the same way.

"Yeah, you had great puck control," Jacob agreed, as his dad let go of him.

Jacob didn't touch him but Finn could tell he wanted to. His gaze was as good as a caress across his cheek.

"Food?" Morgan asked.

Finn glanced over at Jacob again. He wanted to have dinner with his boyfriend—not his dad—but he didn't know how to suggest it.

Until Morgan blew his mind and continued, "Braun, you should come with us."

Finn looked at him, aware that he was staring at his dad like he'd lost his mind. "Are you alright? Do you have some kind of latent concussion syndrome?"

"Don't tell me you don't want to break down the game with him," Morgan said breezily, like this was no big deal. Like he and Jacob hadn't been at each other's throats forever.

"I do," Finn said.

Morgan turned to Jacob. "How about it?"

Jacob looked as floored as Finn felt. "Uh . . .sure. Okay."

"Hey, you're the one who suggested we sit together," Morgan muttered.

This time Finn couldn't keep his astonishment in. "You *sat* together?"

Jacob shrugged, awkwardly. "I had the tickets you left for me at the box office—two of them—and they're good seats and—"

"Don't sprain your few remaining brain cells, Braun," Morgan said, but he was actually honest to God smiling.

Finn wanted to ask if he'd just suddenly been dumped into an alternate universe.

"Seriously," he asked his dad as they walked towards Jimmy's. "Are you okay?"

Morgan elbowed him. "I can be a mature adult."

"No evidence of that so far," Jacob muttered under his breath. Finn caught his gaze and grinned.

"Is this how it's gonna be?" Morgan wanted to know.

Finn wanted to say yes. Wanted to believe that it was true and that it would *stay* true. Pretended, for a single glorious moment, that Morgan already knew the truth and didn't care—but more than that, actually *liked* that Finn had found someone he cared about, who cared about him in return. It was a hazy beautiful possibility that Morgan not only didn't care that it was Jacob, but they got along. Maybe they'd bicker, but only in the way of people who knew the worst of each other a little too well and yet liked each other anyway.

"I wouldn't hate it," Jacob said.

Finn laughed, and Morgan made a face but didn't look *that* upset about the possibility.

Jacob opened the door to Jimmy's and they grabbed a booth in the back, Finn very aware of how more than a few heads turned, watching as they walked in.

Morgan was recognizable of course, but Jacob was harder to pinpoint as he'd spent his career in a helmet and extensive padding.

Still, Finn was pretty sure at least one person, an older guy whose eyes widened comically as they passed, recognized that Morgan Reynolds and Jacob Braun had just walked by and were about to sit down and break bread together.

Finn considered reminding his dad that nothing he did went unobserved, at least for long, but that was only asking for trouble.

Morgan was in a good mood—they *all* were, Finn realized—and was it so much to ask for reality to not shove itself in, uninvited?

"I'm gonna take a leak," Morgan said, after Finn slid into the booth. He put a hand on Finn's shoulder. "Order me a Coke, okay?"

Then he was gone. At least for a minute or two.

"Well," Jacob said, and the corner of his mouth tilted up.

"Don't," Finn said, but he was smiling, too.

"Your dad as a third wheel. That's not weird or anything."

"God, don't remind me," Finn said with a groan. "But maybe . . .maybe if he gets used to this, he won't lose his shit when he finds out there's more."

Jacob didn't look convinced. "He's still going to want to kill me."

"You think so?"

"I know so." Jacob leaned forward. "'Cause he loves you a lot, Finn. And if I was him, I would absolutely want to kick the ass of the older guy who seduced my son."

"*I* seduced *you*," Finn reminded him.

"I don't know if he's going to keep his fists out of my face long enough to hear that part of it," Jacob said wryly. "Or if he's going to *want* to hear it."

"Probably both." Finn's foot brushed Jacob's under the table. "Maybe I can convince him to go home, after this, and you can come back to my room with me."

"Don't get your hopes up," Jacob said.

And yeah, Morgan was suddenly very into this together-ness, which was actually *not* terrible, but it also made it really fucking hard for Finn to have sex.

Morgan came back a second later, taking a seat next to Finn. That wasn't that surprising. Finn wasn't going to assume that he and Jacob were suddenly best friends.

"So," Morgan said, after he'd examined the menu, his grayish-green eyes taking in the list of specials and then dropping it to the table, "how's that guy, Finn?"

Finn had been taking a long drink of water and choked.

"What guy?" he asked, after he managed to get his breath back, even though he knew perfectly well who his dad was referring to.

Jacob.

"You know. The one you wanted to be dating, that you weren't dating yet."

"Uh, well . . ."

"You said you wore the Burberry suit," Morgan said, leaning forward, looking very interested in the answer. "Did you overcome his scruples?"

"Uh, yeah," Finn said.

Jacob smothered a laugh. Finn told himself that was better because if Morgan looked over at him, he'd know the truth in an instant.

"Good for you," Morgan said, patting him on the shoulder supportively. "A chip off the old block. A Reynolds doesn't take no for an answer."

"Is that your dating philosophy?" Jacob asked, and Morgan glared at him.

Finn considered reminding them both about the no blood policy.

"I don't want to hear my dad's dating philosophy," Finn said, hoping they could change the subject. Morgan wasn't ready to hear the truth. *He* wasn't ready for Morgan to hear the truth.

Morgan's grin was shark-like. "Don't tell me you want to hear about it, Braun?"

Jacob shuddered and that didn't feel faked at all. "Ew. No. Please stay far away from my dick."

Finn considered bringing up that Morgan *wouldn't* be interested in Jacob's dick—and that he shouldn't be anyway, because that would be super gross—but instead he settled for an attempt to change the subject.

"So whose idea was it for you two to sit together?" he asked casually.

"Mine," Morgan said and Jacob rolled his eyes which Finn took to mean that it had actually been Jacob's idea.

Interesting. He was going to have to ask Jacob about it—but only after he got him naked and they shared at least a pair of orgasms.

"It was convenient," Jacob said.

The waitress appeared then and took their orders, and it was easy enough for Finn to direct the conversation back towards the game.

"Anyone might've missed that shot," Jacob offered after she'd brought their drinks.

Morgan looked like he didn't believe that, not entirely anyway, but he didn't say anything. For which Finn was *very* grateful.

"The center was taking most of the shots, before that, and I was sure he was going to pass it to him," Finn said. "Made a calculated decision. Except it wasn't right."

"That happens," Jacob said warmly, supportively.

"Does it?" Morgan asked innocently.

"You know it does," Jacob retorted. Finn could tell he wanted to say something along the lines of *happened enough times between the two of us.* But he gave Jacob major props for not doing it.

"That was actually a pretty sick move he made," Morgan said. "I didn't expect it either."

Finn decided that was probably the closest Morgan was going to get to agreeing with Jacob. To supporting Finn.

He was never going to *not* care what his dad thought. He was Morgan Reynolds, sure, so it was easy to look at him and think, *this guy really knows what the hell he's talking about*, but it was more than that, too. Morgan was his dad, and despite all the ways Morgan could be a complete asshole, Finn loved him. He'd been the most consistent force in his life for what felt like all of it.

His mom was around, too, of course, but nobody could really match the power or sheer presence of Morgan.

"You think anyone's gonna figure out if they go for that smaller, quicker forward, that it's gonna piss off that left winger?" Morgan continued. "They seemed really surprised when they did it, and he lost his shit."

"That's . . .uh kind of new," Finn said.

"Oh?"

"Honestly, for last season and most of this season, they were better at chirping at each other than defending each other," Finn said.

"Huh." Morgan sipped his Coke. Looked like he wanted to ask, but he didn't, at least at first. Then he finally burst out. "What changed?"

Finn wasn't sure what the sudden tension in his dad's shoulders was about. Why would he give a shit about Mal and Elliott?

"They got together," Finn said. He met Jacob's gaze across the table and told himself forcibly not to flush.

Morgan's mouth was a tight line, and Finn couldn't understand why. He wasn't homophobic, not at all. In fact, famously, even before Finn had began to consider that he might be gay, his dad had reported one of his teammates for homophobic comments and had gotten him kicked off the team.

It was definitely not that Elliott and Mal were two men. Maybe that they were teammates?

"You ever see that before?" Jacob asked Morgan.

Morgan had an unbelievable control over his own body—was famous for it, in fact—but Finn swore he squirmed on the bench. "No."

"I heard about it, some," Jacob said.

"Not that many out guys in the NHL," Morgan said tightly.

"A few," Jacob said. "The eldest Barnes brother from New Jersey, and Noah Boucher from the Fisher Cats. Oh, and the Sentinels' captain. Hayes Montgomery. He came out in the last offseason, didn't he?"

Finn nodded. He liked Hayes, though he'd only met him a handful of times. "I'm glad he's playing for Tampa now.

Should make it easier when I'm called up." Before, before this, he'd always added a bunch of caveats—internally *and* out loud—about how he might not get there, to the NHL. But he was feeling more confident that he would now.

Could even see the hazy beginnings of it in his mind.

Morgan looked even unhappier, but what he said was the opposite of the awkwardness lurking in his gaze. "I hope so."

A minute later their food came, and conversation slipped from subject to subject, easier than Finn could've imagine, as they demolished it.

After Morgan and Jacob argued over who was paying the bill—Jacob won, and not to be outdone, Morgan tossed a hundred dollar bill on the table for a tip—they headed outside.

"I got to go," Morgan told Finn. "Have an early meeting for some ESPN coverage I'm participating in. But you're good with the plans for Christmas next week?"

That was right, Finn realized, Christmas was only a few days away. He *had* seen the email Morgan had sent and he'd frankly ignored it.

Only Morgan would send a schedule for a holiday.

"Yeah," Finn said. He risked a glance over at Jacob, who stood there, gazing back with a promise in his eyes.

We'll make time for each other, no matter how much Morgan interferes.

"Good," Morgan said. He gave Jacob an abbreviated, but surprisingly mellow nod. "See you around, Braun."

"Reynolds," Jacob said back.

They didn't shake hands, but Finn supposed that was probably asking way too much of the situation. It was amazing they'd sat together at his game and then had dinner together and nobody's face had gotten punched.

"See you later," Morgan said, giving him another long hug, and then he was gone, walking away, back towards the rink's parking lot.

Finn waited until his dad was just out of earshot. "Does he know?"

Jacob shook his head. "You think he'd have left you alone with me if he did?"

Finn laughed. "Good point." He shot Jacob a hot look. "You wanna come back to my room?"

Jacob's returning look lit him up inside. "I thought you'd never ask."

CHAPTER 16

THIS WAS JACOB'S FIRST year having a *real* holiday break—not having it shoved in, in-between practices and games, and he fully intended to enjoy it.

He spent a whole day shopping for gifts, taking his time and not just throwing anything he thought anyone he knew might possibly like into his cart, but really considering what might be the best gift.

On Christmas Eve, he took Jackie and Krista to the Portland Zoo to see the holiday light displays, and plied them with hot fried elephant ears, dripping with butter and cinnamon sugar, and big cups of hot chocolate, ignoring Bryan's protests when he dropped them back at home, hyped and maybe even a little wild.

"Just wait," his brother warned ominously as he waved Jacob into the house.

"'Til what?"

"'Til you have kids of your own and every time you see a food item containing sugar you break into hives," Bryan said.

"I . . .uh . . ." Bryan knew he didn't want kids.

"Okay, fair," Bryan said. "Wait until you end up shuttling around a dozen or so drunk hockey rookies because you're loved up with one of them."

"I'm not . . .we haven't . . .I don't . . ." Jacob hedged. They hadn't talked about it. It wasn't only sex, that was for sure, but they also hadn't used the *L* word yet.

Bryan raised an eyebrow as Jackie tackled Krista into the couch, yelling.

"But we *are* . . .uh . . .together. You know." Jacob felt awkward admitting it, even though if he was doing it, he could surely say it out loud.

"Please tell me you're more articulate with Finn," Bryan said.

Finn didn't seem to have many complaints. He asked for what he wanted and Jacob was more than happy to give it to him as often as they could—which, frankly, between Finn's school and hockey commitments and Morgan being the world's most accomplished cockblocker, was not nearly enough.

"Trust me, he's not complaining. Except about how often his dad accidentally uh . . ." Jacob hesitated, glancing over at where Krista and Jackie were tussling on the couch, but also, possibly listening in.

"Interrupts you?" Bryan laughed. "Hey, at least you aren't pining away alone anymore. That was pathetic."

"Thanks," Jacob said dryly.

Bryan only shrugged. "Just telling it like it is. Did you talk to Finn about tomorrow?"

"Yes. He's spending most of it with his Dad and then uh . . .well, tomorrow night when he finally manages to escape

Morgan's clutches, I'm planning a little celebration at my house, just the two of us."

"Let me guess, you hung some mistletoe over your bed." Bryan laughed. "Subtle, you are not, but hey, that's not a bad thing."

"I did tell him you invited him over and he was really touched. If Morgan wasn't in town . . ."

"I get it," Bryan said briskly. "I can't imagine dealing with that guy full-time."

"He's getting better at it. Or Morgan's trying harder? Or trying less? I'm not sure. But I think it's not entirely a bad thing he's around. As for me and him, well we're never going to be best friends, but we haven't punched each other in the face yet."

"And what happens when he finds out what you and Finn are really doing?"

It was a question Jacob had been asking himself for at least a week.

"No idea," Jacob said. "But there's no reason to tell him right now."

Bryan shot him a look that said, *if you're sure*. Or maybe, *he's going to find out, and be super pissed*. Possibly both.

Probably it *was* both.

"It's too bad he couldn't come with you guys to the zoo," Bryan said.

"Yeah, he had this party with the guys from his team who're still in town," Jacob said. "I'm trying to not get in the way of him enjoying this whole experience."

Bryan rolled his eyes. "You're not going to."

"I've been through this—well, not *this*, not college," Jacob said, shifting uncomfortably. He'd come up through the juniors, instead. But the point remained. He'd already been through this. He'd played his years, and now he was done, and Finn had all his years ahead of him still.

"If you are currently overthinking everything, deciding for him that he couldn't possibly want you, not when you're at two different stages of life, stop it," Bryan said, smacking him. "I'm sure he'd tell you to stop it, too, but he's not here, and I doubt you'd actually get out of your ass long enough to tell him what you're worried about."

Jacob winced.

"I mean it," Bryan said. "Stop it right now."

Jacob did try to stop it, but after he left Bryan's house, he didn't stop thinking about it.

Was still thinking about it when later that night, just after eleven, he was sitting in bed, watching ESPN, when his phone rang.

It was Finn, giggling into the receiver.

"You good?" Jacob said immediately. "You're safe?" He did not want to drag his ass out of his comfortable, warm bed, but he would, if Finn needed help.

"I'm fine," Finn said, and yeah, he'd definitely been drinking. "Totally fine. *So* fine."

Yeah, you are.

Bryan popped into Jacob's head in to lecture him about keeping all these things to himself.

Jacob cleared his throat. "Yeah, you are."

Finn hummed under his breath, sounding pleased that he'd said it out loud. "I'm back at my room, by the way," he said. "Alone."

He didn't love how adept they'd gotten at phone sex recently, but he knew enough now to know what Finn wanted.

What *he* wanted.

"Yeah? All alone?"

"So alone," Finn confirmed. "I nearly took a cab to your place."

"You have to be at Morgan's tomorrow morning for brunch."

"I'm totally capable of doing the walk of shame to my dad's house." Finn paused, like he was still aware, despite the booze, what a bad idea that would've been. After all, he hadn't done it. "But you're right. Annoyingly."

"Bet I could be right again," Jacob murmured, grabbing the remote and muting ESPN before switching speakerphone on.

"I hope so," Finn said.

"I think if I kissed you right now, you'd melt right into me." Jacob hadn't ever thought he was any good at this, but either he'd gotten better because he *had* to—thanks, Morgan—or it was surprisingly easy with Finn.

"Yeah," Finn said breathily. "What else?"

"I bet if I slid my fingers down your chest and then lower, your cock would be hard."

"*Yes.*" Finn groaned, and Jacob didn't need Finn to tell him that he was doing what Jacob wished *he* was doing.

Arousal surged through him, and for a second, he couldn't even form words. Couldn't even *think* them. He just wanted Finn so goddamn bad.

He'd thought once he'd stopped resisting that it would get easier. That the compulsion would feel less desperate.

But his hunger for Finn had only grown. He wanted to take him to bed and keep him there for a full fucking week.

He groaned as he finally let his own hand drift downwards, tucking it under the waistband of his boxer briefs, closing his eyes and imagining that he wasn't experiencing his own touch, but Finn's.

Finn's sure, perfect hands.

"Your hand feels good," Finn panted, breaking the charged silence. "But your mouth feels even better."

Jacob groaned again as he worked his dick. He wanted to feel Finn's cock, hard and twitching against his tongue, deep in his throat. Wanted to make his man moan. Wanted to tuck his fingers inside and fuck him until Finn *screamed*.

"Tomorrow night," Jacob promised, voice rough, desperate. "Tomorrow. Just you and me, my bed. No distractions."

Finn's breathing stuttered and he let out a low moan as he came. Only a second later, Jacob followed him.

"I love the sound of that," Finn said sleepily. "It's gonna get me through all of tomorrow's bullshit."

"Please don't think about having sex with me when you're with your dad," Jacob said, but he couldn't be really worked up about it, because his orgasm had reduced him to a boneless, contented mess.

"How about I just don't tell you?" Finn teased.

"Did you guys have fun tonight?" Jacob finished cleaning up and changed the subject.

"It was good," Finn said. "Missed you, though. Wished I'd bailed and gone to the zoo with you and Jackie and Krista."

"It was fun, but you had plans. Important plans."

Finn gave an exaggerated sigh. "So you keep telling me. When are plans with *you* important?"

"Tomorrow night," Jacob said, saying it like a prayer. "Don't let Morgan fuck this one up."

"There's no way I'd let that happen," Finn promised.

Jacob stewed for a second. Not because he thought Finn would let Morgan ruin their plans, but his mind had already gone back to what he'd been considering earlier. What Bryan had said to him.

"Do you ever feel like we're just . . .wrong place, wrong time?" Jacob wondered. As soon as he said the words he wanted to snatch them back.

"No," Finn said, sounding very sure.

"No?" Jacob wished he could borrow—maybe even keep—some of that certainty.

"I feel like you showed up right when I needed you, right when I was drowning," Finn said softly.

"For hockey, yeah," Jacob pointed out. Why was he even arguing about this? *Just enjoy the afterglow, you stupid idiot.*

"For hockey, yeah," Finn repeated. "But everything else is like an extra super great cherry on top. Something I didn't expect, but . . .but that makes it so much better. Makes everything better." His voice hushed. "I didn't think I was *unhappy* before, but you make me happy, Jacob."

Jacob felt raw. Exposed. Because he was happy, too. Happy to be adjacent to the ice again. Happy to coach, even. And so fucking happy with Finn.

"You make me happy too." He couldn't keep the truth back. Didn't even want to.

"Why do I feel like there's a *but* there?"

Jacob sighed. "It's not a *but*."

"Might be more fun if it was," Finn joked. "My butt specifically."

It would be more fun. Sex with Finn was more fun than it had ever been with anyone before. Jacob had never felt as free to explore, to just *enjoy*, the way he did with Finn. Was it because he was on the brink of coming out? Or was it *just* Finn? He didn't know.

"Why don't you tell me what's got you all worked up?" Finn continued. "I know you. You're worried about something."

Jacob hesitated.

"And," Finn added, "you're not the only one who can tell. I can always tell."

He could. Jacob would find it annoying if it wasn't so absolutely spectacularly wonderful, having someone know him this way.

"You never worry about how you're starting your life and I'm—"

"Don't you dare say you're ending yours," Finn interrupted.

"Okay, that you're *starting* your NHL career and mine's ended?"

"No," Finn said.

"I mean . . ."

"No," Finn repeated again, more firmly this time.

"Oh. Okay. I just…I worried. I don't want to hold you back."

Jacob could hear Finn's ridiculous expression through the phone. "As if you would ever."

"I might," Jacob said. He worried he would. That he'd be a distraction. That he'd be the thing that made Finn take his eyes off the prize. Though at least he could say with one-hundred-dred-percent certainty that it hadn't happened so far. Finn was playing better than ever, with a locked-in focus that Jacob recognized.

He was learning to understand himself. To believe in himself.

It was a beautiful thing to watch and Jacob wanted to be there for every second of it, but not if somehow him being around was the thing that screwed it up.

"No, you wouldn't. I never think of it that way. I think . . ." Finn paused. "Don't freak out, okay, I know we haven't talked about this."

"I'm not freaking out," Jacob said, but his fingers were nervously tapping on his bare thigh, and he wasn't sure he could stop them.

"I think of you next to me, during the hard parts coming up. And I know there's gonna be hard parts. I think about you supporting me. Being there for me. Making me laugh when I only want to cry."

Jacob swallowed hard. "I want to do that."

"And that you've done it before, and that you've gone through it, and you *know,* better than anyone else? That's a gift, Jacob, it's not a curse."

"I'm glad you think so."

"I wish *you* thought so," Finn countered.

"Bryan told me I was being very stupid."

"An older brother's prerogative," Finn teased.

It was. Especially when he was right.

"I . . .I didn't *want* to be right, Finn." Jacob had a feeling Finn already knew this, but he wanted to say it, anyway.

"I know," Finn said. "Just . . .I want you to believe what I believe. That this is great and wonderful and awesome."

"I do. *I do*." And he wanted to believe that it wouldn't be that way only for now. That next year, and the year after that, they'd both believe it still.

But neither of them could make that promise. Not yet anyway. It was still too new. Besides, they still had one huge hurdle to get over before they could even begin to think that way.

Morgan.

"Good." Jacob could hear the affection—maybe even more—in Finn's voice, and he hung on to that, hoped he'd remember exactly the way he sounded now, so in the future when his own certainty wavered, he'd have Finn's.

"I . . ." Jacob hesitated, but he wanted Finn to understand how much he cared without being stupid enough to say the words just yet. "I can't wait to see you tomorrow."

"Yeah?"

"If you'd asked me to get out of my warm bed tonight, I'd have done it," Jacob said.

"Just think about how we're both going to be there, tomorrow," Finn said dreamily.

Finn and his dad had never been much for exchanging gifts.

Morgan never needed anything—if he did, he got it for himself—and he'd made sure Finn never really lacked for anything anyway. Besides, Finn only needed his hockey gear and enough spending money to keep him in Sammy's subs and fries at Jimmy's and occasionally a drink or two at Darcelle's. Anything more felt like an embarrassment of riches.

But it was Christmas, they were spending it together, and so Finn had decided he should get his dad *something*. So he'd taken his last shutout puck, saving it after he'd realized it was his twenty-fifth since he'd started playing goalie and had it framed.

Jacob had wondered if he wouldn't like to keep it for himself, but Finn had enough pucks, and this was something his dad would actually find meaningful.

Success—always a language that Morgan Reynolds understood.

After they'd demolished the brunch that his dad had catered in the high-rise apartment he'd bought after Finn had transferred to Portland, Finn handed him the gift, and Morgan looked surprised.

"You got me something?"

Finn rolled his eyes. "Dad, it's Christmas."

"I know, but I don't really need—"

"Just open it," Finn said.

"Fine, fine," Morgan said. Then he shot him a knowing smile and dug something out of the back pocket of his jeans. "Good thing I got you something, too."

"Well, open yours," Finn said, after Morgan handed him an envelope. Of course he hadn't wrapped it. And of course, after he looked inside noticed that it was cash.

He'd been surprised enough that Morgan had actually had a tree put up—he'd hired someone else to do it, of course—but it had been a surprisingly thoughtful gesture.

Morgan tore open the paper and for a second, just stared at the framed puck and its accompanying engraved plaque.

What if he'd read the situation wrong? What if his dad *didn't* want a reminder that he was good—or that he actually wished Finn had recorded *more* shutouts since he'd switched positions?

But then his dad cleared his throat and looked over at Finn with a surprising amount of emotion in his eyes.

"You'd give this to me?" he asked, tapping at the glass covering the mounted puck.

"Yeah," Finn said. He'd told himself it wasn't a big deal, but was that really true, when it felt like he'd been holding his breath since he'd handed his dad the package?

"Finn . . ." Morgan met his gaze. "Thank you."

He shrugged, trying to shrug off the emotion rising in him. "It's not a big deal."

Morgan sighed. "Yes, *yes*, it is. This should be something you keep for your own cabinet, to remember this year by, and you're giving to *me*. And I haven't been—"

"It's okay, Dad," Finn said awkwardly.

He both wanted the apology, and he *didn't* want it, too.

"No, it's *not* okay," Morgan huffed out. "I've been too hard on you. You're doing great, in spite of me, not because of me."

"I bet that must really chap your ass," Finn said.

Morgan laughed. "Actually, no."

"I play hockey 'cause I love it, you know? But I started . . .I had the desire in the first place, because you did it first. Because you loved it so much."

"Yeah?" Morgan's voice cracked.

"Yeah," Finn said. "I'd see you on the ice and you'd be smiling, like you never wanted to be anyplace else."

He wanted to snatch his words back after he'd said them, because he saw the melancholy bitter twist as Morgan tried to smile.

Finn pulled his dad into a hug. Squeezing him tight. Morgan went and didn't fight him, even as he cleared his throat and mumbled, "No, no, it's good. I'm good."

He gave him one last squeeze. "I know you miss it," Finn said.

Morgan's chin tilted down, like he was agreeing but didn't want to make a big deal out of it. Which . . .typical Morgan. But he said, to Finn's surprise, "I've been putting too much on you."

"I can handle it," Finn said, even though he certainly hadn't been handling it well, before.

"Maybe now," Morgan said wryly. "And not because of anything I've done. I told Braun at the game the other night how proud of you I was, and he asked me if I had ever told you that, *exactly* like that, and I realized that no . . .I didn't. Not like I should've."

"Thanks, Dad," Finn said awkwardly.

"I know it doesn't fix everything, but we'll get there . . .right?"

Finn didn't know, but he remembered how he'd felt last night, when Jacob had confessed his worries. He believed, despite all the cards stacked against them.

The cards were *definitely* stacked against him and Morgan fixing their shit.

But for the first time, Finn thought that if Morgan tried, then he could try too.

"We'll get there," he told his dad. "Now where are we going to hang this?" He tapped the plaque.

"Oh, I'm not anywhere long enough to hang it on a wall," Morgan said seriously. "It's going right into my suitcase so I can take it wherever I go. Look at it every single day."

And maybe they really would be okay.

They spent the afternoon watching football—and ordering in pizza—his dad complaining about how the NHL no longer played on Christmas so he was forced to watch the NFL.

"My friend Brody's boyfriend is going to be a really famous football player," Finn offered. "I know Ramsey went with him to a game, and I was thinking I should too."

"So how's *your* boyfriend and when am I gonna get to meet him?" Morgan wondered.

"What happened to all those warnings about dating someone during the season?"

Morgan shrugged. "You seem determined to do whatever you want, so what am I going to say about it? Besides, you were right, I married your mom during the season. Sometimes . . .sometimes we do things that don't seem like they make a lot of sense, but they make us happy."

"That why you married Mom?"

Morgan was gazing at the TV, but it didn't really look like he was seeing it at all.

"Uh . . .yes. Yeah. Of course."

But Finn wasn't sure that he'd understood at all. He was just glad Morgan had gotten distracted from asking to meet Jacob.

An hour later he got out of the Uber at Jacob's place and headed towards the door.

Jacob had it open before he was even halfway down the path.

"Hey," Finn said, tilting his mouth up for a kiss hello.

Jacob brushed a kiss across his mouth. "Merry Christmas," Jacob murmured. He closed the door behind them, his arm winding around Finn's waist and pulling him in tighter against him.

Finn went easily, kissing Jacob back. He was hoping, with each passing moment and with how passionately Jacob was kissing him, like he couldn't get enough of his mouth, that they might end up heading straight to bed.

Phone sex was all well and good, but he wanted Jacob's hard, solid body under him and over him and around him.

But Jacob didn't tug him towards the staircase and disappointingly, he broke the kiss, pulling away from Finn a fraction.

"Come on," he said, sounding breathless. He took Finn's hand and led him into the living room. There was a fire in the fireplace, wood crackling, and a small tree in the corner. A bottle of wine sat next to a trio of flickering candles on the coffee table, two glasses already poured.

"This is . . .really nice," Finn said.

He wouldn't have thought Jacob was a romantic, and wouldn't have thought he'd need that, but it turned out he really, really liked it.

Jacob produced a small velvet box from his pocket.

"I just thought . . ." He sounded self-conscious. "I didn't know if we were exchanging gifts, but I wanted you to have these."

"Not a ring then?" Finn teased, enjoying the way Jacob flushed, as he tugged him down to the comfortable couch, tucking him under his arm.

"Little soon for that, don't you think?" Jacob asked. "Your dad doesn't know. The world doesn't know."

"But they will," Finn said, even though he knew Jacob was right. Besides, the box wasn't even the right size for a ring.

"True."

Jacob looked nervous, anyway, as Finn opened the box.

A pair of silver cufflinks shone in the dim flickering light of the room. He lifted one and made a pleased noise in the back of his throat at the engraved evergreen tree on one and his initials on the other.

The metal was heavy, substantial and smooth in his palm as he stroked them.

"These are gorgeous," Finn said, tilting his head so he could look at Jacob's face better. "You had these made just for me."

"This is such an exciting time of your life . . .I want you to remember it," Jacob said, clearing his throat. "You really like them?"

And suddenly Finn's throat felt a little tight, too. He'd come here expecting sex, and well, maybe a little bit of holiday romance, but he hadn't been expecting *this*. "I love them."

"Good," Jacob said.

Carefully, Finn nestled the cufflinks back into the box. "I feel bad I didn't have anything for you . . ."

"I've got every single thing I could possibly want, right here," Jacob said firmly, and the look in his eyes, content and happy, helped Finn to believe that was true.

They stayed like that for a long while. Sipping wine and just pressed up together, watching the fire.

Finn had already told him about the gift he'd given Morgan, but he hadn't told Jacob how Morgan had reacted.

"I keep saying this, and I kinda wish he'd do it from farther away, but the man really seems to want to make things right with you," Jacob said after Finn had told him.

"I think so," Finn said.

Jacob's arm squeezed him tighter, tugging him fractionally closer. "How do you feel about that?"

"Good. But also frustrated. Because why didn't he do this two years ago?" Before Jacob could answer that question—as if anyone really could—he continued. "He's never going to be perfect, though. He's still going to fuck up." The wad of cash his dad had tossed into an envelope and shoved at him promised that. But then the look in Morgan's eyes when he'd unwrapped Finn's plaque told another side of the story.

"No question. He's Morgan, so he'll do everything he can to screw it up, but in the end, you gotta believe he means well," Jacob reminded him.

"Ugh, I don't even want to," Finn complained.

"I won't, then," Jacob teased. "What else could I do instead?"

"Kiss me," Finn murmured, tilting his face closer.

Jacob didn't need another invitation. His hands cupped Finn's face and his tongue slipped into his mouth, and buoyed with emotion and all this undeniable romance, Finn gave himself over to it. Draped his body over Jacob's, loving the solid warmth of it underneath him, the way his heartbeat accelerated as Finn settled into his lap and kissed him even deeper.

"Feels so good," Jacob murmured into his mouth. "Can't get enough."

Finn couldn't either. He squirmed closer, feeling Jacob's cock growing hard underneath him, his own trapped in his pants, pressing into Jacob's stomach.

He kept expecting Jacob to put the brakes on, but he didn't, hand sliding confident and sure underneath Finn's shirt, finding his bare skin, stroking it like he owned it.

Finn settled lower into Jacob's lap, grinding against him, no hesitation at all. His hands gripped Jacob's shoulders, loving the width and the breadth and the flex of them, then slid over, to pick apart the buttons on his shirt.

"Need you," Finn gasped as Jacob's touch swept up and down his back and then went lower still, tucking two fingertips under his belt.

Finn had gotten all the buttons undone that he could reach and spread the two halves of his shirt open, curling his fingers into his chest, feeling where his heart beat hard against them.

"What do you want?" Jacob asked.

Finn pulled back a fraction and shot him a hot look. "I want you inside me, *yesterday.*"

"Hang on," Jacob said and with an impressive demonstration of strength, lifted them both off the couch.

Finn's feet wrapped around his back and groaned as he stumbled in the direction of the bedroom. Jacob deposited Finn on the edge of the bed, and Finn reached out, tugging his shirt off the rest of the way, then started in on his pants, pushing Jacob's jeans down.

"Want to look at you this time," Jacob murmured, leaning in and kissing him again. It was impossibly sweet and also dirty, his tongue sweeping into Finn's mouth.

"Yes," Finn panted as he broke the kiss.

"Don't move," Jacob said, like Finn had *any* intention of moving from this spot. He skirted around the bed, only wearing a pair of tight black boxer briefs, and Finn watched, loving the view.

Already looking forward to the view he'd be treated with when he convinced Jacob to lose those, too.

Jacob returned, tossing lube on the bed next to Finn and then tugged off his shirt, kissing him again, hard and insistent this time. His pants were the next to go, Jacob's hands finding every bit of bare skin to touch, to caress.

There was a part of Finn that wanted to tell Jacob to get on with it, that he didn't need the kissing and the foreplay, but the more it continued, the more Finn realized he liked it.

That he *loved* it.

Each and every touch of Jacob's felt like fire trailing over his skin, building up his arousal but also banking it.

Finally, Jacob slipped off his briefs, but to Finn's frustration, he didn't go for his cock first thing. Just lowered himself to his knees and pressed his lips to the crease of Finn's hip, then traced his tongue along the cut muscle there. "Gorgeous," he murmured. "My perfect, gorgeous Finn."

Finn gasped, cock twitching as Jacob finally curled his tongue around the head.

He was only giving him little, teasing touches of his mouth, though, keeping him floating, not overwhelming him with pleasure. Then he slipped a lube-wet finger lower and circled Finn's hole.

He cried out as Jacob pressed it in. "More," he begged, suddenly not content to just float along that plateau of feeling good but wanting to be overwhelmed by it.

"I got you, baby," Jacob murmured, and Finn felt the pressure of two of his big, calloused fingers sliding into him. He bent his head and licked Finn's cock, and Finn's back bowed with it.

Jacob's fingers hit that spot inside that lit him up and he groaned again.

"You ready?" he asked, lifting himself up and draping his body over Finn's. Brushing a kiss against his lips.

"Yes," Finn said and went to reach for Jacob's cock as he slipped out of his underwear, but Jacob's jaw tightened.

"If you do that, this is going to be over really fucking quick," Jacob warned. "I'm . . .I want you too bad, Finn."

"Same," Finn agreed breathily. "Come on."

Jacob didn't need any more encouragement, fitting the head of his cock to Finn's hole and pushing in gently as he leaned over his chest, fingers gripping Finn's thigh tightly.

Every time they did this—and it had only been a handful of times before now—Finn felt overwhelmed. But this time unwound and wound him at the exact same goddamn time.

He panted into Jacob's mouth as their lips met, Jacob kissing him deeply as he bottomed out.

"Feel good?" Jacob murmured and Finn could only nod.

Wanted to beg for more, to feel like this always—protected by the warm cage of Jacob's body and set free by it, too—but he didn't have the words and then Jacob began to move anyway.

It started slow and considerate, but Finn twitched his body and began to meet Jacob's thrusts and after that, it was a hot sweaty race to the end. Jacob's gaze searing Finn's face as Finn groaned and came between them, only from the way Jacob's cock felt inside him and the way his dick rocked up against Jacob's abs.

Jacob followed only a second later, groaning into Finn's mouth, a litany of praise falling from his lips about how good and right and amazing Finn was. How he didn't know how he'd ever lived without him. How Finn made him happier than he'd ever been.

It was just sex, Finn told himself. Maybe, finally, the really good sex they'd discussed weeks ago, on the way home from the Salem game.

But it felt like more than that, too. A turning point.

Jacob got up and grabbed them a washcloth, helping Finn clean up and then tucking him up against his chest as they lazed in bed.

Finn's gaze caught on something above them. "Did you—" He burst out laughing before he could finish the question. "You did not."

"I don't know, it kinda looks like I hung mistletoe above the bed," Jacob teased. "You like?"

"Yeah, it's perfect." Finn paused. Thinking of everything Jacob had murmured into his skin at the end. Everything he felt. "Kind of like you."

He could feel Jacob smile, lips pressed to the side of his head. "Yeah?"

"Mean it," Finn said.

CHAPTER 17

A heavy knock on the door woke Jacob from a deep, dreamless, perfect sleep. He was warm and currently wrapped around Finn, face full of curls, and he didn't want to move.

No. Correction. He wasn't *going* to move.

The pounding continued. Louder, this time.

"Are you—what *is* that?" Finn mumbled.

"Nothing," Jacob said. He stroked his arm. "Go back to sleep. You've got nowhere to be."

But it was hard to relax again, because the noise didn't stop.

"Do you get . . .do you get crazy people out here? Like fans?" Finn wanted to know, partially sitting up.

Jacob snatched back a groan of frustration. "Actually, no. Never."

Finn looked dubious. "Are you sure? Are you just trying to make me feel better?"

He was. He absolutely was. He wanted Finn to go back to sleep and for him to follow.

But then it occurred to him why Finn suddenly sounded edgy. Morgan probably had and *did* have creepy fans show up to his house. He probably needed security. A *lot* of security. It made sense that Finn would be apprehensive.

"Listen," Jacob soothed, "I promise. If people know who I am, which mostly they don't, they don't give a shit. Portland's not really a hockey town." It was one of the many reasons he'd come here after retiring. It was wonderful how much Pittsburgh cared about its hockey team, but it could also be suffocating.

Finn turned and shot him a look. "But you're *Jacob Braun*," he hissed.

"Yes, well, good news is not many people know who that is," he said, chuckling under his breath. "It's probably just my landscaper or kids selling Girl Scout Cookies."

"That's no kid," Finn said, tilting his head as the knocking intensified again.

"Big doors, lots of sound," Jacob said.

Finn looked at him again, and Jacob sighed. "I'm not getting out of going to see who it is, am I?"

Finn shook his head. "And when you do, bring a baseball bat or something."

"A *baseball bat?*" Jacob laughed, even though he wanted to cry about how unfair it was, as he slid out of his warm, soft bed with its gorgeous, naked occupant. "I can do one better than that."

Which is how he ended up in only sweatpants and carrying a hockey stick to open the door.

It was not his landscaper. Or the Girl Scouts. Or a crazed fan, desperately wanting an autograph or a selfie at seven in the morning the day after Christmas.

It was Morgan, and he looked angry enough to spit nails.

"Shit," Jacob said reflexively and closed the door in his face.

"What is it?"

Jacob glanced behind him, and sure enough, there was Finn. He hadn't even bothered with sweatpants, only his briefs, but he had run downstairs to the gym to grab another of Jacob's hockey sticks.

Because of course he had.

Jacob's heart wanted to clench at how sweet, how *thoughtful* that was—and also how insanely fucking hot it was that Finn's first instinct was to protect him—but he couldn't do that now, because Morgan was standing right outside the door and had resumed his pounding and was now yelling.

He took a deep breath. "It's your dad," he said. Morgan's voice was now loud enough that he could hear some of the words through the heavy wood of his door. Jacob caught *betrayed* and *my son* and *fuck*. The last one a whole bunch of times.

"Morgan is *here*?" Finn's face turned red and then white. His fist clenched around the hockey stick and Jacob didn't miss that he hadn't put it down yet.

Well, maybe they *would* have to fight their way out of this one.

Morgan sounded pissed enough.

"Yes," Jacob said. Pretending wasn't going to make their Morgan-sized problem evaporate.

"And he knows."

Jacob didn't answer right away. Just listened. And yeah, it seemed inevitable, because there was a whole litany going now, of *how dare you, you fucking backstabbing pedophile*—that one was a little much, but Morgan was clearly worked up and nobody had ever said that Morgan Reynolds didn't go overboard in the midst of a meltdown—and *he's too young,* and *you're too old.* Something additional about being too old to get it up, too, and Jacob almost smiled at that one.

Almost.

"Yeah, he knows," Finn said heavily.

"How did he find out?" Jacob asked, mystified. They'd told almost nobody.

"Does it matter?"

"Well, *yeah,* it does," Jacob said, though maybe not. Maybe it was just easier to contemplate how their boat was leaking than to consider how many different ways Morgan was going to attempt to kill him in the next five minutes.

"Positively," Finn said, "we're in your house and he's not."

"I don't suppose he's going to calm down the longer he's out there," Jacob said.

Suddenly the doorknob rattled, and they both jumped back.

"I know you're in there," Morgan yelled. "Come out and face me like a man." The doorknob rattled again. "Or I'm coming in."

"You didn't lock the door?" Finn looked worried at that. "Maybe yeah, if we could wait him out, he'll get tired. Or wet. Or cold. Or just give up."

Jacob shot him a look. "This is Morgan Reynolds we're talking about here. Does he do those things? Or the better question is, does he give a shit about those things?"

Finn's groan of resignation was answer enough.

Re-gripping his hockey stick and taking a step back, pushing Finn behind him, he said a mental prayer that he wouldn't get fucked up today, and opened the door.

Morgan immediately shoved a foot between the door and the doorjamb.

"What the actual fuck," he spit out as Jacob held out his stick, holding him at its length.

"That's far enough," Jacob warned as Morgan hesitated on the threshold.

Jacob had seen Morgan angry plenty of times, but he'd never seen him like this.

Then he must've seen Finn behind Jacob, and his face grew even darker.

"I thought you might be here," Morgan said to him, but suddenly he didn't sound pissed at all, only upset and really, really tired.

"Yeah, I'm here," Finn said.

Jacob sighed, trying not to shiver in the cold early morning air. "Come on," he said to Morgan, "you can come in, if you promise to keep your fists to yourself."

Morgan didn't look like he wanted to promise that, at all, but he finally nodded, pulling the door shut behind him.

Then he saw how Finn was dressed—or how he wasn't—and he went dull, brick red. "I should—I should go—I shouldn't be here."

"Why?" Finn said.

"Yeah, you woke us up at ass o'clock, dragged us out of bed, you might as well yell at us now," Jacob said dryly. "You want coffee?"

"I want coffee," Finn announced and tucked himself under Jacob's arm, hand stroking Jacob's back as it curled around his waist.

Morgan made a horrible noise behind them as they walked into the kitchen.

"Are you trying to get me killed?" Jacob muttered under his breath.

But Finn only batted his eyelashes at him innocently and said, "He's got to get used to the idea. For better or worse."

"It's gonna be worse," Jacob predicted.

Sure enough, Morgan hesitated in the entry to the kitchen, glaring at where Finn remained attached to Jacob's hip, like they'd been glued together.

"At least," Jacob hissed, "go put some clothes on. Aren't you cold? I think he's got the idea. You were naked—or mostly—naked in my bed."

"Yes," Morgan said in a clipped voice. "'Cause on top of being dumb enough to do this, you should catch pneumonia too, only to prove some stupid point to me."

"It's not stupid," Finn argued.

But Jacob shot him another look and Finn finally nodded. "Fine."

"And bring me a shirt, too, while you're at it," Jacob said, even though he probably didn't need one. The house, once they were out of the open doorway, was warm enough. Was he trying to push Morgan's buttons, too, just a little, by letting him know that Finn knew exactly where his shirts were?

Sure, he might be retired, but he was still a hockey player.

That would never change.

"As long as you two keep your promise. No blood," Finn reminded both of them.

Jacob nodded easily—though if Morgan attacked him, he would defend himself. But finally Morgan nodded too, very reluctantly.

"Alright, baby," Finn said to Jacob as he stepped out of the room.

Jacob braced himself in front of the coffee maker. Ready to punch back if he had to.

"You fucking took advantage of him," Morgan said, hitting Jacob square in the face without touching him at all.

Jacob winced. "No," he said, but he could hear the uncertainty in his voice. He *knew* he hadn't, that he'd done everything in his power to *not* take advantage of Finn, but right now, with Morgan's eyes boring into him accusatorially, it was hard to remember that.

He pressed the button on the coffee maker and turned around. "I know you aren't going to believe me—"

"What, are you going to try to work me around again? Convince me that you being with Finn is somehow good for his hockey? That I should want it too?" Morgan shook his head like he was trying to clear it. "No fucking way. You're not good enough to lick his shoes."

"Probably not," Jacob agreed. "But you're going to have to convince him of that."

Morgan made an angry noise in the back of his throat.

A second later, Finn was back, dressed in loose sweatpants and an old, worn tank scooped low under the armpits. He tossed Jacob a T-shirt, who caught it and shrugged it on.

"Oh good, you didn't kill each other," Finn said. He leaned against the counter, opposite his father, and crossed his arms. Jacob told himself he was happy—relieved, even—that Finn had stopped trying to pack on the PDA to freak his dad out, but it had had the accidental effect of making him feel like they were a team.

Like they were in this together.

"You told me no blood," Morgan muttered. "Even though he deserves it!" He shoved a thumb towards Jacob.

"He does not," Finn said flatly.

"But—"

"No. You've said plenty," Finn said. "Your feelings have been clear, for . . .I don't know . . .the last twenty-plus years?"

"We didn't play together that long," Jacob muttered under his breath. He wasn't *that* old, okay?

"Why does that matter?" Finn asked, forehead creasing with confusion.

"It matters because—"

"Because he doesn't want you to think he's too old. That he's as old as he actually is," Morgan interrupted.

Ugh.

"Jacob is thirty-five. I know exactly how old he is," Finn said, rolling his eyes.

"Great," Jacob said weakly.

"It's not fucking great," Morgan argued. "It's disgusting."

"No, it's not," Finn said. He didn't sound angry even. Frustrated maybe, and a little annoyed, but no more annoyed than if Jacob's landscapers had woken them up at seven a.m. the day after Christmas.

"I'm going to add—"

"Nobody wants to hear what *you* have to say," Morgan muttered.

"I'm going to add," Jacob continued again, raising his voice, "that not only is it *not* disgusting, it's also not any of your business what Finn does and who he does it with."

"Bullshit," Morgan said bluntly.

"Please, for the love of fucking God, do not say because he's your son," Jacob said. Now *he* was getting angry, even though, honestly, so far none of Morgan's reaction had been much of a surprise. In fact, the only shocking part of all of this so far was that Jacob's jaw was currently intact.

But he was pissed. Pissed that Morgan was pissed, even though he and Finn had both expected it to go this way.

Did Morgan really think Finn was some stupid idiot incapable of mature decisions who only thought with his dick?

Morgan made a rough noise in his throat, and shit, he'd said that out loud, hadn't he? Out loud and now Morgan might actually kick his ass.

Or at least Morgan might *try*.

"Dad," Finn said, clearly trying to play peacemaker. Except then he added, "Jacob's right."

"Oh yes, well, of course you'd think that. Course you'd think this is a good idea. That *he's* a good idea."

"He's not a bad one," Finn said steadily.

"Wait. *Wait*." Morgan suddenly grimaced. "He's the guy, isn't he? The guy who wouldn't date you, that you convinced to date you. With the Burberry!"

Jacob turned to the cupboard and pulled out the biggest mug he owned. If the conversation was going down this particular rabbit hole, he needed coffee. A lot of fucking coffee.

"Yes," Finn said bluntly, with apparently no concept of softening the news. "And remember how you told me to go get him? To not let him get away if I wanted him? Well, I didn't. I got him."

"But…but…*but*…" Morgan spluttered. "You didn't tell me it was Jacob fucking Braun."

"Yes, I did. I told you he was older than I was. I told you he was interested in charity work. I told you he was a good guy. Actually…" Finn paused, an unholy grin sneaking across his face. "I think *you* actually told me he was a good guy."

"I didn't mean it." Morgan looked like he wanted to sink through the floor.

Jacob pulled out a second mug and poured coffee for Finn.

"But you did. You told me that his hesitation meant he cared about me. That he wanted to do right by me." Finn smiled at Jacob as he handed him the mug. "And you were right."

"He is," Jacob agreed.

"I can't…you *can't*," Morgan said, looking angry enough now that Jacob wanted to lean in and remind Finn that they didn't need to make this any worse than it already was. Maybe he should be laying off the hard truths for the next little bit.

But Finn clearly didn't want to. Finn wanted to go for the jugular.

"You can say that all day long," Finn said calmly, sipping his coffee, "but it doesn't mean anything. I already did, and I'm going to do it again. And I'm not going to stop. Not anytime soon."

Morgan went red and then white.

Like father, like son, Jacob realized.

"I can't be here anymore, listening to this fucking garbage," Morgan ground out and stalked off, slamming the door behind him so hard the whole house shuddered.

"Well, that could've gone better," Finn said, but he didn't look upset. Not particularly, anyway.

He looked . . .resigned. Accepting. But also . . .*free*.

And it occurred to Jacob then that they were. The worst person to tell had just been told—or however he'd found out. And yes, Morgan was pissed, but it wasn't like he was going to get *more* pissed.

"Could've gone worse, too," Jacob said. "I could have two black eyes right now."

"He wouldn't have hit you." Finn sounded annoyingly sure of that particular fact.

"At least one of us believes that," Jacob muttered morosely.

"I wonder how he found out," Finn said, this time actually sounding interested. Probably because he wasn't currently fending off a furious Morgan.

"You said your guys—Elliott and Mal and Ramsey—they wouldn't tell anyone." Jacob made sure to remove as much judgment from his voice as possible. He trusted Finn, and he knew Finn trusted his teammates, and the last thing Jacob wanted was for Finn to believe he was wrong.

"They wouldn't," Finn said. "Who else knew?"

"The valet at Andina?"

Finn laughed. "Yes, his first act after licking his wounds of rejection was to call my father, with his extremely well-protected phone number, and tattle on me."

"You should be a lot more upset about this," Jacob said. "He was *pissed*."

"Yeah. I guess. More though because I think he believes that he should be. Frankly," and Finn was smiling now, "I'm just relieved it's over."

"It could get worse," Jacob pointed out. He didn't want to be the Debbie Downer here, but this was Morgan they were talking about.

Finn shook his head. "No. His heart wasn't in it. You couldn't tell?"

Now that Jacob looked back, compared the fire of Morgan today to the fire of years prior, he could see what Finn was saying. He'd been angry, for sure, but also just going through the motions.

"Yeah, I can see it," Jacob agreed. Hesitated. This wasn't his place to say, but Finn should know. "Retirement isn't easy, you know? I'm honest-ish about how I struggle with it. But Morgan?"

"Naturally he'd pretend he was fine," Finn said, sighing.

"Might be why he's in town. Besides of course wanting to see you," Jacob said.

"Of course," Finn teased, elbowing Jacob gently in the ribs.

"Hey, I know it's still early . . ." They'd intended to have a late, lazy morning. Breakfast and then getting to training whenever it happened.

"I'm up, and you're up," Finn said shrugging. "You want breakfast?"

"Sounds good," Jacob said, kissing the side of his head. "Grab the eggs, okay?"

Jacob was entering some new wine he'd just had shipped to his wine inventory app when the phone rang.

It was two days after the holiday, and despite the rude awakening on the day after Christmas, Morgan had been suspiciously silent.

Jacob had texted Finn this morning, asking if he'd heard from his dad, and Finn had sent a quick reply of **No.** Then a longer message a minute later. **No, and I don't know whether to be pissed or relieved. Or hurt, I guess.**

He hated it, because he cared so much for Finn. *Loved him,* actually, and even though he'd made the *no blood* promise twice now, he wanted to break it because surely Morgan hurting Finn made that promise obsolete.

Then Finn had sent a third message. **Doesn't change the no blood rule, no matter how much you want it to.**

Damn it. It sucked how well Finn knew him. Well, sucked and was also totally fucking great. Jacob decided the latter won out over the former, every time.

Okay. How'd you guess?

Finn texted back. **Silent too long. Don't worry, this is just a reprieve. I'm sure my dad's thinking of some new, fresh hell.**

And here it was, now, when Jacob answered the phone.

Unlike the resignation of this morning's texts, Finn sounded nearly frantic.

"Jacob?" Finn said.

"Yeah, what's going on? Are you okay?" Jacob told himself to stay calm; that Finn was clearly upset enough for the two of them.

"I'm fine. I'm not the problem. I just got a call from a bar over by 23rd. Apparently Morgan's drunk. Really fucking drunk, and they want me to come get him, but I can't. I've got an optional skate I told Coach I'd be at, and I really don't want to skip it."

"Can't they pour him into a cab or an Uber or something?"

"He won't go. And he's my dad." Finn sounded utterly frustrated. "So they're not going to force it on him, right?"

Right. Because Morgan was enough of an asshole on a good day to decide to take a swing. And because he was also Morgan fucking Reynolds.

"It's three in the afternoon," Jacob said, glancing down at his watch. "He got drunk at three in the afternoon?"

"Your guess is as good as mine," Finn said with resignation.

"This isn't . . .he hasn't done this before, has he?" Had Morgan been hiding an addiction? Jacob swore he would've been able to tell—they'd spent enough time with him recently that if he wasn't sharp, wasn't in charge of all his faculties, Jacob would've picked up on it right away.

But actually, Morgan had seemed *sharper* than usual.

"No," Finn said. "I'll give you two guesses why today and the first one doesn't count." He sighed heavily.

"Finding out about us," Jacob said.

"Yep. I know . . .I know it's asking a lot. But . . .can you go get him? He might take a swing at you, too, but you know how to deal with him."

He always had.

Jacob just really, really didn't want to. But he also really, *really* didn't want to ignore that pleading tone in Finn's voice. They'd done this—*he'd* done this, with his eyes wide open to the possible consequences—and now they were here, and it seemed unfair to ignore them just because Morgan was a handful and a half.

"Okay," Jacob said. Paused. "What about the no blood rule?"

Finn groaned in the back of his throat. "If he takes a swing first, you're free to defend yourself. I'm not gonna make you a martyr here. Besides . . .I like your face. A whole lot."

"I like yours, too," Jacob said. *I love it, in fact.*

"Good." Finn sounded relieved, and that was all the payment Jacob needed to do this probably awful thing. "Text me when you drop him off at his place, okay? I'll probably be on the ice, but I'll get it when I'm done."

"Yep," Jacob said. "What bar is it?"

Finn recited him the address, and ten minutes later, he was parking around the corner from the nondescript squat brick building. It wasn't the swanky, A-list type of place that he knew Morgan liked to frequent. In fact, it looked downright dive-ish.

When he pulled the door open, Morgan was at the bar, the only person in the bar in fact, laughing uproariously at something the young female bartender had said to him. She was short, at least a foot shorter than Morgan, even with him perched precariously on a stool, and had spiked lavender hair, a nose ring and a whole chain of bright pink studs running up each ear.

If she recognized Jacob, she didn't show it. She only looked relieved as he walked in. Clearly, whether she knew he was Jacob Braun or not, she had correctly guessed that he was here to collect Morgan.

"Finally," she said, half-groaning, half-laughing under her breath. "Morgan, someone's here for you."

Jacob braced as Morgan turned around.

He was definitely as drunk as promised, and the booze did nothing to obscure or temper the anger that spilled out of him when he saw Jacob.

"What the fuck are *you* doing here? Where's Finn?"

"You're welcome for coming down here to save this poor woman from your inebriated and pathetic attempts at flirting," Jacob said, bracing himself again.

"It's alright, I'm a lesbian," she said, shooting Morgan a fond but *I'm-over-it* look. "Plus," she added, her mouth quirking up, "he's old. Tips well though."

Morgan made an outraged noise. Jacob wasn't sure if it was *his* comment Morgan was just now reacting to, the words finally filtering through all the booze he'd drunk, or that the bartender had called him old.

Well, it was his turn. Two days ago, Morgan had called Jacob old half a dozen different ways, each one less complimentary than the last.

"Come on," Jacob said, approaching Morgan more carefully now as he got closer. He didn't want to spook him or maybe make him decide he'd been saving up all his punches for this one golden opportunity.

"Where's Finn?" Morgan repeated somewhat belligerently, setting his jaw.

Jacob almost said, *I know it's strange but your son has other, better things to do than pick your drunk ass up.* But he didn't, because he liked the bartender, and he didn't want to cause more trouble for her.

"Practice," Jacob said, because that was both the truth and the one thing that might pacify Morgan about Jacob's presence.

Morgan turned back towards the bartender.

Jacob sighed as he skirted around the side, giving Morgan a three-stool berth.

He tapped his glass and the bartender shot him a look, then shook her head. "You're done here," Jacob said firmly. "Come on, let's go and leave this poor lady alone."

"She's not poor now," Morgan muttered. He looked up, met the bartender's eyes. "A hundred bucks a shot," he said. "If you keep them coming."

She looked unimpressed.

"I've got booze at my place," Jacob said, deciding that maybe for once in his whole life, the carrot might work better for Morgan than the stick.

"I don't want your booze," Morgan sniffed.

"If you want booze, it's gonna be mine," Jacob said.

"Ugh, you're such a fucking boy scout, aren't you?" Morgan sneered.

"I thought we established two days ago that I'm not."

Morgan's face went white, and that was the only warning Jacob got before he swung a fist at him.

As a goalie, Jacob hadn't been in that many fights, but he knew how to defend himself. He also knew how to duck, especially when Morgan was about four times slower than he normally was.

Jacob dodged the punch and then wrapped his arms around Morgan's middle.

Morgan kicked out, but Jacob told him warningly, "I *will* kick your ass, and I promised Finn no blood. I'd rather not break that promise."

Surprisingly, Morgan went still. Jacob had been sure he'd have to put him in some complicated headlock to get him to stop fighting him, but he went slack, so suddenly Jacob almost dropped him.

"You're gonna tell him, aren't you?" Morgan's voice was plaintive.

"About?"

"Me punching you."

"Good try, but you didn't connect," Jacob said, really trying to hide his amusement. "No blood, no foul. I think we can keep that moment of shame between us."

Morgan sighed heavily and struggled out of Jacob's grasp.

Jacob made a warning noise, but Morgan just shrugged, all the fight gone out of him as he slumped against the bar.

"What does he owe you?" Jacob asked.

The bartender looked over at the pair of them and reported what was left on his tab. He gave her props because it didn't seem inflated, despite the fact that she had to know by now that Morgan was rich.

Morgan squawked as Jacob reached over and pulled his wallet out of the back pocket of his jeans.

He pulled a couple hundred dollar bills out and set them on the bar. It more than covered the tab—with a *lot* to spare.

"It's your own fault," Jacob said unrepentantly as he tossed the wallet back to Morgan, who barely caught it. "Now come on, let's go."

"To your house? With the booze?" Morgan asked, still sounding disgruntled but to Jacob's surprise, he did follow him, a little unsteadily, out of the bar and down the street to his car.

He paused as Jacob opened the driver's side door.

"Am I—" Morgan bit off a swear word. "Am I not gonna want to sit in this seat?"

Jacob rolled his eyes. "Don't worry, I didn't defile your son there. I've got a whole house for that."

Morgan didn't look exactly pleased by this but at least he got in, and while he was, Jacob muttered under his breath, "Just don't go into the backseat."

But thankfully Morgan missed that in his struggle to get the seat belt on.

He was quiet on the drive to Jacob's house.

He hadn't really wanted to bring him here—the last time Morgan had been here, he'd been spitting venom and pissed as hell. But he didn't want to drop him at his apartment because no doubt he'd just find another place to pickle his liver.

At least if he was with Jacob, Jacob could keep an eye on him.

Morgan flopped down bonelessly onto the sofa in the living room.

Jacob was glad he hadn't asked about whether he'd defiled Finn there, because he absolutely one-hundred-percent had. A very mutual, very pleasurable defiling.

Then, of course Morgan opened his mouth.

"You promised me another drink," he said mulishly.

He had, but only to get him to leave. "You don't need any-more, you've had plenty."

"But—"

"You really want Finn to come get you and find you obliter-ated on my couch?"

Morgan grimaced, and that reminded Jacob to pull his phone out and send a reassuring text to Finn. **Have Morgan at my place. No blood.**

He slipped his phone back into his pocket.

"I can hold my booze," Morgan argued.

"And this is just a great example of that skill set?" Jacob questioned.

Morgan looked even more annoyed than before. "So you're a liar now, too."

Jacob decided if Morgan was going to antagonize him, he could dish it right back. He walked into the kitchen, grabbed two bottles of water from the little fridge under the counter where he stored all his drinks and handed one to Morgan who made a face at it.

"You wanted a beverage, I brought you a beverage," Jacob said. "Drink it, it might help you feel less like death later."

Morgan made another face, but he did open it and take a sip.

"Not likely," Morgan muttered darkly. "Unless water is gonna erase my memory."

He wasn't stupid enough to ask what he wanted removed from his memory; Jacob already knew.

"No," Jacob agreed.

Morgan stood abruptly and began to wander around the living room. First he looked at some books stacked in the built-ins, and a few pictures Jacob had lying around—one of him with the Cup, several others with the Vezina trophies he'd won—and then he wandered over by the wine.

Tensing, Jacob watched as he silently absorbed the information on several of the labels. Wondering if he was going to decide to forcibly take that drink and Jacob would have to physically wrestle him away from it.

Just when Jacob was sure he'd have to, and hoping that whatever bottle Morgan plucked from the rack wasn't valuable because it was extremely likely to get broken in the ensuing scuffle, Morgan said without even turning around, "Why are you fucking my son?"

Jacob froze and felt his face flush bright, brick red.

Of course, that was when Morgan chose to look right at him, pinning him in place with a sharp look that he shouldn't have been able to drag out, not as drunk as he was.

"I . . . uh . . ." Jacob rubbed his neck, viscerally uncomfortable in a way he hadn't been in a very long time. Maybe ever.

"'Cause he's young and hot, right?" Morgan pushed.

Shame and awkwardness crawled up Jacob's spine. "Well, he *is* both of those things."

Morgan shot him a disgusted look.

"Not just because of that, of those things, in fact . . ." Jacob sighed. "I'd feel easier about it if he was a few years older, but . . ."

"Would you?" Morgan demanded.

God, Finn wouldn't be here for awhile yet. An hour at least, probably longer. Could he pour Morgan into an Uber and send him off God knew where? He *could*, but guilt would dog him after. Morgan was a grown ass man, and he could take care of himself. He'd been doing it for a long fucking time. Why then, did he suddenly feel responsible for the asshole?

Jacob swore under his breath and crossed over to the wet bar set into the built-ins. Pulled out a bottle of whiskey. Not usually his thing, but it was Morgan's, and well, if they were gonna talk about this, he was going to need some liquid courage. More than a glass of wine could give him.

He poured an inch or so into two glasses and handed one to Morgan, who just looked unimpressed.

Jacob itched under his collar. It would be easier to break his promise and punch Morgan in the face for pushing on this.

"I think it's a pretty damn good plan, don't you?" Morgan said conversationally, taking a long drink of his whiskey. "Recapture the youth you miss, the hockey you miss, the *life* you miss."

"No," Jacob said.

But Morgan was on a roll. "You can't live through him. You'll *ruin* him, drag him down, suck him dry, when he should be *free*."

Now it was Jacob's fist that was itching.

"No," he repeated.

Morgan didn't continue, just shot him a knowing look and went back to drinking his whiskey.

"He *is* free. He's . . .freer than he's ever been," Jacob said quietly. *He's happy. We're happy together.*

For once, Morgan didn't argue.

Jacob finished his whiskey and got up and refilled both their glasses, all in silence.

He told himself it was the whiskey that unstuck his tongue, but the truth was he'd been wondering since Morgan had confessed the truth last week.

"That why you did it?"

Morgan glanced over. "Did what?"

"Hooked up with a player." It was only a guess, but the way Morgan's fingers clenched white around the glass told him he'd hit the nail on the head.

"Never said I did," Morgan said, but his voice wavered on the last word.

"Yeah, okay." Jacob wasn't convinced.

"We're not talking about this," Morgan announced, pulling himself up and walking over towards the wet bar and the bottle, still unsteady on his feet.

"Good," Jacob said. "Does that mean you're gonna stop being pissed at Finn for me?" He didn't ask Morgan if he would ever stop being pissed at *him*. That was way too much to ask for, and besides, he'd lived with Morgan's bitter anger for years. He could tolerate it.

"No," Morgan muttered. "I just don't want him to get his hopes up. To think this is something it's not. That you're something you're not."

"And what's that?"

Morgan turned and leaned back against the counter. "He's smart, you know? Bright. He could do so much."

"Believe me, I know that," Jacob said dryly. "And you didn't answer the question."

"You're gonna lean on him, fuck him, use him, trying to remember something you lost, and then when you realize it's not gonna work, that there's no going back, you're gonna ditch him, and it's gonna . . ." Morgan looked away.

Jacob itched again. He wasn't happy about Morgan's assessment of the situation, but it was more than that. He wanted to know what had made Morgan so bitter.

Who had made him so bitter?

"I'm definitely not leaning on him, and while I *am* fucking him—" Morgan glared at him with a dark, disgusted look, but *hey,* he was just using Morgan's terminology here. "I'm not ever going to use him. I'm not trying to recapture my youth, and I'm certainly not gonna *ditch* him after. It's not about that."

Morgan had the nerve to look surprised. "No?"

"*No.* I care about him, I like him so much, I even—" Jacob stopped abruptly, because he might be new to relationships but he did know the first time he said out loud that he loved Finn shouldn't be to his *father.*

"It's not just sex," Jacob continued.

"Well, I sure fucking hope not," Morgan said.

It was Jacob's turn to be astonished. "What? You weren't pissed that it was *me,* you were pissed I was just going to . . .what . . .fuck and leave him?"

"Stop saying it." Morgan's voice was sullen, matching his expression. He tipped the glass back, finishing his drink.

"Hey, you said it first," Jacob reminded him.

"I'm not saying I'm *happy* it was you. Finn knows how . . .how I feel about it, about you." Morgan cleared his throat. "I don't want to fucking look at you across the breakfast table, every day, but if he really liked you—if you really liked him . . ."

Jacob was floored.

"I can't fucking believe that you thought it was just sex, and *that's* why you were pissed." Jacob heard the amazement in his own voice.

"Hey, you know how hockey players can be," Morgan said darkly. "Would you want one of us around *your* son?"

Probably not.

"You're such a dick," Jacob muttered, grateful and annoyed at the same time. "You should have been talking to *Finn* about this."

"Too mad. Too confused. Too something."

"So you decided to drink half a bar. Yeah, that tracks."

Morgan glared.

"Well, I'm happy I could explain it to you," Jacob said, trying not to smile. Trying not to let the relief he felt show on his face.

"Asshole," Morgan mumbled under his breath.

His phone dinged then and he pulled it out of his pocket.

It was Finn, saying he'd be there in ten minutes.

"When you sober up," Jacob said, "you're gonna explain *all* this to him."

"Not now?" Morgan asked, raising an eyebrow.

"Fuck no. You're a mess. He's going to be understandably pissed about that first. Maybe give him a minute to get over that, first." Jacob shot him a triumphant grin. "Besides, you're not very good with your words even when you're sober. Want to put your best foot forward, you know?"

Morgan pointed at him, but Jacob could see the smile twisting the corner of his mouth. "Fuck you."

"Fuck you right back," Jacob said.

CHAPTER 18

Finn dropped his bag in the locker room and looked around. Jacob had said he'd meet him today for extra ice time but he didn't seem to be here yet. He was about to pull out his phone to ask how far away he was when a noise at the doorway made him look up.

It was not Jacob, but his dad, looking sheepish and almost a little ashamed.

"What are you doing here?" Finn asked, trying to keep his voice level.

"To see you," Morgan said, walking into the locker room the same way he always had—like he belonged there. Like he *owned* it.

They'd barely talked when he'd picked up his dad, drunk, from Jacob's house two days ago.

Jacob had leaned in and kissed him briefly, and Finn had figured out pretty quickly *he* wasn't sober either. At least he wasn't as drunk as Morgan, but still. "Take it a little easy on him, okay?" Jacob had murmured, unexpectedly.

Finn hadn't been easy on him or hard or anything. How could he have, when his dad wasn't talking to him still, at least about anything important? They'd barely exchanged half a dozen sentences before he'd dropped his dad off at his condo to sleep it off.

When Finn had asked Jacob what they'd talked about, he'd only shaken his head and gave a vague answer about clearing up some misconceptions.

And now Morgan was here.

Finn didn't think Jacob had sold him out, but . . .

"Did Jacob tell you I'd be here?"

Morgan looked confused. "Gavin sent me the rink schedule. I like to . . ." He cleared his throat. "Thought maybe you wouldn't mind sharing the ice with an old man."

"You're not old," Finn retorted. "Old men don't get day drunk."

Morgan winced. "They feel it the next day, though."

"Oh, is that why you've been so quiet?" Finn began to dig his equipment out of his bag.

"Partly yeah. And partly . . .Braun told me to get my head on straight before I talked to you, and as much as I hate to admit it, he was right."

Morgan took a seat next to Finn, a few stalls away, but close enough.

"So what, you're listening to Jacob's advice, now? I thought he was what . . .*a backstabbing pedophile?* Isn't that what you called him?"

"I was . . .surprised. Upset." Morgan had the nerve to look ashamed, and Finn almost felt guilty for bringing it up. He *knew* his dad had a temper.

"Gee, I had no clue," Finn retorted.

"Finn," Morgan admonished. "I won't keep you. I know you're here to skate. But I wanted to clear the air."

"Okay." Finn sat and waited.

"You like him."

Finn supposed he shouldn't be surprised that his dad would start with a blunt statement like that, and not, say . . .*an apology for being a complete fucking asshole*.

"Yeah," Finn said.

"I knew you did, before I even knew who he was. And then I found out who he was, and . . ." Morgan made a face. "I went insane. When Monica called me and told me she'd heard it from Braun's PR woman's assistant, I was sure it wasn't true, but then I showed up at his house, and there you were, and *ugh*, I lost my mind a little."

Finn raised an eyebrow. "A little?"

"Fair. That's fair." Morgan hesitated. "I fucked this up a lot. A whole lot. But more than me being angry that it was *Braun* you were all starry-eyed over, it was . . .I was worried about you. I worried what he was doing to you. What he was going to do with you."

"Dad, I know how to practice safe sex."

Morgan looked like he wanted to drop through the floor and die. Now they were *almost* even for all the things Morgan had yelled the other day. "Of course you do, you're smart. So smart. Smarter than me, for sure."

"Then what the fuck were you so angry about?"

"I thought he was using you! I thought he was trying to . . .I don't know . . .find his youth again. Pretend that he wasn't old and retired. Use you up for everything you are that's bright and .

. .wonderful. And I couldn't stand that. I couldn't stand anyone doing that to you, but that it was Braun?" Morgan shook his head. "I couldn't handle it. And I'm sorry about that, but not that sorry."

"Not that sorry?"

Morgan shrugged, looking a little embarrassed. "I know you're all grown-up now. Self-sufficient. You take care of yourself. You always have. But forgive an old man for still worrying about you. For loving you." He looked down at the ground, at his shoes, and Finn felt his throat tighten.

"You didn't have to call him those things, you know," Finn said quietly. "He's a good man. He . . .it was exactly what you said, why he didn't want to make a move on me. He liked me too much. Didn't want to take advantage or force me into something I wasn't ready for."

"I know." Morgan looked like he was admitting this only under duress.

"I really care about him. I . . ." Finn moistened his lips. Realizing suddenly what he'd nearly said.

"You love him," Morgan said with resignation.

Finn felt like he'd just been plugged into the nearest socket and lit up inside. Why hadn't he noticed this before? Because it hadn't felt any different than before—like a slow, gradual, *inevitable* slide into love. "I think so, yeah. *Yeah.*"

Morgan cleared his throat. "I . . .I want to say I'm angry about that, but I'm not. At all. He's . . .well, he'll do right by you, I think. He *is* doing right by you. You're playing so great, Finn. Like . . ." He hesitated, and Finn braced himself for what was coming next. An old habit that seemed sometimes like it was impossible to break. "Like for the first time you don't give a shit what anyone thinks about you. Only what you think of yourself. I wanted you to find that for so long, and I didn't think you could, I was worried you never would, and that's why I pushed so hard and made everything terrible—"

"You didn't make everything terrible." Okay, not *everything*, anyway. Finn could see their history with clearer eyes than he ever had before. Maybe Morgan had been overenthusiastic, but he'd been oversensitive. They'd fed into the worst of each other's pain.

Morgan looked at him with hope in his eyes. "No?"

Finn stood and pulled his dad into a tight hug. "No. I kind of made them terrible, too."

Morgan gripped him tight and Finn thought the lump in his throat couldn't expand any farther, but it did.

"Let's not make them terrible anymore," he murmured into Finn's shoulder, and he could only nod, words lost in his tight throat.

They broke apart.

Morgan surreptitiously wiped his eyes and Finn could only laugh.

"I should . . . uh . . ." Morgan gestured towards the door.

Suddenly, it was very obvious what he should say. Something he couldn't even have imagined three months ago but now seemed like the most natural thing in the world.

"Hey, I thought you said you wanted to share the ice?" Finn asked. "Come skate with me."

Finn was almost done getting dressed before finishing his warmups on the ice when Jacob showed up.

"Sorry," he said, dropping his bag down on the bench. "I got caught up with chatting with Neal about the podcast, and I totally lost track of time."

"Yeah?" Finn asked. "It's going well?"

"I knew I would like him, but I really like him," Jacob said.

Finn grinned. "Should I be jealous?"

"Not at all." Jacob glanced over and the look in his eyes was as good as a kiss. "You almost ready?"

How did he not know he loved Jacob? It was so obvious now, now that he was looking for it. Now that he had acknowledged it was true.

"Yeah," Finn said. He opened his mouth to tell Jacob that his dad was here and that he was going to skate with them, but before he could, Morgan walked through the door from the bathroom, dressed for the ice.

Jacob raised an eyebrow. "What did I miss?"

"Everything, as usual," Morgan retorted.

"Do I need to repeat the rule?" Finn threatened. Morgan looked ashamed—slightly, anyway. He turned to Jacob and said, "He's going to skate with us."

"Yeah? You want that?" Jacob asked.

Morgan started to splutter something, but Jacob just held a hand up and shot him a warning look.

"I'm asking Finn," he said and turned back to Finn.

Finn moistened his lips. It had felt so natural to invite his dad onto the ice. He hadn't even stopped to think if he wanted it, but now that he was considering it, of course he did.

"Yeah," Finn said.

Jacob's eyes glowed with pride and affection. "Good. Okay." He leaned in and broke the other, more unspoken, no-PDA-at-the-rink rule and pressed a quick kiss to the side of Finn's head. "I'd better get ready then."

Morgan picked up his stick and tapped it on the floor, clearly impatient. "Cute that you think it'll make a difference."

Finn braced for Jacob's frustration to boil over, but he only laughed.

"Yeah, you comin' for me?" Jacob questioned.

Morgan nodded sharply and turned to head towards the ice.

"Hey, I want you to work on some of those specific movement drills first," Jacob said, as he pulled his skates out of his bag. "If you're okay with that."

"Yeah. After I finish my warmups." He stood, stretching a little. "See you out there?"

"Hey," Jacob said, and he turned back. "You're really okay with him being here, aren't you?"

"Yeah. We . . .uh . . .talked some, before you came." Finn paused. "It was good. It was actually *great*."

Jacob's smile was so bright. "Yeah?"

Finn nudged him with his glove. "I know you gave him advice, and he actually used it."

"Nobody is more surprised than me," Jacob said, still grinning and actually *not* looking all that surprised.

"I know you thought—and *I* thought—it was all him, and it was definitely *some* him, but it was me too, wasn't it?"

Jacob's gaze was so warm. "Maybe, yeah. A little. Which nobody could blame you for, by the way. You had—*have*—a lot of pressure on your shoulders. Some he's put there, sure. Some *you've* put there, and some that's just on there 'cause of who he is. What your last name is."

"Yeah. But it's just me out there, isn't it? Just me."

"Just you," Jacob agreed easily.

It felt like everything was slotting into place. His play and his confidence. His relationship with his dad, which he'd never thought would be *better* after he'd found out about him and Jacob, but miraculously was. And then there was Jacob, and Finn's heart practically fucking expanded, just thinking of how good it was with him.

How he wanted it to be good with him forever. How he wanted to love him forever.

"Couldn't have done it without you," Finn said, feeling that lump in his throat grow again.

Jacob's look was affectionate but chiding. "Yeah, you could've," he said. "But it was absolutely my honor to be there. To remind you of what you're capable of."

"Still. Thanks." Finn wanted to tell him he loved him so badly it was right there on the tip of his tongue but what if it was too early?

What if it freaked Jacob out? He didn't look freaked out, particularly, but that could change so easily.

"Of course." Jacob tapped his glove. "Now go out there and make me proud."

You'll get there, Finn promised and made himself walk off.

When he got to the ice, his dad was already skating in slow, sweeping circles, his stick leaning against the far boards.

Morgan nodded at him, and Finn went to the opposite end and, after he finished his stretches, began to work through some of the specific movement drills that he and Jacob had been working on. Drills to make his reaction time quicker, to help him move faster and more fluidly from position to position.

For so long, he'd thought these basic drills were a waste of time. But now, not only did they reassure and ground him, Finn could feel the echo of them in every save he made during a game.

He could hear his dad's stick against the ice, a rhythmic tapping as he took the puck down the ice towards the other net. But as Finn's focus narrowed, even the noise of his dad skating and drilling puck after puck into an empty net began to fade away.

Maybe he was deep in the zone, but Finn *did* notice when Jacob came on the ice. He hadn't put a full set of gear on, but he had his gloves on and his kneepads and a helmet, one of the ones he'd worn playing for Team USA, a bald eagle spreading its wings across one side.

But he didn't come in Finn's direction first. Instead, he skated over to where Morgan was circling the other net.

They were *probably* not going to kill each other, but Finn called out, "Do I need to remind either of you of the rule?"

Jacob pushed his helmet up. Shot him a knowing look, hot even across the ice. "No, we'll behave."

"Speak for yourself," Morgan retorted.

But Finn already knew his dad was full of talk and nothing else, and it wasn't like Jacob couldn't dish it right back.

"Alright," Finn said and went back to his drill, satisfied he'd done his due diligence, and actually, *yes*, trusting that they might not kill each other.

Jacob had noticed as soon as he'd skated onto the ice how deep Finn's focus was, and he was worried him heading in Morgan's direction might be distracting, but he did it anyway.

"How about it?" Morgan said, gesturing with his stick towards the net after Finn had warned them, and to Jacob's relief, had gone right back to his drills.

Jacob raised an eyebrow. "You really wanna go?"

"Just like old times," Morgan said.

"Not *that* old," Jacob reminded him. "I retired two years after you did."

Morgan patted his still-flat stomach. "Best shape of my life," he claimed. Which knowing Morgan was probably true.

"Kept up with you then, and nothing's changed," Jacob said.

Morgan grinned, and to Jacob's surprise, he was smiling right back. And even more than that, Jacob was actually *enjoying* this.

They'd always chirped back and forth, but before, the comments had been sharp as knives. Morgan—and after a time, Jacob, too—had meant them to cut. To slice each other open.

But now, the exchanges felt normal, almost like a routine. Exactly what Jacob had traded back and forth with hundreds of other hockey players over the years. He didn't know why it suddenly hurt less. Maybe because now, finally, they were born out of respect for each other's skill and not lingering resentment or anger.

"Well, get warm then," Morgan said. "Let's see what you've got."

As Jacob finished warming up, he watched out of the corner of his eye as Morgan made sweeping circles around the ice, gaining speed as he went.

Morgan's speed had always been deceptive; he had another gear that nobody imagined existed until he turned it on, and then he was charging so fast it felt impossible to react in time.

He'd be a hair slower now, at forty-one, but he was still Morgan Reynolds.

"You ready?" Morgan asked as Jacob settled himself into the goal, stick in front of him.

"Yeah," Jacob said, nodding. Neither of them was wearing their full set of gear. Morgan didn't even have a helmet on. But they'd played long enough they knew the limitations.

Even six months ago, Jacob never would've agreed to do this, because he wouldn't have necessarily trusted that Morgan, the most competitive person on the fucking planet, *would* follow any kind of limitation. But he'd begun to know the man better, behind the facade, and that had changed everything.

Morgan didn't warn him, but then Jacob hadn't expected that he would.

He just came in hard.

Exactly the way Jacob remembered he always had.

"He's going glove-side," Finn called out from the other side of the ice, and Jacob supposed he couldn't be surprised that Finn was watching.

He'd be watching if he was Finn.

But he didn't actually agree with Finn. How many times had he seen Morgan skate in like this? Too many to count. He didn't always have a tell—that was part of what had made him so damn good—but Jacob tracked his gaze and had a feeling he wasn't going to do anything as simple as going glove-side.

He'd want to be fancy, to be *impressive*. To show off his Morgan goddamn Reynolds skills.

Jacob braced himself, keeping his weight perfectly balanced so he *could* change his mind, but he wasn't surprised in the least when at the last second, instead of shooting the puck, Morgan curved around the back of the net.

Jacob reacted instantly, dropping to his knee pad and sliding his stick around the side of the crease. It wasn't the fastest reaction he'd ever had, but it must have been pretty damn good because Finn catcalled from the other side of the ice.

The puck bounced off Jacob's pad, and Morgan swore, loudly.

"How'd you know I'd go around?" he demanded. He looked mildly perturbed but not burning up from the inside out with anger. Like he had so many times when they'd played each other.

Every time Jacob had denied him a goal, Morgan had always looked ready to kill Jacob. Or maybe worse, turn that anger onto himself.

"Lucky guess," Jacob said, shrugging. "You always want to go so fucking fancy. Remind everyone you're Morgan Reynolds."

Morgan rolled his eyes but plucked another puck from the pile by the boards and started in another round.

They went for maybe ten minutes, taking longer and longer and breaks in between.

Jacob forgot how many shots he deflected, and how many goals Morgan scored on him, but he wasn't really surprised when Morgan pulled up short, ice spraying from his skates, and said, "We're even. Ten and ten."

"Yeah?" Jacob pushed his helmet up and his sweaty hair back. This was as good as the machine back home—or maybe better, actually. Because as good as Morgan's physical skills had always been, it was his conniving mind that was the toughest challenge.

"Yeah." Morgan set his stick against the boards and grabbed his water bottle.

"You wanna call it?" Jacob asked, but he already knew what Morgan was going to say.

Morgan shrugged, and Jacob decided that he wouldn't make him actually utter the words out loud.

"I think that's a good place to leave it," Jacob said. Then he glanced over towards the back of the rink. "Unless you want to give Finn some work."

Morgan had the nerve to look shocked at that. "You're actually gonna let me go against him?"

"Let you? *Let you*?" Jacob laughed. "I'm not his keeper."

"No, just his boyfriend. And his coach."

"He can handle you, if you don't lose your mind," Jacob said.

"Did I do that with you?" Morgan demanded.

"Nope. Which is why I suggested it in the first place," Jacob pointed out dryly.

"Okay. Um. Yeah." Morgan was floundering. Apparently he really hadn't anticipated this.

"Take a break. I know you're old now," Jacob joked, ignoring it when Morgan flipped him off. He skated down to where Finn was finishing up his own drills.

"Hey," Finn said. "Looking sharp out there." His gaze was full of approval and heat. Jacob being good turned him on. Well, that wasn't surprising, because Finn being downright fucking *amazing* turned Jacob on too.

"Thanks," Jacob said. "Hey, you good with your dad taking some shots at you?"

Finn leveled him with a flat stare. "Really?"

"I mean . . ."

"You don't have to ask," Finn said. "Send him over."

Jacob skated back and grabbed his water bottle from the top of the net, watching as Morgan did a few additional sets of stretches.

He would probably regret this but he knew he should say it.

"Hey," he said, lowering his voice and skating over to where Morgan was stretching. "I . . .uh . . .thought you should know. I'm going on a podcast, in a few days. Coming out."

Morgan looked up. "Yeah?"

"I know you told me about you—"

Morgan's face totally closed over. "You can't keep fucking bringing that up."

Jacob had only brought it up *twice*.

"You called me a *pedophile*," Jacob reminded him.

"And? I was pissed."

"I'm just saying, you don't have any room to complain here." Jacob took a short breath. Knowing Morgan wasn't going to take this well but believing he should say it anyway. "I just think you should tell Finn."

"Don't like keeping secrets from him?"

Jacob didn't hold back. Figured that he and Morgan had come to a place where he didn't have to. Not anymore. "About you? Fuck no."

Morgan sighed. Scrubbed a hand over his sweaty face. "I don't want to tell him. I don't want to talk about it. Not at all. Not because of the . . ."

"The queer thing?" Jacob said gently.

Morgan nodded. "It didn't end well. I . . .I didn't want it to end that way. I don't know how else it could've ended, honestly, but, I still didn't like it. I *don't* like it."

It suddenly occurred to Jacob that Morgan Reynolds could fall in love. It should've occurred to him before this. After all, he'd married Finn's mom and had him with her, but he'd never seemed affected by their marriage or frankly by their divorce either.

Not like he was now.

Because that was what he was saying, without saying it, wasn't he? He'd loved this guy. Jacob didn't want to feel sorry for Morgan, but it was kind of impossible not to.

"You don't have to tell Finn any of that."

"He's going to ask," Morgan said bluntly.

"Well, probably. Doesn't mean you have to talk about that part of it."

Morgan actually seemed to consider this for a long moment. "Do you think it's gonna help you to be honest on this podcast?"

Jacob noticed that he didn't specify what it would help. Jacob already knew it; so did Morgan. They finally understood each other. They'd just had to both retire to get there.

"I don't think it's gonna hurt, if that's what you're asking." He'd been so uncertain about doing this, forever, not wanting to make a big deal out of it. This *still* wouldn't be a big deal, but Jacob had begun to understand how hard it had been on him to hide forever, and he never wanted to do it again.

"You don't care about what people are gonna say about you? *Think* about you?" Morgan wondered.

"I never cared what anyone thought or said about me. Even you," Jacob said.

Morgan made a face. "That's so fucking true," he muttered.

"You don't have to tell him. I'm not going to tell him. But I think you should."

"I'll think about it," Morgan said, and Jacob actually thought he would. Shockingly.

"Come on," Jacob said, patting Morgan on the arm. "Let's show Finn what you can do."

"Aren't I supposed to be seeing what *he's* made of?" Morgan questioned.

Jacob grinned. "Oh, what *he's* capable of was never in question. But you're old now."

Morgan spluttered. "You fucking asshole. I *hate* you."

"Yeah, yeah," Jacob said, laughing, and he was pretty damn sure what Morgan meant was actually the opposite.

Finn took a breath in and then let it out slowly, watching as his dad skated towards him.

"You got this," Jacob called out, but Finn didn't look over.

Instead, he kept his gaze glued to where Morgan was coming in hard, his speed still strong even though he was old.

But that would be the first mistake he'd make, if he underestimated how good his dad still was, even three years after retirement.

He'd watched a little of Morgan versus Jacob, on the other side of the rink, mostly because it was impossible not to, with their level of skill on display. They were both so ridiculously good still and still had each other's number.

But watching had given Finn a good refresher course on Morgan's habits.

He liked to skate not just with his body, but with his mind, to outmaneuver the goalie. To turn it into a game of chess, not just a game of hockey.

The first move of Morgan's wouldn't be his last, and Finn needed to prepare for that.

Morgan came in hot, wiggling the puck around on the tape of his stick like he was trying to deflect Finn's attention, but Finn didn't let himself be shook.

He also didn't let himself think of the last time they'd done this—last summer, they'd only done it once, and Finn had ended up breaking his stick afterwards.

Not his finest moment.

But today, he wasn't going to let Morgan get to him.

Maybe his dad was Morgan Reynolds, but he was *Finn Reynolds*.

Morgan streaked around the right of the goal and then circled back, swooping past the dot. Finn nearly went to the ice, sure Morgan would try to flick the puck into the five hole, but he held for a second longer, listening to his instincts, instead of the fear that had always screamed louder, that always screamed that he had to do *something* before someone scored on him. Before an opposing player—or even worse, *his dad*—humiliated him.

But the only person who could humiliate him was *him*.

Finn held for another breathless moment and then, as Morgan changed direction, sliding to the right and shooting the puck high, he lifted his pad and knocked the puck away.

Jacob crowed on the other side of the ice, and there was no denying that felt damn good, but it felt even better when Morgan came to a stop in front of him and lifted his chin.

"Great save," he said.

But it felt even *more* amazing when Finn could respond, "Yeah, I know," and for the first time in a very long time when faced with his dad, *believed* it.

CHAPTER 19

"I HAD NO IDEA they planned podcasts out so thoroughly ahead of time," Finn said, staring at the sheet of questions in his hands.

They were in Jacob's bed—Jacob was hard-pressed these days to not think of it as *theirs*—and already naked. Finn had surprised him with a mind-blowing blowjob on the couch and then Jacob had returned the favor after he'd pulled him to bed. Fingering him nice and slow, dragging the pads of his fingers over his prostate until Finn was squirming and begging for it.

Jacob felt a pulse of heat spike inside him, just thinking of how good it had been.

Of how good Finn looked, propped up against his pillows. How *right*.

Jacob cleared his throat, trying to focus. Finn had agreed to help him with the last of his podcast preparation—he was flying out first thing in the morning and by tomorrow night it would be done—and he *needed* it.

"I don't think they typically do, but this is more . . .uh . . .delicate than the norm," Jacob said.

Finn nodded in understanding. "Okay, let's go over some of these questions. From the top or is there a particular one you want to work on?"

The only question he hadn't worked on yet. Had he been putting it off? Maybe. Okay, *definitely*.

"Uh . . .the last section."

Finn's eyes scanned the page and then he glanced up at Jacob. "This is the coming out question."

Jacob picked at a thread coming loose from the comforter. "Yeah. I . . .uh . . .was saving the best for last?"

"Is that what it is, really?" Finn asked and Jacob wanted to hide his face, but he didn't, because that seemed horribly cowardly and he wasn't a coward.

But geez, how often was Finn going to hold his hand through this?

"I'm going to do it," Jacob said firmly. That was not up for debate. Sophie had found the one way to do this that he could actually stand, and Neal was great—supportive and smart and savvy—and Jacob had learned enough to know that if he did want the focus to be where it was supposed to be, then he had to do this.

But that didn't mean he had to *like* it.

"I didn't think you wouldn't," Finn said quietly. "Do you want to talk about it?"

Did he? No. But he thought he probably should.

"It's not that I care what people think. I don't. I don't care what they say even, even if it's to my face—"

"It wouldn't be," Finn said soothingly, reaching out and gripping his hand. "They wouldn't dare."

"They might," Jacob said. He'd prepared himself for it. "It's not any of those things. It's that they're gonna be talking about me *at all*. I just didn't want to make a big deal out of this. I just wanted to live my life, the way I wanted to live it."

"Like I did." Finn cleared his throat. "I never really 'came out.' I just did whatever the fuck I wanted to. Which was guys." He smiled then, dimples showing, and Jacob had never loved him as much as he did in that moment, because Jacob couldn't help but smile too.

"I can't do that, I get that. I was . . .too much time's gone by with me in the closet, and now the foundation I'm starting . . .I *get* it. But I don't like it."

"You're allowed to be afraid, too, you know?"

Jacob shot Finn a look. "Is that what you think?"

"I think you'd have to be a lot stupider to *not* be afraid at all. It's scary, and it's okay to admit that."

Jacob was floored. He shouldn't have been, but every time he thought he knew how beautiful, inside and out, Finn was, he was surprised again.

"Okay," Jacob admitted softly. "I'm a little afraid, too. Less than I was, but . . ."

"It's fine, it's gonna be okay." Finn squeezed his hand. "I wish I could be there for you."

Finn hadn't been able to swing the trip, because he had class and then practice, but he'd made enough noise about skipping both that Jacob had had to put his foot down. He'd be fine. He'd have Mark and Sophie there, and Neal was on his side, too.

There'd be plenty of support.

"It's okay really. You've been here for the hardest part. The part—" Jacob's voice cracked. "The part I needed you for. 'Cause you're good at this, you know? So supportive. You'd be so good at this."

"Counseling people about to come out? I'll keep that in my back pocket for twenty years from now."

"You should. You're wonderful. Amazing." Jacob was aware he'd lost control of his own mouth, and it was making sounds and forming words maybe it shouldn't. But he couldn't stop it. Not any longer. He pressed a kiss to Finn's head. "Perfect. The most perfect. And I love you."

Finn was completely still for a second, staring at Jacob with his jaw dropped, and then he threw his arms around Jacob and hugged him tightly.

"God," Finn murmured into his ear. "I love you too. So fucking much."

Jacob had hoped, but when he heard Finn, everything inside him settled, wildly happy and painfully content.

"Yeah," Jacob said roughly into Finn's hair. He kissed Finn's perfect shoulder.

Finn pulled back. "I wanted to tell you before, but I didn't want to freak you out, especially not before . . ." He gestured at the sheet of paper that had fallen, forgotten, to the comforter.

It was so thoughtful and so *Finn* Jacob could only kiss him.

The kiss got hot and heavy immediately, Finn's tongue stroking into his mouth and his thigh rubbing alongside Jacob's like he couldn't get close enough.

Jacob buried his hands in Finn's hair and just hung on.

But just when he thought Finn might be edging them closer to round two, he pulled back. "Don't think you're getting off that easily," Finn teased. He resettled himself next to Jacob and grabbed the paper.

"You want me to answer the question *now*?" Jacob glanced down at his mostly hard dick, which had really believed they'd been about to go for round two. "I'm not sure how good I'll be at this now."

But Finn only grinned and patted him on the thigh—a little too close to where he really wanted Finn's touch, and his cock twitched—then said, "You're going to be distracted tomorrow, too. This is good practice."

He cleared his throat and changed to a very formal, officious tone, which didn't sound anything like Neal Fisher, but that was okay. Jacob got it. "Let's talk more about your decision to start a foundation aiming to help LGBTQ kids play sports?"

Jacob had thought about this a lot so it wasn't like it was hard to answer. Maybe hard to voice. "I decided to do it, because I thought, what if I'd had this kind of organization backing me, when I was a kid? Helping me understand that I wasn't alone?"

Finn kept his "Neal Fisher" voice going to ask the next question on the paper. "Do you want to talk specifically about what kind of support you might have wanted or needed?"

Sophie had told him this interview was not a time to be vague, and Jacob *had* already decided he would just go for it, like ripping off a Band-Aid. "I'm gay, and I had the support of my parents and my friends, always. My coaches always knew, and a lot of teammates, and they were mostly supportive—"

"Mostly?" Finn asked this question in his own voice, raising an eyebrow and looking like he wanted to interrogate Jacob on just which teammates *hadn't* been supportive and exact slow, painful revenge.

"Nothing's ever perfect," Jacob said with a shrug. "It's stupid to assume it would be."

Finn harrumphed in annoyance and gestured for Jacob to keep going.

"But even when the support was strong from people in my corner, I think it would have gone a long way to knowing how much the wider world would be supportive. That's the aim of the foundation. To build support systems for those kids, like me. Like you. And liaise with the wider sports community to build awareness and understanding."

Finn didn't say anything at first. Just set down the paper and stared at Jacob, gaze warm and affectionate. He reached up and cupped Jacob's cheek and then leaned in and kissed him. It was hot and soft and sweet, and Jacob, still half-aroused, groaned in the back of his throat as Finn's tongue brushed his.

He pulled back a little, even though he didn't want to. "So," he said breathlessly, "that was good?"

"It was goddamn perfect," Finn said and went back to kissing him.

Jacob knew he was turning into a total sap, but it was *Finn* who was perfection. The way his skin felt under his hands, the softness and the muscle rippling under it, so full of power and control. It was such a turn-on, and he was done pretending that it wasn't.

His hand slid down Finn's bare back, glorying in the feel and the closeness of him, and dug his fingertips into an ass cheek, making Finn moan.

"Yeah, you want more?" Jacob murmured into Finn's mouth and he nodded, eyes bright and pupils dilated.

Grabbing the lube from where he'd tossed it earlier, he slicked up his fingers and crooked his wrist, sliding one in experimentally.

Finn moaned harder. "Come on," he begged, cheeks flushed now. "I'm good."

"But I like this so much." He did. It was entrancing, watching Finn fall apart on his hand, grinding down, trying to get his finger deeper. He added a second and found that spot that made Finn squirm.

"God, yes," Finn groaned. "Feels so fucking good." He slid a hand down and wrapped it around Jacob's cock.

Pleasure spiked inside him but he didn't want just Finn's hand. He wanted Finn hot and tight around his dick as he fell apart.

"More?" Jacob murmured, pressing his mouth against Finn's lips, red and wet from his.

"Yeah, *more*," Finn begged.

Jacob shifted his hand and tucked a third finger in, no longer thrusting, just pressing the pads of his fingers against that place that made Finn shudder.

"Fuck," Finn cried.

He was thrusting in tiny movements now, rubbing the wet head of his dick against Jacob's stomach.

"No," Jacob said, reduced to single words now by the fire pulsing inside his stomach. He curled his other hand around Finn's hip, stopping him.

Finn's eyes were wild and he bit his lip. "Close," he said.

Maybe the savage surge of satisfaction that shot through him was ridiculous—Jacob knew how good it was between them, and how much Finn wanted it—but he felt it anyway.

Reluctantly, he pulled his fingers out and stroked his cock with the excess lube, then pressed into Finn's hole.

Finn gasped as he slid all the way down, his thighs meeting Jacob's.

He didn't thrust right away, just ground against his dick, and he was just as wondrous as he felt around Jacob's fingers—but so much more.

"Like that?" Jacob managed two words this time, but that was all he had as Finn kissed him, grinding harder, his hips sinuous and so fucking perfect.

Finn gasped into his mouth as Jacob grabbed his ass with both hands, hoping that he'd found the right angle, and thrust hard.

This was going to be over really quick, and he needed to send Finn over the edge first. He'd confessed awhile back that sometimes, the second time he got fingered or fucked, he could come just from that, and *God* that had been the hottest thing Jacob had ever heard and he wanted it so goddamn bad. Not just for him, not as some kind of badge of sexual prowess, but he wanted to give it to Finn. Give him *everything*.

Finn was fucking back down on his dick, now, panting hard, and Jacob thought from the way all his muscles were quivering he was close.

"Come on," Jacob begged him, "I know you want it, and I want it too. Give it to me."

Finn arched, his whole body a gorgeous fucking line, and clenched down hard, coming around Jacob.

It was glorious and perfect.

Jacob managed half a thrust more and exploded.

"Fuck," Finn half-moaned, half-chuckled, as he collapsed onto Jacob. "That was . . ."

"Yeah," Jacob agreed. Single words were still easier.

"Love you," Finn murmured into his sweaty skin.

They really needed to move, or the mess would be tremendous.

Jacob's grip tightened on him, deciding that he didn't care.

He found one additional word. "Love you more," Jacob said.

⟫⟫⟫ ⟪⟪⟪

The interview had been going for forty minutes now—thirty-seven actually, if the clock on the wall of Neal Fisher's setup was any indication.

He filmed his podcast in one of the rooms of his house, two comfortable armchairs in a peaceful, relaxing lavender blue, and memorabilia from his NFL career dotting the walls.

It had been an unsurprisingly effortless conversation. He and Neal had had several phone calls leading up to this podcast recording, and he'd immediately liked the guy. He was easygoing and funny, in a dry, laid-back way, but even more than that Neal Fisher *understood*.

Maybe he'd been a football player and not a hockey player. Maybe he'd been a kicker and not a goalie. But neither of them had gotten to define the terms of their retirement and they'd both struggled with the aftermath.

Neal because, after missing the game-winning kick in the Super Bowl, he had been summarily released from his team. Jacob because his hip had refused to cooperate and his only choice had been to continue playing in a diminished capacity or to not play at all.

They'd talked about retirement at length. Specifically, the lack of support from most—if not all—professional sports organizations post-retirement and how ex-players were largely responsible for their own emotional health once they were no longer signed to a team.

"I've been upfront about how I should have gone to therapy sooner than I did," Neal confessed. "I spent practically a whole year hiding in my house, after the Super Bowl. Because yeah I didn't want to see anyone, and wonder what they were going to say about the kick I'd missed, but also because I was more worried how I'd feel about myself if they did."

"I figured out pretty quickly I needed the therapy," Jacob said wryly. "My agent found me one day, sink full of empty wine bottles and a week out from a shower, and he sent me a number that same day. She's been amazing, but even as amazing as she is, it's not easy."

Neal shook his head. "Nope. The process kind of sucks, right?"

"Totally sucks, but still totally worth it."

"Is that who recommended that you start your new foundation?" Neal asked.

Jacob braced himself. They were coming into the meat of the interview. The part he'd practiced with Finn last night.

Early, early this morning, before he'd left for the airport, Finn had kissed him sleepily, told him he loved him and he was proud of him, and honestly that memory had been keeping him going.

"Yeah, it was her idea that I find something new to care about. The foundation was a no-brainer because I wish there'd been something like this when I was growing up."

Neal gave him a soft, supportive smile and read the mission statement Jacob and Carla, their brand-new director, had spent the last week refining.

"So," Neal added, "this is really great. I think LGBTQ kids could really use this support system. And it sounds like you're committed to giving it to them."

"Totally committed," Jacob agreed.

"Sounds personal," Neal said, and there was the prompt. Not exactly as it had been written on the sheet, but there it was regardless.

Jacob was afraid. There was no way around it. He was afraid, but he also trusted that in the next minute, he'd be less afraid.

Less afraid and free, and the latter was all that mattered in this moment.

"I'm gay," Jacob said. And there it was. Recorded and not released but that didn't matter, because tomorrow everyone on the planet could hear him say those words. Most of them wouldn't know who he was and most wouldn't even care, but *he* cared.

He took a breath and kept going. "I wish I'd had someone to tell me that I wasn't alone. That I wasn't a freak. My family and friends were supportive. My coaches always knew, and a lot of teammates, and they were mostly supportive, too."

Neal shrugged, and Jacob knew from the look on his face that he understood, more than maybe Finn had, who'd grown up in a more accepting time, with more out pro athletes, that nothing *was* ever perfect. "It's sad that we were forced to accept *mostly* supportive, but *mostly* is better than *not*," Neal said.

"Yeah. I was luckier than some. But even when I had great people in my corner, I think it would have gone a long way if I'd believed that the wider world was also supportive. That's really the idea behind this foundation. We want to build support systems for those kids. Kids like you, and like me. But even more importantly, I want to raise awareness in the wider sports community and build collaboration and understanding."

"I think there's this really terrible fallacy out there," Neal said, nodding, "that the sports community *isn't* supportive, and I think it's great you're going to try to bring the truth of what it means to be a queer person in both non-professional *and* professional sports out to the wider public."

"Nothing's perfect," Jacob said, borrowing Finn's words, because he *was* perfect.

"Nope, but we're making it better one day at a time," Neal agreed.

The interview wound down. When it finally ended, Neal rose and Jacob met him halfway between the chairs, holding out his hand to shake, but to his surprise, Neal pulled him in for a hug instead.

"Congratulations, Jacob," he said, when he let him go. "I'm so happy for you. Great interview. I can't wait for people to hear it."

"Thanks for having me," Jacob said.

"You know, we contacted some of your teammates and players you skated against, for extra material," Neal said.

Jacob tensed. He hadn't known they were doing that.

"Sophie," Neal continued, "suggested a list, and it had one really interesting addition."

God, Jacob just bet she'd done it. He wanted to yell at her, but he supposed Neal was bringing this up for a reason. Either to tell him he needed to fire Sophie—and it would be terrible timing to do that, since she was standing just behind the camera, listening to every word—or to tell him that the result had been surprising.

"Hayes Montgomery had something to say, and Noah Boucher and Avery Barnes too. But the most fascinating addition was Morgan Reynolds. You know, his son Finn's gay?"

"I know," Jacob said, trying to keep a straight face.

"Well, I know you and Morgan never got along."

"Never," Jacob agreed, failing to keep his smile under wraps now.

"Well, to my shock, he sent along a super complimentary bit about you. About your bravery and steadfastness." Neal shook his head, like he was still surprised. "I thought you guys had some crazy rivalry. Didn't you two get into a brawl at your last All Star Game? And he wasn't even *playing*?"

"Uh, that was highly exaggerated," Jacob said. Even though it really hadn't been. Morgan had said something exceptionally shitty and he'd have punched him in the face if a teammate hadn't held him back. "But we've . . .uh . . .buried the hatchet. So to speak."

"Sounds like it," Neal said. He paused. "I'm just sorry that you can't stay. I was hoping you could meet my husband, Jamie, but he's at practice right now. We thought we might convince you to hang around for dinner, but Sophie said you needed to get back home."

Jacob figured that they were being very honest *and* he trusted Neal so he might as well keep going. "I wish I could, but I've got some responsibilities back home. My boyfriend has a hockey game tomorrow, and I'm helping him out with some stuff."

The corner of Neal's mouth quirked up. "Yeah, a boyfriend, and a boyfriend who plays hockey?"

"Yeah, uh . . .well, funny that." Jacob grinned. "The boyfriend is Finn Reynolds. *My* boyfriend is Finn Reynolds."

Neal's jaw dropped gratifyingly. "You're fucking kidding me."

"Nope," Jacob said.

Neal still looked shell-shocked, but Jacob was impressed at how quickly he seemed to recover. He patted Jacob on the arm. "Well, congrats are in order, I guess? And I suppose it wasn't all that interesting that Morgan said such nice things about you."

"Actually, it is," Jacob said, chuckling. "I can't say we're friends, maybe we'll never be friends but . . .we're working on it?"

"If you want my two cents," Neal said, dropping his voice and looking very amused, "I think that statement he made to my team tells me exactly what side of that argument Morgan falls on."

Jacob wanted to disagree but as he said goodbye to Neal and his team, he and Sophie grabbing a cab to the airport, he thought that actually maybe Neal was right.

"Hey," he said to Sophie as they were waiting for the plane, "did you tell Neal's team to contact Morgan for a quote?"

She had the nerve to look slightly embarrassed. "Yes," she said, "and before you freak out, I think it was the right call. It means more coming from him than it means coming from someone you were close to when you were playing."

"How did you know he'd say anything civil?"

Sophie rolled her eyes. "If he didn't, he wasn't getting any face time on the podcast and he's *Morgan Reynolds*."

Jacob laughed. "True," he said. "Still."

"I know you didn't want him to be part of this, but . . ."

"With me and Finn, he's part of this, now," Jacob finished for her.

"Yeah. Yeah. I wouldn't have been so blunt about it but the truth is yes, he is. And if you want to be public with Finn—"

"I do," Jacob said with absolute certainty. "I'm not hiding him."

"Then this is good. Him saying good stuff about you in public? That's only good. Those are the quotes people are gonna dig out when they write gossipy stories about you and Finn."

"Right. Right." Jacob reached down and squeezed her hand. "Thanks for always looking out for me."

Sophie smiled. "Thanks for *mostly* making it easy."

CHAPTER 20

Finn would never get tired of seeing Jacob walk towards him, wearing his black and green Evergreens jacket, his access credentials swinging around his neck.

"Hey," Jacob said, putting a hand on Finn's shoulder as he sat on the bench finishing getting dressed for the game. "How are you feeling?"

Finn could feel the warmth of his touch even through all the layers of equipment and he lifted his chin up, wishing that he could have more than a reassuring touch.

Wishing, maybe a little, for a good luck kiss.

"Good," Finn said, tilting his head back. Was pretty sure Jacob was also wishing for a good luck kiss from the way his gaze lingered on Finn's lips.

Mal and Elliott knew what was going on between them, and Ramsey and, Finn was pretty sure, Brody suspected, but nobody else knew, and it gave Finn a little charge every time he had to interact with Jacob in front of the team. Like he was getting away with stealing all the cake and nobody else knew.

Of course, that wouldn't be the case forever. Jacob's podcast had released a few days ago, and Sophie was already cc'ing him on emails about preparing for another slow reveal, in a month or two.

Jacob had asked him very seriously if he wanted to wait, and Finn hadn't been sure what there was to wait for. He'd said this, confused, and Jacob had only laughed. "Guess you're not getting rid of me that easily," he'd said.

And okay, it *was* soon, they'd only been dating for two months. But Finn knew what he wanted and who he loved, and he wasn't going to hide him away forever.

Not when Jacob had just taken that first precious step into the light.

"You've looked great in practice," Jacob said, jamming his hands into the pockets of his jeans.

Finn smiled, wondering if Jacob had done that on purpose so he'd stop touching him.

"Had someone really great helping me get there," Finn said, enjoying more than he should how much Jacob was squirming.

"Watch out for their second line center," Jacob warned. "He likes to charge the crease."

"Brody and Ramsey'll have my back," Finn said. "And if he gets too close, I'll take care of it."

Jacob nodded, digging his fingers deeper into his pockets.

"You coming with us after the game?" Finn asked. A handful of them were headed to Darcelle's, to grab what they hoped was a celebratory drink and to catch the drag show. He'd invited Jacob who'd hesitated for so long that Finn had teased him about spraining his brain.

"It's just Ramsey and Ivan. Brody and his football player boyfriend. Have you met Dean? Enormous guy?" Finn had asked and Jacob said he'd think about it.

"I . . .uh . . .are you sure you want me to go?" Jacob asked under his breath.

"*I asked you*," Finn reminded him sweetly.

"I'm just saying . . ."

"And I'm just saying, I don't want to hide anymore. You don't want to hide anymore."

Jacob nodded so sharply in agreement, the movement so clearly instinctual that it was clear he didn't.

Talking about his sexuality and being public about it was never something that would come to easily to Jacob—he was too private of a person and just wanted to be left alone to live his life—but it was one thing to not want to proclaim their love to the masses and another to go out for a drink after a game.

"Come on, come with me," Finn said, tongue flicking out and tasting his lower lip. "And after . . ."

Jacob laughed and scrubbed a hand across his face. "Okay. Yes. I'm absolute shit at resisting you."

"Which is okay 'cause you really don't want to."

Jacob's expression went unbearably fond, love radiating out of it, and Finn understood why Sophie seemed to be accelerating their timetable every day, because he saw the way Jacob looked at him. And Finn couldn't imagine that the way he looked back was much different.

They wouldn't be able to keep this under wraps much longer.

"No, not at all," Jacob agreed. He leaned down and for a split second, brushed the bottom of his chin against the top of

Finn's head. "Kick some ass out there, and we'll go out with your guys."

"Can do," Finn said, grinning. "You gonna sit with my dad again?"

Jacob rolled his eyes. "Who do you think's already texted me four times about the second line center?"

Finn laughed.

Three months ago, those messages would've gone to him, and three months ago, those messages would've made him believe unequivocally that his dad didn't have any faith in him to deal with some team's second line center.

Witnessing his dad's attempts to show how much he believed in Finn and loved him was great. What was even better was feeling this bone-deep certainty, no matter what anyone said or did, that he was capable of anything he set his mind to.

"We need to stop him from watching so much tape," Finn said.

"No," Jacob said, and the word was as good as a caress, "'cause then we have to occupy his time instead and we've got a lot better things to do."

"Yeah," Finn agreed, lighting up just thinking about it. "Maybe someone he could date?" Then he made a face. "Ugh, then he'd want to double date."

Jacob's expression made it clear he didn't want to double date with Morgan either.

"Well, at least *you're* getting the texts now?"

"And I'm probably gonna hear about it the whole game, every time that center is on the goddamn ice," Jacob said. But he didn't seem honestly that annoyed about it, really.

Finn had a feeling that one morning he'd wake up and suddenly his boyfriend and his dad would actually be friends.

There was no way they'd ever stop chirping each other, but it had gotten downright good-natured in comparison and Finn couldn't say he hated it.

"Well, I uh . . ." Jacob gestured towards the door. "Guess I'd better go find him."

Finn loved him so much. It was adorable and ridiculous how much he was fighting the compulsion to just lean down and take what they both wanted.

"Come here," Finn said, before Jacob could turn away.

"I'm . . . but . . ." Jacob's protest wasn't real though. He didn't even sound convinced by it himself.

"Just this," Finn said and tilted his head up. "Say 'good luck, Finn' and give me a quick kiss. Nobody's paying attention." That wasn't really true, but Finn didn't care. Elliott and Malcolm were five seconds away from fucking in a treatment room these days, and they all barely blinked at that.

He could have this.

"You really want me to?" Jacob asked.

"Yes," Finn said. He didn't ask if Jacob wanted to. It was obvious he did, from the careful way he held himself a scrupulous six inches away from Finn and his eyes kept snagging on Finn's mouth.

Jacob's hands moved from his pockets to Finn's shoulders. He leaned in, close, and Finn felt his breath go out in a hard, unsteady whoosh.

"Good luck," he murmured into his ear, and then Finn tilted his head, Jacob's mouth brushing against his. It was fairly PG as their kisses went but it *wasn't* short, not like Finn had imagined when he suggested it, but that was okay, because this was even better.

And so was the way Jacob lingered in the bubble of his personal space, his dark eyes full of promises Finn knew he'd keep, and said, "I love you."

Finn nearly chased his lips after that, greedy and wanting a second kiss. But Jacob pulled back.

"And that's what I *really* wanted to do," Jacob said, and then he was turning and walking out to more than a few catcalls, leaving Finn to stare goofily after him.

"Well, congratulations," Brody said, nudging him. "I think we're all pregnant now."

"You're a bio major; you know that's an impossibility," Finn argued.

"But if it *was*, we'd all be pregnant," Brody said sagely. "That's my way of saying, congrats, Finn, we're happy for you. He's hot, but even more important, he's hot for you."

"Yeah, seriously," Ivan said, leaning over and joining in. "Nabbing Jacob fucking Braun. You're my new hero."

Finn flushed happily. "Yeah?"

"Even better that it probably drove your dad *insane*," Ivan said. "Someone needs to take that guy down a peg. Or ten."

Brody looked like he agreed with this assessment, but Brody was awesome and had always, and would probably never stop, taking Finn's side.

"Who needs taking down a peg?" Ramsey sauntered over. Everyone else looked semi-stupid walking in skates except Ramsey.

Elliott liked to say that was how he got so much dick, but they all knew that wasn't even remotely close to the only reason why.

"Finn's dad," Ivan said.

There was a commotion at the door to the locker room, a few gasps and Finn looked up and *God*, there he was, outlined in the doorway.

"Shit," Ivan muttered under his breath.

"Yeah, Ivy, where's your balls now?" Ramsey asked loudly. "You gonna go do it right now?"

"No, no, *no*," Ivan hissed.

Finn laughed.

Coach G walked in, flanked on one side by Zach and on the other side by his dad.

He was wearing black and green, and their eyes met across the room. Morgan had told him that Coach had asked him if he could do this, at some point, and he'd actually asked Finn if it was okay with him.

Finn had said yes, but he hadn't had a clue it was happening *tonight*.

Well, maybe better Jacob was already gone and his dad hadn't had to witness Jacob claiming him in front of the entire locker room.

"We've got a special guest tonight," Coach said, eyes scanning the room. "A future Hall of Famer, and one of the best players to ever take the ice, Morgan Reynolds."

They all cheered.

Even Finn.

And for once, that felt okay.

For a split second, when he'd seen his dad walk in, he'd thought, horribly, *no, no, not now*, but after his initial reaction, he realized that it wasn't terrible. It was actually okay. *More* than okay.

Morgan met his gaze from across the room. Finn's chin went up and then Morgan's did and they both smiled.

It's gonna be good. It's gonna be great.

"Happy to be here, boys," Morgan said, glancing around the room as the cheers grew. "Let's kick this off with our starting left wing, number nine and your Captain, Malcolm McCoy." Morgan paused as cheers spiked again. "At center, number seventy-one, Ivan Sokolov. Starting right wing, number eighty-eight, Elliott Jones. In the back, Brody Faulkner, number seventy-four. And opposite him, Ramsey Andresen, number eight. And last, but definitely not least. Between the pipes tonight, with one of the highest save percentages in the nation, number twenty-nine, from Rochester, New York, my son and your goalie, Finn Reynolds."

The room erupted as Morgan walked down the center of the room and Finn met him halfway, embracing him firmly.

Morgan's eyes weren't entirely dry and Finn didn't think his were either. He decided he didn't give a shit. His teammates had been present for the worst of this relationship—maybe now they could see the other side of the coin, the way Finn was.

"Kill it out there today," Morgan murmured, and Finn nodded.

When he pulled back, Morgan's eyes were still bright with unshed tears.

"Yeah," Finn said.

"Proud of you."

And Finn realized that not only did his dad mean it, but that *he* meant it.

He was proud of himself.

Time to go to work.

EPILOGUE

A year later

Jacob told himself he wasn't freaking out, but he kind of was.

They were sitting on the couch, watching ESPN, Finn curled up next to him, breathing relaxed and even, and Jacob felt like a rubber band about to snap.

At least he wasn't alone. He'd had to silence his phone because Morgan had sent too many texts in the last few hours.

Jacob wasn't sure which of them was more enthusiastic than Finn was finally making his NHL debut tomorrow night. Finn seemed ready. Calm and prepared. Jacob was excited for him. Morgan was . . .well, Morgan was Morgan-ing all over the place.

"Hey, you need to relax," Finn said sleepily next to him. It was early still, not quite eight, but Jacob knew in an hour or two Finn would head to bed, to get a good night's rest, and it seemed he'd actually sleep.

Jacob didn't know how he was going to sleep.

"I'm relaxed," Jacob claimed.

It wasn't like he didn't think Finn was prepared; he'd never been more ready. He was physically and mentally in such a great spot right now, and everyone in the Sentinels' organization was eager for him to get on the ice.

But Jacob still remembered his own debut. How he'd not slept a wink the night before. How he'd been sure he'd collapse right there on the ice from sheer nerves.

Was Finn hiding it? Would he eventually realize what was about to happen and panic the same way Jacob had? And what if Jacob wasn't there to calm him down?

If that happens, it'll still be okay, because Finn has Finn.

Jacob tried to even out his breathing and knew he'd failed because Finn looked over at him, amusement in his eyes.

"You're the last thing from relaxed," Finn teased. He ran his fingertips up Jacob's T-shirt-clad chest. "Maybe I should do something about that."

Jacob cleared his throat, wishing that was going to be enough. But Finn had already given him a spine-meltingly good blowjob a few hours ago. If that hadn't taken care of his anxiety, nothing was going to do it.

"Do you . . .are you really not nervous?" Jacob wanted to smack himself the moment the words escaped him.

Finn smiled. "No, not really. Excited, yeah. But nothing bad."

"Good. Good." Jacob felt like a useless lump.

"I couldn't be more ready, you know?" Finn's eyes glowed with happiness and contentment.

"Yeah?"

"Yeah. And you should take some of the credit for that," Finn said seriously.

"Some?"

"Well, not *all*," Finn said, chuckling. "But yeah, some. I told you, I wanted you to help me, and you did. And I told you I wanted you next to me, that it would be meaningful to have someone who'd gone through it, and you were there. Every step of the way."

It hadn't been easy, always.

Jacob hadn't really wanted to leave the house in Portland and move to Tampa, for example. But he'd done it. After all, he'd come to realize during this last year that home wasn't a four-walled structure, but a *person*.

Finn was his happy place, his touchstone, his everything.

Besides, the house in Portland would always be there, whenever Finn was finished being extraordinary at hockey and ready to tackle being extraordinary at something else.

"Of course. I love you."

Finn sighed, all comfortable contentment as his fingers dug into the fabric of Jacob's shirt. "Love you, too. You and my dad sitting together tomorrow?"

"Morgan says so." He had, *at length*. To the point where the last text Jacob had read before he'd silenced Morgan was, **you'd better be there tomorrow with me or I'm gonna lose my shit.**

"You've done a pretty good job keeping him in line," Finn said.

And yes, that was true, but the more accurate truth was that Morgan had done a much better job keeping *himself* in line.

Point in fact: Morgan had texted *him* that, not Finn.

"I'd do worse, for you," Jacob said, and that was way too fucking true.

Finn's smile was like the sun. "Yeah? Well, then I've got something for you."

"What is it?"

Finn poked him in the pectoral muscle. "Calm the hell down, okay?"

Jacob let out a short breath. Tried not to laugh, because this was serious. Well, sort of serious. "Yeah. Yeah. I can do that."

"Good." Finn's head dropped back down to his shoulder. "One more episode and then we'll go to bed?"

"Sounds perfect," Jacob said, dropping a kiss onto Finn's head. He wasn't going to mention that when Finn fell asleep, he was probably going to lie awake, staring at the ceiling.

There was only so much relaxation ability in him right now.

"You're perfect," Finn said, and Jacob felt the warmth of that declaration all the way down to his toes. Then the corner of his mouth turned up in a tiny irresistible smirk. "Even though I know you're lying and you'll let *me* go to bed and you'll stay awake, freaking out beside me."

"Uh," Jacob said, and Finn laughed.

"It's alright, you're still perfect."

"Did you tell him about the way he's got to watch the loose puck around the net? The Pens are aggressive on that shit, and if Crosby—"

"You need to take a fucking breath," Jacob told Morgan, though that didn't stop him. Not much could.

But then, probably nobody else other than Jacob knew how Morgan could be, when he got like this.

Jacob used to hate it, and he couldn't say he *liked* it now, but he'd accepted it, and could even, on occasion, be amused by it.

Like now.

"Fuck you," Morgan said. "This is important! He needs to know this."

"Finn knows this. I think if a puck and Sidney Crosby get near the net, he's going to be paying attention," Jacob said dryly.

Morgan's knee bounced up and down, which it had done nearly from the moment they'd taken their seats in the Sentinels' arena. It was nearly full to capacity. Jacob liked to think a lot of these fans were here to see the Tampa Sentinels' new and very promising rookie goalie make his first start, but the more accurate assumption was that they were here to see the Crosby-Malkin farewell tour.

Regardless, Finn would have a full house for his debut, and Jacob loved that for him.

"It's not that I don't think he's capable, right? Or that he doesn't know how to do this, but I just . . ." Morgan turned to him helplessly.

"You're just going out of your mind?" Jacob asked.

Morgan's lips were a flat line. "Don't tell me you're not."

"Oh, I am." As he'd predicted, Jacob hadn't slept a wink last night. Finn, on the other hand, had slept like a baby.

"Doesn't seem like it," Morgan muttered.

"That's because you're emoting enough for both of us right now."

Morgan made a disgruntled noise.

"Also," Jacob continued, "it turns out being amused by your total meltdown is a good distraction from my own anxiety."

"I stayed up all night watching game tape," Morgan said.

"Yeah, that's really obvious."

Morgan shoved an elbow into his side. Jacob had discovered over the last year, as they'd learned to tolerate each other off ice and had gradually actually become friends, Morgan had really fucking sharp elbows. Jacob yelped, shooting Morgan a dirty look.

"What? You're being an unsupportive asshole," Morgan said sulkily.

"Sucks, doesn't it?"

Morgan shoved another elbow into his side and this time Jacob just accepted the pain as a matter of course.

He'd do *anything* for Finn, even tolerate Morgan's pointy elbows.

"I'm supportive," Morgan squawked. "I'm even wearing his sweater! I haven't worn one since—" He stopped abruptly.

Jacob glanced over at him and they shared a look.

He remembered the first time he'd put on a jersey that wasn't his own. It had been Finn's, during the Evergreens' playoff run last year. He'd wanted to be supportive in any way he could and doing something had felt better than doing nothing. But his fingers had still slid over the fabric uncomfortably before he'd finally pulled it over his head.

"It's gonna mean a lot to Finn that you're wearing it," Jacob said, more gently than Morgan probably deserved. Finn had gifted it to him for Christmas this year, his autograph proudly scrawled over the two and the nine on the back.

Finn had told Jacob later that night, as they'd cuddled naked in bed, that he didn't think his dad would ever wear it, but he hoped he'd carry it with him either way. Jacob had told him that he knew he would. Because he could say a lot about Morgan Reynolds, but these days, the man was dedicated to showing his son just how much he cared about him.

"And he's going to laugh his ass off that we're sitting here, like fucking twins in a Sears photoshoot," Morgan grumbled.

"Yeah, probably." Jacob smiled. Inside, *he* was laughing his ass off that they now looked like twins. "Don't you dare shove that elbow into me again. I *will* kick your ass if you do."

"No, you won't," Morgan said, sounding very confident.

Kind of the way he'd used to talk in press conferences and with reporters' microphones shoved in front of him. *"Oh yeah, I'm definitely gonna get points tonight against Braun. There's no way he can stop me, not when I'm skating like this."* Morgan being confident in relation to him in such a different way had taken a lot of getting used to.

Jacob wasn't sure he'd quite accomplished it yet.

But then, when Morgan Reynolds was your future father-in-law, could you ever sleep easy?

"Did I tell you that I'm cutting back on some of my ESPN commitments?" Morgan asked.

Jacob considered telling Morgan that no, he hadn't told Jacob but he'd told Finn and that was as good as telling Jacob. But Morgan was clearly making an effort to not freak out, or not *keep* freaking out, and Jacob wanted to encourage that.

"No."

"Well, I am. I want to be present for this, for Finn. It feels important, you know? I'm still doing a few segments, but they said I can do those from my rental house."

Jacob ping-ponged, much the same way Finn did, on how he felt about Morgan abruptly decamping from New York and moving, in some kind of long-term capacity, to a rental house a mile from theirs in Tampa.

On one hand, it was a very good thing for Finn to have a better relationship with Morgan, and to everyone's surprise, it *was* becoming a better relationship.

On the other hand, Morgan liked to annoyingly show up just when Jacob wanted to get Finn naked.

"Good. Do more of those," Jacob said and then laughed at the horrible expression that crossed over Morgan's face.

"For the hundredth time, I don't want to hear about your sex life," Morgan muttered.

"Then stop interfering," Jacob said easily, fully expecting and accepting the elbow that got shoved into his gut.

"Do you . . .should I . . ." Morgan trailed off, suddenly looking not only anxious, but also like he might be about to vomit.

"Spit it out, Reynolds."

"Should I have not come?"

"To this game? I don't think Finn would've ever forgiven you for missing it." Jacob knew what Morgan had actually meant, but it was fun to misunderstand him, just to watch him splutter in annoyance.

"No, *no*. I mean . . .should I have not come down here? Rented the house?"

"Oh, well, no the house rental thing was a good idea. You'd have *really* cramped our style if you'd insisted on moving in," Jacob said seriously.

Morgan made a face. "I was never going to do that."

"Thank God for that." Jacob paused. "But seriously, I think it's good you're here. Finn respects you a lot, and you give him a good perspective, and well . . .this is a big time in his life. You've been there, too. You get it."

"So do you," Morgan said quietly. Jacob understood then that this was another way of Morgan saying, without actually admitting it out loud, in actual words, that he approved of Jacob and Finn's relationship.

Jacob wished he could go back in time and tell his past self, *look at what you're going to have, if you're brave and face down your fear. A man you love more than anything on earth and even his annoying, meddling father, who it turns out could actually be your best friend.*

"Yeah, I'm his boyfriend. But you're his father." Jacob cleared his throat. "It's okay you're here. I promise. If it hadn't been, you'd have known."

Finn would've made it clear. He did that these days, setting boundaries in that clear-eyed, blunt way he'd adopted. Boundaries shouldn't have turned Jacob on. But then pretty much everything about Finn turned him on.

"Good," Morgan said, turned back to the ice. "Oh, look, it's . . .uh . . .it's starting."

They'd gotten to their seats way early, because neither of them wanted to miss the special tradition of a rookie warming up on the ice for the first time, solo—of Finn doing it for the first time.

"Did you bring—" Jacob didn't even get the words out before Morgan slapped something into his hand.

Jacob looked down and smiled.

It was a pack of tissues.

The ice spread out before him, perfect and glossy.

Untouched. *It's all for you, now.*

Finn's heart beat unsteadily and he gripped his stick harder.

"You ready?"

He glanced over and there, deep back in the tunnel, was Hayes, waiting for him to make his debut rookie lap before he let the rest of the team onto the ice to warm up.

"Yeah," Finn said. "I feel good."

"You *are* good," Hayes said.

As he'd expected, he liked Hayes Montgomery, who wore the C for the Sentinels, a lot. He'd been as welcoming as any captain of a team would be, but there'd been an extra addition of comfort on top of that, because with Hayes out and in charge of the locker room, there'd never be a reason for Finn to worry a teammate would start shit.

"Thanks," Finn said. He was still trying to adjust to the thinking that his NHL debut, something he'd worked so long and hard for, was actually *happening*, like right fucking now, and that was overwhelming enough. Not to mention that Hayes Montgomery thought he was *good*.

"There's no reason to be nervous, okay? You've got this. The ice runs in your veins."

It did.

Cold and solid, it ran true for Morgan and it would for Finn, too.

For so long, he'd worried that he wouldn't be enough. That he'd let his dad down. That he'd never live up to the potential of his last name.

But in the last year he'd begun to discover that it actually was insanely fucking cool that they both had gotten this chance. Morgan had made the most of his, and Finn was going to do the same.

If he could get through his rookie lap without tripping, or falling, or otherwise humiliating himself.

"Yeah," Finn agreed. "I got this."

Hayes clapped him on the shoulder. "Have fun and remember to take it in, okay? Every moment. Don't let it go to waste."

"Thanks, Cap." Finn gave him a last nod, and Hayes melted back into the tunnel.

"You ready?" a Sentinels staffer asked Finn.

Finn took a deep breath, pulled his mask down, and found himself grinning wildly as he nodded.

The ice felt as smooth as it looked, his blades cutting through it sharply, perfectly.

He could imagine Jacob up there in the stands, watching him—and loving him—and his heart felt so full it nearly burst with happiness.

He'd have been here with or without him, maybe, but Finn loved him enough, loved him more with each passing day, that he knew he'd never want to do it alone.

He was better, *they* were better, with each other.

Morgan would be there too, sitting next to Jacob.

Probably freaking out.

Probably happier than Finn could remember him being.

Finn nailed a puck right into the net and swung around, loving the feel of the ice, loving the crowd, loving the lights, loving his life, and then, just like that, they all disappeared.

It was just him and the ice.

And he was ready.

-

Don't miss the final Evergreens book, with Coach Gavin and Zach. Coming in June 2025. Preorder here!

-

And of course, Morgan is going to get a book! (He was too pushy to be denied LOL). Preorder *Breakaway Goals* here.

-

Imagine if Brody and Dean (from *Melting the Ice)* decided to swap jerseys. Read all about it here.

INTERESTED IN READING MORE OF
BETH'S BOOKS?

CHECK OUT A FULL LIST OF TILES
BY SCANNING THE QR CODE
OR VISITING HER WEBSITE

WWW.BETHBOLDEN.COM/BOOKLIST

WANT TO FOLLOW BETH?

MAKE SURE YOU NEVER
MISS A RELEASE?

SCAN THE QR CODE BELOW
OR VISIT HER WEBSITE
FOR A SOCIAL MEDIA LIST,
NEWSLETTER SIGNUP,
AND SO MUCH MORE!

WWW.BETHBOLDEN.COM/ABOUT

www.ingramcontent.com/pod-product-compliance
Lightning Source LLC
Chambersburg PA
CBHW070309310726
48976CB00005B/1639